SPIES OF THE BALKANS

ALAN FURST

THORNDIKE
WINDSOR
PARAGON

LIBRARY OF CONGRESS CATALOGING-IN-PUBLICATION DATA

Furst, Alan.
    Spies of the Balkans / by Alan Furst.
        p. cm. — (Thorndike Press large print basic)
    ISBN-13: 978-1-4104-2858-5
    ISBN-10: 1-4104-2858-3
        1. World War, 1939–1945—Underground movements—Greece—Fiction.
    2. Greece—History—1917–1944—Fiction. 3. Thessalonike (Greece)—
    Fiction. 4. Large type books. I. Title.
    PS3556.U76S73 2010b
    813'.54—dc22   2010013175

BRITISH LIBRARY CATALOGUING-IN-PUBLICATION DATA AVAILABLE
Published in the U.S. in 2010 by arrangement with Random House, Inc.
Published in the U.K. in 2011 by arrangement with The Orion
Publishing Group Limited.
U.K. Hardcover: 978 1 408 48754 9 (Windsor Large Print)
U.K. Softcover: 978 1 408 48755 6 (Paragon Large Print)

Printed and bound in Great Britain by the MPG Books Group
1 2 3 4 5 6 7 14 13 12 11 10

In August of 1939, General Ioannis Metaxas, the prime minister of Greece, told a Roumanian diplomat "that the old Europe would end when the swastika flew over the Acropolis."

DYING IN BYZANTIUM

In autumn, the rains came to Macedonia.

The storm began in the north — on the fifth day of October in the year 1940 — where sullen cloud lay over the mountain villages on the border of Bulgaria and Greece. By midday it had drifted south, heavier now, rolling down the valley of the Vardar River until, at dusk, it reached the heights of the city of Salonika and, by the time the streetlamps came on, rain dripped from the roof tiles in the ancient alleyways of the port and dappled the surface of the flat, dark sea.

Just after six in the evening, Costa Zannis, known to the city as *a senior police official* — whatever that meant, perhaps no more than a suit instead of a uniform — left his office on the top floor of an anonymous building on the Via Egnatia, walked down five flights of creaky wooden stairs, stepped out into the street, and snapped his umbrella aloft. Earlier that day he'd had a telephone call from the port captain, something to do with the arrival of the Turkish tramp freighter *Bakir* — "an irregularity" was the phrase the captain used, adding that he preferred to pursue the matter in person. "You understand me, Costa," he'd said. Oh yes, Zannis understood all too well. At that moment, Greece had been ruled by the Metaxas dictatorship since 1936 — the length of women's skirts was regulated; it was forbidden to read aloud the funeral oration of Pericles — and people were cautious about what they said on the telephone. And, with much of Europe occupied by Nazi Germany, and Mussolini's armies in Albania, on the Greek frontier, one wasn't sure what came next. So, *don't trust the telephone.* Or the newspapers. Or the radio. Or tomorrow.

Entering the vast street market on Aristotle Square, Zannis furled his umbrella and worked his way through the narrow aisles. Rain pattered on the tin roofing above the stalls, fishmongers shouted to the crowd, and, as Zannis passed by, the merchants smiled or nodded or avoided his eyes, depending on where they thought they stood with the Salonika police that evening. A skeletal old woman from the countryside,

10

black dress, black head scarf, offered him a dried fig. He smiled politely and declined, but she thrust it toward him, the mock ferocity of her expression meaning that he had no choice. He tore the stem off, flicked it into the gutter, then ate the fig, which was fat and sweet, raised his eyebrows in appreciation, said, "It's very good, thank you," and went on his way. At the far end of the market, a sponge peddler, a huge sack slung over his shoulder, peered anxiously out at the rain. Marooned, he could only wait, for if his sponges got wet he'd have to carry the weight for the rest of the night.

The customshouse stood at the center of the city's two main piers, its function stated on a broad sign above the main entry, first in Greek, then with the word *Douane.* On the upper floor, the port captain occupied a corner office, the sort of office that had over the years become a home; warm in the chilly weather, the still air scented with wood smoke and cigarettes, one of the port cats asleep by the woodstove. On the wall behind the desk hung a brightly colored oleograph of Archbishop Alexandros, in long black beard and hair flowing to his shoulders, hands clasped piously across his ample stomach. By his side, formal photographs of a stern General Metaxas and a succession of port officials of the past, two of them, in fading sepia prints, wearing the Turkish fez. On the adjoining wall, handsomely framed, were the wife and children of the present occupant, well fed, dressed to the hilt, and looking very dignified.

The present occupant was in no hurry; a brief call on the telephone produced, in a few minutes, a waiter from a nearby *kafeneion* — coffeehouse — with two tiny cups of Turkish coffee on a brass tray. After a sip, the captain lit a cigarette and said, "I hope I didn't get you down here for nothing, Costa. In such miserable fucking weather."

Zannis didn't mind. "It's always good to see you," he said. "The *Bakir*, I think you said. Where's she berthed?"

"Number eight, on the left-hand side. Just behind a Dutch grain freighter — a German grain freighter now, I guess."

"For the time being," Zannis said.

They paused briefly to savor the good things the future might hold, then the captain said, "*Bakir* docked this morning. I waited an hour, the captain never showed up, so I went to find him. Nothing unusual, gangplank down, nobody about, so I went on board and headed for the captain's office, which is pretty much always in the same place, just by the bridge. A few sailors at work, but it was quiet on board, and going down the passageway toward the bridge I passed the wardroom. Two officers, gossiping in Turkish and drinking coffee, and a little man in a suit, with shiny shoes, reading a newspaper. German newspaper. Oh, I thought, a passenger."

"See his face?"

"Actually I didn't. He was behind his newspaper — *Völkischer Beobachter?* I believe it was. Anyhow, I didn't think much about it. People get around these days any way they can, and they don't go anywhere at all unless they have to."

"Submarines."

The captain nodded. "You may just have to swim. Eventually I found the captain up on the bridge — a man I've known for years, by the way — and we went back to his office so I could have a look at the manifest. But — no passenger. So, I asked. 'Who's the gent in the wardroom?' The captain just looked at me. What a look!"

"Meaning . . . ?"

"Meaning *Don't ask me that.* Life's hard enough these days without this sort of nonsense."

Zannis's smile was ironic. "Oh dear," he said.

The captain laughed, relieved. "Don't be concerned, you mean."

From Zannis, a small sigh. "No, but it's me who has to be concerned. On the other hand, as long as he stays where he is . . . What's she carrying?"

"In ballast. She's here to load baled tobacco, then headed up to Hamburg."

"You didn't happen to see the passenger come this way, did you?"

"No, he hasn't left the ship."

Zannis raised an eyebrow. "You're sure?"

"I've had a taxi waiting out there all afternoon. If he tries to enter the city, two beeps on the horn."

This time the sigh was deeper, because Zannis's plans for the evening had vanished into the night. "I'll use your telephone," he said. "And then I'll take a little walk."

Zannis walked past the taxi on the pier — the driver awake, to his surprise — then continued until he could see the *Bakir*. Nothing unusual; a rust-streaked gray hull, a cook tossing a pail of kitchen garbage into the bay. He'd thought about ordering up a pair of detectives, then decided not to get them out in the rain. But now the rain had stopped, leaving in its place a heavy mist that made halos around the streetlamps.

14

Zannis stood there, the city behind him quiet, a foghorn moaning somewhere out in the darkness.

He'd turned forty that summer, not a welcome event but what could you do. He was of average height, with a thick muscular body and only an inch of belly above his belt. Skin a pale olive color, not bad-looking at all though more boxer than movie star, a tough guy, in the way he moved, in the way he held himself. Until you looked at his face, which suggested quite a different sort of person. Wide generous mouth and, behind steel-framed eyeglasses, very blue eyes: lively eyes. He had dry black hair which, despite being combed with water in the morning, was tousled by the time he reached the office and fell down on his forehead and made him look younger, and softer, than he was. All in all, an expressive face, rarely still — when you spoke to him you could always see what he thought about whatever you said, amusement or sympathy or curiosity, but always something. So, maybe a tough guy, but your friend the tough guy. The policeman. And, in his black suit and soft gray shirt, tie knot always pulled down and the collar button of the shirt open, a rather gentle version of the breed. On purpose, of course.

15

He'd certainly never meant to be a cop. And — once he fell into being a cop — never a detective, and — once promoted to that position — never what he was now. He'd never even known such a job existed. Neither of his parents had been educated beyond the first six years; his grandmother could neither read nor write, his mother doing so only with difficulty. His father had worked his way into half ownership of a florist shop in the good part of Salonika, so the family was never poor; they managed, pretty much like everyone else he knew. Zannis wasn't much of a student, which didn't matter because in time he'd work in the shop. And, until 1912, Salonika had remained a part of the Ottoman Empire — Athens and the western part of the nation having fought free of the Turks in 1832 — so to be Greek was to know your place and the sort of ambition that drew attention wasn't such a good idea.

By age twelve, as the Greek army marched in to end the Second Balkan War, Zannis's private dreams had mostly involved escape; foreign places called to him, so maybe work on a ship or a train. Not unusual. His mother's brother had emigrated to America, to a mysterious place called Altoona, in the state of Pennsylvania, from whence postal cards arrived showing the main street or the railway station. Until 1912, at times when the money ran out, the Zannis family considered joining him, working in his diner, a silvery building with rounded corners. Yes, maybe they should go there; they'd have to talk about it. Soon.

And, six years later, they did leave, but they didn't go to Altoona. In 1917, as Anglo-French and Greek forces fought the Bulgarians in Macedonia, a sideshow to the war in France, Salonika burned, in what came to be known as the Great Fire. The Zannis house, up in the heights by the ancient battlements, survived, but the florist shop did not, and there was no money to rebuild. Now what?

It was his father's brother who saved the day. He had, as a young man, involved himself in fighting the Turks, with a pistol, and the day came when, threatened with life in a Turkish prison, he had to run away. He ran to Paris, mostly walking or riding trains without a ticket until they threw him off, but in time he got there.

And, with luck and determination, with playing cards for money, and with the advent of a jolly French widow of a certain age, he had managed to buy a stall in the flea market in Clignancourt, in the well-

17

visited section known as Serpette. "Forget Alteena," he wrote in a letter to his brother. "I need you here." A little money was sent and the Zannis family, parents and grandmother, Costa and his younger brother — an older sister had earlier married an electrician and emigrated to Argentina — got on a fruit ship and worked their way to Le Havre. And there, waving up at them from the wharf, was the benevolent uncle and his jolly wife. On the train, Zannis's heart rose with every beat of the rails.

Two hours later, he'd found his destiny: Paris. The girls adored him — soon enough he fell in love — and he had a lot of money for a seventeen-year-old boy from Greece. He worked for his uncle as an *antiquaire,* an antiques dealer, selling massive armoires and all sorts of junk to tourists and the very occasional Parisian. They had a magnificent old rogue with a great white beard who turned out Monets and Rubenses by the yard. "Well, I can't say, because it isn't signed, maybe you should have somebody look at it, but if the nice lady comes back in twenty minutes, as she swore she would, we'll have to sell it, so if I were you . . ."

The happiest time of his life, those twelve years.

At least, he thought later, it lasted that

long. In 1929, as the markets crashed, Zannis's father went to bed with what seemed like a bad cold then died a day later of influenza, while they were still waiting for the doctor. Bravely, Zannis's mother insisted they stay where they were — Costa was doing so well. By then he spoke good French — the lingua franca of Salonika — and he'd taken courses in German and learned to speak it well: some day the stall would be his, he'd met a woman, Laurette, a few years older than he and raising two children, and he was enchanted with her. A year earlier they'd started living together in Saint-Ouen, home to the Clignancourt market. But, as winter turned to spring, his mother's grief did not subside and she wanted to go home. Back to where she could see her family and gossip with friends.

She never said it aloud but Zannis, now head of the household, knew what she felt and so they went home. Laurette could not, or would not, leave with him, would not take her children to a foreign place, so her heart was broken. As was his. But family was family.

Back in Salonika, and urgently needing to make a living, he took a job as a policeman. He didn't much care for it, but he worked hard and did well. In a city where the

19

quarter known as the Bara held the largest red-light district in eastern Europe, in a city of waterfront dives and sailors of every nation, there was always plenty of work for a policeman. Especially the tolerant sort of policeman who settled matters before they got out of hand and never took money.

By 1934 he was promoted to detective and, three years later, to, technically, the rank of sub-commander, though nobody ever used that title. This advancement did not just happen by itself. An old and honored expression, from the time of the Turkish occupation, said that it was most fortunate to have a *barba sto palati,* an uncle in the palace, and it turned out, to Zannis's surprise, that he had that very thing. His particular talent, a kind of rough diplomacy, getting people to do what he wanted without hitting them, had been observed from on high by the head of the Salonika police, a near mystic presence in the city. Vangelis was at least eighty years old, some said older, with the smile of a saint — thus St. Vangelis, at least to those who could appreciate irony and veneration in the same phrase. For fifty years, nothing had gone on in Salonika that the old man didn't know about, and he'd watched Zannis's career with interest. So in 1937, when Zannis decided to resign his position, Vangelis offered him a new one. His own office, a detective, a clerk, and a greatly improved salary. "I need someone to handle these matters," Vangelis told him, and went on to describe what he needed. Zannis understood right away and in time became known to the world at large as *a senior police official,* but to those with knowledge of the subterranean intricacies of the city's life, and soon enough to the Salonika street, he was simply "Zannis."

Was the Belgian consul being blackmailed by a prostitute? Call Zannis.

Had the son of an Athenian politician taken a diamond ring from a jeweler and "forgotten" to pay for it? Call Zannis.

Did a German civilian arrive "unofficially" in Salonika on the freighter of a neutral nation?

When Zannis walked back to the foot of the pier he found his assistant, Gabriel — Gabi — Saltiel, waiting for him, smoking a cigarette, leaning back in the driver's seat. Saltiel loved his car, a hard-sprung black Skoda 420, built by the Czechs for Balkan roads. "Pull over behind the wall, Gabi," Zannis said. "Out of sight, where we can just see the pier."

21

Saltiel pushed the ignition button, the engine rumbled to life, and he swung the car around and headed for the customs-house. A gray fifty-five, Saltiel, tall and shambling, slump-shouldered and myopic, who viewed the world, with a mixture of patience and cynicism, through thick-framed eyeglasses. A Sephardic Jew, from the large community in Salonika, he'd somehow become a policeman and pros-pered at the job because he was intelligent, sharp, very smart about people — who they really were — and persistent: a courteous, diffident bulldog. On the day that Vangelis offered Zannis the new job, saying, "And find somebody you can work with," he had telephoned Gabi Saltiel, explained what he'd be doing, and asked Saltiel to join him. "What's it called, this department?" Saltiel said. "It doesn't need a name," Zannis answered. Ten seconds passed, a long time on the telephone. Finally, Saltiel said, "When do I start?"

Now Zannis headed for the taxi, gave the driver some money, thanked him, and sent him home. When Zannis slid into the pas-senger seat of the Skoda, Saltiel said, "So, what's going on?"

Zannis repeated the port captain's story, then said, "As long as he doesn't enter the

22

city, we leave him alone. We'll give him a few hours to do something, then, if he's still holed up in the ship, I'll get some detectives to replace us."

"What if he waits until morning, strolls down here and shows a passport to the control officer?"

"Follow him," Zannis said. "I don't want him running loose in the city."

"German, you said."

"Reads a German newspaper, who knows what he is."

"A spy, you think?"

"Could be. The Turkish captain more or less said he was. With a look."

Saltiel laughed. "The Levant," he said. "A look indeed — I wouldn't live anywhere else." After a moment he added, "What's a spy after in Salonika? Any idea?"

"Who knows. Maybe just the war, coming south."

"Don't say such things, Costa. Down here, at the ass-end of the Balkans, who cares?"

"Not Hitler. Not according to the newspapers. And he has to know what goes on here, up in the mountains, when we're occupied."

Saltiel looked thoughtful. "Still," he said.

"What?"

"Well, I have a nephew who teaches at the technical school. Geography, among other things. A smart boy, Manni, he says that as long as Hitler stays allied with the Russians, we're safe. But, if he attacks them, we could be in for it. On the map of Europe we're the right flank — if somebody's headed east, the right flank that goes to the Caucasus, for the oil. Anyhow, that's Manni's theory."

"Believe it?"

Saltiel shrugged. "Hitler's cunning, I wouldn't say intelligent, but cunning. Jews he attacks, Russians he leaves alone."

Zannis nodded, it sounded reasonable. "Before I forget," he said, "did you bring what I asked for?"

"In the glove box."

Zannis opened the glove box and took out a Walther PPK automatic, the German weapon preferred by Balkan detectives. There were bright metal scratches on the base of the grip. "What have you been doing with this?"

"Hanging pictures," Saltiel said. "The last time I saw my hammer, one of the grandkids was playing with it."

"Kids," Zannis said, with a smile.

"I'm blessed," Saltiel said. "You ought to get busy, Costa, you're not getting any younger."

Zannis's smile widened. "With Roxanne?" he said, naming his English girlfriend.

"Well . . . ," Saltiel said. "I guess not."

8:20 P.M. It had started to rain again, a few lightning flashes out in the Aegean. "You awake?" Zannis said.

"Just barely."

"You want a nap, go ahead."

"No thanks. Maybe later."

10:30 P.M. "By the way," Zannis said, "did you telephone Madam Pappas?"

"This morning, about eleven."

"And she said?"

"That she hated her husband and she's glad he's dead."

"That's honest."

"I thought so."

"Anything else?"

"No, she was getting ready to scream at me, so I got off the phone — you said to go easy."

Zannis nodded. "Let the detectives deal with her."

"She kill him?"

"She did."

"Naughty girl."

1:15 A.M. Quiet, in the city behind them.

25

Only faint music from the tavernas on the seafront corniche and the creaking of the pier as the tide worked at the pilings. The sound was hypnotic and Zannis fought to stay awake. He took a cigarette from the flat box in his pocket — a Papastratos No. 1, top of the line in Greece — and struck a wooden match alight with his thumbnail. Expensive, these things, so a luxury for him. He made good money now, Vangelis had seen to that, but good money for a cop, which wasn't very much, not with four people to feed. His younger brother Ari, for Aristotle, sometimes made a few drachmas by carrying messages in the city. Poor soul, he did the best he could but he wasn't quite right, had always been "different," and the family had long ago accepted him for who he was.

It was getting smoky in the car and Saltiel rolled down the window. "Do you think there are men on the moon?" he said.

"I don't know. I suppose anything's possible."

"They were arguing about it, yesterday, in the barbershop."

"Little green men? With one eye? Like in Buck Rogers?"

"I guess so."

"Somebody in your barbershop thinks

26

those movies are true?"

"That's what it sounded like."

"I'd change barbers, if I were you."

3:30 A.M. "Wake up, Gabi."

"I wasn't sleeping. Not really."

"Here he comes."

Of medium height, the man wore a raincoat and carried a briefcase. He had a hard, bony, chinless face beneath a hat with the brim tilted over his eyes. As he neared the end of the pier, Zannis and Saltiel ducked down below the windshield. By now they could hear footsteps, determined and in a hurry, that approached, then faded away from them, headed around the east side of the customshouse, toward the city — to the west lay the warehouse district and the railway station. Zannis made sure of the Walther in the pocket of his jacket, slid out of the passenger seat, and was careful not to slam the door, leaving it ajar. "Give me thirty seconds, Gabi," he said. "Then follow along, nice and slow, headlights off, and keep your distance."

Zannis walked quickly to the east side of the customshouse, paused at the corner, and had a quick look around it. Nobody. Where the hell had he gone? There was only one street he could have taken, which served

27

the warehouses. Zannis, moving at a fast trot, reached the street, turned the corner, and there he was — there somebody was — about two blocks away. Now Zannis realized he was getting wet, put up his umbrella, and moved into the shelter of the high brick wall of the first warehouse. Up ahead the German sped on, with long strides, as though, Zannis thought, he was taking his evening constitutional on a path in some Deutschland forest. A few seconds later the Skoda turned the corner behind him and Zannis signaled, waving his hand backward, for Saltiel to stay where he was. Zannis could hear the engine idling as the Skoda rolled to a stop. Could the German hear it? Doubtful, especially in the rain, but Zannis couldn't be sure — the street was dead silent.

Then the German glanced over his shoulder and turned right, down a narrow alley. He'd likely seen Zannis, but so what? Just a man with an umbrella, trudging along, shoulders hunched, on a miserable night. Zannis walked past the alley, ignoring it, eyes on the ground ahead of him, until he passed the far corner and moved out of sight. He didn't stop there but went farther down the street — if he could hear the German, the German could hear him — then looked for a place to hide. He saw a loading dock across from him and moved quickly, soaking one foot in a puddle between broken cobblestones, hurried up the steps and stood in the angle of the shuttered entryway and the wall, which was blind from the street — as far as the alley, anyhow. The German wasn't going anywhere, Zannis realized, not from this alley, where, a few years earlier, a porter had stabbed Hamid the moneylender in an argument over a few lepta — not even a drachma — and it was blocked by a high stone wall covered with a wisteria vine. Hamid had staggered as far as the wall and pulled at the wisteria, thinking to climb over, but the vine came away from the crumbling stone and he died right there. The porter covered him up with the vine but in a few hours — it was summertime — Hamid had made his presence known and the crime was discovered. A sad business, Zannis thought, the moneylenders preyed on the waterfront laborers like hawks on pigeons. Was this a law of nature? Perhaps it was. A real hawk had once tried to get at one of his little brother's canaries, in a cage on the windowsill, and bent the hell out of the wire frame.

Zannis looked at his watch, 3:39, and settled down to wait. This was a meeting, of course, and somebody was going to show up, sooner or later. If he was dumb enough to walk past the idling Skoda, they'd get both of them. If not, just the German, though Saltiel would likely take off after the second man. Woman? Maybe, anything was possible.

3:48 A.M. *Hurry up, you bastards, have your fucking meeting and let me go home to bed.* After arrest, and a trip to the police station, where they'd get what they could, then run him back to the ship. After all, he hadn't done much — entered Salonika without having his passport stamped. No point in keeping him. The German consul would squawk, Vangelis would be irritated, the hell with it.

4:00 A.M. What was the German doing down there? Was there a way through to another street that Zannis didn't know about? Oh, a fine thing that would be! *I stood there in the rain until dawn but I never saw him again.* Zannis sighed, shifted from his wet foot to his dry one, and thought about Roxanne, about making love, which was what they did. Sure, a restaurant now and . . . Suddenly, his mind snapped back to full attention.

30

From the other end of the street, at the corner of a distant alley, headlights — no car yet, just beams probing the mist. What? Could you get through down there? Zannis didn't know, but obviously somebody did because the lights swung left into the street and now pointed directly at him. He scurried along the iron shutter to the opposite corner and wound up facing the Skoda. What would Saltiel do? Nothing. The lights stayed off. *Good, Gabi, that's the way.*

And next, he thought, addressing the unseen driver of the car, *you'll turn into the alley.* It was a Renault sedan that muttered past him, going very slowly, but his prediction was off. The Renault paused at the alley, moved forward a few feet, and backed in. *Clever,* Zannis thought, ready for a fast getaway. What was this? Another murder in the alley? Was it cursed? Was this long, boring, stupid night going to end in melodrama?

Whatever happened down there didn't take long. It happened in the alley and it happened quickly and it happened where Zannis couldn't see it. A car door slammed, an engine roared, and the Renault reappeared, taking a fast left turn into the street and speeding off. Zannis squinted into the rain, trying to see through the

31

cloudy rear window — someone in the passenger seat? No, he didn't think so. As he hurried down the steps from the loading dock, he watched the Renault as it flew past the Skoda. *Count: one, two, three, four;* then the Skoda's lights came on and Saltiel made a nice easy turn and followed the Renault, which had turned east up the deserted corniche.

As Zannis approached the alley, the German came out. They stopped dead, facing each other, maybe thirty feet apart, then the German, like Hamid the moneylender, went scuttling back down the alley. Heading for the wisteria vine? No, he had a better idea, because by the time Zannis entered the alley, he'd disappeared. The magic German. Where? Zannis trotted along the sheer wall, very tense about some sort of unseen cover at his back, very certain that he was about to be shot. But then, just at the foot of the alley, a door. A door that, he guessed, would lead into the office of the warehouse. Had he forgotten it? Had it even been there, back then?

Walther. Yes, the time had come, work the slide, arm it, assume Gabi kept it loaded, assume he'd put the bullets back in the clip when he'd got done hanging up his picture. For he'd surely *unloaded* it, knowing full well that banging loaded weapons on hard surfaces wasn't such a good idea — the very least you could hope for was embarrassment and it got quickly worse from there. Grampa! The cat! No, Gabi had done the right thing because Gabi always did the right thing. No?

Zannis closed the umbrella and set it by the wall, freed the Walther's clip, found it fully loaded and locked it back in place. Then he stood to one side of the door and, making sure of his balance, raised his foot and kicked at the knob, intending to make it rattle on the other side. No bullets from inside so he reached over, turned the knob, and opened the door. Unlocked. Always unlocked? Unlocked at the moment. Keeping to the cover of the wall as much as he could, he swung the door wide, waited a beat, then rushed in low, Walther pointed ahead of him.

He'd expected an office, and hoped for a telephone. Right, then wrong. It was an office, open to the warehouse floor — filing cabinets, two desks, and an old-fashioned telephone, no dial, on the wall. But the line had been cut a few inches below the wooden box. Cut years ago? Or thirty seconds ago? He didn't know. But he did know where he was — the Albala spice warehouse. The air was thick with scent; a dense compound of fennel, opium poppies, foul silk cocoons, and Mediterranean herbs; sage and thyme and the rest. Stacked in burlap-covered bales and wooden crates out in the darkness, ready to be shipped.

He listened for a time, but heard only silence. Then waited, hoping his eyes would adjust to the darkness but the only light in the warehouse seeped through closed louvers, set high on the walls. One hand ahead of him, he moved forward, but he knew it was hopeless, he wasn't going to find the German crouched behind a bale of fennel. So he returned to the office, took hold of the door handle, and slammed it shut, then walked out into the darkness, making no attempt to move quietly.

Something moved, something much bigger than a rat. The sound, weight shifting on boards, came from somewhere above him. He waited, changed gun hands, and wiped his sweaty palm on his pants leg. Again he heard it, almost directly above his head. So, the second floor. How did one get up there? No idea. He reached in his pocket, lit a match, discovered he was in an aisle with stacked bales on both sides. Lighting a second match, he saw what looked like a stairway on the far wall.

It wasn't a stairway but a wooden ramp and, when he got there, he found what he was looking for. At the foot of the ramp was a metal cabinet with a lever affixed to one side. He pulled the lever down and the lights went on. Not a lot of light, a few bare bulbs in outlets screwed to the boards of the ceiling, and only on the first floor, but enough. Whatever was up there moved again, fast, running, then stopped.

Zannis was finding it hard to breathe — how the hell did people work in here? — the air was so charged, so chemically sharp, his eyes were watering and he had to take his glasses off and wipe away the tears. Then, in a crouch, he scurried up the ramp and dove flat at the top, his head just below floor level. Quickly, he raised up to get a look but, even with some ambient light from the first floor, the gloom at the top of the ramp quickly faded into darkness. He sniffed — this place was really reaching him — then spoke, not loud and not angry, in German. "Sir, please come out from wherever you're hiding, and let me see your hands. Please. You won't be harmed."

That did it.

Running footsteps on the far side of the second floor, then a series of thumps punctuated by a cry of panic, and, after a few beats of silence, a moan. Using two matches to reach the opposite wall, Zannis realized what had happened. There was another ramp over there but, if you didn't want to use it, there was an alternative; a square cut in the floor with a narrow and very steep set of stairs, almost a ladder, that descended to the floor below. The German's descent had clearly taken him by surprise and he was lying face down with his head on the boards and his feet on the steps above — Zannis saw that he was wearing green socks — briefcase still clutched in one hand. Carefully, Walther still held ready for use, Zannis walked down the stairs. The German said something — it sounded as though he were pleading but his voice was muffled and Zannis couldn't make out the words. He checked for weapons, found none, then took the German under the arms, turned him over, hauled him upright, and managed to get him seated on a step. For a moment he just sat there, eyes shut, nose bleeding, then he pressed a hand to the center of his chest and said, "Hospital. Hospital."

Well, Zannis thought later, I tried. He'd put one arm around the man, held him up, and walked him along a step at a time, meanwhile carrying the briefcase in his other

36

hand. It was awkward and slow; by the time they reached the street that led to the customshouse, dawn had turned the sky a dark gray. There they were lucky — a taxi was cruising slowly along the corniche, looking for the last revelers of the night. Zannis waved it down and settled the German in the backseat and the driver sped off, reaching the hospital only a few minutes later. And when they pulled up to the emergency entrance a doctor showed up right away and climbed into the back of the taxi. But then, the doctor shook his head and said, "Can't help him here. You might as well take him to the morgue, or maybe you want us to use the ambulance."

"You're sure?"

The doctor nodded and said, "I'm sorry."

By ten the next morning he was on the phone with Vangelis, who said, after hearing a brief version of the story, "And what was in the briefcase?"

"Photographs. Seventy photographs. And a sketch, in sharp pencil, a freehand map of the area around Fort Rupel."

"How do you know it was Fort Rupel?"

"It's labeled. Printed in Roman letters. The pictures were taken from a distance: roads, barbed wire, the fort itself." The line hissed, finally Zannis said, "Hello?"

"Yes. I'm here." A conventional answer, but the tone was sad and grim.

Zannis repeated what he'd said to Saltiel in the car. "Maybe just the war, coming south." Fort Rupel protected the Rupel Pass on the Bulgarian border, directly north of Salonika. The invasion route from there, down the Struma valley, was more than two thousand years old. Farmers' plows turned up spearheads, broken swords, bayonets, and bones.

"Not yet," Vangelis said. "The Nazis don't care about us. Yet. What are you doing about the Renault?"

"Saltiel never could catch him, but he did get the license plate number. Local car, so all I have to do is call the clerk."

"All right, Costa, just proceed as you think best."

"I called some friends at the newspapers — German tourist found dead on the sidewalk near his hotel. Heart attack the apparent cause. I gave them the information on the passport: Albert Heinrich, domiciled in Essen, fifty-three years old." He paused, then said, "You wouldn't prefer a spy scandal, would you?"

Vangelis snorted and said, "Oh fine! Good idea!" then added a version of a local

38

Albanian expression. "Let's fart up Hitler's nose. We'll have them down here in no time at all."

"I thought you would see it that way. As for the photographs, what's your pleasure?"

"Drop them off here, I'll send them over to the army."

"And Spiraki?"

"I was afraid you'd ask that. Tell him what happened; write him a report — he'll like that; have your clerk type it up, on Salonika police stationery. And Costa? Make damn sure you get rid of the passport before you contact Spiraki — those people love passports."

"It should go to the German consulate."

"It must. Tell me, was it really a heart attack? You didn't, ah, do anything to him, did you? Not that I'd blame you if you did."

"No, sir, he did it to himself. He was scared — afraid of being caught, afraid of failure — he was running around up there like a rat. Falling down the stairs didn't help, but if I had to have a theory I'd say he frightened himself to death."

Vangelis's voice was disgusted. "Miserable business," he said. Then, "Oh well, keep me informed."

When he'd hung up, Zannis took a piece of paper from his drawer and began to write

39

the first draft of a report to Spiraki. Formerly an Athenian lawyer, Spiraki ran the local office of the Geniki Asphalia, the State Security Bureau. It had changed names several times, becoming the Defense Intelligence Bureau in 1936; then, a few months later, as the Metaxas dictatorship took hold, the General Directorate of Foreign Citizens, but most people still called it "state security."

Zannis found Spiraki himself not so easy to deal with. Tall, heavy, balding, somber, with a thick mustache, he was given to light-blue suits, formal language, and cold-eyed stares. He never responded immediately to anything you said, there was always a dead moment before he spoke. On the other hand, he could've been worse. His office was supposed to ensure obedience to the dictatorship's morality laws, forbidding hashish and prostitution, the traditional targets, and they'd tried to go beyond that, prohibiting lewd music, the *rembetika* — filthy, criminal, passionate, and very dear to Salonika's heart. But Spiraki didn't insist, and the police were tolerant. You couldn't stop these things, not in this city. And, after four hundred years of Turkish occupation, it was unwise to press Greeks too hard.

■ ■ ■ ■

The gray sky wouldn't go away, seagulls circled above the port, their cries doing nothing to disperse the melancholy. Saltiel showed up at eleven, tired and slumped, and he and Zannis tried to finish up the investigation. The clerk at the city hall found the plate number, to her great delight. It belonged to a Renault registered by one K. L. Stacho. Zannis knew who he was, a Bulgarian undertaker, third-generation proprietor of a funeral home that buried Bulgarians, Albanians, Serbs, and Vlachs, who died with sufficient regularity to provide Stacho with a handsome villa in Salonika's wealthy neighborhood, by the sea east of the city.

Zannis telephoned and Saltiel drove them out there ten minutes later. Poor Madam Stacho, red-eyed, a balled-up handkerchief clenched in her fist, Zannis felt sorry for her. Her husband had left the house, to take care of some unspecified business, long after midnight. And he never returned. She'd been frantic of course but, at eight in the morning, a neighbor had come knocking at her door to say that Stacho had telephoned and asked her to relay a message: he would

41

not be coming home. Not for a long time. He was well, she was not to worry. Beyond that, Madam Stacho didn't know a thing.

So, did Mr. Stacho have German friends?

Not as far as she knew.

A camera?

Well, yes, he did have one, photography was a hobby of his.

For how long, a hobby. Years?

No, only a few months.

And, please Madam Stacho, excuse us, we're only doing our job, may we take a look around the house?

No answer, a wave of the hand, *Do what you like, I don't care any more.*

They did take a look. Rooms crowded with heavy furniture, thick drapes, tiled floors, a frightened maid, but no undertaker in a closet or beneath a bed.

When they returned to the parlor, Madam Stacho wondered what her husband had done to provoke the interest of the police.

They couldn't tell her, but he might have information they needed for an investigation that was currently under way.

"And that's all?" she said, obviously brightening.

"Is that not enough?"

"When he left, when I learned he wasn't coming home . . ."

42

"Yes?"

"I thought it was a woman."

"Nothing like that."

Now she was very close to beaming, held Zannis's hand warmly at the door. "Thank you, gentlemen," she said. "Thank you."

"Perhaps you would notify us, if he returns; he can clear his name by answering a few questions."

Oh definitely, surely, absolutely, no doubt about it.

In the Skoda, Zannis had Saltiel drive him back to the alley behind the Albala spice warehouse.

But the umbrella was gone.

That night, he was supposed to take Roxanne to the movies, a Turkish Western — *Slade Visits Wyoming* was his attempt at translation — but by the time he reached the Pension Bastasini, the hotel where she lived, he was in another kind of mood. His love affair with Roxanne Brown had gone on for more than a year and had reached that pleasantly intimate plateau where plans were casually made and just as easily changed. "Perhaps the Balthazar," he suggested. The name of a taverna but it meant much more than that.

"Then we shan't be visiting Wyoming?

43

With Effendi Slade?" This in English, but for the Turkish title. Her Greek was close to perfect but she knew how her English voice affected him. Prim, upper-class, clipped, and chilly, a voice perfectly suited to her firm horsewoman's body, weathered face, mouth barely touched with lipstick.

"Perhaps we could go later. Or now, if you prefer."

"No," she said. "I prefer depravity."

Balthazar, tucked away in a cellar beneath lowlife Vardar Square, wasn't far away so they walked, protected by her umbrella, a hideous thing with pink polka dots on a green field. Very much a couple; his arm reached around her shoulders — they were just about the same height — hers around his waist. "Is the world being good to you, this week?" he said.

"Not too bad. The school has a recital coming up this weekend but I refuse to worry about it." Arriving in Salonika in 1938, by way of expatriate years spent first in southern France, then in Capri, she had purchased the Mount Olympus School of Ballet and, once every eight weeks, the daughters of the city's bourgeoisie, *all* shapes and sizes, twirled around the stage to Tchaikovsky. As rendered by a victrola that ran, in its old age, not as fast as it once did, so the dance was perhaps a little on the stately side, which frankly suited some of the statelier daughters.

"Am I invited to the recital?" he asked.

She pressed her cheek against his. "Many things I might ask of you, my dear, but . . ."

"Do you perform?"

"In tights? I think not."

"Don't tell *me* you can't wear tights."

"*That* is for you to look at, not the butcher and his wife."

Balthazar was delighted to see them and offered a solemn bow. "So pleased," he said, "it's been too long," and led them to a very small, very private room. Filled with ottomans, wool carpets, and low brass tables, the soft, shadowy darkness barely disturbed by a spirit lamp flickering in one corner. Balthazar lit some incense, then prepared two narghilehs, each with a generous lump of ochre-colored hashish. "You will eat later?" he said. "A nice meze?" Small appetizers — eggplant, feta, hummus.

"Perhaps we will."

He well knew they would but didn't make a point of it, saying only, "As you wish," and closing the door carefully — their privacy his personal responsibility.

Music would have been nice and, as it turned out, music there was. If not from

45

Balthazar itself, from the taverna next door, a bouzouki band and a woman singer, muffled by the wall, so just the right volume. They sat on a low loveseat, shoulders and hips touching, and leaned over a worked-brass table. When Zannis inhaled, the water in the narghileh bubbled and took the harsh edge off the hashish so he could hold the smoke in for a long time.

They were silent for a while, but eventually she said, "Quite nice tonight. The smoke tastes good, like . . . what? Lemon and lime?"

"Did you ever eat it?"

"No."

"Best not."

"Oh?"

"Very powerful. It will take you, ah, far away. Far, far away."

"I'm rather far away as it is." After a moment she said, "You see that little lamp in the corner? It reminds me of Aladdin, I believe it might have been in a book I had, as a child." She stared into the distance, then said, "Do you suppose, if I rubbed it . . . ?"

"You'd burn your fingers, the genie keeps it hot."

"Doesn't want to come out?"

"Not in this weather."

She giggled. "Not in this weather." She tossed the tube of the narghileh on the table, turned sideways, rested her head on his shoulder, and began to unbutton his shirt. That done, she spread it apart and laid her cheek on his chest — hairless and smooth, with broad, flat plates. Putting her lips against his skin, she said, "You *smell* good."

"I do? I took a bath, maybe it's the soap."

"No, it isn't soap, it's something about you, something sweet."

For a time they drifted, then, returning from wherever he'd been, he said, "Would you like to sit on my lap?"

"I always like that." She stood, hiked up her dress, settled herself on his thighs, leaned her weight against him, and raised her knees, so that, as if by magic, his hand covered her bottom. On the other side of the wall, the singer's voice grew plaintive. That made them both laugh, as though she could see through the wall. "Can you understand the lyric?" he said.

She shook her head.

"She's singing about her flower."

"In her garden?"

He moved her top knee a little and said, "No, this one." The tips of his index and middle fingers rested on tight cotton. She

47

was, he thought, so very clever, wearing white cotton panties, just right for a proper Englishwoman, but they were cut to provide a snug fit, and the cotton felt very fine, very soft, to his fingers. After a few moments, a breath escaped her; he could feel it and he could almost, but not quite, hear it. Delicately, he moved his fingers, not ambitious, simply savoring the warm reception, and much more pleased than proud.

On. And on. Until she raised her head and spoke quietly by his ear, in the King's English: "Let's have those off, shall we?"

Later, after Zannis had gone out into the public room and Balthazar had brought them — now famished — the meze, she scooped up some hummus with a triangle of pita bread and said, "Strange, but it just now occurs to me that the ottoman is an extraordinary piece of furniture, ingenious."

"Yes?"

"Oh yes. Because you can, you know, also sit on it."

After such a night, going back to work the next day was something like a punishment. Sibylla, the office clerk, always starched and taut, was wound especially tight that morning — neither Saltiel nor Zannis would admit it but they were both afraid of her.

She stood straight as a stick, with fair hair set every Wednesday in a warrior's helmet. And *warrior* was, at the moment, the very word, for she had come to work in a bad mood and was taking it out on the files.

Of these, there were two distinct sets. The first lived in a row of wooden filing cabinets in what was called *the other room* — there were two, with a bathroom in the hall — and included all the various paper that flowed through a government bloodstream: directions from on high, carbons of correspondence, letters from the citizenry, and various oddments, like newspaper clippings, that got themselves into the files and stayed there. Though sometimes — as witness Sibylla's attack *du jour* — not forever.

"Gabi," she said, holding a paper so that Saltiel could read it, "is this important?"

Saltiel didn't want to read it. "Probably not."

"A memorandum, from Station Six. It seems to concern the cemetery."

"Which one?"

"The old Turkish one. The subject is 'Copulation at Night.' "

"By the living?"

"If not, keep it," Zannis said, looking up from his desk. They couldn't really get Sibylla to laugh, but they never stopped trying.

Instead, a sigh. What bad boys they were. "Dated 10 September, 1938."

"By now, they're likely done copulating," Saltiel said. "Get rid of it."

The other file was maintained by Zannis, on five-by-eight cards in shoeboxes, and, taken altogether, was a working map of the power centers — and there were many — of Salonika. Thus it included cards for ship-owners and bankers, Greek Orthodox prelates, consuls, spies, resident foreigners, journalists, politicians, high-class criminals, and courtesans — anybody who mattered. For an official whose job was to work behind the scenes, it was crucial to keep track of the cast of characters.

The files, both sets, played a central role in the unnamed office on the Via Egnatia, with support from three typewriters, three telephones, and one more device which, from time to time, would remind them of its presence by ringing a little bell. As it did at that moment, producing a mumbled *"Skata,"* from Zannis — the Greek equivalent of the French *merde* — by which he meant *now what*. The device, on its own private table in the corner, was a Model 15 Siemens teleprinter, and now, all by itself, it began to type, fast and furious, a page rising slowly from a slot above its keyboard.

Zannis stood by the table and read the text as it appeared.

AS PER YOUR QUERY 6 OCTOBER 1940 STOP MAIN BORDER STATIONS REPORT NO RECORD RENAULT MODEL UN-KNOWN LICENSE SK 549 ENTERING BULGARIA LAST 48 HOURS STOP NO RECORD GREEK NATIONAL K L STACHO THIS OFFICE STOP SIGNED LAZAREFF END

The teleprinter waited, making its *thucka-thucka-thucka* sound, for thirty seconds, then shut down. Well, Zannis thought, I gave it a try. On a hunch that Stacho had fled up to Bulgaria, he'd had Sibylla send a teletype to his old friend, Ivan Lazareff, in Sofia. If he'd thought that Stacho was spying for Bulgaria — a perfectly reasonable assumption — he wouldn't have done it, but the undertaker, a Greek citizen of Bulgarian descent, was spying for Germany, or at least for a man carrying German documents, so he'd taken a chance. And why not? He'd known Lazareff for years; they'd had plenty of good times in Greek and Bulgarian bars back when they'd both been detectives. At one time they'd talked on the telephone — mostly in German — but now that Zannis

51

was a police official and Lazareff a chief of detectives, they communicated back and forth by teletype.

Logically, the purchase of the Siemens equipment should have been animated by some urge for progress, but it wasn't so. As German power surged in Europe, German corporations drove deep into the Balkans, buying up raw materials at preferential prices and selling — often trading — technology in return. Roumanian wheat moved east; back the other way came Leica cameras, aspirin, harmonicas, and, in some of the police stations in the cities and towns of southern Europe, teletype systems. In many cases, the purchase wasn't optional, was instead dictated by a very apprehensive foreign policy — *we must appease these people, buy the damn machine!* And yes, there were stories of hens nesting atop teleprinters in Serbian villages, and no, you really weren't going to hunt down the goat thief sought by a Roumanian police officer, but the system did work and, soon enough, some Balkan policemen found that it had its uses.

10 October. Hotel Lux Palace, Salonika.
Maybe just the war, moving south.
The end of her cigarette was marked with

lipstick, dark red, a color that emphasized her black hair and pale skin. *Stunning,* Zannis thought, was the word for her. And seductive, future delights suggested in the depths of her glance. And a liar, because she had no intention of going to bed with him or anybody else. She was important, this woman; she would never do such things. She was, however, scared, and not used to it, so she flirted a little with the handsome policeman, because she needed help.

He was here, in the best suite the best hotel in the city had to offer, at Saltiel's suggestion. No, request, though put mildly enough. This was a Jewish matter, originating with some pillar of the Sephardic community who knew to reach Zannis by way of Saltiel.

She ordered coffee, sat Zannis in a brown velvet armchair, turned the chair that went with the escritoire halfway and perched on its edge, facing him. Heels together, posture erect. "Frau Krebs is terribly formal," she said, her voice in cultured and well-modulated German. "Everybody calls me Emmi, for Emilia."

"And I'm Costa, for Constantine. My last name is Zannis. And they are?"

He referred to two children, the boy seven,

53

he guessed, the girl perhaps nine, in a staged tableau beyond the open bedroom door. They were perfectly dressed, Jewish by their looks, the girl reading a book, the boy coloring with crayons.

"Nathanial and Paula." The girl looked up from her book, smiled at Zannis, then went back to reading — or pretending to read.

"Attractive children, no doubt you're proud of them."

Silence. She hesitated, a shall-I-lie hesitation that Zannis had seen many times before. She inhaled her cigarette, tapped it above the ashtray, and finally said, "No."

"Not proud?" He smiled, of course she meant no such thing.

"They're not my children." Then, regret. "Does it matter?" She was worried that she'd made a mistake.

"It doesn't matter, but it is interesting. I'm sure you'll explain."

The waiter arrived, bringing croissants, butter, jam, Greek pastry, and coffee. In ordering, she'd covered all the possibilities. "I thought you might like something to eat."

"Maybe later."

The tray was set on a table and she tipped the waiter.

"Two days ago, I arrived at the Turkish border on what used to be called the Orient

Express. But we were turned back by a customs officer, so here we are, in Salonika."

"A Turkish customs officer?" he said. Then made the classic baksheesh gesture, thumb rubbed across the first two fingers, and raised his eyebrows.

She appreciated the theatre. "Oh, I tried, but I somehow managed to find the only honest official in the Levant."

"For what reason, Emmi, turned back?"

"Some question about papers."

"Are they legitimate?"

"I thought they were. I was told they were."

"By . . . ?"

"A lawyer in Berlin. I paid him to obtain the right papers, Turkish entry visas, but what I got were — um, cooked up. False papers. That's what the officer said."

"And then you offered a bribe."

"I started to but, oh, you should have seen his face. I think he might have put us in prison."

Sympathetic, Zannis nodded. "Always best, we think here, to avoid time in Turkish prisons. Emmi, if they're not your children, whose are they?"

"A friend's. An old school friend. A Jewish friend. She can't get out of Germany;

she asked for help, I volunteered to take the children out. To Istanbul — where there are people who will take care of them."

"And where you will live."

Slowly, she shook her head, then put her cigarette out, pressing the end against the glass. "No, I will go back."

"Forgive me, I assumed you were Jewish."

"I am."

Zannis didn't answer. It was properly hushed on the top floor of the Lux Palace; from the corridor outside the room he could hear the whir of a vacuum cleaner. He stood up, walked over to the window and looked out to sea, at a steamship and its column of smoke against the sky. As he returned to the chair she met his eyes. Stunning, he thought again, and hard, much harder than he'd first thought. *What have I stumbled on?* Back in the chair, he leaned forward and spoke quietly. "You don't *have* to say anything, if you don't want to. I'll still help you."

She nodded, grateful for his understanding. In the bedroom, the boy said, his voice just above a whisper, "Should this be green?"

"No, blue," the girl said.

Emilia Krebs bent toward him and lowered her voice. "It was very hard for them. They couldn't go to school, they couldn't

56

really go outdoors — Berlin is brutal now. Do you understand?"

His expression said that he understood perfectly.

"So, my friend asked me to get them out, somewhere safe. Because she knew I could go in and out of Germany. *Krebs* is Colonel Hugo Krebs, my husband, and a very powerful man."

"In the party?" He meant the Nazi party, and kept his voice light and neutral.

"Never." She was offended that he could even suggest such a thing, and her voice knew how to be offended. "No, he isn't like that. He's a career officer; he serves on the General Staff of the Wehrmacht, a manager of logistics — trains getting where they're needed on time, enough socks — it's not glamorous, but it is quite important."

"I know what it is," Zannis said. "Is there a *J* stamped in your passport?" That was now a legal requirement in Germany, a *J* for Juden, Jew.

"Oh no, not mine; they wouldn't dare."

"No, likely they wouldn't, not with you married to a man in his position, and he's probably not Jewish — he couldn't be, the way things are in Germany."

"A Lutheran, from a solid old family, though nothing special. We met, we fell in love, and we married — he's a wonderful man. We were never able to have children, but we lived a good life, then Hitler came to power. Hugo would have resigned his commission but he realized that, with a Jewish wife, it was better for us if he stayed where he was."

Zannis nodded, acknowledging an unfortunate truth. *And,* he thought, *logistics is the word.* How to get this woman and the two children to Turkey? "Could you tell me how, once you reached Istanbul, you planned to return to Berlin?"

"I didn't see it as a problem," she said, hesitant, not sure what he had in mind.

"By steamship?"

"Heavens no. It's faster to fly. From Istanbul to Bucharest, then on to Berlin. Lufthansa has routes to all the neutral countries."

"But you didn't fly to Istanbul. I imagine, with two children, it would have been expensive."

"It wasn't that, I don't care about money. Hugo and I thought the three of us might be a little too noticeable at Tempelhof — Gestapo everywhere, at the airport — so better to go on the train. By stages, you see, first to Vienna, then Budapest, Belgrade, Sofia, and on to Istanbul. We got as far as

58

the border control at Edirne, in Turkey."

"But you came back to Salonika."

"Because I knew there were Jews in Salonika — 'the Jerusalem of the Balkans,' all that."

"Yes, at one time a majority here, and still a large community."

"I couldn't think what else to do. Going back to Berlin was out of the question, of course."

"Why?"

"Because" — she paused, then said — "that would have been, well, failure."

"And you don't fail."

"How could I?" With a shift of her eyes, she referred to the children in the bedroom.

Zannis thought for a moment; then he said, "There *is* one thing I wondered about."

"Anything." She encouraged him with a smile; certainly they had become, almost, friends, she hoped.

"You said, 'I don't care about money,' and I don't mean to pry, but I suspect you weren't talking about the pay of an army colonel."

"You don't mean to pry?" Arch and amused.

Zannis's turn to smile.

"I have money of my own. I am Emilia Krebs but I used to be, I guess I still am,

59

Emilia Adler. A name you might recognize, if you were German. Emilia Adler, of the Frankfurt Adlers, private bankers since the Middle Ages and very, very rich. There, it's out."

Zannis was puzzled and showed it. "Now? Under the Nazis? My impression was that they'd stolen all the Jewish money in Germany, forced the sale of Jewish businesses, prevented funds from leaving the country. Not true?"

"Not quite. Because once the Nazis got hold of the money they had to do something with it. Much of it went to Switzerland, but a substantial amount was deposited with my grandfather, at the Adler Bank in Frankfurt. That's because he pays interest of twelve percent — which the Swiss, believe me, don't."

Zannis was impressed. "Twelve percent."

"There's no way he can invest at that level, of course, though the Nazis think he can — the cunning Jew, working in secret. . . . But, in fact, the money is coming from his own resources, it is a rather elegant form of bribery."

After a moment, Zannis said, "Forever?"

"No. But for a time, maybe a year, maybe more. He knew they would come after him, in 1936, he knew, so he went after them.

Gently. He is on the surface a very gentle man, though he's not really like that."

"Nor are you."

"Nor am I."

"And your father, works for the bank?"

"My father died ten years ago."

"I'm sorry."

"In Persia, where we held bonds for the building of water systems."

"Of . . . an illness?"

"Of passion. A heart attack in a bordello. We like to believe he died happy. So there, Herr Zannis, now you have it all."

"Almost. I'd like to know how you managed to secure exit papers for the children."

"The lawyer *did* do that — at least he got something right."

"How was it done? Do you know?"

"With a bribe, according to the lawyer. Fifty thousand reichsmark. Anyhow, that's what I paid him, besides his fee, but all I have is his word." She shrugged. "It might have been less."

Zannis raised his eyebrows — a *lot* of money. "What, in dollars: twenty-five thousand? People could live on that for years."

"Closer to twenty, I believe. Still, a substantial sum; this kind of transaction has become very expensive in the Reich. The Nazis are vicious and criminal but, thank

61

God, they are also venal. The ideology, for many of them, is only skin-deep — they like power, and they *love* money."

"Well, I'll need the exit papers, for a day or two, maybe longer."

As she went for her purse, Zannis rose to his feet and said, "Now I think I will have a coffee — may I pour one for you?"

"Please."

"Nathanial?" Zannis said. "Paula? Would you like a pastry?"

12 October. The Club de Salonique.

It was *the* place in the city, so much so that even the mighty Vangelis had had a difficult time getting Zannis a membership. "Not only did I have to put my thumb in a certain place," the old man told him, "but I had to press hard." Nonetheless, it was crucial for Zannis to belong, because some of the most important business in Salonika was done there, in the club's own building on the fancy end of the corniche. The atmosphere in the dark mahogany dining room, with its view over the sea and its hushed luncheon ritual — subdued conversation, just the barest music of china and silverware — was privilege transcendent.

Just the setting for Celebi, the Turkish consul. Easily a film version of the diplomat,

62

Celebi — silver hair, serene smile, ivory cigarette holder; Roxanne had once described him as *debonair.* The waiter arrived, they ordered indifferently — the food was too polite to be good — and Zannis was properly grateful for Celebi's seeing him on such short notice. Aperitifs were served, Zannis said he needed a favor, Celebi's expression changed only slightly — *oh?* So it was to be a sophisticated sort of a luncheon, based on the most sophisticated sort of understanding about life and politics, though somewhat less sophisticated was the view out the window, where a merchant freighter, torpedoed that morning, burned while they dined. Mostly black smoke but, if one of your sideways glances came at just the right moment, you might catch a bright dot of fire.

"She's a very cultivated woman," Zannis said. "Jewish, and a person of some standing in the social world of Berlin."

"Really?"

"So it seems."

"She must be terribly rich, then. I'm afraid the rest of them . . ."

"I know."

"She's in difficulties?"

"In a way. She's trying to get a friend's children out of Berlin."

"And into Turkey?"

"Yes. Will you have another one?"

"Oh, I don't know . . ."

"Waiter?"

"Sir?"

"Two more, please."

"I shouldn't . . ."

"Let's go to hell a little, no? A nap this afternoon . . ."

"Maybe *you* can . . ."

"You're busy?"

"It's frightful. Half the world trying to get in the door. I'm over *January's* limit now, for entry visas, and my superiors in Istanbul are becoming tiresome."

Zannis shook his head. "Damned war."

"We could've done without, that's certain. Why don't you just smuggle them in? Everyone else does."

"They're kids, Ahmet. Sweet kids. I don't want them to pee their pants every time some cop looks at them in the street."

"Oh, yes, well, you're right then. They'll need real documents."

"Can you reason with Istanbul?"

"Umm, yes and no. But, truth is, I may have to sweeten somebody."

"Well, *that* won't be a problem."

"No?"

"No, I don't think so."

64

Celebi took a cigarette from a silver case and twisted it into his cigarette holder.

Zannis flicked a lighter and, as Celebi bent toward the flame, said, "What do you think, four hundred?"

"I assume you don't mean drachmas."

"Dollars."

"Apiece?"

"Yes. An adult and two children."

"Can she get dollars?"

"In Salonika?"

Celebi nodded, amused, to himself: *of course.* "I'll send Madam Urglu along, say, tomorrow afternoon?"

"I'll expect her. I have an envelope with me — German exit visas, you can get the information from them."

"On the way out," Celebi said.

Zannis nodded in agreement. So elegant, the dining room of the Club de Salonique, not a place to be passing envelopes across the table.

Blue sky, that afternoon, sparkling air after the rain, the snow-capped Mount Olympus visible across the bay. Zannis walked back to the office along the busy Via Egnatia, taking his time, pausing to look at the windows of the shops. He made a mental note to contact Emilia Krebs when he reached the

65

office, giving her time to arrange the money for the bribe — he doubted any of it would ever reach Istanbul — so that by the following afternoon he could give an envelope to Madam Urglu.

He didn't much care for Madam Urglu, said to be Celebi's chief spy. In her fifties, pigeon-breasted and stout, with glasses on a chain around her neck and a sharp tongue. Spiraki at state security claimed she served as a spymaster for various secret agents — "coded wireless transmission Monday and Thursday nights," he'd said, "from the top floor of the legation." Probably he was right, Zannis thought, staring at a display of tennis rackets and a poster of a blond woman in mid-backhand, but he wondered what intelligence, secret intelligence, the Turks wanted in Salonika. Whatever it might be, he was hardly shocked.

After all, they'd been fighting the Turks forever — famously in Troy, in Homeric days, but that surely wasn't the first time. The last time it started was in 1919, when the Greek armies had gone up into Turkey and occupied the coastal city of Smyrna. There was even talk in those days about getting Constantinople — Byzantium — back, the great capital of the Byzantine Empire, taken by Moslem Turks in 1453. They'd had

66

it long enough, no?

Well, they still had it, now Istanbul. And the Turkish armies had retaken Smyrna in 1922: burned the town, slaughtered the Greek population, and changed the name to Izmir. In the following year a treaty was signed: three hundred and fifty thousand Turks left Greece, and a million and a half Greeks came to Greece from Turkey, came back home, where they hadn't lived for a thousand years. Thus, in the autumn of 1940, there was still a taverna called Smyrna Betrayed, located on what had once been known as Basil-the-Slayer-of-Bulgars Street. Renamed the Street of the Franks, in memory of yet another conquest. Easy enough to find new names in a city where the wars outnumbered the streets.

Back at the office, he telephoned Emilia Krebs at the Lux Palace. She was very emotional, close to tears — as close as she ever came, he thought, and these would've been tears of relief. Yes, she had the money, and the minute she got off the phone she'd go out and buy dollars. Victory. He supposed you had to call it that: two kids off to grow up in a foreign country, perhaps never to see their parents again, but at least alive. And late in the afternoon on 16 October, he rode in a taxi to the railway station so Emilia and the children could board the 17:20 express to Istanbul. In the waiting room, Nathanial and Paula sat quietly — too quietly, too much had happened to them — and Emilia Krebs gave him a sheet of Lux Palace notepaper with her address and telephone number in Berlin. "There may come a time," she said, "when I can return the favor."

"Maybe," he said, meaning *likely never.*

"The way the world is going now, you can't tell about the future." The approaching train sounded its whistle and she put a hand on his arm. "I can never thank you enough," she said. "For helping me."

"You don't have to thank me," he said. "Who could say no?"

He left the office early that day and headed back to his apartment — two small rooms on a cobbled lane called Santaroza, between the railway station and the port. Not the best part of town, on the border of what had been the Jewish district before the Great Fire. He would play with his big mountain sheepdog, Melissa — honeybee — who would be waiting for him in the doorway after a hard day's work in the neighborhood. This was a night, one of two or three every week, when he would go to his mother's house for dinner. Melissa always accompanied him and would stay until he returned for the next visit.

She was a big girl, eighty pounds, with a thick soft black-and-white coat and a smooth face, long muzzle, and beautiful eyes — not unlike the Great Pyrenees. Queen of the street, she started her morning by walking him a few blocks toward the office, to a point where, instinct told her, he was no longer in danger of being attacked by wolves. Next, she returned home to protect the local kids on their way to school, then accompanied the postman on his rounds. That done, she would guard the chicken coop in a neighbor's courtyard, head resting on massive paws. If a marauding fox didn't show up, she'd wait until it was time to trot off to the school and see the kids safely home.

Nobody taught her any of this, it was all in her bloodline, coming from the mountains where her ancestors — perhaps descendants of Turkish Akbash dogs — guarded flocks but didn't herd them. Thus she would never trot in front of or behind her charges, but stayed always to one side. Watchful. And independent; when Zannis had tried putting her on a leash she'd responded by lying down and refusing to move. Nonetheless, a splendid girl, from a mountain village where these dogs were highly valued. Zannis counted himself lucky to have been able to buy a puppy from a good litter.

She stood when he appeared, gave a single low bark of greeting, then had her pretty ears smoothed back, her muzzle flapped, and her ruff given a few affectionate tugs. Across the lane, two old ladies sitting on kitchen chairs — always brought out in good weather — beamed at the spectacle. Then he took her up to his apartment. There were two floors in the narrow building; he had the second. "We're going to see Grandma tonight," he told her. Melissa's ears shot up. At the house in the old Turkish quarter by the battlements, Zannis's grandmother always brought home the most succulent butcher's scraps on the nights when Melissa came for dinner.

But the shopping didn't end there. Accompanied by Zannis's mother and his brother, Ari, his grandmother campaigned through the markets, coming home with fresh creamy feta, baby red mullet, calamari, or a chicken with yellow skin — the best kind of chicken, the *only* kind of chicken — making sure that she got extra feet for the soup pot. Oh they spoiled him rotten, begged him to stay over, which he often did, then sent him off with two of his shirts, boiled white and perfectly ironed.

17 October. Life back to normal, thank heaven. A few cases referred to the office — not much to be done with most of them. A local politician's wife had gone missing; they could work on that, likely to discover she'd run off with her lover. Otherwise it was quiet. Strange — with half the continent occupied by Germany, and Great Britain standing alone in opposition and fighting for its life — but quiet. At one time, Zannis had received letters from Laurette, in Paris, but now, with the occupation, the letters came only once in a great while. He answered them, carefully, carefully, because they would be read by the German censor. So Laurette would know he was well, that he often thought of her, and something of the Salonika weather.

On the evening of the seventeenth, a party. At the house of a young professor of literature at the university, more Roxanne's friend than his, but he was happy enough to go. Roxanne had a huge appetite for parties; Zannis went along, smiled, talked, looked covertly at his watch. This particular party was nothing new — Salonika's high bohemian caste gathered for wine and retsina, seductions physical and social — but it was apparently one of the more important parties that autumn, because Elias showed up. Elias, the king of the city's poets, and of sufficient stature and self-esteem to call himself by one name only, perhaps his first, perhaps his last, perhaps neither — maybe chosen for mellifluous sonority, who knew. Elias certainly looked like the king of the poets, with snow-white prophet's beard and Einstein hair. "He doesn't own a comb," went the local witticism. "He just unscrews the bulb and sticks his finger in a lamp." Discovering Zannis — they'd met several times — hiding in a corner, Elias rocked back on his heels and squinted his eyes, like a zoologist encountering an interesting animal. "Ah Zannis, you're here."

"Nice to see you, Elias."

"So, how goes life with the bullyboys?"

"Myself, I avoid them."

"Really? So do I."

"Are you hard at work, these days?"

"I am, yes I am. Perhaps a new book next year."

"I look forward to reading it."

"Do you have the others?"

"I've given a couple of them as gifts, and I

have one of my own. *Dawn* — um . . ."

"Dawn of the Goddess."

"That's it."

"Maybe not my best. Early work."

"I liked it," Zannis said. "The one about the owl."

Elias thought for a time. " 'Night in the Field'?"

"Could be. I don't exactly remember."

" 'In the late night, the huntress wakes to hunt'? That one?"

"Right. That one."

"Zannis, it isn't about an owl. It's about — well, a woman, a woman I knew."

You knew a woman who ate mice? Skata! "Elias," he said, "I'm just a policeman." He didn't say, "just a *simple* policeman," but even so Elias heard the *simple,* which meant that Zannis had pushed the proper button, because the word made him a *worker,* a *worker of the world* who would, in some misty future, *unite.*

"Well, maybe you have a point," Elias said, his voice not unkind. "If you take it literally."

Zannis sensed that Elias was preparing to escape, but Zannis wasn't ready to let him go. "Tell me, Elias, do you ever go up into the mountains? See old friends?" It was said of Elias, and Zannis believed it to be true,

73

that as a young man he'd gone to the mountains and fought alongside the klephts. This was the name given to the men from the mountain villages who'd fought the Turks — essentially resistance fighters — and who were sometimes shepherds and sometimes bandits, as well as guerrillas.

Elias changed; his party-guest hauteur vanished. "No," he said ruefully, now the Elias of a former life. "No, I don't. I don't see them. I do go up there, especially in the spring, because it is so beautiful, but what you're talking about, no, that was a long time ago."

"True, many years ago. But I'd guess your old friends are still around. The ones who survived."

Elias had the last sip of his wine. "Are you asking as a policeman?"

Zannis didn't care for the question. "No, not at all. Those days are long gone, and people in my family did the same thing, against the Turks. I was only curious and, if you really want to know, I was wondering if you'd ever write about it."

Elias shook his head. "Not me, not ever. Up there, secrecy is a religion, and even though it was long ago you keep faith with it. Not that I'd mind seeing them again; when you fight alongside people, their life is in your hands, yours in theirs; it's beyond anything else — family, love, anything. And they aren't like people down here. To them, freedom is everything. You know how they refer to themselves, as *adespotoi.* Masterless."

"Yes, I know the word. They aren't the only ones."

"Well, maybe not, we'll see."

"We'll see?"

"The war."

"You think it will come here?"

"The Four Horsemen of the Apocalypse, yes, all of it, and there will be cowardice and bravery." Elias paused for a moment, then said, "Of course I hope I'm wrong. The Turkish gendarmerie was bad enough, believe me, but these people . . ." He looked down at his glass and said, "It appears I'm going to need some more of this."

"I'm glad we had a chance to talk," Zannis said.

Maybe Elias wasn't so glad. His expression, as he nodded a brusque farewell and went off to refill his glass, was vaguely troubled. But not for long. As he reached the middle of the room, he cried out, "Helena! My heart's desire! Where've you been hiding?"

■ ■ ■ ■

People arrived, nobody left, the room grew warmer, the party got louder, somebody put on a *rembetika* record, a woman closed her eyes and danced without moving her feet. Zannis talked to a lawyer's wife, to an actor — "It's like Sophocles, only modern" — to the professor host, to the cultural attaché from the German embassy in Athens — "We are madly Hellenophile; you know, we have a great passion for Greece" — and was happily engaged with a woman painter when Roxanne appeared and towed him away. "Somebody you must meet," she said.

A tall fellow leaning against a doorframe smiled expectantly as Roxanne led Zannis toward him. Zannis knew immediately that he was English: sand-colored hair swept across a handsome forehead, lines of early middle age graven in a youthful face that made him look like an old boy.

"This is Francis Escovil," Roxanne said. She gave the name some extra flavor, as though Zannis was expected to know who he was. "The travel writer," she added.

"Hello," Escovil said, smiling as he shook hands. He wore his shirt with collar open and one button undone, had an old tweed jacket draped over his shoulders, and was drinking beer from a bottle.

"Please, to meet you," Zannis said, in his shaky English.

"I hope you'll be patient with my Greek," Escovil said, in Greek.

"Francis did classics at Cambridge," Roxanne said.

"Ancient Greek," Escovil said, apologetic. "I'm trying to learn the demotic. You'll have to forgive me if I say odd things."

"We all say odd things. In all sorts of languages."

Escovil found the remark amusing. "I see why Roxanne likes you."

"You're writing about Salonika?"

"I believe I will. Will try."

Zannis was puzzled. "You didn't come here from *Britain,* did you?"

Escovil laughed. "Now there's an idea! 'Despite the war' " — with a dramatic shading of his voice he implied quotation marks — " 'I was off to old Salonika. On the merry battleship — umm, *Valorious!*' No, no, when we declared war in 'thirty-nine I happened to be in Alexandria, so I took a job with the local English newspaper. Not much of a job — it barely pays, you know — but they allow me to do the occasional travel piece."

Out of the corner of his eye, Zannis could

see that Roxanne had the glow of a woman whose two attractive male friends are getting along well. He nodded, *now I understand,* then said, "Still, it must be hard to find places to write about, with a war going on."

"Only the neutrals. 'On Skis in Frosty Switzerland!' 'A Visit to Sunny Spain!' And, truth to tell, it's hard to reach even those countries."

"At least there is Salonika," Zannis said. "Or anywhere in Greece, or Turkey."

"And so I'm here. Not for the old come-and-see-it travel writing, but more wishful thinking, these days, a reminder of better times."

"Just for readers in Alexandria?"

"Oh, I expect the pieces will appear in the British papers. In the *Daily Express* anyhow, they've always run my stories."

"Well, if I can be of help . . . Where are you staying?"

"I've been lucky, Roxanne helped me find a place in a fishing village down on the peninsula. It's all whitewashed houses, little alleys with stone steps, cypress trees — you know."

"Picturesque," Roxanne said, in English.

"Gawd, Roxy, don't say that word."

"It means . . . ?" Zannis said.

"Cute." Now she was tormenting Escovil. Then, to Zannis, "Beautiful in an old-fashioned way."

"They *are* beautiful, these villages," Zannis said. "And you can buy wonderful food from the fishermen. By the way, I meant what I said, about help. Having your own place, it sounds like you'll be here for a while."

"Maybe a month — it's a kind of working vacation. And, frankly, I'm glad to get away. Alexandria's impossible now — soldiers and sailors everywhere, a lot of the old families have left for the countryside." He paused, reflectively, then answered a question Zannis hadn't asked. "I *did* try to join up, in 'thirty-nine, but . . ." He tapped his heart, then shook his head at the idiocy of it all. "Hard to believe they turned me down — I've climbed mountains, run for trains, ridden camels — but they say my heart's no good."

Liar, Zannis thought, with a sympathetic smile.

Roxanne put a hand on Escovil's arm. "You have a perfectly fine heart, my dear."

"*I* think so. Anyhow, we're fighting the Italians now, out in the Libyan desert. Pretty much a stalemate, but if things go wrong I expect they might reconsider."

79

"Until then," Zannis said, "I hope you'll enjoy your stay in Salonika, Mr. Escovil."

"Please, call me Francis."

It was very late, not long until dawn, in Roxanne's saggy bed at the Pension Bastasini. Tired — from too many people — and groggy — from too much wine — Zannis had intended to drop Roxanne off and go back to his apartment, but she'd insisted he come up for a drink, and one thing had led to another. Parties always aroused her, so she'd been avid, and that had had a powerful effect on him. Which led in turn to her present condition: content, feline, and sleepy, her damp middle clamped to his thigh as they lay facing each other on their sides. Intimate, and warm, but temporary. In time, he knew, she would move a little, and then a little more. But not quite yet, so Zannis gazed idly at the red glow at the end of his cigarette.

"What went on with you and Elias?" she said.

"Nothing much."

"It looked like more than gossip."

"Oh, his misspent youth."

"Misspent youth? Misspent entire life, you mean, the old satyr."

"He's tried to make love to you?"

"Of course. To every woman he meets."

"Well, it wasn't about that. He fought with the guerrillas, the klephts, a long time ago, and we talked about it. Briefly."

"Hardly misspent, from the Greek point of view."

Oh let's talk politics. Instead of answering, Zannis yawned.

"You're not going to sleep, are you?"

"Not yet."

"What did you think of Francis?"

"Pleasant fellow. And a spy, of course."

"He *is? Francis?*"

"Yes, can't you tell?"

"No. How do you know?"

"Silly story, about a working vacation in the middle of a war."

"Really." She thought it over. "A British spy."

"Or a secret agent. This, that, the other thing, call it whatever you like, but he's working for one of the intelligence services, and maybe for a long time. Is he really a travel writer?"

"Oh yes, and top class. Up there with Robert Byron and Leigh Fermor and Waugh. Are they all spies?"

"It's possible. More likely they were recruited, one, two, or all of them, after 'thirty-eight, when it was pretty damn clear

81

to everyone but Chamberlain that Britain was going to have to go to war."

"Will you, I don't know, will you *watch* him?"

"I doubt it. The British are our friends. In fact, the British are just about our *only* friends. I don't know what he wants here, but I don't think he, I should say *they,* mean us harm." Tired of the conversation, he lowered his head and brushed her nipple with his lips. "Anyhow *you're* British, and you're *my* friend."

She didn't answer.

Instead, a luxuriant stretch and then, down below, she moved. Ran her hand beneath his arm and pressed it against his backside, drawing him closer and resettling her legs around his thigh. Said a barely audible "Mm," and again moved, slid.

27 October. Late in the afternoon, a call from one of the detectives — detective-inspector in rank — at the CID, Salonika's Criminal Investigation Division. One of Salonika's most prominent citizens, a banker, had not shown up at his bank for three days. His second-in-command had telephoned, no answer, then gone out to the house and knocked on the door. Again, no answer. Back at the bank, it was discovered that a

82

great deal of cash — large-denomination drachma notes, Swiss francs, British pounds — was missing.

Zannis knew the detective, who was young for the job, ambitious and vain, and wore a vain little mustache and a very expensive fawn-colored hat. He picked Zannis up at the office and drove him out to the city's fanciest quarter, where, in front of a splendid villa — portico, columns — a locksmith was waiting. "Thought I'd better call him," the detective said; this was not a neighborhood where one kicked in doors. Likely they couldn't have kicked it in even if they'd wanted to. The villa, built by some Turkish bey around the turn of the century, was massive and well-secured.

Even better inside: dark, silent, perfectly maintained, and, Zannis's sense of smell told him, not host to a corpse. *Thank God for that.* Only a note for the maids, in the kitchen. Here were two thousand drachma for each of them — a lot of money, almost two hundred dollars — thank you for being such good girls, we'll be back some day. The money itself was gone, the house was clean, sheets covered the furniture.

They searched the rooms, finding wardrobe trunks but no hand luggage. "Do you have a theory, sir?" the detective asked.

83

"Been stealing for years, perhaps?"

"Always possible," Zannis said. But he knew better; he knew what this meant and the more he thought about it the more he knew. Suddenly, he didn't feel so good, tightness in the chest. He went to the kitchen cabinet, found a glass, filled it with cold water, and drank most of it. Then he lit a cigarette. The detective went to the parlor and returned with an ashtray.

When he was done with the cigarette, they continued the search. No passports, no bankbooks, a dog's rubber ball with a bell inside it but no dog and no dog leash. On a desk, family photographs and three empty frames. In the wife's dresser, expensive scarves but no underwear. Fashionable dresses in the closet, and three empty hangers. "Very nice," the detective said. "Quilted hangers." A datebook in the desk drawer. Pages from 15 October to 5 November cut, not ripped, out.

"Carefully done," Zannis said. "Likely reservations, a ship maybe, or hotels somewhere."

"I suspect you're right, sir," the detective said. "They just took off. Left town. Because of the missing money."

"No, I expect that when we look at his accounts we'll find they've been cleaned out.

The day before he left, but normal before that. I think this is somebody who decided to take his family out of Europe, now, before anything else happens. And he might have figured that this money would vanish, so why not take it for himself? One thing about flight: the more money you have, the easier it's going to be."

"Where do you think they went?"

"I'd say you'll find him listed on the manifest of some ship, out of some Greek port, maybe not here, maybe Athens, or Istanbul. As to where he went, it's anybody's guess. Argentina? America? Mexico?"

"Anywhere safe from the guns," the detective said. "Are you feeling better, sir?"

"I am, thanks."

"Maybe you need a day off." Then, "What became of the dog?"

"With the maids. You might look for a car, though if they parked it at a dock somewhere it's probably stolen by now."

The detective began turning off the lights. "I'll write this up as a theft from the bank. And issue a fugitive warrant."

"Not much else you can do," Zannis said.

They locked up the house and walked toward the detective's car. *This banker knew it was coming,* Zannis thought. Knew somebody who knew somebody, and they told

85

him, "get out, while you still can." And maybe he, or she, whoever it was, nameless, faceless, wasn't wrong. *Enough,* Zannis told himself. *Forget it, at least for today.*

But it didn't forget him, and he wasn't done for the day. Because when he returned to the office, Sibylla told him that the telephone operator at a hotel in Basel was trying to reach him.

So Zannis couldn't go home. He waited at the office, Sibylla left at five-thirty, and Saltiel went home an hour later. The phone didn't ring until after nine. On the other end of the line, "Hello? Hello?" It was a bad connection, charged with crackling and static, the woman's voice faint. Zannis put a hand to his other ear and said, "Yes? Can you hear me?"

"Hotel Mont Blanc operator, sir. I have to send a bellman to find your caller. *Please* hold the line."

"Yes, fine," Zannis said.

Three minutes later, another distant voice. "Hello? Herr Zannis?" The woman was almost shouting.

"Yes?"

"This is Emilia Krebs."

"Hello. Are you all right?"

"I'm in Basel. I came here in order to call you."

"Oh?"

"It's about the two sisters. Called Rosen-blum."

"Who?"

"Two sisters, in their forties. They were librarians, in Berlin. Have they . . ."

The line went dead. Zannis said, "Hello? Hello?"

Then the static returned. ". . . to Salonika. Hello?"

"Hello. Yes, I'm here. What did you say?"

"I gave them your name."

You did? "Of course, I see."

"Have they called?" Her voice was tense, barely under control.

"No, I'm sorry, they . . ." Again, the line went dead, and this time it stayed dead. Zannis wasn't sure what to do. Wait for the connection to return? Or hang up so the operator could make a new call? He looked at his watch, let two minutes go by, then placed the receiver back on the cradle. What had she done? Clearly she'd sent fugitives, two Jewish women from Berlin, to Salonika. Where he was to help them. *She could have asked, at least.* But maybe she couldn't, he thought. He sat there, his mind working, staring out the window at a streetlamp on the Via Egnatia. Then the phone rang and he snatched the receiver.

"Hotel Operator, Mont Blanc. Your call is reconnected, one mo — . . ."

The static was worse on the new connection. Emilia Krebs shouted, "Hello? Herr Zannis?"

"Listen to me." Zannis's voice was loud and urgent and he spoke quickly. "I don't know where these people are, they haven't contacted me, but if they do, I'll send you a postal card. It won't say anything special, simply a greeting from abroad."

"Meaning they've arrived safely."

"That's it. Now, if you want to write to me, just buy Panadon tablets, the aspirin. Are they available in Berlin?"

"Yes."

"Melt them in cold water, then write with the water between the lines of a letter and, if you get a letter from Greece, iron it, not too hot, the writing will appear."

"How ma — . . ." Again, the line went dead.

It came back a few seconds later. Zannis said, "Hello?" and started to speak, but, after a click, a new connection. Now the voice of a woman, some operator in some country, spoke angrily in a language Zannis couldn't identify, and then, with another click, the connection was cut off. He waited at the desk until ten-thirty, staring at the telephone, but it was silent.

He would never hear from the sisters, he was almost certain of that. Evidently they'd set out from Berlin, some days earlier, trying to make their way to Salonika, where Zannis could help them get to Turkey, or Palestine, or wherever they could manage to slip over a border. Slip over, or bribe their way over, because as Jews in flight they were welcome nowhere in the world. Nowhere. Not one single country. And now, not as adept and forceful as their friend in Berlin, they had vanished. Well, lately people did. And they were never heard of again.

Back in his apartment, Zannis couldn't sleep. He was exhausted, had expected to be dead to the world the instant his head hit the pillow, but he'd been wrong. He tossed and turned, his mind racing. What had happened to him at the banker's villa — that tight band across the chest? He'd always been healthy, he had to be, there was no choice. Now what? Or maybe it was just nerves, which was, he thought, maybe even worse. But it had *reached* him, he had to admit that, the almost certain knowledge that invasion was imminent. This banker was a certain type of man, a type Zannis knew well. He had friends who knew things, and you couldn't plan an invasion — recall soldiers from leave, resupply your army with ammunition, medical stores, and everything else — without people finding out about it. So the banker fled, and fled in a hurry — grabbed all the money he could and ran. *Sauve qui peut!* Run for your life! Write a note to the maids, do something about the dog, lock up the house, and go. Poor dog. They were, the dogs, considered special spirits in Greece: faithful friends, fearless guardians. *I'm sure I was right about the dog,* Zannis thought, flipping his pillow over. The maids, the "good girls," would take care of it.

And they were special spirits, faithful guardians.

Thus it was Melissa who figured it out, sensed it, before he did. Zannis must have dozed because, just after dawn, she growled, a subdued, speculative sort of growl — *what's this?* And Zannis woke up.

"Melissa? What goes on?"

She stood at the window, *out there,* turned her head and stared at him as he unwound himself from the snarled bedding. What had caught her attention, he realized, were

90

voices, coming from below, on Santaroza Lane. Agitated, fearful voices. Somebody across the street had a window open and a radio on. It wasn't music — Zannis couldn't make out the words but he could hear the tone of voice, pitched low and grim.

He opened the window. One of the ladies who sat in a kitchen chair on sunny days was standing in the street, her black shawl pulled tight around her head and shoulders, gesticulating with her hands as she talked to a neighbor.

Zannis leaned out the window, called her by name, and said, "What's going on?"

She looked up at him. "The Italians," she said. "They've invaded us."

Poor Mussolini.

Such a puffed-up, strutting horse's ass. Not a man to be ignored, the way he saw it. And surely he had been ignored. Left standing there, shouting slogans from the balcony, thrusting his chubby fist in the air, while that sneaky Hitler conquered the world. Took Austria, Czechoslovakia, Poland, France, Belgium, the Netherlands, Norway, and Denmark. Now *that* was an empire!

And Mussolini? And his new Roman Empire? What glory had it won? Not much.

Occupied Albania, publicly scorned as "a handful of rocks." And Ethiopia. What would you call that, a handful of mud? And Libya, a handful of sand? And oh yes, not to forget that when Hitler invaded France, Mussolini rushed in ten days later and took . . . Nice! So now the doorman at the Negresco would have to bow down to the might of Rome.

Ha-ha!

Said the world. But the worst thing you can do to a dictator is laugh at him — that's contempt, not awe, and it made Mussolini mad. Well, he'd show the world, he'd take Greece. So there, still laughing? And he didn't tell Hitler about it, he didn't ask permission, he just went ahead and did it. And when Hitler heard the news, as dawn broke on the twenty-eighth of October, he was reportedly enraged. Known to be a *tepik fresser,* a carpet chewer, he'd likely gone down on his knees, once he was alone, and given his favorite rug a good thorough grinding.

Zannis got the details on his way to work, from headlines on the newspaper kiosks, from the newspaper he bought — which he read while walking — and from people in the street. Greece was at war, everybody was talking to everybody, there were no strangers that day. Least of all the soldiers, reservists called to duty, hundreds of them, many accompanied by wives and children so they could say good-bye at the railway station. And not a soul abroad that morning didn't stop to wish them well.

"Be careful, my child."

"Remember, keep your head down!"

"You give them a good kick in the ass for me, and don't forget!"

"So maybe you need a little extra money? A few drachmas?"

"Here, have a cigarette. I *see* you're smoking, take it anyhow, for later."

"Good luck, take care of yourself."

This from Zannis, looking up from his newspaper. He might well be joining them, he thought, before the day was done. In 1934, when he'd become a detective, he had automatically been assigned to a General Staff reserve unit in Salonika. If Greece went to war, the army could call up however many detective-grade officers it required because, in a small country, every male below the age of sixty had to be available to serve.

According to the paper, there had been a grand dinner party the night before, in Athens. Count Grazzi, the Italian ambas-

93

sador, had invited the most important people in the city, including General Metaxas. Seated beneath the crossed flags of Italy and Greece, the guests drank "to our eternal friendship for Greece," Count Grazzi himself having stood to propose the toast. Eventually, they all went home. But then, at three in the morning, Grazzi was driven to the home of General Metaxas, who came to the door in his dressing gown. Grazzi presented an ultimatum: Let our army march into your country and occupy the cities. Metaxas's answer wasn't complicated; it could be seen at the top of every front page of every newspaper.

"No."

When Zannis opened the office door, he saw that Sibylla was knitting. She worked feverishly; hands moving quickly, needles clicking, a ball of gray wool in her lap. "By the time I got to the store," she said, "and they had it open at six-thirty, all the khaki was gone. Imagine that! Not yet seven-thirty when I got there, and all the khaki wool bought up."

"What will it be?"

"A sweater. One has a choice, sweater or socks, but I'm good at it, so I decided to make sweaters."

All over the country, women were knitting warm clothes for the Greek boys who would be fighting in the cold mountains. A poor country, less than eight million in population, they had to improvise. So Sibylla's fingers flew and, when the phone rang, she propped the receiver between chin and shoulder and never dropped a stitch. Producing, Zannis thought, a rather curious juxtaposition. "And what time did you say he was murdered?" Click, click.

Zannis tried to telephone Vangelis but the line was busy, so he looked over at Saltiel and said, "What about you, Gabi? Are you leaving today?"

"Too old to fight. Officially. For the time being, I'm to take the place of an ambulance driver who's going up to the border with the medical corps. So I get to drive around the city at night with a siren on. So what's new."

"And days?"

"I'll be here. What about you?"

"I'm waiting for orders," Zannis said. "I'm in a reserve group, we're a communications unit, and I'm liaison with an officer of the Yugoslav General Staff. Not really sure what that means, but I guess I'll find out."

It was late in the morning when he finally got through to Vangelis. "I'm waiting," Zannis explained, "for a call or a telegram. But I could be ordered to report. Maybe even today, or tomorrow."

"Have you given any thought to what you might do if they occupy the city?"

"No, but I suppose I should."

"We wouldn't want them to have the files," Vangelis said. "After that, it will be up to you. Just remember, if you decide to work underground, be careful with your address book. Just in case." He paused, then said, "For the moment, who will run the office?"

"Saltiel and Sibylla. They'll do fine."

Vangelis didn't answer immediately, his way of saying that it wasn't true. "I'm not sure what lies ahead, Costa, but if I need you, I may have you brought back. We'll just have to see how it goes."

"We may surprise them," Zannis said.

"Yes, I think we will," Vangelis said. "If we don't run out of bullets."

Late in the afternoon, a telephone call for Zannis. Not the General Staff, but Roxanne. She sounded rattled, almost desperate. This was something new — she'd been cool and composed from the first day he'd met her. "I didn't want to call you," she said, "but I didn't know what else to do."

"What's wrong?"

"I have to get to the airport. But there isn't a taxi to be found in the whole city, and my friends with cars don't answer their phones, or they're driving somebody to Athens, or — or *something!*"

"Roxanne . . ."

"What?"

"Calm down."

"Sorry, I've just had —"

"There's no point in going to the airport, all commercial flights are canceled; we're at *war* — the military has taken over out there. Now, tell me where you need to go and I'll see what I can do."

"I need to go to the airport. Please."

"Are we going to fight about this? You think I didn't tell you the truth?"

"Costa, can you borrow a car? Or get one from the police?"

After a moment, he said, in a different tone of voice, "What is this?"

"A favor. I have never asked you for a favor, not ever, but I'm asking now. And part of the favor is not trying to make me explain on the telephone, because I have to be there right away."

"Hold on." He turned to Saltiel and said, "Gabi, may I use your car for an hour?"

Saltiel stared at him. *I don't let anyone drive my car.* "Well, I guess you can, if you need it." He was clearly not happy.

"Did you hear that?" Zannis said, on the phone.

"Yes."

"I'll pick you up in ten minutes."

It was a rough ride to the airport, some fifteen miles east of the city. Convoys of army trucks were rolling west, toward them, headed for the roads that went up to the Albanian border. And, being army convoys on the first day of a war, saw no reason, in the national interest, not to use both lanes. So more than once Zannis had to swerve off the road, the Skoda bumping over a rocky field. Teeth clamped together, he waited for the blown-out tire or the broken spring, though it happened, over and over again, only in his imagination. But that was bad enough.

Meanwhile, from Roxanne, stony silence, broken occasionally by English oaths, *bloody* this and *bloody* that, delivered under her breath every time the trucks came at them. Finally, answering the unasked question, she said, "If you must know, it's just some friends who want me *out* of here."

"Powerful friends," Zannis said. "Friends with airplanes."

"Yes, powerful friends. I know you have

them; well, so do I."

"Then I'm happy for you."

"Bloody . . ." A muttered syllable followed.

"What?"

"Never mind. Just drive."

Coming around a curve, they were suddenly confronted by a pair of gasoline tankers, side by side, horns blaring. Zannis swung the wheel over, the back end broke free, and they went skidding sideways into a field. The car stalled, Zannis pressed the ignition button, the Skoda coughed, then started. But the army wasn't done with them. Just before they reached the airport, a long convoy came speeding right at them — and this time they almost didn't make it. The car idled by the side of the road, pebbles hit the windshield, soldiers waved, Roxanne swore, Zannis fumed.

The airport was deserted. The Royal Hellenic Air Force — about a hundred planes: a few PZL P.24s, Polish-built fighters, and whatever else they'd managed to buy over the years — was operating from airbases in the west. A sign on the door of the terminal building said ALL FLIGHTS CANCELED, and the only signs of life were a small group of soldiers on guard duty and a crew gathered beside its antiaircraft gun. They'd built a fire and were roasting somebody's chicken on a bayonet.

Roxanne had only a small valise — Zannis offered to carry it but she wouldn't let him. They walked around the terminal building and there, parked in a weedy field by the single paved runway, was a small monoplane, a Lysander, with a British RAF roundel on the fuselage. The pilot, sitting on the ground with his back against the wheel, was smoking a cigarette and reading a Donald Duck comic book. He stood when he saw them coming and flicked his cigarette away. Very short, and very small, he looked, to Zannis's eyes, no more than seventeen.

"Sorry I'm late," Roxanne said.

The pilot peered up at the gathering darkness and strolled back toward the observer's cockpit, directly behind the pilot's — both were open, no canopies to be seen. "Getting dark," he said. "We'd better be going."

Roxanne turned to Zannis and said, "Thank you."

He stared at her and finally said, "You're not going to England, are you."

"No, only to Alexandria. I may well be back; it's simply a precaution."

"Of course, I understand." His voice was flat and dead because he was heartsick. *"Now,"* he added, "I understand." *And how*

100

could I have been so dumb I never saw it? The British government didn't send Lysanders to rescue the expatriate owners of ballet schools, they sent them to rescue secret service operatives.

Her eyes flashed; she moved toward him and spoke, intensely but privately, so the pilot wouldn't hear. "It wasn't to do with you," she said. "It wasn't to do with you."

"No, of course not."

Suddenly she grabbed a handful of his shirt, just below the collar, and twisted it, her knuckles sharp where they pressed against his chest. It surprised him, how strong she was, and the violence was a shock — this hand, in the past, had been very nice to him. "Wasn't," she said. Her eyes were dry, but he could see she was as close to tears as she ever came. And then he realized that the hand clutching his shirt wasn't there in anger, it was furiously, almost unconsciously, trying to hold on to something it had lost.

The pilot cleared his throat. "Getting dark," he said. He knotted his fingers, making a cup out of his hands, nodded up at the observer cockpit, and said, "Up we go, luv."

Zannis walked with Roxanne the few feet to the plane. She turned and looked at him,

101

then rested her foot on the waiting hands and was hoisted upward, floundered for a moment, skirt rising to reveal the backs of her thighs, then swung her legs over into the cockpit. The pilot smiled at Zannis, a boyish grin which made him look even younger than seventeen, and said, "Don't worry, mate, I'm good at this." He handed Roxanne her valise, jumped up on the wheel housing, and climbed into the pilot's cockpit. A moment later, the engine roared to life and the propeller spun. Zannis watched the Lysander as it taxied, then lifted into the air and turned south, heading out over the Aegean toward Egypt.

Back in the office, a yellow sheet of teletype paper lay on his desk. From Lazareff in Sofia.

COSTA: DO US ALL A FAVOR AND CHASE THESE BASTARDS BACK WHERE THEY CAME FROM

The message was in Bulgarian, but Zannis had grown up in Salonika, "a city where even the bootblacks speak seven languages," and was able to figure it out. Normally, he would have enjoyed Lazareff's gesture, but now he just sat there, his mood dark and melancholy, and stared at the wall.

He came to believe, after going back over their time together, that Roxanne hadn't lied, that he'd not been the target of a British spy operation. He could not recall a single time when she'd asked him anything that might touch on the sort of information that spies sought. So, in fact, it wasn't to do with him. He'd had a love affair with a woman who'd been sent to Salonika as part of an intelligence operation. Then, when war came, when occupation by an Axis force was more than possible, they'd snatched her away. Or maybe she simply did have friends in high places, friends with the power to organize an RAF Lysander flight to Greece. No, she'd actually confessed. "It wasn't to do with you." The *it.* To do with somebody else. The Germans, the Italians, the Vichy French consul; there were many possibilities.

Should he tell somebody? What, exactly, would he tell? And to who? Spiraki? Never. Vangelis? Why? His job was discretion; his job was to keep things quiet. Well, he would. And if she returned? It might be easier if she didn't. At the least, they'd have to come to some sort of understanding. Or pretend it had never happened? Slowly, he shook his head. *This war — look what it does.* In truth, he missed her already. Maybe they weren't in love but they'd been passionate lovers — she'd been his warm place in a cold world. And now he had to go up north and kill Italians, so maybe he was the one who wouldn't be coming back.

The telephone rang and Saltiel answered it, said, "I see" and "very well" a few times, made notes, and hung up.

"What was that?" Zannis said.

"The mayor's chief assistant." He rubbed his hands back through his hair and sighed. "Sometimes I don't know whether to laugh or cry."

Sibylla looked up from her sweater.

"It seems the mayor has a niece, a favorite niece, recently married; she lives out by Queen Olga Street."

"I know who she is," Zannis said. "Pretty girl."

"Well, maybe she was distracted by the war, maybe, I don't know, something else. Anyhow, this afternoon she went to feed her pet bird, a parakeet. And, unfortunately, she left the door of the cage open, and it flew away."

Zannis waited a moment, then said, "And that's it?"

"Yes."

Sibylla turned away, and, as she started to

knit, made a small noise — not a laugh, but a snort.

"It's true? You're not just saying this to be funny?"

"No. It's true."

Now it was Zannis's turn to sigh. "Well, I guess you'll have to call her," he said. "And tell her . . . what? Put an advertisement in the newspaper? We can't go out and look for it."

"Tell her to leave the window open," Sibylla said, "and the door of the cage, and have her put some of its food in there."

Saltiel made the call, his voice soothing and sympathetic, and he was on for a long time. Then, ten minutes later, the telephone rang again and, this time, it *was* the General Staff.

8:35 P.M. It began to rain, softly, no downpour, just enough to make the pavement shine beneath the streetlamps. Still, it meant that it would be snowing in the mountains. Zannis waited on the corner of the Via Egnatia closest to Santaroza Lane, a canvas knapsack slung on his shoulder. The Vardari, the wind that blew down the Vardar valley, was sharp and Zannis turned away from it, faced the port and watched the lightning as it lit the clouds above the sea.

105

Moments later the thunder followed, distant rumblings, far to the south.

He'd had a hectic time of it since he left the office. Had taken a taxi back to Santaroza Lane, packed some underwear, socks, and a sweater, then threw in his old detective's sidearm, the same detective's version of the Walther PPK that Saltiel had, and a box of bullets. Then he changed into his reservist's uniform, a close cousin to what British officers wore, with a Sam Browne belt that looped over one shoulder. He searched for, and eventually found, inside a valise, his officer's cap, and, Melissa by his side, hurried out the door to find another taxi.

Up at his mother's house in the heights, the mood was quiet and determined — basically acceptance. They fussed over Melissa, fed her and set out her water bowl and blanket, and gave Zannis a heavy parcel wrapped in newspaper — sandwiches of roast lamb in pita bread — which he stowed in his knapsack atop the gun and the underwear. For some reason, this brought to mind a scene in Homer, dimly remembered from school, where one of the heroes prepares to go to war. Probably, Zannis thought, given some version of the lamb and pita, though that didn't get into the story. After he buckled the knapsack, his brother, mother, and grandmother each embraced him; then his grandmother pressed an Orthodox medal into his hand. "It saved your grandfather's life," she said. "Keep it with you always. You promise, Constantine?" He promised. Melissa sat by his side as he was saying a final good-bye, and, last thing before he went out the door, he bent over and she gave him one lick on the ear. She knew.

On the corner, Zannis looked at his watch and shifted his feet. Well, he thought, if you had to go to war you might as well leave from the Via Egnatia. An ancient street, built first in the second century B.C. as a military road for the Roman Empire. It began as the Via Appia, the Appian Way, in Rome, went over to Brindisi, where one crossed the Adriatic to Albanian Durrës and the road took the name Via Egnatia. Then it ran down to Salonika and went east, eventually reaching Byzantium — Constantinople. Thus it linked the two halves of the Byzantine Empire, Roman Catholic and Italian in the west, Eastern Orthodox and Greek in the east. Sixteen hundred years of it, until the Turks won a war.

Zannis lit a cigarette and looked at his

watch again, then saw a pair of headlights coming toward him down the street. A French-built staff car, old and boxy, a relic, with a blue-and-white Greek pennant flown from the whippy radio aerial. When the car drew up in front of him, a General Staff captain in the passenger seat opened the back door from inside. "Lieutenant Zannis," he said. Zannis saluted and climbed in; two other men in the backseat moved over and made room for him. It was smoky in the car, and rain dripped through a tear in the canvas top.

The driver worked hard, winding up into the mountains on dark roads, the wiper brushing across the windshield. He was employed, he said, by the telephone company in Salonika, as a maintenance supervisor, "but I spent years working on the lines, relay stations, the whole system." The other two men simply gave their names and, still civilians, shook hands, though they were sergeants, and Zannis, who'd signed up for the reserves as an officer in the police department, a lieutenant. The captain was a real serving captain, very smart-looking in his uniform, with a small mustache and eyeglasses. "I'm in signals," he said, "communications of all sorts," and let it go at that.

For a time, the mountain roads were deserted; then, climbing a steep grade that curved sharply to the right, they came up behind an army truck. The headlights revealed soldiers, rifles between their knees, sitting on two benches that ran the length of the truck bed. One of them waved.

"Evzones," the captain said. The word meant sharpshooters. Their ceremonial uniforms — white kilt and hat with tassel — were derived from the klephts who'd fought the Turks. In fact, once the ceremonial uniforms were changed for traditional battlefield dress, the Evzones were the elite combat units of the army. "I don't think," the captain said, "the Italians will be glad to see them coming."

"Well, I am," said the man next to Zannis. In his late forties, he'd served in the army as a wireless/telegraph operator. "But that was years ago," he said. "Now I work in a pharmacy."

The curve in the road seemed to go on forever, jagged walls of stone rising above them in silhouette against the night sky. When at last the road straightened out, the driver swung over into the left lane and tried to pass the crawling truck. A foot at a time, the staff car gained ground.

"Can we do this?" the captain said.

"Skata," the driver said. "My foot is on the floor."

As they drew even with the cabin of the truck, its driver rolled down his window, turned and grinned at them, stuck his hand out and waved it forward with comic impatience: *faster, faster.* Zannis watched the horizon for headlights coming toward them but there was nothing out there. "A snail race," said the man next to Zannis. The driver of the army truck leaned out the window and shouted.

The captain said, "What did he say?"

"Move your ass," Zannis said.

The captain laughed. "Poor old thing, she fought in France."

They were rounding another curve before they finally got back into the right lane. "Can you tell us where we're going?" Zannis asked.

"Can't be sure," the captain said. "Right now, we're supposed to be based in Trikkala, but that might change. As of five this afternoon, the Italians — the Alpini division, the mountain troops — have advanced ten miles into Greece. They are going for Janina, supported by a tank column, the center of a three-pronged attack which will cut the only rail line and the two main roads — that would mean no reinforcements from Macedonia. It's the plan you draw up in military school, however —" He paused as the staff car skidded and the driver swore and fought the wheel. When the car steadied he said, "However, I doubt they'll reach Janina, and likely not Trikkala."

"Why not?" the wireless operator said.

"Oh . . . let's just say we knew they were coming. Not when, but we knew where and how. So we prepared . . . a few things."

The silence following that admission was appreciative. The wireless operator said, "Hunh," which meant something like *that's the way.* Then he said, "Fucking *makaronades.*" Greek for macaronis, the national insult name for the Italians. There was a sneer in the expression, as though their ancient enemies, Bulgarians, Albanians, and Turks, were at least serious opponents, whereas the attack by Italy was somehow worthy of contempt. In August, off the island of Tenos, an Italian submarine had torpedoed the cruiser *Helle,* in harbor, in full view of the people on the island, and on a religious holiday. This was seen more as cowardice than aggression, a Roman Catholic attack on an Eastern Orthodox religious festival, thus especially dishonorable. Not that they hadn't disliked the Italians before that. They had, for centuries.

111

A few minutes later, the driver stopped the car — there was nowhere to pull over — and, shoulder to shoulder, they all peed off the side of the mountain. It was a long way down, Zannis saw, a long, long way. As he rebuttoned his fly, the truck carrying the Evzones came chugging up the road, its engine laboring hard. When the driver saw the staff car, he swung around it and, passing close to the men standing at the edge of the mountain, and observing what occupied them, he blew a mighty blast on his klaxon horn, which echoed off the mountainside. Then it was the turn of the soldiers who, as their truck rumbled away, called out a variety of suggestions and insults, all of them obscene.

The driver, standing next to Zannis, swore and said, "Now I'll have to pass them all over again."

"Oh well," the captain said, giving himself a couple of shakes, "the fortunes of war."

■ ■ ■ ■

THE BACK DOOR TO HELL

Poor Mussolini.

He, like everybody else in Europe who went to the movies, had seen the Pathé newsreels. First a title, in the local language, flashed on a black screen: GERMANY INVADES POLAND! Followed by combat footage, the Panzer tanks of the Wehrmacht charging across the Polish steppe, accompanied by dire and dramatic music. Loud music. And the words of a narrator with a rich, deep, theatrical voice. The effect was powerful — here was *history* being made, right before your eyes.

Mussolini hated it, couldn't get the images out of his mind. For he sensed that whatever made Hitler look powerful made him look meagre, but, fifteen months later, here came a chance to put things right — he'd had more than enough of being mocked as the conqueror of . . . Nice! Now he'd show the world who was who and what was what. Because he had tanks of his own, an armoured formation known as the Centauri Division, named for the mythic Greek figure called the centaur, half man, half horse. Shown always as the top of the man and the back of the horse, though there were those who suggested that, in the case of Mussolini's army, it should be the other way round.

Mussolini paced the rooms of his palace in Rome and brooded. Was the lightning attack known as Blitzkrieg the private property of Adolf Hitler? Oh no it wasn't! He would storm into Greece just as Hitler's Panzers had done in Poland. And his generals, whose politics carefully conformed with his own, encouraged him. The Centauri would smash through the vineyards and olive groves of southern Greece; nothing could stop them, because the Greek army hadn't a single tank, not one. Hah! He'd crush them!

Alas, it was not to be. The problem was the geography of *northern* Greece, massive ranges of steep jagged mountains — after all, this was the Balkans, and "balkan" meant "mountain" in Turkish. So Mussolini's Blitzkrieg would have to attack down the narrow valleys, protected by Alpini troops occupying the heights above them.

116

Which might have worked out but for the Evzones, one regiment of them opposing the Alpini division.

The Greeks, contrary to Italian expectations, fought to the death.

Took terrible casualties, but defeated the Alpini, who broke and fled back toward the Albanian border. Now the Greeks held the mountains and when the Centauri came roaring down the valleys two things happened. First, many of the tanks plunged into a massive ditch that had been dug in their path, often winding up on their backs, and second, those that escaped the ditch were subject to shelling from above, by short-barreled, high-wheeled mountain guns. These guns, accompanied by ammunition, had been hauled over the mountains by mules and then, when the mules collapsed and died of exhaustion, by men.

As the first week in November drew to a close, it was clear that the Italian invasion had stalled. Mussolini raged, Mussolini fired generals, Greek reinforcements reached the mountain villages, and it began to snow. The unstoppable Axis had, for the first time, been stopped. And of this the world press took notice: headlines in boldface, everywhere in Europe. Which included Berlin, where these developments were viewed

117

with, to put it mildly, considerable irritation. Meanwhile, poor Mussolini had once again been humiliated, and now the Greek army was poised to enter Albania.

In Trikkala, an ancient town divided by a river, the snow-capped peaks of the Pindus Mountains were visible when the sun came out. Which, fortunately, the first week in November, it did not do. The sky stayed overcast, a solid mass of gray cloud that showered down an icy rain. The sky stayed overcast, and the Italian bomber pilots, at the airfields up in Albania, played cards in their barracks.

The Salonika communications unit was at least indoors, having bivouacked in the local school along with other reservists. They'd stacked the chairs against the wall and slept on the floor. Dry, but bored. Each member of the unit had been armed for war by the issue of a blanket, a helmet, and a French Lebel rifle made in 1917. The captain took Zannis aside and said, "Ever fire one of these?"

"No, never."

"Too bad. It would be good for you to practice, but we can't spare the ammunition." He chambered a bullet, closed the bolt, and handed the weapon to Zannis. "It has a three-round tube. You work the bolt, look through the sight, find an Italian, and pull the trigger. It isn't complicated."

There was, that first week, little enough to do. The General Staff was based in Athens, with a forward position in Janina. But if things went wrong at Janina they would have to serve as a relay station, take information coming in over the telephone — the lines ended at Trikkala — and transmit it to front-line officers by wireless/telegraph. "We are," the captain said, "simply a reserve unit. And let's hope it stays that way."

As for Zannis, his liaison counterpart from the Yugoslav General Staff was apparently still trying to reach Trikkala. Where he, if and when he ever showed up, could join the unit in waiting around. Yugoslavia had not entered the war. In the past, Greeks and Serbs had been allies in the First Balkan War in 1912, and again in the Balkan campaigns against Germany, Bulgaria, and Turkey in the 1914 war, and greatly respected each other's abilities on the battlefield. But now, if Yugoslavia attacked Mussolini, it was well understood that Hitler would attack Yugoslavia, so Belgrade remained *on alert,* but the army had not mobilized.

Meanwhile, they waited. Early one morn-

119

ing, Spyro, the pharmacist-turned-wireless-operator, sat at a teacher's desk and tapped out a message. He had been ordered to do this, to practice daily, and send one message every morning, to make sure the system worked. As Zannis watched, he sent and received, back and forth, while keeping a record on a scrap of paper. When he took off the headset, he smiled.

"What's going on?" Zannis said.

"This guy up in Metsovon . . ." He handed Zannis the paper. "Here, take a look for yourself."

TRIKKALA REPORTING 9 NOVEMBER.
WHY DO YOU SEND ME MESSAGES?
I AM ORDERED TO SEND ONCE A DAY.
DON'T YOU KNOW WE'RE BUSY UP HERE?
I HAVE TO FOLLOW ORDERS.
WHAT SORT OF MAN ARE YOU?
A SOLDIER.
THEN COME UP HERE AND FIGHT.
THAT WOULD BE FINE WITH ME.
LOOKING FORWARD TO SEEING YOU.

Every day it rained, and every day long lines of Italian prisoners moved through Trikkala, on their way to a POW camp somewhere south of the town. Zannis

120

couldn't help feeling sorry for them, cold and wet and miserable, eyes down as they trudged past the school. When the columns appeared, the reservists would bring out food or cigarettes, whatever they could spare, for the exhausted Greek soldiers guarding the prisoners.

Late one afternoon, Zannis walked along with one of the soldiers and gave him a chocolate bar he'd bought at the market. "How is it up there?" he said.

"We try not to freeze," the soldier said. "It's gotten to a point where fighting's a relief."

"A lot of fighting?"

"Depends. Sometimes we advance, and they retreat. Every now and then they decide to fight, but, as you can see, much of the time they just surrender. Throw away their rifles and call out, *'Bella Grecia! Bella Grecia!'* " When he said this, one of the prisoners turned to look at him.

"Beautiful Greece?"

The soldier shrugged and adjusted the rifle strap on his shoulder. "That's what they say."

"What do they mean? That Greece is beautiful and they like it and they never wanted to fight us?"

"Maybe so. But then, what the fuck are

they doing down here?"

"Mussolini sent them."

The soldier nodded and said, "Then fuck him too." He marched on, tearing the paper off his chocolate bar and eating it slowly. When he was done he turned and waved to Zannis and called out, "Thank you!"

By the second week in November, Greek forces had crossed the Albanian border and taken the important town of Koritsa, several small villages, and the port of Santi Quaranta, which meant that Greece's British ally could resupply the advance more efficiently. At the beginning of the war, they'd had to bring their ships into the port of Piraeus. Also, on Tuesday of that week, Zannis's Yugoslav counterpart showed up. He was accompanied by a corporal who carried, along with his knapsack, a metal suitcase of the sort used to transport a wireless/telegraph. The two of them stood there, dripping on the tiles just inside the doorway of the school.

"Let's go find a taverna," Zannis said to the officer. "Your corporal can get himself settled in upstairs."

Zannis led the way toward the main square, a waterproof groundcloth draped over his head and shoulders. The reservists had discovered that their overcoats, once soaked, never dried out, so they used what was available and walked around Trikkala looking like monks in green cowls.

"I'm called Pavlic," the officer said. "Captain Pavlic. Reserve captain, anyhow."

"Costa Zannis. Lieutenant Zannis, officially."

They shook hands awkwardly as they walked. Zannis thought Pavlic was a few years older than he was, with a weather-beaten face, sand-colored hair, and narrow eyes with deep crow's-feet at the corners, as though he'd spent his life at sea, perpetually on watch.

"Your Greek is very good," Zannis said.

"It should be. I grew up down here, in Volos; my mother was half Greek and my father worked for her family. I guess that's why I got this job." They walked for a time, then Pavlic said, "Sorry I'm so late, by the way. I was on a British freighter and we broke down — had to go into port for repairs."

"You didn't miss anything, not too much happens around here."

"Still, I'm supposed to report in, every day. We have another officer in Janina, and there's a big hat, a colonel, at your General Staff headquarters in Athens. It's all a

123

formality, of course, unless we mobilize. And, believe me, we won't do any such thing."

In the taverna, rough plank tables were crowded with local men and reservists, the air was dense with cigarette smoke and the smell of spilled retsina, and a fire of damp grapevine prunings crackled and sputtered on a clay hearth. It didn't provide much heat but it was a very loud fire, and comforting in its way. The boy who served drinks saw them standing there, rushed over and said, "Find a place to sit," but there was no table available so they stood at the bar. Zannis ordered two retsinas. "The retsina is good here," he said. "Local." When the drinks came, Zannis raised his glass. "To your health."

"And to yours." When he'd had a sip, Pavlic said, "You're right, it is good. Where are you from?"

"Salonika. I'm a policeman there."

"No!"

"Don't like the police?"

"Hell, it isn't that, I'm one also."

"You are? Really? Where?"

"Zagreb."

"*Skata!* A coincidence?"

"Maybe your General Staff did it on purpose."

124

"Oh, yes, of course you're right. You can trust a policeman."

From Pavlic, a wry smile. "Most of the time," he said.

Zannis laughed. "We do what we have to, it's true," he said. "Are you a detective, in Zagreb?"

"I was, for twenty years, and I expect you know all about that. But now, the last year or so, I'm in charge of the cars, the motor pool."

"Your preference?"

"Not at all. It was a, how should I put this, it was a *political* transfer. The people who run the department, the commissioner and his friends at city hall, were reached."

"Reached." Such things happened all the time, but Zannis couldn't stop himself from being shocked when he heard about it. "Bribed?"

"No, not bribed. Intimidated? Persuaded? Who knows, I don't. What happened was that I didn't hold back, in fact worked extra hard, investigating certain crimes. Crimes committed by the Ustashi — Croatian fascists, and great friends with Mussolini; they take money from him. Maybe you're aware of that."

"I'm not. But it's no surprise."

"Of course they consider themselves *patri-*

125

ots, fighters in the struggle for Croatian independence — they sing about it, in the bars — but in fact they're terrorists, Balkan Nazis. And when it was reported that they'd beaten somebody up, or burned his house down, or murdered him in front of his family — their favored method, by the way — I went after them. I hunted them down. Not that they stayed in jail, they didn't, but it was a matter of honor for me. And not just me. There were plenty of us."

Zannis's face showed what he felt: disgust. "Still," he said, after a moment, "it could have been worse."

"That's true. I'm lucky to be alive. But you know how it goes — you can't take that into account, not when you do what we do."

"No, you can't. At least I can't. I'm a fatalist, I guess." Zannis drank the last of his retsina, caught the eye of the woman behind the bar, raised his empty glass and wiggled it. The woman quickly brought two more. Pavlic started to pay but Zannis beat him to it, tossing coins on the bar. "I'm the host," he said. "Here in scenic Trikkala."

"All right. My turn next time." Pavlic raised his glass to Zannis, drank some retsina, reached into the inside pocket of his uniform tunic, and brought out a packet of cigarettes. "Do you smoke? Try one of these."

On the packet, a bearded sailor looked out through a life preserver. "Players," Zannis said. "English?"

"Yes. I got them on the freighter." Pavlic lit their cigarettes with a steel lighter. "What do you do, in Salonika?"

"I run a small office where we take care of . . . special cases. We deal with the rich and powerful, foreigners, diplomats — whatever's a little too sensitive for the regular detectives. I report to the commissioner, who's been a good friend to me, for a long time."

"Lucky."

"Yes."

"But you have something similar to the Ustashi: the IMRO — they used to work together, if I have my history right. What is it, Internal Macedonian Revolutionary Organization?"

"It is. And founded in Salonika, back in the last century. They're slavic Macedonians, Bulgarians mostly, who think they're going to have a separate Macedonia. But, thank heaven, they've been quiet for a few years."

"More luck — especially for your Salonika Jews. Because our Jews, in Zagreb, are right at the top of the Ustashi *list*. They'd like to get rid of the Serbs, and the Croat politicians who oppose them, but they really have it in for the Jews. If the Ustashi ever took control of the city, well . . ."

Zannis heard the words *our Jews* as though Pavlic had emphasized them. For some reason, a fleeting image of Emilia Krebs crossed his mind. "That won't happen in Salonika," he said. "Not with IMRO, not with anybody."

"It's a damn shame, what's being done to them, up in Germany. And the police just stand there and watch." Pavlic's face showed anger, his policeman's heart offended by the idea of criminals allowed to do whatever they wanted. "Politics," he said, as though the word were an oath.

For a time they stood in silence, sipping their retsinas, and smoked their English cigarettes. Then Pavlic nodded toward the window and said, "Here's *some* good news, anyhow."

Through the cloudy glass, past the dead flies on the windowsill, Zannis saw that the wet street in front of the tavern was steaming. "At last," he said. "It's been raining for days."

Pavlic stubbed out his cigarette, making ready to leave the taverna. "Once my corporal gets his wireless running, I'll let them know up in Belgrade: 'Pavlic reporting. The sun's come out.' "

Zannis smiled as he followed Pavlic through the door. The captain stopped for a moment and closed his eyes as he raised his face to the sun. "By the way," he said, "I'm called Marko."

"Costa," Zannis said. And they headed back to the school.

The officers did their best to keep the reservists busy — calisthenics, marching drills, whatever they could think up — but the soldiers were there to wait until they were needed, waiting was their job, and so time passed very slowly. At night, as the chill of the schoolroom floor rose through his blanket, Zannis found it hard to sleep. He thought about Roxanne, reliving some of their warmer moments together: the way her face looked at climax; times when she'd thought something up that particularly, spontaneously, excited her. Or maybe such ideas came to her when she was by herself, lost in fantasy, and she tried them out when she got the chance. That was true of him, likely true of her as well. A lot of love got made when lovers were apart, he thought.

But, with snoring men on either side of

him, fantasy of this sort led nowhere. Instead, his mind drifted back to recent life in Salonika, which now seemed remote and distant. He sometimes recalled the German agent; more often Emilia Krebs and the two children. But, most often, the Rosenblum sisters he'd heard about during the frantic, disrupted telephone call from Switzerland. Unmarried sisters, he guessed: older, librarians. Helpless, vulnerable, trying to make their way through some dark night in Budapest, or wherever they'd been caught. No ability whatever to deal with clandestine life, with border patrols, police raids, informers, or conscientious fascist citizens who knew a Jew when they saw one, no matter the quality of their false papers.

Could he have helped them? How? He was absolutely sure that Emilia Krebs would not stop what she was doing — Germany was now the very essence of hell; continuous torment, no escape. And so her fugitives would be taken by the machine built to hunt them down. Again and again. This thought reached a very sore place inside him, and he could not stop thinking it.

The military population of Trikkala began to thin out as reservists were sent up to the fighting to replace the dead and wounded.

Pavlic and Zannis worked together, Zannis receiving situation reports from the captain and handing them on to Pavlic for translation and transmission to the Yugoslav General Staff. Now and then Pavlic wanted to know more, and now and then Zannis went to the captain and requested more, and now and then clarification or expansion was provided. Mostly the reports included the daily numbers — enemy dead, wounded, and captured — and names — villages, rivers, and positions, taken or abandoned — as the Greek infantry labored over the snow-covered mountains of Albania. The Yugoslavs read the reports, but their support wasn't needed, and so they did nothing. What help the Greeks had came from their British ally.

A senior officer, for example, who appeared with a truck one morning, a truck stacked with wooden crates. Almost a stage presence, this officer, who stood ramrod straight, had a splendid cavalry mustache, and lacked only the monocle. Some forty reservists, Zannis among them, were organized to move the truck's cargo up to a village a few miles behind the front lines. The reservists stood in front of the school while the British officer addressed them in classical Greek — as though Shakespeare were making a speech to a platoon of East London sappers. But nobody smiled.

"Men," the officer said, at a volume meant for the parade ground, "these crates are important. They hold antitank rifles, fifty-five-calibre weapons with tripods that are fired by a single soldier, like Bren guns. The square crates contain antitank rounds, and you will take turns carrying them, because the ammunition is heavy."

There were two trucks for the reservists, and they managed to drive some way north on the rutted dirt roads, but with altitude the snow deepened and soon enough they were spending more time pushing their vehicles than driving them. So, unload the crates, and start walking. Which was hard work, in the snow. Zannis sweated, then shivered as the sweat dried in the icy chill of the mountain air. One reservist sprained an ankle, another had pains in the chest; none of them were really in fighting shape.

When darkness fell, Zannis rolled up in his blanket and groundcloth and slept in the snow. The wind sighed through the trees all night long and when the cold woke him up he heard wolves in the distance. In the morning he was exhausted and needed force of will to keep going. Spyro, the former pharmacist, said, "I don't know how much longer I can do this"; then he re-gripped the rope handle at his end of the crate and the two of them plodded forward. High above them, an eagle circled in the gray sky.

They reached the village late in the afternoon, where men from the forward positions would take the antitank rifles the rest of the way. When the small cluster of houses came into view, the dogs appeared — *Melissa's cousins,* Zannis thought — barking and threatening until a piercing whistle sent them trotting back home. When the column reached the center of the village, the reservists went silent. The village well, which might have been there for a thousand years, was no more — some of the stonework remained, shattered and blackened, but that was all. And the houses on either side of the well were in ruins. "A bomb," the villagers said. They'd seen the planes above them; one of them descended toward the village and dropped a bomb. They'd watched it as it tumbled from the plane. It had killed two women, a child, and a goat, and blown up their well. "Why?" the villagers asked. "Why did they do this to us?"

At the end of October, when war came to Trikkala, Behar saw it as an opportunity.

133

He was Albanian, his family had lived in Trikkala since the time of the Ottoman Turks, but he was no less Albanian for that. Age twenty-five when the war began, Behar had been a thief since the age of fourteen. Not that he was very good at it, he wasn't. As a teenager he'd spent a few months in the local jail for stealing a radio and, later on, a year in prison for trying to sell stolen tires, on behalf of a man called Pappou. The name meant *grampa*, a nickname, not so much because he was old and gray, but because he'd been a criminal for a long time and people were afraid of him so he could call himself whatever he liked. Sometimes Pappou, just like a grampa, would help out his little Trikkala "family": give them something to sell and let them keep some of the money. Thus, for Behar, better to stay on the good side of Pappou.

With the war, and the soldiers crowding into Trikkala, Behar thought he would prosper. These people came from cities in the south; to Behar they looked rich, and rich people spent lavishly — perhaps they'd like a nice girl to keep them warm, or maybe a little hashish. They were, it was said, going to free Albania from the Italians, but Behar had never been to Albania and couldn't have cared less who ruled there.

No, what mattered to Behar was that these people might want things or, if they didn't, could be separated from what they had: wristwatches, for example, or rifles. One way or the other, Behar knew they were meant to put money in his empty pockets.

But the soldiers weren't such easy targets, they were always together, they didn't pass out drunk in an alley — at least not in the alleys where he searched for them — and they went to the brothel for their girls. After a few days, Behar began to despair, war was not going to turn out to be much of an opportunity at all.

But then, in the second week of the war, Pappou came to his rescue. Behar lived in a shack at the edge of the city, with his mother and two sisters. They never had enough wood for the stove, so they froze during the winter and waited anxiously for spring. He was lying on his cot one afternoon when a boy came with a message: he was to go and see Pappou the following day. Two o'clock, the boy said, at the barbershop Pappou owned, where he did business in the back room.

Behar was excited. He walked to the edge of Trikkala to find his eldest brother, who owned a razor, and there scraped his face. Painful, using the icy water, because his

135

brother was not so prosperous as to own soap. Behar made sure he got to the barbershop on time. He wore his grimy old suit, the only clothing he had, but he'd combed his hair and settled his short-brimmed cap at just the proper angle, down over his left eye. It was the best he could do. On the way to the shop he looked at himself in the glass of a display window; scrawny and hunched, hands in pockets, not such a bad face, he thought, though they'd broken his nose when he'd tried to steal food in the prison.

To Behar, the barbershop was a land of enchantment, where polished mirrors reflected white tile, where the air was warmed — by a nickel-plated drum that heated towels with steam, and scented — by the luxurious, sugary smell of rosewater, used to perfume the customers when they were done being barbered. There were two men in the chairs when Behar arrived, one with his face swathed in a towel, apparently asleep, though the cigar in his dangling hand was still smoking, the other in the midst of a haircut. The barber, as he snipped, spoke to his customer in a low, soothing voice. The weather might change, or maybe not.

When Behar entered the back room, Pappou, sitting at a table, spread his arms in welcome. "Behar! Here you are, right on time! Good boy." Sitting across from Pappou was a man who simply smiled and nodded. His friend here, Pappou explained, was not from Trikkala and needed a reliable fellow for a simple little job. Which he would explain in a minute. Again, the man nodded. "It will pay you very well," Pappou said, "if you are careful and do exactly as you're told. Can you do that, my boy?" With great enthusiasm, Behar said he could. Then, to his considerable surprise, Pappou stood up, left the room, and closed the door behind him. Outside, Pappou could be heard as he joked with the barbers, so he wasn't listening at the door.

The man leaned forward and asked Behar a few questions. He was, from the way he spoke, a foreigner. Clean-shaven, thick-lipped, and prosperously jowly, he had a tight smile that Behar found, for no reason he could think of, rather chilling, and eyes that did not smile at all. The questions were not complicated. Where did he live? Did he like Trikkala? Was he treated well here? Behar answered with monosyllables, accompanied by what he hoped was an endearing smile. And did he, the foreigner wanted to know, wish to make a thousand drachma? Behar gasped. The foreigner's smile broadened — that was a good answer.

The foreigner leaned closer and spoke in a confidential voice. Here were all these soldiers who had come to Trikkala; did Behar know where they lived? Well, they seemed to be everywhere. They'd taken over the two hotels, some of them stayed at the school, others in vacant houses — wherever they could find a roof to keep them out of the rain. Very well, now for the first part of the job. The foreigner could see that Behar was a smart lad, didn't need to write anything down, and so shouldn't. Mustn't. Behar promised not to do that. An easy promise, he couldn't have written anything down even if he'd wanted to, for he could neither read nor write. "Now then," the foreigner said, "all you have to do is . . ." When he was done, he explained again, then had Behar repeat the instructions. Clearly, Behar thought, a very careful foreigner.

He went to work that very afternoon, three hundred drachma already in his pocket. A fortune. At one time he'd tried his hand — disastrously — at changing money for tourists, and he knew that a thousand drachma was equal to ninety American dollars. To Behar, that was *more* than a thousand drachma, that was like something in a dream, or a movie.

But then, delight was replaced by misery. As the light faded from the November afternoon, he walked the streets of Trikkala, his eyes searching the rooftops. He knew where the reservists lived, or thought he did, and went from one to the next, crisscrossing the town, but no luck. In time, he became desperate. What if the foreigner was *wrong?* What if the accursed object didn't exist? What then? Give back the three hundred drachma? Well, he no longer had the three hundred drachma. Because, immediately after leaving the foreigner he had, maddened by good fortune, visited a pastry shop where he'd bought a cream-filled slice of *bougatsa* with powdered sugar on top. So good! And then — he was rich, why not? — another, this one with cheese, even more expensive. Now what? Make good what he'd spent? How?

Thirty minutes later, fate intervened. In, for a change, Behar's favor, as, for the third time in an hour, he paced the street in front of the school. A building that held, for Behar, nothing but terrible memories. The reservist soldiers went in and out, busy, occupied with important military matters. Up above, the sky had grown dark as it prepared to shower down some nice cold rain. Then, just for a moment, a thick cloud drifted aside and a few rays of sun, now low on the horizon, struck the school's chimney at just the proper angle. And Behar caught a single silver glint. Finally! There it was! Just as the foreigner had described it. A wire, run up from somewhere in the building and fixed in place by a rock atop the cement surround that topped the stuccoed plaster. Immediately, he looked away.

The rain held off. Fortunately, for Behar, it went away and found somewhere else to fall, because, for the second part of the job, he required sunshine. Which, the following morning, poured through the window of the shack and sent him off whistling to the better part of town, that part of town where people were used to certain luxuries. But this too turned out to be a difficult search, since the little gardens behind these houses were walled, so that Behar had to find a deserted street, check for broken glass cemented to the top of the wall — he'd learned about that years ago, the hard way — get a good grip, and hoist himself up. His first few attempts were unproductive. Then, at the very end of a quiet street, he found what he was looking for: a garden with two fig trees, a clothesline strung between them, laundry out to dry. Underpants, panties, two towels, two pillowcases, and two big white sheets.

He hauled himself the rest of the way and lay on the wall. Anyone home? Should he go and knock on the front door? *Does Panos live here?* No. He stared at the house; shutters closed over the windows, all silent and still. He took a deep breath, counted to three, and was over the wall. *Steal the underwear.* But he resisted the urge, snatched one of the sheets off the line, and sprinted back to the wall. He hauled himself up, made sure the street was still deserted, and sprang down. He folded the sheet, held it inside the front of his jacket, and walked away.

Back home, he experimented. Working with concentration — the remaining seven hundred drachma shimmered in his mind — he found he could wrap the sheet around his bare upper body and then button his shirt almost to the top, as long as he didn't tuck it into his trousers.

Now for the hard part. He stayed home through the early evening, going out only after the bell in the town hall rang midnight. When he reached the school, the street was empty, though there were lights shining in the windows on both floors. But he had no intention of going in there, there wasn't a bluff in the world that would get him past

141

all those soldiers. No, for the Behars of the world there was only the drainpipe, at a corner toward the back of the building. He knew these pipes, fixed together in flanged sections, the flanges extending from the curve every three feet or so, he'd climbed them many times in his stealthy life. First, shoes off — the soles worn so thin and smooth he'd get no traction at all. He had no socks, so he climbed barefoot, his toes pressed against the flange, his fingers pulling him up to the next level.

In a few minutes he was on the roof. He crouched down, keeping his silhouette below the sight line from the street, and crawled over to the chimney. Yes, here was the wire. He wanted to touch it, this ribbon of metal worth a thousand drachma, but he had no idea what it might be for; perhaps it was charged with some mysterious form of electrical current and would burn his fingers with its magic. It was certainly a secret wire — that much he'd sensed in the voice of the foreigner — so, *leave it alone.* He took off his jacket and shirt, unwound the sheet, and laid it flat on the roof.

What if the wind . . . ? He searched the dark rooftop, looking for weight, but found only some loose stucco where a crack ran along one corner. He pried up a few pieces, not very heavy, and distributed them at the corners of the sheet. They would have to do. Below him, on the second floor of the school, he could hear voices, a laugh, another voice, another laugh. He scuttled back to the drainpipe, descended to the ground, put on his shoes, and, feeling better than he'd felt in a long time, walked home. What did it mean, the sheet on the roof? He didn't know, he didn't care, he knew only what it meant to him.

The following morning he hurried off to the barbershop. In the back room, Pappou was cold and frightening. "Is it done? Whatever it is — done properly?" Behar said yes. Pappou sat still, his eyes boring into Behar's soul, then he picked up the telephone and made a brief call. Asked for somebody with a Greek name, waited, finally said, "You can have your hair cut any time you want, the barber is waiting for you." That was all. The foreigner appeared ten minutes later, and Pappou went out into the shop.

The foreigner asked where he'd found the wire; Behar told him. "Maybe I'll go up to the roof myself," he said. "What will I see?"

"A big white sheet, sir."

"Flat?"

"Yes, sir."

"Behar." A pause. "If you ever, *ever,* tell anybody about this, we will *know.* Understand?" With a slow, meticulous grace he drew an index finger across his throat, a gesture so eloquently performed that Behar thought he could actually see the knife. "Understand?" the foreigner said again, raising his eyebrows.

A frightened Behar nodded emphatically. He understood all too well. The foreigner held his eyes for a time, then reached into his pocket and counted out seven one-hundred-drachma notes.

28 November. For Costa Zannis, it began as a normal day, but then it changed. He was standing next to the captain in the school's narrow cloakroom, which, with the addition of a teacher's desk, had been turned into what passed for a liaison office. Pavlic was just about to join them, it was the most common moment imaginable; pleasant morning, daily chore, quiet talk. Zannis and the captain were looking down at a hand-drawn map, with elevations noted on lines indicating terrain, of some hilltop in Albania.

Then the captain grabbed his upper arm. A grip like a vice — sudden, instinctive.

Zannis started to speak — "What . . ." —

144

but the captain waved him into silence and stood frozen and alert, his head cocked like a listening dog. In the distance, Zannis heard a drone, aircraft engines, coming toward them. Coming low, not like the usual sound, high above. The captain let him go and ran out the door, Zannis followed. From the north, two planes were approaching, one slightly above the other. The captain hurried back into the school and grabbed the Bren gun that stood, resting on its stock, in one corner of the entry hall. The windows rattled as the planes roared over the rooftop and the captain took off toward the street, Zannis right behind him. But the captain shouted for him to stay inside, Zannis followed orders, and stopped in the doorway, so lived.

In front of the school, the captain searched the sky, swinging the Bren left and right. The sound of the planes' engines faded — going somewhere else. But that was a false hope, because the volume rose sharply as they circled back toward the school. The captain faced them and raised the Bren, the muzzle flashed, a few spent shells tumbled to the ground, then machine guns fired in the distance, the captain staggered, fought for his balance, and sank to his knees.

What happened next was unclear. Zannis

never heard an explosion, the world went black, and when his senses returned he found he was lying on his stomach and struggling to breathe. He forced his eyes open, saw nothing but gray dust cut by a bar of sunlight, tried to move, couldn't, and reached behind him to discover that he was pinned to the floor by a beam that had fallen across the backs of his legs. In panic, he fought free of a terrible weight. Then he smelled fire, his heart hammered, and he somehow stood up. *Get out.* He tried, but his first step — it was then he discovered his shoe was gone — landed on something soft. Covered with gray dust, a body lying face down. Somebody ran past him, Zannis could see he was shouting but heard nothing. He turned back to the body. Let it burn? He couldn't. He grabbed the feet, and, as he pulled, the body gave a violent spasm. Now he saw that one of the legs was bleeding, so he took the other leg which, as he hauled, turned the body over and he saw it was Pavlic.

As he pulled Pavlic's body toward the entry, there was a grinding roar and the rear section of the second story came crashing down onto the first floor. Zannis heaved again, Pavlic's body moved. He could see an orange flicker now and then, and could feel heat on the skin of his face. Was Pavlic alive? He peered down, found his vision blurred, realized his glasses weren't there, and was suddenly infuriated. He almost wanted — for an instant a scared ten-year-old — to look for them, almost, then understood he was in shock and his mind wasn't quite working. He took a deep breath, which burned in his chest and made him cough, steadied himself, and dragged the body out of the building, the back of Pavlic's head bouncing down the steps that led to the doorway. Immediately there was someone by his side, a woman he recognized, who worked in the post office across from the school. "Easy with him," she said. "Easy, easy, I think he's still alive." She circled Zannis and took Pavlic under the arms and slid him across the pavement.

With one bare foot, and unable to see very much of anything, he headed back toward the school. As he entered the building, a reservist came crawling out of the doorway, and Zannis realized there were still people alive inside. But the smoke blinded him completely and the heat physically forced him backward. In the street, he sat down and held his head in his hands. Not far from him, he saw what he thought were the captain's boots, heels apart, toes pointing in. Zannis looked away, tried to rub his ankle, and discovered his hand was wet. Blood was running from beneath his trouser cuff, across the top of his foot, and into the gray powder that covered the street. Very well, he would go to the hospital but, when he tried to stand, he couldn't, so he sat there, holding his head, in front of the burning school.

He wasn't hurt so much. They told him that later, in a dentist's office where the lightly wounded had been taken because the town clinic — there was no hospital in Trikkala — was reserved for the badly injured. The reservists lay on the floor of the reception area, the dentist had tried to make them comfortable by putting the pillows of his waiting room couch under their heads. Zannis could hear out of one ear now, a wound in his leg had been stitched up, and there was something wrong with his left wrist. He kept opening and closing his hand, trying to make it better, but motion only made the pain worse.

As dusk fell, he realized he was tired of being wounded and decided to seek out whatever remained of his unit. In the street, people noticed him, likely because a nurse had cut off the leg of his trousers. Zannis met their eyes and smiled — *oh well* — but the people looked sorrowful and shook their heads. Not so much at a soldier with a bare leg and one shoe. At the bombing of their school and the men who'd been killed, at how war had come to their town.

And it wasn't done with them. And they knew it.

Two days later, Zannis went to the clinic to see Pavlic. Some of the wounded lay on mattresses on the floor, but Pavlic had one of the beds, a wad of gauze bandage taped to one side of his face. He brightened when he saw Zannis, now fully dressed. After they shook hands he thanked Zannis for coming. "It is very boring here," he said, then thanked him also, as he put it, "for everything else."

Zannis simply made a dismissive gesture: *we don't have to talk about it.*

"I know," Pavlic said. "But even so, thanks."

"Here," Zannis said. He handed Pavlic three packs of cigarettes, a box of matches, the morning newspaper from Athens, and two magazines. German magazines. Pavlic held one of them up to admire it; Brunhilde, naked, full-breasted and thickly bushed, had been photographed in the act of serving a

149

volleyball. Pavlic said, "*Modern Nudist.* Thanks, I'll share these."

"You should see what we have in Salonika."

"I can imagine. What becomes of you now?"

"Back home, so they tell me. I've lost the hearing in one ear. And they say I might get a little medal if there are any left. And you?"

"A concussion, cuts and bruises." He shrugged. "I have to stay for a few days, then I'm ordered back to Zagreb. I suspect they don't think what I was doing was so important. They'd rather I keep the police cars running."

"Marko," Zannis said. Something in his voice made Pavlic attentive. "I want to ask you to do something."

"Go ahead."

Zannis paused, then said, "We have Jews coming into Salonika now. Fugitives from Germany, in flight. At least some of them have disappeared on the way. Where I don't know."

"I thought they went to the port of Constanta."

"Some of them do," Zannis said.

"But the way things are going in Roumania these days, it may be easier for them to get away if they try from Greece."

"As long as I'm there, it will be. And we have more ships, and more smugglers. For Europe, it's like slipping out the back door." After a moment, he said, "What do you think about it, this flight?"

Pavlic said, "I don't know," then hesitated, finally adding, "God help them, I guess that's the way I'd put it."

"Would *you* help them?"

For a time, Pavlic didn't answer. He was still holding the nudist magazine. "Costa, the truth is I never thought about — about something like that. I don't know if I . . . , no, that's not true, I could, of course I could. Not by myself, maybe, but I, I have friends."

Zannis said, "Because —" but Pavlic cut him off. "I don't know about you, but I saw this coming. Not what you're talking about, exactly, but something like it. That was in 'thirty-eight, September. When Chamberlain made a separate peace with Hitler. I remember very well, I thought, So much for Czechoslovakia, who's next? It's going to be our turn, sooner or later. So, what do I do if we're occupied? Nothing?" The word produced, from Pavlic, the thin smile of a man who's been told a bad joke.

"Well," he went on, " 'nothing' doesn't exist, not for the police. When somebody

151

takes your country, you help them or you fight them. Because they will come after you; they'll ask, they'll *order:* 'Find this man, this house, this organization. You're from Zagreb — or Budapest, or Salonika — you know your way around; give us a hand.' And if you *obey* them, or if you obey them during the day and don't do something else at night, then —"

"Then?"

For a moment, Pavlic was silent. Finally he said, "How to put it? You're ruined. Dishonored. You won't ever be the same again."

"Not everybody thinks that way, Marko. There are some who will be eager to work for them."

"I know, you can't change human nature. But there are those who will resist. It goes back in time forever, how conquerors and the conquered deal with each other. So everyone — well, maybe not everyone, but everyone like you and me — will have to take sides."

"I guess I have," Zannis said, as though he almost wished he hadn't.

"How would you do it, Berlin to Vienna? Cross into Hungary, then down through Yugoslavia into Greece? That's by rail, of course. If you went city to city you'd have to transit Roumania, I mean Budapest to Bucharest, and if you did *that* you'd better have some dependable contacts, Costa, or a lot — and I mean a *lot* — of money. And even then it's not a sure thing, you know; the way life goes these days, if you buy somebody they're just liable to turn around and sell you to somebody else."

"Better to stay west of Roumania," Zannis said. "The rail line goes down through Nis and into Salonika. Or even go from Nis into Bulgaria. I have a friend in Sofia I think I can count on."

"You don't know?"

"You never know."

"How do we communicate? *Telephone?*" He meant that it was beneath consideration.

"Does your office have a teletype machine?"

"Oh yes, accursed fucking thing. The Germans wished it on us — never shuts up, awful."

"That's how. Something like, 'We're looking for Mr. X, we think he's coming into Zagreb railway station on the eleven-thirty from Budapest.' Then a description. And if somebody taps into the line, so what? We're looking for a criminal."

Pavlic's expression was speculative: *could this work?* Then, slowly, he nodded, more to himself than to Zannis. "Not bad," he said. "Pretty good."

"But, I have to say this, dangerous."

"Of course it is. But so is crossing the street."

"Do you know your teletype number?"

Pavlic stared, then said, "No idea. So much for conspiracy." Then he added, "Actually, a typist works the thing."

"I know mine," Zannis said. "Could I borrow that for a moment?"

Pavlic handed over the *Modern Nudist*. Zannis took a pencil from the pocket of his tunic and flipped to the last page, where a group of naked men and women, arms around one another's shoulders, were smiling into the camera below the legend SUN-SHINE CHUMS, DÜSSELDORF. Zannis wrote 811305 SAGR. "The letters are for Salonika, Greece. You use the rotary dial on the machine. After it connects, the machine will type the initials for 'who are you' and you type the 'answer-back,' your number." He returned the magazine to Pavlic. "Perhaps you shouldn't share this."

"Does the message move on a telephone line?"

"Telegraph. Through the post office in Athens."

"I think I'd better have the typist teach

154

me how to do it."

"Someone you trust?"

Pavlic thought it over and said, "No."

Pushing a cart with a squeaky wheel, a nurse was moving down the aisle between the beds. "Here's lunch," Pavlic said.

Zannis rose to leave. "We ought to talk about this some more, while we have the chance."

"Come back tonight," Pavlic said. "I'm not going anywhere."

7 December, Salonika. Zannis wasn't sorry to be home, but he wasn't all that happy about it either. This he kept hidden; why ruin the family pleasure? His mother was very tender with him, his grandmother cooked everything she thought he liked, and, wherever he went that first week, room to room or outdoors, Melissa stayed by his side — she wasn't going to let him escape again. As for his brother, Ari, he had exciting news, which he saved during the first joyous minutes of homecoming, only to be upstaged by his mother. "And Ari has a job!" she said. With so many men away at the fighting, there was work for anybody who wanted to work, and Ari had been hired as a conductor on the tram line.

And, he insisted, this was something his

big brother had to see for himself. So Zannis had ridden the Number Four trolley out to Ano Toumba and let his pride show — sidelong glances from Ari made certain Zannis's smile was still in place — as Ari collected tickets and punched them with a silver-colored device. He was extremely conscientious and took his time, making sure to get it right. Inevitably, some of the passengers were rushed and irritable, but they sensed that Ari was one of those delicate souls who require a bit of compassion — was this a national trait? Zannis suspected it might be — and hardly anybody barked at him.

So Zannis returned to daily life, but a certain restless discomfort would not leave him. Able to hear out of only one ear, he was occasionally startled by sudden sounds, and he found that to be humiliating. A feeling in no way ameliorated by the fact that, just before he returned to Salonika, the Greek army *had* managed to find him a little medal, which he refused to wear, being disinclined to answer questions about how he came to have it. And, worst of all, he felt the absence of a love affair, felt it in the lack of commonplace affection, felt it while eating alone in restaurants, but felt it most keenly in bed, or out of bed but thinking about bed, or, in truth, all the time. In the chaos that followed the bombing of the Trikkala school, whatever goddess had charge of his mortality had brushed her lips across his cheek and this had, he guessed, affected that part of him where desire lived. Or maybe it was just the war.

On the evening of the seventh, Vangelis threw him a welcome-home party. Almost all were people Zannis knew, if, in some cases, only distantly. Gabi Saltiel, grayer and wearier than ever, was still driving an ambulance at night but traded shifts with another driver and brought his wife to the party. Sibylla, her helmet of hair highly lacquered for the occasion, was accompanied by her husband, who worked as a bookkeeper at one of the hotels. There were a couple of detectives, a shipping broker, a criminal lawyer, a prosecutor, two ballet teachers he'd met through Roxanne, an economics professor from the university, even a former girlfriend, Tasia Loukas, who worked at the Salonika city hall.

Tasia — for Anastasia — showed up late and held both his hands while he got a good strong whiff of some very sultry perfume. She was small and lively, dressed exclusively in black, had thick black hair, strong black eyebrows, and dark eyes — fierce dark eyes

157

— that challenged the world from behind eyeglasses with gray-tinted lenses. Did Vangelis have something in mind for him when he invited Tasia? Zannis wondered. He'd had two brief, fiery love affairs with her, the first six years earlier, the second a few months before he'd met Roxanne. Very free, Tasia, and determined to remain so. "I'll never marry," she'd once told him. "For the truth is, I like to go with a woman from time to time — I get something from a woman I can never get with a man." She'd meant that to be provocative, he thought, but he wasn't especially provoked and had let her know that he didn't particularly care. And he truly didn't. "It's exciting," she'd said. "Especially when it must be kept a secret." A flicker of remembrance had lit her face as she spoke, accompanied by a most deliciously wicked smile, as though she were smiling, once again, at the first moment of the remembered conquest.

Vangelis gave famously good parties — excellent red wine, bottles and bottles of it — and had stacks of Duke Ellington records. As the party swirled around them, Zannis and Tasia had two conversations. The spoken one was nothing special — how was he, fine, how was she — the unspoken one much more interesting. "I better go say hello to Vangelis," she said, and reluctantly, he could tell, let go of his hands.

"Don't leave without telling me, Tasia."

"I won't."

She was replaced by the economics professor and his lady friend, who Zannis recollected was a niece or cousin to the poet Elias. They'd been hovering, waiting their turn to greet the returning hero. Asked about his war, Zannis offered a brief and highly edited version of the weeks in Trikkala, which ended, "Anyhow, at least we're winning."

The professor looked up from his wineglass. "Do you really believe that?"

"I saw it," Zannis said. "And the newspapers aren't telling lies."

From the professor, a low grumbling sound that meant *yes, but.* "On the battlefield, it's true, we are winning. And if we don't chase them back into Italy, we'll have a stalemate, which is just as good. But *winning,* maybe not."

"Such a cynic," his lady friend said gently. She had a long intelligent face. Turning to the table at her side, she speared a dolma, an oily, stuffed grape leaf, put it on a plate and worked at cutting it with the side of her fork.

"How do you mean?" Zannis said.

159

"The longer this goes on," the professor said, "the more Hitler has to stop it. The Axis can't be seen to be weak."

"I've heard that," Zannis said. "It's one theory. There are others."

The professor sipped his wine; his friend chewed away at her dolma.

Zannis felt dismissed from the conversation. "Maybe you're right. Well then, what can we do about it?" he said. "Retreat?"

"Can't do that either."

"So, damned if we do, damned if we don't."

"Yes," the professor said.

"Don't listen to him," the professor's friend said. "He always finds the gloomy side."

The warrior in Zannis wanted to argue — *what about the British army?* Because if Germany attacked them, their British ally would arrive in full force from across the Mediterranean. To date, Britain and Germany were bombing each other's cities, but their armies, after the debacle that ended in Dunkirk, had not engaged. Hitler, the theory went, had been taught a lesson the previous autumn, when his plans to invade Britain had been thwarted by the RAF.

But the professor was bored with politics and addressed the buffet — "The eggplant spread is very tasty," he said, by way of a parting shot. Then gave way to one of Zannis's former colleagues from his days as a detective — insider jokes and nostalgic anecdotes — who in turn was replaced by a woman who taught at the Mount Olympus School of Ballet. Had Zannis heard anything from Roxanne? No, had she? Not a word, very troubling, she hoped Roxanne wasn't in difficulties.

Minutes later, Zannis knew she wasn't. Francis Escovil, the English travel writer and, Zannis suspected, British spy, appeared magically at his side. "Oh, she's perfectly all right," Escovil said. "I had a postal card, two weeks ago. Back in Blighty, she is. Dodging bombs but happy to be home."

"I'm glad to hear it."

"Yes, no doubt busy as a bee. Likely that's why you haven't heard from her."

"Of course," Zannis said. He started to say *give her my best* but thought better of it. That could, in a certain *context,* be taken the wrong way. Instead, he asked, "How do you come to know Vangelis?"

"Never met him. I'm here with Sophia, who teaches at the school."

"Oh." That raised more questions than it answered, but Zannis knew he'd never hear anything useful from the infinitely deflective

Englishman. In fact, Zannis didn't like Escovil, and Escovil knew it.

"Say, could we have lunch sometime?" Escovil said, trying to be casual, not succeeding.

What do you want? "We might, I'm pretty busy myself. Try me at the office — you have the number?"

"I think I might . . ."

I'll bet you do.

". . . somewhere. Roxanne put it on a scrap of paper."

Escovil stood there, smiling at him, not going away.

"Are you writing articles?" Zannis asked, seeking safe ground.

"Trying to. I've been to all sorts of monasteries, got monks coming out of my ears. Went to one where they haul you up the side of a cliff; that's the only way to get there. Just a basket and a frayed old rope. I asked the priest, 'When do you replace the rope?' Know what he said?"

"What?"

"When it breaks!" Escovil laughed, a loud *haw-haw* with teeth showing.

"Well, that's a good story," Zannis said, "as long as you're not the one in the basket." Out of the corner of his eye, he saw that Tasia was headed toward him. "We'll talk

162

later," he said to Escovil, and turned to meet her.

"I'm going home," she said.

"Could you stay a while?"

"I guess I could. Why?"

"I'm the guest of honor, I can't leave yet."

"True," she said. She met his eyes, no smile to be seen but it was playing with the corners of her mouth. "Then I'll stay. But not too long, Costa. I don't really know these people."

He touched her arm, lightly, with two fingers. "Just a little while," he said.

She had a large apartment, near the city hall and obviously expensive. One always wondered about Tasia and money but she never said anything about it. Maybe her family, he thought. Once inside, she fed her cats, poured two small glasses of ouzo, and sat Zannis on a white couch. Settling herself at the other end, she curled into the corner, kicked off her shoes, rested her legs on the cushions, said, "Salute," and raised her glass.

After they drank she said, "Mmm. I wanted that all night — I hate drinking wine. Take your shoes off, put your feet up. That's better, right? Parties hurt your feet? They do mine — high heels, you know? I'm

163

such a peasant. Oh yes, rub harder, good . . . good . . . don't stop, yes, there . . . ahh, that's perfect, now the other one, wouldn't want it to feel neglected . . . yes, just like that, a little higher, maybe . . . no, I meant higher, keep going, keep going . . . . . . no, don't take them all the way off, just down, just below my ass . . . there, perfect, you'll like that later. Remember?"

He was tired the following day, and nothing seemed all that important. It had been a long while between lovers for Tasia, as it had for Zannis, they were both intent on making up for lost time, and did. But then, a little after eleven, on what seemed like just another morning at work, he got something else he'd wanted. Wanted much more than he'd realized.

A letter. Carried by the postman, who appeared at the door of the office. Not his usual practice, the mail was typically delivered to a letter box in the building's vestibule, but not that day, that day the postman hauled his leather bag up five flights of stairs, came to Zannis's desk, took a moment to catch his breath, held up an envelope, and said, "Is this for you?"

Obviously a business letter, the return address printed in the upper left corner:

164

Hofbau und Sohn Maschinenfabrik
   GmbH
28, Helgenstrasse
Brandenburg
DEUTSCHLAND

With a typewritten address:

Herr C. N. Zannis
Behilfliches Generaldirektor
Das Royale Kleidersteller
122, via Egnatia
Salonika
HELLAS

"Yes," Zannis said. "That's for me." The letter was from, apparently, a manufacturer of industrial knitting machines in Brandenburg — not far from Berlin — to the assistant general manager of the Royale Garment Company in Salonika. *Well done,* he thought.

The postman leaned toward Zannis and spoke in a confidential voice, as though Saltiel and Sibylla might not be in on the game. "I don't care if you want to do this kind of thing. These days . . . well, you know what I mean. But I almost took this back to the post office, so in future leave me a note in the letter box, all right?"

"I will," Zannis said. "But if you'd keep

an eye out for, for this sort of *arrangement,* I'd appreciate it."

The postman winked. "Count on me," he said.

As the postman left, Zannis slit the envelope with a letter opener, carefully, and slid out a single sheet of folded commercial stationery; the address printed at the top of the page, the text typewritten below.

30 November 1940

Dear Sir:
I refer to your letter of 17 November.
We are in receipt of your postal money order for RM 232.
I am pleased to inform you that 4 replacement motors, 11 replacement spindles, and 14 replacement bobbins for our model 25-C knitting machine have been shipped to you by rail as of this date.
Thank you for your order. Hofbau und Sohn trusts you will continue to be satisfied with its products.

Yours truly,
S. Weickel

"Sibylla?" Zannis said. He was about to ask her about an iron. Then he stopped cold. She said, "Yes?" but he told her it was nothing, he'd take care of it himself.

Because he saw the future.

Because there was some possibility that the darkest theories of the war's evolution were correct: Germany would rescue the dignity of her Italian partner and invade Greece. Yes, the British would send an expeditionary force, would honor her treaty with an ally. But Zannis well knew what had happened in Belgium and France — the chaotic retreat from Dunkirk. So it hadn't worked then, and it might not work this time. The Greek army would fight hard, but it would be overwhelmed; they had no answer to German armour and aircraft. Salonika would be occupied, and its people would resist. *He* would resist. And that meant, what? It meant clandestine leaflets and radio, it meant sabotage, it meant killing Germans. Which would bring reprisal, and investigation, and interrogation. Saltiel and Sibylla might be questioned, so he could not, would not, compromise them, endanger them, with information they should not have. If they knew, they were guilty.

So Zannis left the office at noon, walked down to the market, found a stall with used irons in every state of age and decay, and bought the best electric model they had. "It works good," the stall owner said.

"How do you know?"

"I can tell," the man said. "I understand them. This one was left in the Hotel *Lux Palace,* and the settings are in *English.*"

Zannis walked back to his apartment, set the iron on his kitchen table, returned to the office, couldn't bear to wait all afternoon, and went home early.

First, he practiced, scorched a few pieces of paper, finally set the dial on WARM. Then he laid the letter flat on a sheet of newspaper on the wooden table in the kitchen and pressed the iron down on the letter's salutation. Nothing. He moved to the text in the middle — "I am pleased to inform you that 4 replacement motors" — but, again, nothing. No! A faint mark had appeared above the *p* of "pleased." *More heat.* He turned the dial to low, waited as the iron warmed, pressed for a count of five, and produced parts of three letters. He tried once more, counting slowly to ten, and there it was: ". . . ress KALCHER UND KRO . . ."

Ten minutes later he had the whole message, in tiny sepia-colored block letters between the lines of the commercial text:

Reply to address KALCHER UND KROHN, attorneys, 17, Arbenstrasse, Berlin. Write as H. H. STRAUB. 26 December man and wife traveling under name HARTMANN arrive Budapest from Vienna via 3-day excursion steamer LEVERKUSEN. He 55 years old, wears green tie, she 52 years old, wears green slouch hat. Can you assist Budapest to Belgrade? Believe last shipment lost there to Gestapo agents. Can you find boat out your port? Please help.

Last shipment meant the Rosenblum sisters, he thought, unless there had been others he didn't know about. Also lost. Budapest? How the hell could he help in *Budapest?* He didn't know a soul in Hungary; why would he? Why would Emilia Krebs think he did? What was wrong with this woman? *No, calm down,* he told himself. It isn't arrogance. It is desperation. And, on second thought, there might be one possibility. Anyhow, he would try.

He never really slept, that night. Staring at the ceiling gave way to fitful dozing and awful dreams which woke him, to once again stare at the ceiling, his mind racing. Finally he gave up and was at the office by seven-thirty. December weather had reached them: the clammy chill of the Mediterranean winter, the same grisaille, gray days, gray city, that he'd come to know in Paris. He turned on the lights in the office and set out his box of five-by-eight cards. Yes, his memory had not betrayed him: *Sami Pal.* His real — as far as anybody knew — Hungarian name, *Pal* not an uncommon surname in Hungary. Or, perhaps, a permanent alias.

Szamuel "Sami" Pal. Born Budapest 1904. Hungarian passport B91-427 issued 3 January, 1922, possibly counterfeit or altered. Also uses Nansen passport HK33156. Resident in Salonika since 4 May, 1931 (renewable visa) at various rooming houses. Operates business at 14, Vardar Square, cellar room rented from tenant above, Madame Zizi, Fortune Teller and Astrologer. Business known as Worldwide Agency — Confidential Inquiries. Telephone Salonika 38-727.

According to Salonika police records: investigated (not charged) for removal of documents from office of French consul, May '33. Arrested, September '34, accused by British oil executive R. J.

Wilson of espionage approach to valet. Released, valet refused to testify, likely bribed. Arrested June '38, accused of selling stolen passport. Released when witness could not be found. Investigated by State Security Bureau (Spiraki) November '39. (Salonika police consulted.) No conclusion reported to this office.

Previous to arrival in Salonika, Sami Pal is thought to have escaped from prison, city unknown, country said to be Switzerland by local informant, who claims Pal deals in merchandise stolen from port storage, also in stolen passports and papers.

9 December. For this interview, Zannis borrowed an interrogation room at the police station in the Second District — his last headquarters when he'd worked as a detective. His old friends were pleased to see him. "Hey Costa, you fancy sonofabitch, come back to join the slaves?"

Sami Pal was waiting on a bench in the reception area — had been waiting for a long time, Zannis had made sure of that — amid the miserable crowd of victims and thugs always to be found in the police stations. For the occasion, Zannis had chosen two props: a shoulder holster bearing

171

Saltiel's automatic — his own weapon having disappeared in the collapse of the Trikkala school — and a badge, clipped to his belt near the buckle, where Sami Pal was sure to see it.

Summoned by telephone the previous afternoon, Sami was looking his best. But he always was. A few years earlier, he'd been pointed out by a fellow detective in a taverna amid the bordellos of the Bara and, as the saying went, Zannis had seen him around. Natty, he was, in the sharpest cheap suit he could buy, a metallic gray, with florid tie, trench coat folded in his lap, boutonniere — a white carnation that afternoon — worn in the buttonhole of his jacket, a big expensive-looking watch that might have been gold, a ring with what surely wasn't a diamond, and a nervous but very brave smile. As Zannis got close to him — "Hello, Sami, we'll talk in a little while" — he realized from the near-dizzying aroma of cloves that Sami had visited the barber. To Zannis, and to the world at large, Sami Pal, with the face of a vicious imp, was the perfection of that old saying, "After he left, we counted the spoons."

The interrogation room had a high window with a wire grille, a battered desk, and two hard chairs. Zannis introduced himself

172

by saying, "I'm Captain Zannis," lowering his rank for the interview.

"Yes, sir. I know who you are, sir."

"Oh? Who am I, Sami?"

Sami's prominent Adam's apple went up, then down. "You're important, sir."

"Important to you, Sami. That's the truth."

"Yes, sir. I know, sir."

"You like it here, in Salonika?"

"Um, yes. Yes, sir. A fine city."

"You plan on staying here?"

After a pause, Sami said, "I'd like to, sir."

Zannis nodded. Who wouldn't want to stay in such a fine city? "Well, I think it's possible. Yes, definitely possible. Do you have enough work?"

"Yes, sir. I keep busy. Always husbands and wives, suspecting the worst, it's the way of love, sir."

"And passports, Sami? Doing any business there?"

Once again, the Adam's apple rose and fell. "No, sir. Never. I never did that."

"Don't lie to me, you —" Zannis let Sami Pal find his own word.

"Not now, sir. Maybe in the past, when I needed the money, I might've, but not now, I swear it."

"Allright, let's say I believe you."

173

"Thank you, sir. You can believe Sami."

"Now, what if I needed a favor?"

Sami Pal's face flooded with relief, this wasn't about what he'd feared, and he'd had twenty-four hours to consider his recent sins. He fingered his carnation and said, "Anything. Anything at all. Name it, sir."

Zannis lit a cigarette, taking his time. "Care for one of these?" He could see that Sami did want one but was afraid to take it.

"No, sir. Many thanks, though."

"Sami, tell me, do you have any connections in Budapest?"

Sami Pal was stunned; that was the very last thing he'd thought he might hear, but he rallied quickly. "I do," he said. "I travel up there two or three times a year, see a few friends, guys I grew up with. And my family. I see them too."

"These friends, they work at jobs? Five days a week? Take the pay home to the wife? Is that what they do?"

"Some of them . . . do that. They're just, regular people."

"But not all."

"Well . . ." Sami's mouth stayed open, but no words came out.

"Sami, please don't fuck with me, all-right?"

"I wasn't, I mean, no, yes, not all of them,

174

do that. One or two of them, um, make their own way."

"Criminals."

"Some would say that."

"This *is* the favor, Sami. This *is* what will keep you in this fine city. This *is* what may stop me from putting your sorry ass on a train up to Geneva. And I can do that, because you were right, I am important, and, just now, *very* important to you."

"They are criminals, Captain Zannis. It's how life goes in that city, if you aren't born to a good family, if you don't bow down to the bosses, you have to find a way to stay alive. So maybe you do a little of this and a little of that, and the day comes when you can't go back, your life is what it is, and your friends, the people who protect you, who help you out, are just like you, outside the law. Well, too bad. Because you wind up with the cops chasing you, or, lately, some other guy, from another part of town, putting a bullet in your belly. Then, time to go, it's been great, good-bye world. That's how it is, up there. That's how it's always been."

"These friends, they're not what you'd call 'lone wolves.' "

"Oh no, not up there. You won't last long by yourself."

"So then, gangs? That the word? Like the

175

Sicilians?"

"Yes, sir."

"With names?"

Sami Pal thought it over, either preparing to lie or honestly uncertain, Zannis wasn't sure which. Finally he said, "Sometimes we use the — um, that is, sometimes *they* use the name of a leader."

This errant pronoun *we* interested Zannis. One end of a string, perhaps, that could be carefully pulled until it led somewhere, maybe stolen merchandise or prostitutes traveling between the two cities. And not years ago, this week. But the clue was of interest only to Zannis the detective, not to Zannis the operator of a clandestine network. So he said, "And which one did you belong to, Sami? Back in the days when you lived up there?"

Sami Pal looked down at the desk. Whatever he was, he wasn't a rat, an informer. Zannis's first instinct was to show anger, but he suppressed it. "He won't be investigated if you tell me his name, Sami. You have my word on that."

Sami Pal took a breath, looked up, and said, "Gypsy Gus."

"Who?"

"Gypsy Gus. You don't know Gypsy Gus?"

"Why would I? He's a Gypsy?"

Sami Pal laughed. "No, no. He left Hungary, when he was young, and became a wrestler, a famous wrestler, in *America,* captain, in *Chicago.* I thought maybe you would know who he was, he was famous."

"Then what's his real name?"

After a moment Sami Pal said, "Gustav Husar."

Zannis repeated the name, silently, until he felt he'd memorized it. He was not going to write anything down in front of Sami Pal, not yet. "Tell me, what do they do, Husar and his friends."

"The usual things. Loan money, protect the neighborhood merchants, help somebody to sell something they don't need."

Zannis had a hard time not laughing at the way Sami Pal thought about crime. *Boy scouts.*

"That's the way it used to be, anyhow." *In the good old days.*

"And now?"

"There's bad blood now. Didn't use to be like that, everybody kept to their own part of town, everybody minded their own business. But then, about three years ago, some of the, well, what you call gangs got friendly with a few individuals on the police force, maybe money changed hands, and the idea was to help certain people and maybe hurt

177

some other people. It was after Hitler took over in Germany, sir, we had the same thing in Budapest, guys in uniforms, marching in the streets. There were some people in the city who liked what Hitler said, who thought that was the way life should go in Hungary. But not my crowd, captain, not my crowd."

"Why not, Sami? Why not your crowd?"

"Well, we were always over in Pest, across the river from the snobs in Buda. Pest is for the working class, see? And when the politics came in, that's the way we had to go. We're not reds, never, like the Russians, but we couldn't let these other guys get away with it. That meant fighting. Because if the workers were just having a drink somewhere, and here came some guys with iron bars, looking to cause trouble, we helped out. Maybe one of our guys had a gun, and he knew how to use it, understand?"

Gold! But Zannis merely nodded. "What about the Jews, in Budapest?"

Sami shrugged. "What about them?"

"What does . . . your crowd, think about them?"

"Who cares? There was one who used to work with us, he's in jail now, but it didn't matter to anybody, what he was." After a pause, Sami Pal said, "We knew he was a Jew, but he didn't have sidelocks or a beard or anything, he didn't wear a hat."

Zannis drummed his fingers on the desk. Would it work? "This Gypsy Gus, Gustav Husar," he said. "He looks like a Gypsy?"

"No, sir." Sami Pal grinned at the idea. "They made him a Gypsy because he came from Hungary, he's got the photographs. Big mustache, like an organ-grinder, a gold hoop in his ear, and he wore a fancy sort of a shirt, and that little hat. You know, captain, *Gypsy Gus.*"

"And where would I find him, if I went to Budapest?"

Sami Pal froze. In his mind's eye, he saw his old boss taken by the police — guns drawn, handcuffs out — and all because it was Sami Pal who'd sold him to the cops in Salonika.

Zannis read him perfectly. With hand flat, palm turned toward the desk, he made the gesture that meant *calm down.* And softened his voice. "Remember my promise, Sami? I meant it. Nobody's going to do anything to your friend, I only want to talk to him. Not about a crime, I don't care what he's done, I need his help, nothing more. You know the sign on your door, in Vardar Square? It says CONFIDENTIAL INQUIRIES? Well, now you've had one." He paused to let that sink in, then continued. "And I mean *confiden-*

179

tial, Sami, secret, forever, between you and me. You don't go blabbing to your girl-friends, you don't go playing the big shot about your friend on the police force. Understand?"

"Yes, sir. I have your promise." He sounded like a schoolboy.

"And . . . ?"

"It's called Ilka's Bar. When Gypsy Gus was a strong man in the circus, in Esztergom, before he went to Chicago, Ilka was his, um, assistant, on the stage, with a little skirt."

Now Zannis set pad and pencil on the desk in front of Sami Pal. "Write it down for me, Sami, so I don't forget. The name of the bar and the address."

"I can only write in Hungarian, captain."

"Then do that."

Zannis waited patiently while Sami Pal carved the letters, one at a time, onto the paper. "Takes me a minute," Sami said. "I don't know the address, I only know it's under the Szechenyi Bridge, the chain bridge, on the Pest side, in an alley off Zrinyi Street. There's no sign, but everybody knows Ilka's Bar."

"And how does it work? You leave a message at the bar?"

"No, the bar is his . . . office, I guess you'd

call it. But don't show up until the after-noon, captain. Gypsy Gus likes to sleep late."

11 December. *Now for the hard part.* He had to tell Vangelis. He could do what he meant to do behind the back of the entire world — all but Vangelis. Zannis telephoned, then walked up to the office in the central police headquarters on the same square as the municipal building. Vangelis was as always: shaggy white hair, shaggy white mustache stained yellow by nicotine because he'd smoked his way through a long and eventful life, and more and more mischief in his face, in his eyes and in the set of his mouth, as time went by — *I know the world, what a joke.* Vangelis had coffee brought from a *kafeneion,* and they both lit Papastratos No. 1 cigarettes.

They spent a few minutes on health and family. "Your brother makes a wonderful tram conductor, doesn't he?" Vangelis said, his pleasure in this change of fortune producing a particularly beatific, St. Vange-lis smile. Which vanished when he said, "The mayor is still telephoning me about his niece, Costa. The lost parakeet?"

Zannis shook his head. "Write another report? That we're still looking?"

"*Anything,* please, to get that idiot off my back."

Zannis said he would write the report, then told Vangelis what he was going to do. No names, no specifics, just that he intended to help some of the fugitives moving through the Balkans, and to that end he might be spending a day or two in Budapest.

Vangelis didn't react. Or perhaps his reaction was that he didn't react. He took a sip of coffee, put the cup down and said, "A long time, the train to Budapest. If it's better for you not to be away from your work for so long, perhaps you ought to fly. The planes are flying again, for the moment."

"I don't think I have the money for airplanes."

"Oh. Well. If that's all it is." He reached into the bottom drawer of his desk and brought out a checkbook. As he wrote, he said, "It's drawn on the Bank of Commerce and Deposit, on Victoros Hougo Street, near the Spanish legation." Carefully, Vangelis separated the check from the stub and handed it to Zannis. The signature read *Alexandros Manos,* and the amount was for one thousand Swiss francs. "Don't present this at the cashier's window, Costa. Take it to Mr. Pereira, the manager."

Zannis looked up from the check and

raised his eyebrows.

"Did you know Mr. Manos? A fine fellow, owned an umbrella shop in Monastir. Been dead for a long time, sorry to say."

"No, I didn't know him," Zannis said, echoing the irony in Vangelis's voice.

"One must have such resources, Costa, in a job like mine. They've been useful, over the years. Crucial."

Zannis nodded.

"And, Costa? Gun and badge for your trip to Hungary, my boy, servant of the law, official business."

"Thank you, commissioner," Zannis said.

"Oh, you're welcome. Come to think of it, maybe the time has come for you to have one of these accounts for yourself, considering . . . your, intentions. Now, let, me, see . . ." Vangelis thought for a time, leaning back in his chair. Then he sat upright. "Do you know Nikolas Vasilou?"

"I know who he is, of course, but I've never met him." Vasilou was one of the richest men in Salonika, likely in all Greece. He was said to buy and sell ships, particularly oil tankers, like penny candy.

"You should meet him. Let me know when you return and I'll arrange something."

Zannis started to say thank you once more

183

but Vangelis cut him off. "You will need money, Costa."

Zannis sensed it was time to go and stood up. Vangelis rose halfway from his chair and extended his hand. Zannis took it — frail and weightless in his grasp. This reached him; he never thought of the commissioner as an old man, but he was.

Vangelis smiled and flipped the backs of his fingers toward the door, shooing Zannis from his office. *Now go and do what you have to,* it meant, a brusque gesture, affectionate beyond words.

He was busy the following day. For one thing, because of absent personnel — the war, the fucking war, how it *manifested* itself — the office had to handle a few commonplace criminal investigations. So now they'd been assigned a murder in Ano Toumba, a dockworker found stabbed to death in his bed. Nobody had any idea who'd done this, or why. By noon, Zannis and Saltiel had talked to the stevedores on the wharf, then some of the man's relatives. He wasn't married, couldn't afford it, didn't gamble or patronize the girls up in the Bara, gave no offense to anybody. He worked hard, played dominoes in the taverna, such was life. So, why? Nobody knew, nobody even offered the usual dumb theories.

After lunch he cashed Vangelis's check, visited the Hungarian legation and was given a visa, then bought a ticket at the TAE office: up to Sofia, then Lufthansa to Budapest. The ticket in his hand was not unexciting — he'd never flown in an airplane. Well, now he would. He wasn't afraid, not at all.

It was after six by the time he got to his front door, greeted the waiting Melissa, trudged up the stairs, and found his door unlocked and Tasia Loukas naked in his bed. "I remembered your key," she said. "Above the door." She was propped on one elbow, wearing her tinted glasses and reading the Greek version of one of Zannis's French spy novels, *The Man from Damascus.* "You aren't sorry to see me, are you?"

He drew the sheet down to her waist and kissed her softly, twice, by way of answer. Then he went into the kitchen, gave Melissa a mutton bone, a hunk of bread, and two eggs. "I have to take a shower," he said as he returned to the bedroom. "Really I have to, it's been that kind of day."

"I have a surprise for you," Tasia said.

"Oh?"

"But not until later. At eleven we have to go back out."

"What is it?"

185

"You'll see. It's a nice surprise."

He began to unbutton his shirt, she watched attentively as he undressed.

"I see you're ironing your own clothes now," she said.

The iron was still sitting on the table in the kitchen. "Yes," he said. "A small economy."

"I'd like to watch you do it," she said, amused at the idea. "Can you?"

"I'm learning," he said. He stepped out of his underpants and bent over to pick them up.

"Come and sit with me for a little," she said. "I don't care if you smell."

How to say no?

He sat on the edge of the bed, she began to stroke him, observing the result like an artist. "I daydreamed all day, at work," she said, voice tender. "A little voice in my head. It kept saying, 'Tasia, you need a good fucking,' so here I am. Did you think you were too tired?"

"I did wonder."

"But you are not, as we can see."

He woke up suddenly and looked at his watch. 9:33. He could hear rain pattering down on Santaroza Lane, a gentle snore from Melissa, which now stopped abruptly because she'd also woken up, the instant after he had. She always knew. How? A dog mystery. Tasia was asleep on her stomach, arm beneath the pillow, mouth open, face delicately troubled by a dream. Her lips moved, who was she talking to? As he watched, one eye opened. "You're awake," she said.

"It's raining." The first attack of a campaign to stay home.

She sat up, sniffed, then got out of bed and, haunches shifting, walked to the bathroom, closed the door almost all the way, and called out, "What time is it?"

"Nine-thirty."

"Hmm."

When she emerged, she began to sort through her clothes, which lay folded on a chair. "I have a funny story for you," she said, stepping into her panties.

Oh no, she still wants to go out. They had eaten nothing, so he'd have to take her somewhere, though, for him, making love was a substitute for food. "You do?"

"I forgot to tell you," she said.

He waited as she put on her bra, hooking it in front then twisting it around.

"I have a little nephew. A cute kid, maybe four years old. And you know what he did? You won't believe it when I tell you."

187

"What?"

"He tried to kill Hitler."

"He *what?*"

"Tried to kill Hitler. Really. They have one of those shortwave radios, and they were listening to some music program. Eventually the news came on and there was Hitler, shouting and screaming, the crowd cheering. You know what it sounds like. Anyhow, the kid listens for a while, then he picks up a pencil and shoves it into the speaker."

Tasia laughed. Zannis laughed along with her and said, "That's funny. It really happened?"

"It did," she said. She put on a black sweater, combing her hair back in place with her fingers once she had it on. "Aren't you hungry?" she said.

The surprise was, in truth, a surprise. They left the apartment, then stopped at a taverna for fried calamari and a glass of wine, and Tasia told him what she'd planned. A friend of hers owned the movie theatre in what had been, until the population exchange of 1923, a Turkish mosque, and he had gotten hold, somehow, of a print of Charlie Chaplin's *The Great Dictator.* "It won't have subtitles," she said, "but you understand English, don't you?"

188

"Some. Not much."

"Never mind, you'll manage. He's showing it for friends, so we'll at least have a chance to see it. Otherwise, we'd have to wait a long time, for the official release."

The film was accompanied by considerable whispering, as people asked their neighbors to explain the dialogue, but that didn't matter. Hitler was called Adenoid Hynkel, Mussolini appeared as Benzino Napaloni, which Zannis supposed was amusing if you spoke English. Mussolini teased and tormented and manipulated his fellow dictator — that didn't need translation either. Still, even though it was Chaplin's first talking picture, the physical comedy was the best part. Everybody laughed at the food fight and applauded Hitler's dance with an inflated globe, literally kicking the world around. The political speech at the end was spoken out in Greek by the theatre owner, who stood to one side of the screen and read from notes.

Zannis didn't find it all that funny, the way Mussolini provoked Hitler. The movie was banned in Germany, but Hitler would no doubt be treated to a private screening — trust that little snake Goebbels to make sure he saw it. Hitler wouldn't like it. So, some comedian thought the Axis partners were comic? Perhaps he'd show him otherwise. When the movie was over, and the crowd dispersed in front of the mosque, Zannis wasn't smiling. And in that, he saw, he wasn't alone.

"So!" said a triumphant Tasia. "What will Adolf think of *this?*"

"I wouldn't know," Zannis said. "I'll ask him when he gets here."

14 December. The Bréguet airplane bumped and quivered as it fought the turbulence above the mountains. Zannis was alarmed at first, then relaxed and enjoyed the view. Too soon they descended above Sofia airport, then zoomed toward the runway — *too fast, too fast* — and then, just as the wheels bounced on the tarmac and Zannis held a death grip on the arms of his seat, something popped in his left ear and the sound of the engines got suddenly louder. He could hear in both ears! He was overjoyed, smiling grandly at a dour Bulgarian customs official, which made the officer more suspicious than usual.

It was dusk when they landed in Budapest. Zannis took a taxi to the railway station and checked into one of the travelers' hotels across the square. In his room, he looked out the window. Looked, as big windblown snowflakes danced across his vision, at the people hurrying to and from their trains, holding on to their hats in the wind. Looked for surveillance, looked for men watching the station. What happened to the fugitives who came here? Who was hunting them? How was it managed?

The following day, he waited until one in the afternoon, rode a taxi across the Szechenyi Bridge, and made his way to Ilka's Bar. Which was small and dark and almost deserted — only one other customer, a tall attractive woman wearing a hat with a veil. She was not a casual patron but sat nervously upright, staring straight ahead, a handkerchief twisted in her hands.

As for Gustav Husar, he was nowhere to be seen. Except on the walls: a glossy publicity photograph of a menacing Gypsy Gus applying a headlock to a bald fellow in white spangled tights, and framed clippings from newspapers: Gypsy Gus with his arm around a blond actress, a cigarette holder posed at an angle in her gloved hand; Gypsy Gus flanked by four men who could only have been Chicago gangsters; Gypsy Gus sitting on another wrestler as the referee raised his hand to slap the canvas, signaling a pin.

Zannis had a cup of coffee, and another.

Then, some forty-five minutes after he'd arrived, two men strolled into the bar, one with a slight bulge beneath the left-hand shoulder of his overcoat. He nodded to the barman, glanced at the woman, and had a long look at Zannis, who stared into his coffee cup. As the other man left, the barman took an orange, cut it in half, and began squeezing it in a juicer. Very quiet at Ilka's, the sound of juice splashing into a glass seemed quite loud to Zannis.

The barman's timing was exquisite — so that Gustav Husar, entering the bar, could take his glass of orange juice to a table in the corner. Zannis started to rise, but the tall woman was already hurrying toward the table. There was not much to be seen of the wrestling Gypsy, Zannis realized, only the rounded shoulders and thick body of a man born to natural strength, now dressed in a cashmere overcoat and a stylish silk scarf. On his huge head, where only a fringe of graying hair remained, a black beret. He had blunt features and, flesh thickened at the edges, cauliflower ears. His eyes were close-set and sharp. *Cunning* was the word that came to Zannis.

As Husar and the woman spoke in hushed tones, she reached beneath her veil and dabbed at her eyes with the handkerchief.

192

Husar patted her arm, she opened her purse, and took out an envelope. This she handed to Husar, who slid it in the pocket of his overcoat. Then she hurried out the door, head held high but still dabbing at her eyes. The man with the bulging overcoat was suddenly at Zannis's table and said something in Hungarian. Zannis indicated he didn't understand. "I can speak German," he said in that language. "Or maybe English." Foreseeing the difficulties of a Greek needing to speak with a Hungarian, he had studied his English phrasebook, working particularly on words he knew he'd require.

The man turned, walked over to Husar, and spoke to him briefly. Husar stared at Zannis for a time, then beckoned to him. As Zannis seated himself, Husar said, "You speak English?"

"Some."

"Where you from? Ilka's in the office, she speaks everything."

"Greek?"

"Greek!" Husar gazed at him as though he were a novelty, produced for Husar's amusement. "A cop," he said. "All the way from Greece."

"How do you know I'm a cop?" Zannis said, one careful word at a time.

Husar shrugged. "I know," he said. "I always know. What the hell you doing up here?"

"A favor. I need a favor. Sami Pal gave me your name."

Husar didn't like it. "Oh?" was all he said, but it was more than enough.

"Sami gave me the name, Mr. Husar, nothing else."

"Okay. So?"

"A favor. And I will pay for it."

Husar visibly relaxed. A *corrupt* cop. This he understood. "Yeah? How much you pay?"

"Two thousand dollars."

Husar swore in Hungarian and his eyes widened. "Some favor! I don't kill politicians, mister —"

"Zannis. My first name is Costa."

"Your right name? I don't care, but —"

"It is."

"Okay. What you want from me?" *I'm going to say no, but I want to hear it.*

"You know people escape from Germany?"

"Some, yeah. The lucky ones."

"I help them."

Husar gave him a long and troubled look. Finally he said, "You are, maybe, Gestapo?"

"No. Ask Sami."

"Okay, maybe I believe you. Say I let you

194

give me two thousand dollars, then what?"

"People come off the . . ." For a moment, Zannis's English failed him; then it worked. "People come off the excursion steamer from Vienna and get on the train to Yugoslavia. Zagreb, maybe Belgrade. You hide them, help them safe on the train."

Husar puffed his cheeks and blew out a sound, *pouf,* then looked uncertain. "Not what I do, mister. I run business, here in Budapest."

"This is business."

"It ain't business, don't bullshit *me,* it's politics."

Zannis waited. Husar drank some of his juice. "Want some orange juice?"

"No, thank you."

"Why I said Gestapo is, they're *around,* you understand? And they play tricks, these guys. *Smart* tricks." He leaned forward and said, "The Germans try to take over here. And there's Hungarians want to help them. But not me. Not *us,* see? You got this problem? In Greece?"

"No."

"We got it here." He drank more juice, and made a decision. "How I find out what you want? What people? When? Where?"

"You own a cop here, Mr. Husar?"

"Gus."

"Gus."

"Yeah, sure, I do. I own a few."

"We send him . . . It's like a telegram, a police telegram."

"Yeah? Like a 'wanted' notice?"

"Yes. It must be a detective."

"I got that. It's easy."

"Just give me a name."

"First the dollars, mister."

"In a week."

"You don't have with you?"

Zannis shook his head.

Husar almost laughed. "Only a cop —"

"You will have the money."

"Okay. Come back here tonight. Then, maybe."

Zannis stood up. Husar also rose and they shook hands. Husar said, "It's not for me, the money. Me, I might just do it for the hell of it, because I don't like the Germans, and they don't like me. So, let's see about you, I'll call Sami today."

"I'll be back tonight," Zannis said.

It snowed again that evening, big slow flakes drifting past the streetlamps, but Ilka's Bar was warm and bright and crowded with people. A thieves' den, plain to be seen, but the sense of family was heavy in the air. Gustav Husar laughed and joked, rested a big arm across Zannis's shoulders, marking him as *okay* in here, among Husar's boys. Thugs of all sorts, at least two of them with knife scars on the face, their women wearing plenty of makeup. There was even a kid-size mascot, likely still a teenager, with dark skin and quick dark eyes, who told Zannis his name was Akos. He spoke a little German, did Akos, and explained that his name meant "white falcon." He was proud of that. And, Zannis sensed, dangerous. Cops knew. *Very* dangerous. But, that night, friendly as could be. Zannis also met Ilka, once beautiful, still sexy, and it was she who gave him a piece of paper with the name of a detective, a teletype number, and a way to send the money — by wire — to a certain person at a certain bank.

Very organized, Zannis thought, Sami Pal's crowd.

19 December. Vangelis might have waited weeks to connect Zannis with secret money, and Zannis wouldn't have said a word, but there were newspaper headlines every morning, and speeches on the radio, and talk in the tavernas, so nobody waited weeks for anything, not any more they didn't.

Thus Vangelis telephoned on the morning of the nineteenth; come to lunch, he said, at the Club de Salonique at one-thirty, yes? Oh yes. The twenty-sixth of December, when the "Hartmanns" would be leaving Berlin, was closing in fast, and Zannis knew he had to get the two thousand dollars into the account Husar controlled in Budapest.

Zannis was prompt to the minute, but he'd got it wrong — his first thought, anyhow. From the glasses on the table and the ashtray, he could see that Vangelis and Nikolas Vasilou had been there for a while. Then, as both men rose to greet him, Zannis realized this was simply St. Vangelis at work, making time to say things to Vasilou about him that couldn't be said once he'd arrived. "Am I late?" Zannis said.

"*Skata!* My memory!" Vangelis said. Then, "It's all my fault, Costa. But no matter, here we are."

Vasilou was taller than Zannis, lean and straight-backed, with a prominent beak of a nose, sharp cheekbones, ripples of oiled silver hair combed back from his forehead, and a thin line for a mouth. "Very pleased to meet you," he said, his eyes measuring Zannis. Friend? Foe? Prey?

They ordered a second bottle of retsina, with lamb and potatoes to follow, and they talked. The war, the local politics, the city, the weather, the war. Eventually the main course showed up and they talked some more. Zannis contributed little, his status well below that of his partners at luncheon. Smiled at their quips, nodded at their insights, tried not to get food on his tie. Finally, as triangles of tired-looking baklava arrived on the club's French china, Vangelis excused himself to go to the bathroom.

The businessman Vasilou wasted no time. "The commissioner tells me that you need, how shall we say . . . private money? A secret fund?"

"That's true," Zannis said. He sensed that Vasilou had not made up his mind, so the instinct to persuade, to say more, to say too much, was strong inside him but, with difficulty, he fought it off.

"Money that cannot, he tells me, come from the city treasury."

Zannis nodded. After a moment he said, "Would you like me to explain?"

"No, not the details," Vasilou said, protecting himself. "How much are we talking about?"

Zannis gave the number in drachma, two hundred and fifty thousand, his tone neutral, and not dramatic. "It will have to be paid out in dollars," he said, "the way life works in Europe these days."

"A lot of money, my friend. Something

short of twenty-five thousand dollars."

"I know," Zannis said, looking gloomy. "Perhaps too much?"

Vasilou did not take the bait and play the tycoon. He looked, instead, thoughtful — *what am I getting myself into?* The silence grew, Zannis became aware of low conversation at other tables, the discreet music of lunch in a private dining room. Vasilou looked away, toward the window, then met Zannis's eyes and held them. "Can you confirm," he said, "that this money will be spent for the benefit of our country?"

"Of course it will be." That was a lie.

And Vasilou almost knew it, but not quite. "You're sure?" was the best he could do.

"You have my word," Zannis said.

Vasilou paused, then said, "Very well." Not in his voice, it wasn't *very well*, but he'd been trapped and had no way out.

Vangelis returned to the table but did not sit down. "I've got to forgo the baklava," he said, glancing at his watch.

"They will wrap it up for you," Vasilou said, looking for the waiter.

"No, no. Another time. And I really shouldn't." Vangelis shook hands with both of them and made his way out of the dining room.

"A valued friend," Vasilou said. "He

200

speaks well of you, you know."

"I owe him a great deal. Everything. And he believes in . . . what I'm doing."

"Yes, I know he does, he said he did." Vasilou paused, then said, "He also told me you might some day become commissioner of police, here in Salonika."

"Far in the future," Zannis said. "So I don't think about things like that." *But you'd better.*

Vasilou reached inside his jacket — revealing a swath of white silk lining — and took out a checkbook and a silver pen. "Made out to you? In your name?" he said. "You can convert this to dollars at the bank." Vasilou wrote out the check, signed it, and handed it to Zannis.

They spoke briefly, after that, a reprise of the lunch conversation, then left the club together. Walked down the stairs and out the front door, where a white Rolls-Royce was idling at the curb. As they said goodbye, Zannis looked over Vasilou's shoulder. The face of the woman, staring out the window of the backseat, was the most beautiful thing he'd ever seen. Olive skin, golden hair — truly gold, not blond — pulled straight back, eyes just barely suggesting an almond shape, as though wrought by a Byzantine painter.

Vasilou turned to see what Zannis was looking at and waved to the woman. For an instant her face was still, then it came alive, like an actress before the camera: the corners of the full lips turned up, but the rest of the perfect face remained perfectly composed. Flawless.

"Can we drop you somewhere?" Vasilou said. He didn't mean it; Zannis had had from him all he was going to get for one day.

"No, thanks. I'll walk."

Slowly, the window of the Rolls was lowered. She was wearing a bronze-colored silk shirt and a pearl necklace just below her throat. "Can you get in front, darling?" she said. "I've got packages in back."

Vasilou gave Zannis a certain look: *women, they shop.* A chauffeur slid from behind the wheel, circled the car, and opened the front door.

"Again, thank you," Zannis said.

Vasilou nodded, brusque and dismissive, as though Zannis, by taking his money, had become a servant. Then walked quickly to his car.

26 December. Berlin.

Only the wealthy could afford to live in the Dahlem district of Berlin, a neighborhood of private homes with gardens. The houses were powerfully built, of sober stone or brick, often three stories high, sometimes with a corner tower, while the lawns and plantings were kept with the sort of precision achieved only by the employment of gardeners. However, in the last month of 1940, hidden here and there — one didn't want to be seen to acknowledge shortage — were the winter remains of vegetable gardens. Behind a fieldstone wall, a rabbit hutch. And the rising of the weak sun revealed the presence of two or three roosters. In Dahlem! But the war at sea was, in Berlin and all of Germany, having its effect.

At five-thirty, on a morning that seemed to her cruelly cold, wet, and dark, Emilia Krebs rang the chime on the door of the Gruen household. She too lived in Dahlem, not far away, but she might have driven had not gasoline become so severely rationed. When the door was answered, by a tall distinguished-looking gentleman, Emilia said, "Good morning, Herr Hartmann." That was Herr Gruen's new name, his alias for the journey to Salonika.

He nodded, *yes, I know,* and said, "Hello, Emmi."

Emilia carried a thermos of real coffee, hard to find these days, and a bag of freshly

203

baked rolls, made with white flour. Stepping inside, she found the Gruen living room almost barren, what with much of the furniture sold. On the walls, posters had been tacked up to cover the spaces where expensive paintings had once hung. The telephone sat on the floor, its cord unplugged from the wall — the Gestapo could listen to your conversation if the phone was plugged in. She greeted Frau Gruen, as pale and exhausted as her husband, then went to the coat closet in the hall and opened the door. The Gruens' winter coats, recently bought from a used-clothing stall, were heavily worn but acceptable. They mustn't, she knew, look like distressed aristocracy.

Emilia Krebs tried, at least, to be cheerful. The Gruens — he'd been a prominent business attorney — were old friends, faithful friends, but today they would be leaving Germany. Their money was almost all gone, their car was gone, soon the house would be gone, and word had reached them from within the Nazi administration — from Herr Gruen's former law clerk — that by the end of January they would be gone as well. They were on a list, it was simply a matter of time.

Frau Gruen poured coffee into chipped mugs but refused a roll. "I can't eat," she said, apology in her voice. She was short and plump and had, in better times, been the merriest sort of woman — anyone could make her laugh. Now she followed Emilia's eyes to a corner of the living room where a green fedora-like slouch hat rested on a garden chair. "Let me show you, Emmi," she said, retrieving the hat and setting it on her head, tilting the brim over one eye. "So?" she said. "How do I look?"

Like a middle-aged Jewish woman. "You look perfect," Emilia said. "Very Marlene Dietrich."

The hat was meant to provide a kind of shadow, obscuring her friend's face, but if the Gruens, traveling as the Hartmanns, ran into difficulties, it would be because of the way Frau Gruen looked. Their papers, passports and exit visas, were excellent forgeries, because resistance friends of Emilia's had managed to link up with a communist cell — they left anti-Nazi leaflets in public buildings — and with this very dangerous connection had come one of the most desirable people to know these days in Berlin: a commercial printer.

Emilia and the Gruens drank their mugs of coffee in silence, there was nothing more to say. When they were done, Emilia said, "Would you care for company on the way to the tram?"

"Thank you, Emmi," Herr Gruen said, "but we'll go by ourselves, and say farewell to you now."

And so they did.

They left early, seeking the most crowded trains, and they were not disappointed. During the run to Dresden, two and a half hours, they stood in the corridor, packed in with people of all sorts, many with bulky parcels and suitcases. Their own luggage was a simple leather valise, packed for the eyes of customs officers. On this leg of the journey they were ignored, and the passport control on the German side of the Czech border was perfunctory. They were on their way to Vienna, part of the Reich, and so were most of the other passengers. Not quite so smooth was the entry control on the other side of the border — by then it was two-thirty. The officers here were Sudeten Germans, newly empowered, and so conscientious. One of them had a good long look at Frau Gruen, but was not quite so discourteous as to mention that he thought she looked like a Jew. He stared, but that was it, and so failed to notice the thin line of perspiration at her husband's hairline — on a frigid afternoon. But their papers were in order and the officer stamped their visas.

Vienna was a long way from Prague, some eight hours on the express train. Here the Hartmanns were in a first-class compartment, where passengers were rarely subject to unscheduled security checks by Gestapo detectives. One didn't want to annoy powerful people. The Gruens, in preparatory conversation with Emilia and her friends, had determined that friendly chitchat was dangerous, better to remain silent and aloof. But certain travelers, especially the newly prosperous, felt that first-class status was an opportunity to converse with interesting people and were not so easily turned aside. Thus a woman in the seat across from Frau Gruen, who said, "What takes you to Vienna?"

"Unfortunately, my wife's mother has passed away," Herr Gruen said. "We're going for the funeral." After that they were left alone.

A useful lie, they thought. How were they to know that this woman and her mouse of a husband would be on the *Leverkusen,* the excursion steamer to Budapest?

In the war of 1914, the German and Austro-Hungarian empires had fought as allies. After surrender in 1918, Hungary became a separate state but Germany, with a new war on the horizon in the late 1930s, sought to rekindle the alliance, courting the Hungarians in the hope they would join up with Hitler in the planned conquest of Europe. *We must be friends,* said German diplomacy, accent on the *must,* so commercial links of all sorts became important. For example, the round-trip excursion steamer that sailed up and down the Danube between Vienna and Budapest. True, it crossed the border of the Reich, but not the border of national amity. It was *fun.* A band played on the dock in Vienna, another on the dock in Budapest. The food aboard the *Leverkusen,* even in time of rationing, was plentiful — as much potato as you liked. Not that there wasn't a passport control, there was, beneath great swastika banners, but the Austrian SS men kept their Alsatian shepherds muzzled and at a distance, and the officers, on the border with a new ally, were under orders to be genial. "The ice on the river is not too bad, not yet," one of them said to Herr Gruen, who for the occasion wore a Nazi party pin in his lapel.

"One can be glad of that," Herr Gruen said, with his best smile.

"You'll have a jolly time in Budapest, Herr Hartmann."

"We expect to. Then, back to work."

"In Berlin, I see."

"Yes, we love it there, but, always good to get away for a bit."

The officer agreed, stamped the exit visa, raised his right arm, and said, amiably, "Heil Hitler."

"Sieg Heil," said the Gruens, a duet. Then, relieved, they climbed the gangway.

Standing at the rail of the steamer, watching the passengers as they filed past the border control, was the woman from the train and her husband. "Isn't that . . . ?" she said. She had to raise her voice, because the oompah of the tuba in the dockside ensemble was particularly emphatic.

"It is, my dear."

"Very curious, Hansi. He said they were going to a funeral. In Vienna."

"Perhaps you didn't hear properly."

"No, no. I'm sure I did." Now she began to suspect that the pleasure of her company had been contemptuously brushed aside, and she started to get mad.

Poor Hansi. This could go on for days. "Oh, who knows," he said.

"No, Hansi," she said sharply. "They must explain themselves."

But, where were they?

The Gruens had taken a first-class cabin

209

for the overnight trip to Budapest and planned to hide there. Hunger, however, finally drove Herr Gruen to the dining room, where he ate quickly and ordered a cheese sandwich to take back to the cabin. As he left the dining room, here was the woman from the train. Her husband was nowhere to be seen, but she was sitting on a lounge chair just outside the door and rose when she saw him. "Sir," she said.

"Yes?"

"Excuse me, but did you not say on the train that you were attending the funeral of your wife's mother, in Vienna?"

Herr Gruen flinched. Why had this terrifying woman, cheeks flushed, arms folded across her chest, suddenly attacked him? He did not answer, looking like a schoolboy caught out by a teacher, said, "Well," to gain time, then "I did, *meine Frau,* say that. I'm afraid I did not tell the truth."

"Oh?" This was a threat.

"I did not mean to trouble you, *meine Frau,* but I felt I could not honorably respond to your question."

"And why not?" The admission had not appeased her; the prospect of a really nasty confrontation apparently provoking her to a sort of sexual excitement.

"Because we *are* married, but not to each other."

The woman's mouth opened, but no words came out.

"We are in love, *meine Frau,* so much in love, we are." He paused, then said, "Tragically."

Now she went scarlet, and stuttered an apology.

For her, he thought, just as good as a fight. *Humiliation.* Possibly better. It wasn't until he was back inside the cabin that he realized his shirt was soaked with sweat.

27 December. In the sunless light of a winter morning, the Gypsy musicians on the Danube dock seemed oddly out of place, as though they'd become lost on their way to a nightclub. Still, they sawed away on their violins and strummed their guitars as the passengers disembarked from the *Leverkusen.* Holding hands as they walked down the gangplank, the Gruens were as close to peace of mind as they'd been for a long, long time. True, their train to Belgrade didn't leave until the morning of the twenty-ninth, so they would have to spend two nights in a hotel. This didn't bother them at all — they were no longer on German soil, and the hotel would be luxurious. A Hun-

garian officer stamped their passports in the ship's dining room, and they'd begun to feel like normal travelers as they headed for the line of taxis waiting at the pier.

But they were, just then, intercepted.

By a strange creature, small and dark and vaguely threatening, who wore a narrow-brim brown hat with a card stuck in the hatband that said *Hotel Astoria.* Not a bad hotel, but not where they were going. "Hello, hello," said the creature.

"Good morning," said Herr Gruen. "We're not at the Astoria, we're booked at the Danube Palace."

The Gruens started to walk away, but the creature held up a hand, *stop.* "No," he said, "you can't go there." His German was rough but functional.

"Excuse us, please," Herr Gruen said, perhaps less courteous now.

The creature seemed puzzled. "You're the Hartmanns, right? Green tie, green hat?"

Herr Gruen's eyes widened. Frau Gruen said, "Yes, we are. And?"

"I'm called Akos, it means 'white falcon.' I'm sent by your friend in Salonika, and I'm here to tell you that if you set foot in the Palace, well, that's the end of you."

Herr Gruen said, "It is?"

"A big fancy hotel, Herr Hartmann, so

212

Germans all over the place, and they've bribed every waiter, every porter, every maid. You won't last an hour because they *know,* they know fugitives when they see them."

"So it will be the Astoria?"

"What? Oh, I forgot." Akos took off his hat, slipped the card from the hatband and put it in his pocket. "No, I got this just for the dock. It's not so nice where I'm taking you, but you'll be safe." He glanced sideways, at something that had caught his attention, something he didn't like. "Let's go," he said. "And let's make it look good," he added, taking the valise from Herr Gruen. They walked to the line of taxis, then past it, to a taxi parked in a side street just off the waterfront. Akos opened the door for the Gruens, then stared toward the dock as they settled themselves in the backseat.

The taxi sped away, cornering through side streets as Akos, from time to time, turned the rearview mirror so he could see out the back window. The driver said something in Hungarian, Akos answered him briefly. They crossed a bridge, then drove for a few minutes more, entering a narrow street with dead neon signs over nightclub doors. "It gets busy here at night," Akos explained. Midway down the block they

213

stopped in front of a hotel — an old building two windows wide, brick stained black with a century of soot. "Here we are," Akos said. The Gruens peered out the window — *here?* "Don't worry," Akos said. "You'll survive. Wait till you get to Serbia!"

The smell inside was strong: smoke, drains, garlic, God only knew what else. There was no clerk — a bell on the desk, a limp curtain over a doorway — and Akos led them upstairs, up three flights past silent corridors. The room was narrow, so was the bed, with a blanket over a mattress, and the paint had been peeling off the walls for years. "If you want food," Akos said, "just go downstairs and ring the bell, somebody will get you something, but you don't leave the hotel." He stood to one side of the window, moved the curtain an inch with his index finger, and muttered to himself in Hungarian. It sounded like an oath. To the Gruens he said, "I'll be back. Something I have to take care of."

Gus wanted these people kept safe, and Akos was proud that he'd been chosen for the job. But now he had a problem. A man he'd spotted at the dock had stared at every passenger leaving the *Leverkusen,* then a taxi followed his own through a maze of back streets, and now the hotel was being watched by the same man. Not young, with the sort of head that looks like it's been squeezed flat, a brush mustache and waxy complexion, he wore a grimy pearl-gray overcoat. Who was he? A policeman? Akos didn't think so. The guy definitely didn't act like a detective; he was furtive, and he was alone. He was, more likely, some miserable little sneak who sold fugitives for cash — cash from the Budapest cops, or even from the Germans.

These people he'd hidden in the hotel were on the run, surely using false papers. And how did the sneak know that? Because when people ran from the Nazis they ran through Budapest, and when you see something often enough you learn to recognize it; you can smell it. And if the guy was wrong, so what? He was still some cop's lapdog, next time he'd get it right. Cops lived off informers; that was how they did their work. They'd tried it with Akos, but only once: he shrugged, he didn't know anything, I'm the dumbest guy in town. In the gang Gus ran, no rats allowed, there were *stories,* bad stories, better to be loyal. Akos left the hotel, made a sharp turn away from the man in the doorway of an abandoned store, then, head down, in a hurry, he walked around the block, coming up on the man from behind.

Akos carried a little knife, simple thing, a cheap wood handle and a three-inch blade. But that was all you needed, if you knew what you were doing. Only a three-inch blade but he kept it sharp as a razor, so it had to be protected by a leather sheath. As he neared the man, he took the knife out of its sheath and held it behind his leg. What to do? Slide it in and out? That would be that. Put it in the right place and the victim never made a sound, just fell down, as though the air had been let out of him. But now you had a corpse, now you had a murder, so there would be cops on the street, sniffing around. They would search the hotel.

Akos dropped his hand on the man's left shoulder and, as he turned in that direction, circled around on his blind side. Startled, the man opened his mouth, ready to tell some tale but he never got it out. *What an ugly tie,* Akos thought. Maroon, with a gray knight-on-horseback in the middle. Who would wear such a thing? He took the bottom of the tie between thumb and forefinger as though to study it, then the knife flashed, so fast the guy never saw it, just below the knot. Ah, but maybe Akos wasn't as deft as he thought, because the blade not only sliced off the tie but took a shirt button as well, which flew up in the air, landed with a click on the pavement, and rolled away. Still holding the bottom of the tie, Akos folded it in half and stuck it in the pocket of the man's shirt. The man whinnied with fear.

"Could've been an ear," Akos said. "I think maybe you should go back wherever you came from. And forget what happened. Because if you don't . . ." Akos put the knife away.

The man said, "Yes, sir. Yes, sir," turned, and hurried off.

29 December. The train was classified as an express, but it never sped up, just chugged slowly south across the Hungarian plain, past snow-covered fields where crows waited on the bare branches of the trees, through mist and fog, like a countryside in a poem or a dream. The Gruens were nine hours from Belgrade, in the neutral nation of Yugoslavia, as Germany faded away with every beat of the rails.

And so, slowly, they began to believe that they had escaped. The wretched hotel in Budapest had been frightening; neither of them had ever been in such a place. But

217

with the appearance of the little gangster Akos — what a character! — a hand had reached out to protect them. Now all they had to do was watch the scenery and talk about the unknown future, a life different from anything they'd ever contemplated, but at least a life. This optimism, however, proved to be unfounded.

They passed easily through Hungarian customs; then the train stopped in Subotica, the first town in Serbian Yugoslavia, for border control. Ten officers boarded the train and took the Gruens, and many other passengers, into the station. The officers were ferocious — *why? Why? What had they done?* One or two of the officers spoke some German but they didn't explain; that was the ancient prerogative of border guards. They gestured violently, shoved the passengers, swore in Serbian, and took all documents away for examination behind the closed doors of the stationmaster's office. The passengers were forced to stand facing a wall. For more than an hour.

When the officers returned, they took Frau Gruen and two other women into the office and made them undress, down to their slips, while two men in suits and ties ran their hands over every seam and hem in their clothing, then slit the shoulder pads in their dresses and jackets. But, Frau Gruen realized, Emilia Krebs had saved her, had told them both not to *think,* even, of sewing jewels or coins or papers or *anything* in their clothing. And, apparently, the clothing of the other women also hid nothing. As the search proceeded, the women's eyes met: why are they doing this to us? Later, Frau Gruen learned that her husband and several other men had been subjected to the same treatment. And one man, the passengers thought, had been taken away.

They weren't sure. When they were permitted to reboard the train, they gathered in the corridor of the first-class car and, as the engine jerked forward and the station fell away, they argued. Had there not been a fat man with red hair? Perhaps he had simply left the train, perhaps he lived in Subotica. No, one of the passengers didn't think so; she had spoken with this man, and he'd said he was Polish. Well, yes, perhaps he was, but did that mean he didn't live in Subotica? As the train made slow progress through a frozen valley, the dispute went on and on. No one claimed to have actually seen him being led away, but somebody said, "That's the way it's done!" and again they could not agree. Mysterious disappearance? Public arrest? The passengers had stories to tell, had seen arrests, had heard of disappearances. In time, they returned to their compartments, in accord on only one point: the man was gone.

Twenty minutes later, a woman came to see the Gruens. She had been taken into the office alone, an afterthought. While she was there, a senior officer, speaking halting German, had attempted to telephone an office in Berlin. In his hand, she said, was a piece of paper with the name *Hartmann,* and what she thought were passport numbers. "I don't know your name," she said, "but I am telling everybody who was searched." The Gruens were silent; could do no more than stare at her. "Don't worry," she said. "He never got through. Something wrong with the line, maybe a storm in the north. He shouted and carried on, then the operator got tired of him and cut him off." After a moment, Herr Gruen, his heart pounding, admitted they were the Hartmanns, and thanked her. Later he wondered, *Was that safe?* It was surely the decent thing to do but, perhaps, a mistake.

When the train stopped in Novi Sad, the station before Belgrade, a uniformed police lieutenant opened the door of the Gruens' compartment, as though searching for an empty seat. When Herr Gruen looked up, the lieutenant made eye contact with him and gestured, a subtle nod of the head, toward the corridor. He waited there until Herr Gruen joined him; then they walked along the car together. He had a friend in Zagreb, he explained, who'd asked him to see "the Hartmanns" safely through the police control in the Belgrade railway station. He knew they would be changing trains there, for the line that ran south to Nis, not far from the Greek border.

So when they left the train at Belgrade station, the lieutenant accompanied them, spoke briefly to the officers, and the Gruens were waved past. In the station waiting room, he bought a newspaper and sat nearby, keeping an eye on them. When the train for Nis was announced, he followed them along the platform and, once they found seats, paused at the window and gave them a farewell nod.

The train to Nis was slow and dirty and crowded. There was no first-class car. Across the aisle from the Gruens, a woman was traveling with two rabbits in a crate, and at the far end of the car, a group of soldiers got drunk, sang for a time, then went looking for a fight. To the Gruens, none of this mattered at all — they had traveled deep into the Balkans, now far from central Europe, thus the rabbits, the soldiers, the women in black head scarfs, meant safety, meant refuge.

In Skoplje, capital of Yugoslavian Macedonia, they sat in the waiting room all night and, in a slow rain that came with the dawn, boarded the train that followed the Vardar River down to the customs station at Gevgelija, then across the border to Greece, at Polykastro. At last on Greek soil, in sight of the blue-and-white flag, Frau Gruen broke down and wept. Herr Gruen comforted her as best he could while Greek soldiers, manning machine guns and an antiaircraft cannon, stared at them. Greece was at war, and the border guards were courteous but thorough. As the Gruens walked toward the waiting train, a man in civilian clothes was suddenly by their side. "My name is Costa Zannis," he said, adding that he was an officer of the Salonika police, would escort them into Salonika, and arrange for their passage to Turkey. Frau Gruen took his hand in both of hers, again close to tears. "I know," he said gently. "A long journey." He took his hand back and smiled, saying, "We'd better get on the train."

A very old train, that ran to Salonika. Each compartment spanned the width of the car and had its own door to the exterior, where a narrow boardwalk allowed the conductor to move between compartments as he collected tickets. Brass oil lamps flanked the doors and the seats were made of wood, with high curved backs. As the train rattled along, Zannis took a pad and pencil from the pocket of his trench coat. "Forgive me," he said. "I can see you are exhausted, but I must ask you questions, and you must try to be as accurate as possible." He turned to a fresh page on the pad. "It is for the others," he said. "The others who will make this journey."

In Berlin, at the Gestapo headquarters on Prinz-Albrechtstrasse, Hauptsturmführer Albert Hauser kept a photograph of his father on his desk. It had been taken in a portrait studio during the Great War, but it looked older than that, like a portrait from the previous century: a rotund, solemn man, sitting at attention on the regal chair provided by the studio. The subject wore a white handlebar mustache, a Prussian-style helmet, and a uniform, for he had been, like Hauser himself, a police officer in the city of Düsseldorf. A good policeman, the elder Hauser, stern and unrelenting and, in much the same way, a good father. Whose son had followed him into the profession.

Hauser, on a frosty day in mid-January, looked nothing like the photograph. He was heavily, powerfully built, with blunt features, hair worn Prussian-army style: near-shaved on the sides, an inch long on top. Hauser smoked cigars, an old habit from his days as a detective in Düsseldorf, an antidote to the smell of death, sweetish and sickening, that nobody ever got used to. But a policeman's lot was murder, suicide, and week-old corpses who'd died alone, so Hauser smoked cigars.

He'd been very good at his job in Düsseldorf, but as his family grew in the mid-1930s he needed more money. "You should come and work for us," a former colleague told him. "Join the SS, then work for the Gestapo, we are always keen to hire talented men." Hauser didn't much care for politics, he liked quiet evenings at home, and membership in the SS seemed to entail quite a bit of marching and singing, attendance at Nazi rallies, and riotous drinking in beer halls. Though none of this appealed to Hauser, he applied to the SS, was welcomed, and discovered that they didn't insist on marching and singing, they simply wanted his skills: his ability to discover crime, to investigate, and to hunt down criminals and arrest them. Working for the Gestapo, of course, the criminals were different from those he'd pursued in Düsseldorf. No longer burglars, or thieves, or murderers, they were instead Jews and Communists who broke the political laws of the new Nazi state. Laws that concerned flight and false documents, nonpayment of special taxes levied on Jews, and, in the case of the Communists, agitation and propaganda intended to undermine the state. To Hauser, it didn't matter; laws were laws — you simply had to learn how they worked — and those who broke them were criminals. Nothing could be simpler. By January of 1941 he'd risen quickly to the rank of Hauptsturmführer, captain, and by his standards was paid very well indeed.

At nine-thirty that morning he stubbed out his cigar — an expensive cigar, for now he could afford such things — and slipped his arms into the sleeves of his overcoat, an expensive overcoat, so nice and warm. From his office on the third floor, he walked down to the Prinz-Albrechtstrasse, where his partner, a thin, rather bitter fellow called Matzig, waited behind the wheel of a Mercedes automobile. He had to work with Matzig, formerly a detective in Ulm, but didn't much care for him, a man who took his membership in the Nazi party quite seriously, reading, in fact studying, certain books and going endlessly to meetings. Oh well, to each his own, and he didn't see all that much of Matzig, working mostly by himself. But today they were going to make an arrest, a couple called Gruen, a lawyer and his wife, Jews, suspected of affiliation with Communists. His department in the Gestapo had a long list of such people, wealthy Berlin intellectuals for the most part, and was, at a steady pace, arresting and jailing them for interrogation, so that they might be persuaded to confess to their crimes, provide names of others, be tried, and imprisoned.

Matzig drove cautiously, much too slowly for Hauser's taste — the little shrimp was irritating in so many little ways — but soon enough they were in the garden district of Dahlem, one of Berlin's finest neighborhoods, where many on Hauser's list were resident. Matzig parked the car and, as they walked up the path to the Gruen doorway, Hauser instinctively made sure of his sidearm, a Walther PPK, the smaller version of the standard police pistol. Not that he'd need it. These arrests were easy, you had only to open the back door of the car and the criminals climbed in. Not like the old days: much calmer and, important to a family man like Hauser, much safer.

Matzig pressed the button by the door and they heard, from within the house, the sound of a chime.

■ ■ ■ ■

A French King

■ ■ ■ ■

Storms, in January. Snow covered the mountain villages. Down in Salonika, wind-swept rain came sheeting across the corniche, where the locals staggered along, struggling with their umbrellas and scowling each time a gust hit them. When, after work, Zannis returned to Santaroza Lane, a welcoming Melissa shook off a great spray that decorated the wall of the vestibule and the apartment was filled with the musky aroma of wet dog. Lately, Zannis was often alone there — Tasia Loukas didn't visit very often. She sensed in him a certain distraction and she was right. For, again and again, his imagination replayed the scene on the street in front of the Club de Salonique. Behind the window of a white Rolls-Royce, a vision, olive skin and golden hair, then, from perfect composure, the smile of an actress.

Idiot, he called himself. For indulging in

231

such fantasies. *But nothing new,* he thought. Down through the endless halls of time, forever, there wasn't a man in the world who hadn't wanted what he'd never have. "Do you know Vasilou?" he asked Tasia. "And his wife, what's-her-name?"

"Demetria, you mean? The goddess?"

"Yes."

"I know him by sight, he doesn't mix with people like me. What do you want with him?"

"I was just wondering."

"Not about *her.* Were you, little boy?"

"No."

"Better not."

So, he thought, *Demetria.*

And schemed. Absurdly — *Oh no, the house is on fire, I'll have to carry you out.* Or, not so absurdly — *A cocktail party? I'd love to.*

Meanwhile, much realer schemes absorbed his day, schemes involving the Balkan railways and Turkish documents. As the Gruens left for Istanbul, six new refugees — a couple, a single man, a family of three — appeared at Salonika railway station. For reasons of economy, and because the management was sympathetic, Zannis housed them in the Tobacco Hotel, a weary but functional relic of the nineteenth century.

There, gray and exhausted, they tried to recover from long days and nights on the escape route. Tried to recover from the slow brutal succession of torments experienced as Jews living in Nazi Germany. Seven years of it.

As for the final link in the chain, Ahmet Celebi had had his fill of the indifferent food at the Club de Salonique, and now Zannis dealt exclusively with Madam Urglu, nominally a deputy to the commercial attaché, in fact the Turkish legation's intelligence officer. An intimidating presence, Madam Urglu, with her opaque, puffy face, her eyeglasses on a chain, and her — well, *inquisitive* nature. They met at a taverna owned by Greek refugees who'd come to Salonika in the great population exchange, thus called Smyrna Betrayed, where, in the winter damp, Madam Urglu was partial to the fish stew.

"So," she said, "this turns out to be an ongoing, um, project. One might as well call it an 'operation,' no?"

"It is," Zannis said. "Someone has to help these people."

"Can they not remain in Salonika?"

"They would be welcome, this city has always taken in refugees." Zannis tore a piece of bread in half. "But the Wehrmacht is in Roumania — maybe it won't stop there."

"We hope they don't go into Bulgaria. That puts them on our border."

"Only tourists in Bulgaria, right now," Zannis said. "Very fit young men, in pairs, with expensive cameras. Tourists with a passion for the ancient Bulgar culture, like airfields, and port facilities."

Madam Urglu smiled. "Such finesse," she said. "Our Teutonic friends." She retrieved a mussel from her stew, open perhaps a third of the way, stared at it for a moment, then set it beside her bowl. "But at least they're not in Greece. And the English are doing what they can." There were now sixty thousand British Commonwealth troops, divisions from Australia and New Zealand, on the island of Crete.

"We're grateful," Zannis said. "But we can't be sure how Hitler sees it. Provocation? Deterrent? And Mussolini must be screaming at him, because the RAF is bombing the Italians in Albania."

"Which we applaud. Unofficially, of course. And it isn't just a feint, I see they've put shore artillery in Salonika." She gestured with her head toward the waterfront, where long cannon were now facing the Aegean.

"They have."

"One wonders if more is coming."

"It's possible," Zannis said, preparing for the attack.

"Perhaps more guns. Or, even, an RAF squadron."

"We'd be happy to have them," Zannis said.

"You haven't heard?"

"I'm not told such things, Madam Urglu. I'm only a policeman."

"Oh, please. Don't go being coy, not with me."

"Truly, I don't know."

"But I'm sure you could find out. If you cared to."

"Not even that. I expect the military would be informed, but they're known to be secretive."

For just a bare instant, a look of irritation, compressed lips, darkened Madam Urglu's face. Then she said, "Naturally," and with some resignation added, "they are. Still, it would be something of an achievement, for me, to learn of such plans. One always wants to do well in one's job."

"And who doesn't?" Zannis said, meaning *no offense taken.*

"You *would* like to see me do well, wouldn't you?"

235

"You know I would."

"Then, maybe sometime, if you should discover . . ."

"Understood," Zannis said. "It's not impossible."

"Ah me," Madam Urglu said, gently rueful, *how the world goes around.*

Zannis smiled, *yes, it does.* Then he said, "I'll need six visas, this time."

"Six!"

"Yes, it's more desperate every day, up north."

"My, my. Would five help you?"

"Madam Urglu, please."

"All right then, six. It's five hundred dollars each. I trust you have the money with you."

"It was four apiece, the last time."

"I know, but our friend in Istanbul . . ."

"Why don't I give you two thousand, four hundred today, and I'll make up the remainder at our next meeting."

"Oh very well," she said. "If I must. I'll send the papers over when they're ready."

"Thank you, Madam Urglu," Zannis said, meaning it.

"Of course they *could* be free," she said. "It wouldn't take much. Really. It wouldn't."

Her face softened. She was — Zannis saw it — almost pleading. He nodded, sympathy

236

in his eyes. "Yes," he said. "I know."

As to what exactly he knew, he didn't say. Perhaps that it was a hard machine, national interest, which would in time destroy both of them. She was, without doubt, perfectly aware that he would never spy on his British ally — no? Not that he couldn't — and Madam Urglu understood precisely his standing in the politics of Salonika — because he could. He'd seen, of all things, a memorandum from the traffic office of the police department. "Interruption of traffic planned to begin on 2 February, for important waterfront construction." A new municipal garden, perhaps? But he would not, could not, reveal such things, no matter how little it would mean for the Turks to know in advance about the additional armament. They'd *see* it, eventually. But *eventually* was the active word. Until then, well, one didn't spy on a faithful friend, it just wasn't done.

All that much.

The commissionaire — doorman, porter, messenger — at the Tobacco Hotel was a straight-backed old fellow who'd fought valiantly, in his day, against the Turkish gendarmerie. Very solemn and courtly, in the

237

old-world manner. The assistant manager had found for him somewhere, probably in the markets, a doorman's overcoat from some bygone hotel. The epaulets were ragged — more than a few gold braids missing — three of the gold buttons had been replaced, and the original owner had obviously been taller and heavier than the present one. Still, it was the uniform he had, and he wore it with pride.

He was more than aware of the new guests, who spoke German, and who'd clearly had a hard time of it. One in particular touched his heart — she was thin as a rail, with iron-gray hair cut quite short. Likely an aristocrat, in the past, who never failed to give him a gratuity, a pitiful coin or two, when he went out to get her something to eat. Yes, pitiful, but the best she could do, and she never failed him.

Going to work one morning he took a detour through the market, and there was his young nephew, a sweet boy, working at a flower stall. They gossiped for a few minutes and then, as they parted, his nephew handed him a small bouquet and said, "Here, Uncle, take this. Brighten up your room." He said thank you and then, later, on a sudden impulse, took the bouquet up to the nice lady's room. "Please," he said, fixing

238

the bouquet in a water glass. "To brighten up your room." Oh how she was moved, by this generous act. And he would not accept the coin she offered him.

Instead, they talked. Or at least she did. He would not sit down, but stood by the door as she told him her story. She came from Berlin, from a prominent family, at one time, but then the odious Hitler had risen to power and their circumstances declined quickly. Most of them had left, years earlier, and she finally had to follow them. But it had been a dreadful trip, into Hungary and down through the Balkans: unheated railway cars, almost nothing to eat, and police controls every day. Fortunately, some people had helped her, and for this she was grateful. She was no more explicit than that. He said he would hope for, on her behalf, a better future, and left with a nod of the head that suggested a bow. And the flowers did, indeed, brighten up the room.

Two days later, he had his weekly meeting with the British travel writer, not long resident in the city, called Escovil. They met, as usual, in one of the old Byzantine churches, and there the commissionaire passed along bits of gossip about the city and various doings at the hotel — Escovil

239

was always curious about foreign guests. For this the commissionaire was paid a small stipend, money which, given his meagre salary, made all the difference in the way he lived.

Was it wrong? He didn't find it so. He would never have given information to a German, or even a Frenchman, but the British: that was another story. They had been good friends to Greece, as far back as the nineteenth century when the great English poet, Lordos Vyronos himself, Lord Byron, had come to fight in their wars of independence; and the British had fought and died in the hills of Macedonia, in 1917, where they'd faced the Bulgarian army.

That afternoon, the commissionare told the travel writer about the aristocratic German lady and her difficult passage to Salonika. Was she, Escovil wanted to know, the only one? No, there were a few others, and, he'd heard, more were expected. And a good thing too. In these times of war, people didn't travel so often, and there were too many empty rooms at the hotel. And these rooms were paid for in full, promptly, by the well-regarded police official himself, Constantine Zannis, from an old Salonika family.

■ ■ ■

Escape line!

Francis Escovil hurried back to the room he kept at the Pension Bastasini, where his predecessor in Salonika, Roxanne Brown, had stayed. There he wrote a report of his contact with the commissionaire, then drove his car out to a house on the Chalkidiki peninsula, where his assistant encrypted the message and sent it on to London by wireless/telegraph.

The following night, the Secret Intelligence Service wired back. And very excited they were! Could he get at least one name? One true name? There had been, for some years, contact with anti-Nazi Germans in Berlin: intellectuals, lawyers, communist workers, and aristocrats; some Jewish, some not. Were the people using the escape line from that group? Or another, that they didn't know about? Were "the friends" — operatives of the Jewish agencies in Palestine — involved? Could this policeman Zannis be recruited? Bribed? Coerced? Intimidated? Find out more! Most urgent!

Escovil was, despite himself, almost amused. *Hit a tender spot, have I?* It reminded him of something he'd heard about

Churchill, who, excited by some new discovery, would head his minutes, memoranda, with the phrase *Action this day*. Escovil's assistant was less amused; the five-digit groups of numbers took a long time to decrypt. "The hell have you done?" he grumbled. To the fishing village outside the cottage, he was known as Plato, a deaf-mute taken to be Escovil's intimate companion. In fact his name was Geary, formerly a corporal in the Irish Guards and a famous pub brawler. Once, to emphasize the nature of the companionship, Escovil had taken his hand as they walked through the village. This was a practice common enough between any and all Greek men, but Geary didn't like it and said, in an undertone, "Let go me fookin' hand, you damned poofter." To Escovil, a Greek woman radio operator would have been a more credible arrangement, but there weren't any such to be found, so "Plato" had to serve.

In any event, the message radioed back to London wasn't so long. He would try to learn a name. Zannis could be asked to help, but any sort of pressure wouldn't work.

On 18 January, a hand-carried envelope reached Zannis at his office. The message within was typewritten: Colonel Simonides, of the Royal Hellenic Army General Staff, requested his presence at a meeting of "certain residents of Salonika" at a house in the officers' quarters of the army base, east of the city. The meeting was to take place the following day, at six in the evening, and this invitation was, Zannis realized as he reread it, very close to an order. He took a taxi to the base, where he had to show his identity papers to a lieutenant, list in hand, at the guardhouse by the gate. He was then escorted to the residence of, apparently, a senior officer, with fine though well-worn furnishings. On entering a large parlor, Zannis saw that many of the guests had preceded him, to what looked like a social gathering: a number of Salonika's rich and powerful, some with their wives; the city's chief rabbi was there, as was Spiraki, head of the local State Security Bureau; and Vangelis, who waved to him from across the room. In one corner, a professor at the university was talking to a well-regarded journalist. There were, Zannis estimated, close to fifty people in the crowded room, sitting, standing, and drinking coffee, available at a table to one side of the doorway.

A uniformed officer — harsh, slightly reddened face, black mustache — tapped a spoon on a coffee cup to get their attention.

As Zannis looked over the crowd he saw, obscured by two large guests, a flash of golden hair. Was Vasilou there? Of course, he would be. So then, was that who he thought it was? Could it be? His heart raced, and he started to move to a position where he could get a better view.

But then, the officer cleared his throat and said, "Citizens of Salonika, allow me to introduce myself, I am Colonel Simonides, and the first thing I would ask is that you will please consider this a private meeting, not a subject for gossip. Not with associates, or even friends. We — that is, the General Staff of the army — have chosen you carefully. You are crucial to the way our city works; you are crucial, in our opinion, to Greece itself.

"Two further things I would ask: please do not question me when I'm done speaking. For reasons ranging from the unknown future to state security, I won't be able to answer. And, second, please don't seek us out later and ask for our assistance. If this information seems useful and you wish to act on it, you'll do so as you see fit. And if you must share this information, you may do that as well — but choose carefully who you tell and *don't* say where it came from. Do I have your agreement?" He looked around the room, all were silent, their faces deadly serious. Zannis watched as the golden hair moved slightly, then was still.

"Very well," the colonel said, finality in his voice. "Our war with Italy continues, we are certainly winning, though for the moment we've reached stalemate in central Albania, and we anticipate an Italian counteroffensive in the spring. No matter, we'll drive them back. And I know you will agree that the very last word that can describe the Greek armed services, or indeed almost any Greek, is *defeatist*." Again he looked around the room, as though to challenge anyone who might, even privately, contradict this assertion. Then, after a pause, a muscle ticked in his cheek and he said, "However . . ."

What followed was known, in military terminology, as a "strategic appreciation," though phrased for a civilian audience and stripped of any reference that might reveal secret information. Much of what Simonides said was known to the people in the room. Or, rather, it was believed to be true. Roumania and Hungary had signed treaties with Germany; Yugoslavia and Bulgaria had so far refused to do so. So far. The Greek General Staff had undertaken studies — a nice word for it, Zannis thought — indicat-

245

ing that, with the April thaw in the Balkans, this situation would change and, once the Wehrmacht moved across the Yugoslav and Bulgarian borders, Greece would be next. Metaxas, as premier of Greece, would not give way under pressure, so there would be war with Germany. "We," the colonel said, "will fight hard, and the British will fight by our side, but, when a nation of seventy-five million goes to war with a nation of eight million, the outcome will not long be in question. And what we are suggesting tonight is that you prepare yourselves for that eventuality."

Simonides paused and let that sink in. "In time, Hitler will be defeated, after, we calculate, a long and difficult war. Here there will be occupation, resistance, and insurgency, and then, when the war is over, Greece will have to, once again, as we did after we drove out the Turks, restore itself as a state. On that day, we judge that the people in this room will be of significant help, will play an important role in the recovery. So we want you alive. And, by the way, you might give some thought to the fact that the Germans will soon learn who you are. People just like yourselves have been murdered in Poland — an attempt to behead potential resistance — and we don't want you to share that fate."

After a moment, he went on. "As to *what* you may do, and *how* you do it, that's clearly up to you. We invite you here tonight to tell you only that it is not too soon to begin preparation. That is, I fear, the only way you can secure the safety of yourselves and your immediate families." He paused, then said, "Thank you for attending this meeting," turned on his heel, and left the room.

For a time, nobody said a word. Then the man standing next to Zannis turned to him and introduced himself. Mid-fifties, eyeglasses, balding, nobody who would stand out in a crowd. "You're Costa Zannis, aren't you?" he said. "From the police department."

"I am. And what is it that you do in Salonika?"

"I'm the traffic manager for the railroads. What do you make of all this?"

"I'm not sure. 'Get out while you can'? Something like that."

"And will you?"

"No, I'll stay. And you?"

"I hadn't really thought about it. Where would I go?" He shrugged, said he thought he'd get himself a coffee, and headed for the table by the door.

Zannis again searched the room. Now he

was rewarded! Demetria Vasilou was standing in back of a sofa, in conversation with an older woman. She was listening with apparent interest but then, just for a moment, she turned toward him, and smiled. Not the smile of an actress, just the briefest acknowledgment that she was aware of him, that she knew who he was, that she remembered him. Then she returned to the conversation. She wore, that night, an ice-blue blouse, again with a pearl necklace, and a soft, gray wool skirt, not exactly snug, but tight enough to reveal her shape. Now she began to talk to the woman opposite her, not frivolous but making some kind of point. She folded her arms above her waist and leaned backward, so that the top edge of the sofa pressed into the curve of her ample derriere, for one second, then another. As she straightened up, and the woman in front of her began to speak, she glanced at him again and, just for an instant, their eyes met.

His mind raced. Had he seen what he thought he'd seen? Did it mean what he thought it meant? *I want you.* No, no, impossible. Tired of standing, she'd simply taken a moment to lean on a sofa, and desire had led him to believe it was a gesture of seduction. But a voice from within knew better. *A signal.* Not overt, but not subtle either.

That's the way women do things. Don't they? Perhaps? He stared at her; he couldn't stop. Her profile was like, like . . . Now he remembered that Tasia had called her "the goddess," as though people spoke of her in that way. An irony? Not to him. Well, enough, just go over there and talk to her. *Be brave!*

His foot never moved. The traffic manager materialized in front of him with two cups of coffee. Extending one of the cups he said, "I thought you might like a coffee."

Zannis couldn't escape. Heartsick, he watched as Vasilou appeared, took Demetria's arm, and led his prize away.

22 January. His letter confirming yet another arrival in Salonika crossed Emilia Krebs's letter to the Royale Garment Company. Two men would be setting out from Berlin on the twenty-ninth, papers in the names of Brandt and Wald; both were university professors. This time, for a recognition signal, Brandt, who wore a trimmed beard, would carry a pair of gloves in his left hand. After Zannis had informed her of the difficulty at the Subotica border station, the refugees now went west, from Budapest to Zagreb, then back east to Novi Sad, and Belgrade. This deviation added another day

to the journey, and Zannis could only hope they were making the right choice. Dipping his pen in the Panadon solution, he confirmed that day's arrival and the departure of three refugees to Turkey. The following day, in the office, he sent teletype messages to Pavlic in Zagreb and Gustav Husar's detective in Budapest. Wanted for questioning by the Salonika police: one WALD, one BRANDT, who wears a trimmed beard and has been known to carry a pair of gloves in his left hand. Believed to be arriving — then the dates — "by excursion steamer" to Budapest, "by express rail" to Zagreb. When the teletype messages had been confirmed, he returned to his desk. On a pad he printed *Belgrade/Skoplje?* Based on his questioning of the refugees at the Tobacco Hotel, he'd discovered that Emilia Krebs had an operative riding that train. He drew a box around what he'd written and went back over it, darkening the line. Only eye contact, from what the refugees said, but more than once — two or three times. "He was just making sure we were safe." Only some of the refugees said it, and not the Gruens. Still, the ones who did report the man also said that he'd appeared on the platform at Skoplje. Once more, Zannis's pencil traced the box. He would write again, to the Kalcher und

Krohn attorneys, that night. He had to ask her. Who was it? Why hadn't she told him? Because, God forbid, she might not know.

Later that morning he invited Gabi Saltiel to lunch. They left early — Smyrna Betrayed was always crowded — and took the most private table, in the corner. That day the taverna had a freshly caught octopus. A tentacle was hung from a hook in the kitchen ceiling, the customer would proceed to the kitchen, indicate the desired width of the portion, and one of the cooks would slice it off with a fearsomely sharp fish knife. Zannis didn't much care for the knife, he'd too often seen what it could do as a weapon, back when he'd been a detective.

While they waited for their lunch — the slice, grilled over coals, turned sweet and was something like lobster — they lit cigarettes and drank ouzo.

"How are things at home?" Zannis said.

"As usual, nothing too exciting." Saltiel paused, then said, "Thank heaven." He stopped there and waited; he sensed Zannis had something he wanted to discuss.

"Gabi," Zannis said. "I think it wouldn't be such a bad idea to talk about the future."

Saltiel waited, *what now?*

"I've begun to hear things about the

251

Germans. Maybe going into Bulgaria."

"Real things? Or just . . . talk?"

"Real things."

Saltiel's face tightened. "Bad news for us, chief, if that's true, because it's our turn next."

Zannis agreed. "What would *you* want to do, if that happened? Because — well, if the Germans take the city, they'll be interested in our office."

"They know about us?"

"I think we'd better assume they do. And, if they do, once things quiet down they'll come calling. Polite at first, then not."

"Costa?" Saltiel leaned back in his chair. "What are you saying?"

"Make plans, Gabi. Then get out." After a moment he added, "Even if you didn't work for the office you ought to think about it. Because, for the Jews —"

"I know," Saltiel said. "We're all talking about it. Talking and talking." They were silent for a time, then Saltiel forced his attention back to the conversation. "So, get out. When, next week?"

"If the Wehrmacht moves across the Danube, from Roumania to Bulgaria . . ."

"It's very hard to think about this, Costa," Saltiel said, his tone faintly irritated. "To leave the place where you've always lived

252

because something may happen later." He shook his head. "Have you talked to Sibylla?"

"Not yet. I will."

Saltiel thought for a time, then said, "How long will it take, this, this *potential* German advance? Not a lot of bridges over the Danube, you know; those countries don't like each other."

"I don't know," Zannis said. "Days. Not weeks."

"Will they use the railroad bridge, at Vidin?"

"They could use pontoon bridges."

"Here comes the waiter," Saltiel said, stubbing out his cigarette emphatically.

They ate for a time, dutifully, Zannis telling himself that if he didn't eat something he'd be hungry later. Then Saltiel said, "Oh, by the way, did you hear about the man in the synagogue —"

Zannis looked up, knife and fork suspended above his plate. Was this a joke?

"— photographing books?"

"What?"

"You know that the synagogues in Salonika are famous for their sacred texts: ancient books, Talmuds, Torahs, five, six hundred years old. Very valuable, if anybody ever sold anything like that. So last week,

253

the rabbi at the synagogue on Athonos Street left his eyeglasses in his office, then, late that night he went back to get them and discovered some guy, using a desk lamp, had some of the books out and was taking photographs."

"Did the man taking photographs say anything?"

"He ran. The rabbi is eighty years old, he couldn't chase him. Maybe he yelled at him, I don't know. Then he talked to two or three rabbis at other synagogues, and one of them said he'd found his books in the wrong order, though he didn't think anything of it at the time."

Zannis put his knife and fork down on his plate, so much for lunch. "Nothing stolen," he said.

"No. Photographed."

"Which means," Zannis said slowly, "somebody is taking an inventory, in order to know what to steal." He paused, then added, "At some time in the future."

The waiter noticed that Zannis wasn't eating his lunch and walked over to the table. "Everything all right, gentlemen?"

Zannis stared at him. *I've had enough of tentacles for one day.* "It's just," Zannis said, "I'm not hungry."

As they walked back toward the Via Egnatia, they passed Sami Pal, sharp as ever, a red carnation boutonniere in the buttonhole of his jacket, standing in the doorway of a tobacco shop. "Good afternoon, captain," he said.

"Sami," Zannis said.

As they went around the corner, Saltiel said, "Ah, the slick Sami Pal. You're a captain, now?"

"He thinks so."

"There are things you don't tell me, chief."

"There are. And I may have to, one of these days. In the meantime, Turkish visas. What will you need?"

Saltiel turned his head toward Zannis and raised an eyebrow. "What have you been doing, Costa?"

"Private business. How many?"

It took Saltiel a while. "Strange, you never count your family," he said. "There are, with the grandkids, ten of us. Is it possible that you have a way of getting ten Turkish visas?"

"Yes."

"What will this cost?"

"I'll worry about that."

Almost to himself, Saltiel said, "How in God's name would I ever make a living in Turkey?"

"When the Wehrmacht reaches the Macedonian border, something will occur to you."

Saltiel thought for a time. "Don't do anything right away, I have to talk this out with the family. Is there a time limit?"

Zannis thought about that, then said, "Not right now."

Back in the office, Zannis grabbed the telephone and called Vangelis, repeating Saltiel's story, asking what could be done. "Not much," Vangelis said. "I assume they lock the synagogue doors. Beyond that, I don't know."

"This could be coming out of the German legation."

"I suppose," Vangelis said. "It's possible."

"You understand what it means?"

"Of course I do." Vangelis's voice was sharp. "The Nazis have some kind of commission for the study of Jewish culture and religion, maybe it's them. They steal everywhere else, why not here?"

"What if I interviewed the consul? Asked him about it?"

"Von Kragen? He'd just tell you, politely,

to go to hell."

"What about Spiraki?"

"No, he wouldn't be interested."

"Then what?"

"Leave it alone, Costa. Go break your balls on something else."

Zannis, looking out the office window, found himself going back over his conversation with Saltiel. *Ten visas.* He knew that the more visas he requested, the harder Madam Urglu would press him: *tell me something.* And then, how much money did he have left? Enough, he thought, though if Emilia Krebs's operation went on for months, the bribes and the payments to Gustav Husar would deplete his secret bank account. Then he'd have to contact Vasilou. Did he have the telephone number? He thumbed through his card index, yes, there it was, the office on the waterfront, the number at home. The number at home.

The number at home.

There were reasons he shouldn't. One reason: if Vasilou found out . . . *But he won't find out.* And, if he did, there were other wealthy men in the city, including wealthy Jews, who might be the best people to approach. One hand resting on the phone,

Zannis fought it out with himself but the outcome was never really in doubt. In his imagination, Demetria once again pressed herself against the back of the sofa. *Look what I have for you.* That's what she meant. And then? Then this: soon enough the world was going to end, the world he knew, and his life — he wasn't going to run away — would end with it. *So, to love one last time before that day comes . . .*

He dialed the number.

Made a mistake? A man answered and said, "Plakos here."

Tried again. Now, a woman's voice: "The Vasilou residence."

"Is Madam Vasilou there?"

"Just a minute, please."

He could hear a vacuum cleaner, a voice gave instructions, then the telephone was picked up and the voice said, "This is Demetria."

"Hello," he said. "It's Costa Zannis." He waited, ready to turn the call toward some meaningless inquiry, everything depended on what she said next.

Silence. Only the vacuum cleaner. Then: "Oh, Mr. Ionides, please forgive me, I won't be able to come to the office this afternoon. Unfortunately, I must attend a funeral, at the Evangelista cemetery, at four. It will

258

have to be another time."

"I'll be there," Zannis said.

More silence, then the phone was hung up. As he replaced the receiver, he realized that his hand was trembling.

He made a great effort not to leave the office too early, then he did precisely that. *I can't just sit here.* It had drizzled all day, on and off, from a leaden winter sky, so he took an umbrella. By twenty minutes to four he reached the cemetery, decided to walk down to the waterfront, circled the White Tower, a former Turkish prison now pictured on postal cards, then went back up the hill.

As he passed through the entry gates, a group of mourners, led by an Orthodox priest, was on its way out, all dressed in black and wiping their eyes with handkerchiefs. Forcing himself to a slow pace, he walked down the central pathway until he reached the older part of the cemetery, past long rows of graves — headstones askew, clusters of cypress trees, and monuments with pillars and rusted iron doors. He searched as he walked, peering into the misting rain and fading light, but found no living soul, only the dead. Then, with a view from the top of a crumbling stairway, he saw, by the high wall that bordered the cemetery, a figure in a brown raincoat. Head covered by a black kerchief, a bouquet of anemones in clasped hands.

She saw him, as he approached, and stood still, heels properly together, posture erect, waiting. When they were a foot apart, he stopped and they stared at each other, as though uncertain what to do next. At last he said, "Demetria." Then very slowly raised his hand and touched her lips with two fingers. When he did this she closed her eyes, dropped the bouquet, and with her hand pressed his fingers against her. After a moment she let him go and, when he withdrew his hand, said, very quietly, "My God." *I cannot believe that this has happened.* As he leaned forward, as though to kiss her, she said, "Please," her face close to tears. "It isn't safe here."

"Can we go . . . somewhere else?"

Sorrowfully, she shook her head.

"I . . . ," he said. She gazed at him, closer yet to tears. "I have fallen —"

"Don't! I know." She was pleading with him. "You will make me cry."

He didn't understand.

She saw that he didn't, said, "I mustn't. I must not." She stared into his eyes, in love with him, her lips quivered and she turned them inward and pressed them together.

But, he saw, she couldn't hold it in.

"Quick! Think of a monkey!"

A great bark of laughter escaped her and she clapped her hand over her mouth. Then, her composure regained, she moved closer, almost touching him. She was, he thought, beautiful beyond belief; above her brown eyes, the smooth olive skin of her forehead met golden hair at the edge of her kerchief. "You don't," she said, "remember me, do you."

"Remember you?"

"From a long time ago."

He had no idea what to say.

"You don't," she said. "How could you? I was twelve, you must have been, sixteen? Our schools were side by side."

"We *knew* each other?"

"I knew who you were, I looked at you often, we never spoke. I was just a skinny little girl, just a kid. I had long hair, little gold earrings. . . ."

He tried, but he had no memory of her whatsoever. "It's allright now?" he said. "No tears?"

"Thank God. They'd *see* it, they'd know I'd been crying — my eyes would be red. They *watch* me."

"The servants?"

"Yes. He pays them extravagantly, he buys

261

their loyalty."

Not far from them, halfway down a row of graves, a woman was on her knees, despite the wet ground, and was placing flowers at the foot of a headstone. Demetria followed his eyes, then stepped back. "Too many people know me," she said.

"I have an apartment," he said. "On Santaroza Lane."

She didn't answer, and looked down at the ground, her eyes hidden from him. Finally, her voice barely audible, she said, "I am not so brave." The top of her kerchief was turning dark with rain and he extended his umbrella, attempting to cover them both, at least covering her. Then, on the side away from the woman at the grave, he took her hand. Which was cold and damp and, for a moment, lifeless. But it tightened, slowly, until she held him hard and said, "Near the railway station."

Zannis took his hand back and brought out a slip of paper on which he'd written the telephone number at his office. As he held it out to her it moved in the wind. When she'd put it away he said, "If you don't call me, I will call you. In the afternoon."

"Yes," she said. "I know about 'the afternoon.'" Her smile, as she said this, was sad, rueful, *what secret lovers must do.* She thrust both hands deep in the pockets of her raincoat. "I guess I'd better go home now."

"May I kiss you good-bye?"

Slowly, she shook her head. It meant *no,* but it was — the way she did it, the expression on her face — the most seductive gesture that Zannis had ever seen. Hands still in pockets, she turned and walked away, looked back at him once, then, at the end of the path, descended the stairway, and was gone.

The two men from the Secret Intelligence Service came to see Francis Escovil in Salonika. Well, almost in Salonika: out in the bay. They arrived on a small yacht, from Alexandria, anchored beyond the harbor, and sent the captain to the Pension Bastasini with an envelope. Escovil wasn't there, so the captain waited in the lobby, the residents glancing at him, at his uniform — of no country, of the land of yachts — as they came and went. When Escovil returned, the captain let him go upstairs, then followed. In the room, the captain gave Escovil the envelope and then they left together, walking down to the wharf where two sailors in a rowboat awaited them.

Once on board the yacht, he was taken to the salon: grand twenty years earlier, now fallen into gentle decay, the fabrics faded, the brasswork tarnished, mildew in the air. It was, Escovil had noted as the rowboat approached, called the *Amenhotep II,* so, an Egyptian yacht.

Escovil had never before seen these men. Jones and Wilkins, they called themselves and perhaps they were, Jones and Wilkins, or perhaps not. It didn't matter to Escovil who they said they were, he knew what they were. Jones was tall and bony and mournful — Escovil's interior description, adding *though mournful about what God only knows,* while Wilkins was military: stiff, mustached, hostile, and potentially dangerous. To the enemy, to his wife, to his dog. *Maybe not the dog,* Escovil thought. More sentimental, likely. *Only you love me, Fido.* That was very possibly true, Escovil sensed, so was relieved to find Jones in charge. It seemed, anyhow. Perhaps Wilkins had been brought along merely to frighten him, or was eager to have a ride on the yacht.

They gave him a big whiskey soda from the bar and treated themselves to one as well. Settled in the smelly chairs, and smiled. Both of them. It was utterly horrible.

"We have a bit of a nightmare," Jones said. "So you'll have to help us out." He had a high insinuating whine of a voice. "Really, this is somebody else's mess, but we're the ones who have to clean it up."

"Somebody with a name?" Escovil said.

"Oh, we can't tell you *that*," Jones said. He stared at Escovil. *Are you mad?*

"I see," Escovil said, faintly amused.

Which wasn't at all the proper response. "Do you," Wilkins said.

Only in England, Escovil thought, could "Do you" be spoken in such a way that it meant *So now I shall cut your throat.* In full retreat, he took a sip of whiskey and tried to look compliant. This was war, and he'd signed up to fight a filthy enemy, but he would never be one of them, the Joneses and the Wilkinses — they didn't like him and they never would.

"Once upon a time," Jones said — glass in hand, he settled back against the chair and crossed his legs — "there was a little man called Henry Byer. You wouldn't know the name, but if you'd been one of the chaps hanging about in the science labs of Cambridge in the nineteen-twenties, you most certainly would. A physicist, Harry, as he's called, and brilliant. Studied sound waves and radio beams, very theoretical back then, nobody had the faintest idea such things could be used in war, nobody had ever heard of radio navigation. It helps bombers flying at night, who can find their targets only by use of radio beams, locator beams we'd call them now. Who could have known that a radio beam would become a crucial weapon, could win or lose a war? Now the Germans have their own radio beams but, using the methods that Harry Byer discovered, we can alter them. And the Luftwaffe may know we're doing it, but they don't know how. Harry Byer knows how."

Jones stopped for a drink, then went on. "Anyway, life went well for Harry; a lectureship at Cambridge, where he worked in the physics lab, he married his sweetie, a pretty girl —"

"Smashing girl," Wilkins said. "Big bosoms." He indicated the magnitude of the bosoms with his cupped hands.

"Mmm," Escovil offered, raising his eyebrows in appreciation, one of the boys.

Jones cleared his throat and said, "Yes, well." Then, "But, in the summer of nineteen thirty-nine, life went sour for the Byer family, because la wife found somebody she liked better. Harry was, how shall I say, unprepossessing physically, you see, very smart certainly, but came the day when very smart just didn't . . . *compete.*

"And, well, still, who cared? But Harry took it badly, oh, very badly indeed. And just about then the first of September comes rolling around and Adolf sends his tanks into Poland. So Harry Byer, in a terrible huff, marches himself down to London and enlists in the RAF. He'll show the wife what's what, he'll go and get himself killed! Hah! There! Take *that!*"

Something rumbled inside Wilkins which, Escovil figured out a moment later, was laughter.

"Oh, but you know, Escovil, somebody *should* have cared about this fellow who's crucial to the war effort. Because Hitler's got legions of goose-stepping SS goons, but Britain has *scientists.* And scientists win. You see?"

"I do see," Escovil said.

"But the *aristocrat,* who's supposed to be watching, a very *titled* aristocrat I might add, who goes to country houses with *divinely* important people, slips up. Not that he does anything right away, when there's still time to do something about it, no, either he isn't told or he ignores it."

"The latter, I'd say," Wilkins offered.

"And Arthur's got it right. Because that class of individual doesn't make mistakes.

They simply go on. No balls-up here, everything is tickety-boo. But, as you might have guessed, everything really isn't tickety-boo. Now the RAF isn't going to allow Harry Byer to actually *fly* an aircraft, good heavens no, but he is something of a gnome, a little runt, and that qualifies him as a tail gunner because he fits in the turret. So off he goes, in his Wellington bomber, dropping incendiaries on Germany, and good for him."

"Amen," Escovil said.

"Well, it damn near *is* amen, as you say, because early in January, Harry's Wellington is hit by flak over the Ruhr. The pilot makes a valiant effort but it's no good and the crew bails out over France. Now, luck intervenes. Some of the crew are caught right away, but Harry lands in just the right farmer's field and the French, perhaps a resistance group, or simply French, take charge of him and smuggle him up to Paris. And there he sits, as they try to make arrangements to get him out of the country.

"Now, just about here, the aristocrat is told what's become of Harry and gives forth a mighty British roar. And who do you suppose he roars at? To clean up this godawful mess? He roars at us, who else?"

Jones waited. Escovil knew he had been

268

called on to recite, and what came to him was, "And now you're roaring at me."

Impertinent. Wilkins said, "We're not roaring, Francis. Yet."

"So then, what shall I do?"

"Why, get him out. What else?" Jones said. There was a file folder on the table by Jones's chair. Jones opened it, withdrew a photograph, and held it out to Escovil, who had to go and retrieve it. When he'd returned to his chair, Jones said, "There he is. Taken when he reached Paris, just to make sure they have who they say they have."

In the photograph, Harry Byer looked like an owl who'd flown into the side of a barn. Owlish he had always been — hooked beak of a nose, small eyes, pursy little mouth — while the barn wall had left livid bruises by his right eye and the right-hand corner of his mouth. Injured in the airplane? Beaten up? "When was this taken?" he said. He started to rise, intending to return the photograph.

But Jones waved him back down and said, "A week or so after he landed."

"And how did, um, we come to hear about it?"

"Whoever these people are, they were in contact with an underground cell operating a clandestine radio."

269

"Back to London."

"Back to the French in London."

"Oh."

"Quite."

"You don't suppose the Germans are in control of them, do you? Waiting to see who shows up?"

"Haven't a clue."

Silence. Wilkins had now assumed the same posture, drink in hand, legs crossed, as his colleague. They were, Escovil thought, rather good at waiting. Finally he said, "So you'll want me to go up there."

Jones cackled. "Are you daft? Of course not, you'll send your agent, what's-his-name, the policeman."

"Constantine Zannis? He's not my agent. Who told you *that?*"

Wilkins leaned forward and said, "Oh damn-it-all of *course* he is." He glanced at his watch. "Has been for a while — ten minutes, I'd say, more or less."

I'd like to be in the room when you tell Zannis that. But Escovil knew there was no point in starting an argument he couldn't win. "Paris is a long way from here. Why wouldn't you take Byer out by fishing boat, from the French coast?"

"Option closed," Jones said. "For the time being. Somebody got himself caught up

270

there and the Germans shut it down. We'll get it back, in time, but right now you'll have to use your escape line."

"It isn't mine."

"Now it is."

Oh piss off. "And why does *Zannis* have to go?"

"Because Byer will never make it by himself, speaks not a word of any continental language. He can read a scientific journal in German, but he can't order lunch. And, more important, if he's caught, we have to be able to show we did everything we could. We have to show we *care*."

Escovil suppressed a sigh. "Very well, I'll ask him."

"No," Wilkins said, now quite irritated, "you'll *tell* him. 'Ask him' indeed."

Jones said, "Do it any way you like, but keep in mind, Francis, we don't take no for an answer." He stood, collected Wilkins's glass, then Escovil's, and poured fresh drinks. When he'd resettled himself, he said, "Now," in a tone of voice that was new to Escovil, and went on to explain how they thought the thing might actually be done. Bastards they were, to the very bone, Escovil thought, but at least, and thank heaven, smart bastards.

■ ■ ■ ■

27 January. A telephone call from Escovil, early that afternoon. Could they meet? Privately? Zannis's instinctive reaction was to refuse, courteously or not so courteously, because the word "privately" told the tale: the spies wanted something. And it wasn't such a good day to ask Zannis *anything,* because he was miserable. He had waited for a call from Demetria, waited and waited, but it hadn't come. Five long days had crept by, his heart soaring every time the telephone rang: It's her! But it never was. Now, he would either have to assume she'd thought better of the whole thing, or was waiting for him — as he'd promised, very nearly threatened — to call her. Meanwhile, the spies were after him. Back in the autumn, in his time with Roxanne, he would have laughed. But the world had changed, the war *was* coming south, and only the British alliance might save the country.

And didn't they know it.

"It's really rather important," Escovil said. "Is there somewhere . . . ?"

Skata. "You can come to the office after six," Zannis said, a sharp edge to his voice. "Do you know where it is?"

"I don't."

Oh yes you do. Zannis gave him directions, then said, "It's very private here, once everyone's gone home, you needn't be concerned." *And the hell with your damn bookstores and empty churches.*

And so, at five minutes past six, there he was. "Hello."

He'd been drinking, Zannis could smell it on him. And there were shadows beneath his eyes, which made him seem, with his sand-colored hair swept across his forehead, more than ever a boy grown old. Beneath a soiled raincoat, the battered tweed jacket.

Once he was seated on the other side of the desk, Zannis said, "So then, what do you want?"

Such directness caused Escovil to clear his throat. "We must ask a favor of you."

We. Well, now that was out of the way, what next? Not that he wanted to hear it.

"It has to do with your ability to bring refugees, bring them secretly, from northern Europe to Salonika."

"You know about this?"

"We do." Escovil's tone was apologetic — the secret service was what it was and sometimes, regretfully, it worked.

"And so?"

"We need to make use of it, for a fugitive

273

of our own. An important fugitive — that is, important to the British war effort."

Zannis lit a cigarette. That done, he said, "No." Lighting the cigarette had given him an opportunity to amend his first answer, which had been, *Get out of my office.*

Escovil looked sorrowful. "Of course. That's the proper response, for you. It's what I would say, in your place."

Then good-bye.

"You fear," Escovil went on, "that it might jeopardize your operation and the people who run it."

"It could very well destroy it, Escovil. Then what becomes of the men and women trying to get out of Germany? I'll tell you what: they're trapped, they're arrested, and then they are at the mercy of the SS. Want more?"

"No need," Escovil said, very quietly. "I know." He was silent for a time, then he said, "Which might still happen, even if you refuse to help us."

"Which *will* happen."

"Then . . ."

"It's a question of time. The longer we go on, the more lives saved. And if some of our fugitives are caught, we can try to fix the problem, and we can continue. People run away all the time, and the organization

274

designed to catch them adjusts, gets what information it can, and goes to work the next day. But if they discover an *important* fugitive, perhaps a secret agent, it suggests the existence of others, and then the organization starts to multiply — more money, more men, more pressure from above. And that's the end of us."

"He's not a secret agent."

"No?"

"No. He's a downed airman. Who, it turns out, is a scientist, and shouldn't have been allowed to join the RAF, and certainly shouldn't have been allowed to fly bomber missions. But he escaped the attention of the department which — umm, *attends* to such individuals. And now they want him back."

"And you can't get him back on your own? *You?*"

"I don't like saying this, but that's what we're doing."

"And I don't like saying *this,* but you're endangering many lives."

"Well, frankly," Escovil said, "we do nothing else. We don't *want* to, we'd rather *not,* but it seems to work out that way."

Zannis thought for a time. "You have no alternative?"

"Not today."

"I'll tell you something, Escovil, if I find out you're lying to me you'll be on the next boat out of here."

"I take your point, but that won't happen. Don't you see? It's gone beyond that now. The war, everything." He paused, then said, "And I'm not lying."

"Oh, well, in that case . . ."

"I'm not. And you can assure yourself that the individual is precisely who I say he is."

"Really? And how exactly would I do that?"

"Ask him."

Zannis didn't go directly home. He stopped at the neighborhood taverna, had an ouzo, then another, and considered a third but, nagged by guilt over putting off Melissa's dinner, hurried back to Santaroza Lane. Then too, the third ouzo wouldn't, he realized, have much more effect than the first two, which had had no effect whatsoever. His mind was too engaged, too embroiled, to be soothed by alcohol. It lifted briefly, then went back to work. *Sorry!*

He simply could not persuade himself that Escovil was lying. Years of police work had sharpened his instincts in this area, and he trusted them more than ever. After Escovil's little surprise — "Ask him" — he'd gone on to explain the proposed operation, which was artfully conceived and made sense. Made the most perfect sense, as long as Zannis was willing to accept a certain level of danger. And who — given the time and circumstance — wouldn't? Not him. He *had* to go to Paris. *He* had to go to Paris. And do what had to be done. And that was that.

Lying on the bed in his underwear, he reached toward the night table and had a look, yet again, at the photograph he'd been given. Yes, Byer was exactly who Escovil had said he was, bruises and all. And how had Escovil's organization managed to get the photograph out of France? Escovil had claimed not to know and, as before, Zannis believed him. Next he studied the second photograph of Byer, the one in the Sardakis passport, a real passport photo, it seemed, and a real Greek passport. Perhaps for them not so difficult but, even so, impressive. So, was this a man who would murder his wife and her lover in a fit of jealousy? Well, it surely was — the owlish, seemingly harmless intellectual. *Skata!* He'd *seen* such murderers, that was exactly what they looked like!

He returned the passport and the photograph to the night table and turned his mind toward what he had to do in the morning. The gun. Why had he not replaced his Walther, lost in the Trikkala bombing? Why was he so . . .

The telephone. Who would call him here, his mother? She had no telephone, but, in an emergency . . . "Hello?"

"Hello, it's me."

Her! "Demetria. Did . . . did I give you this number?"

"Are you angry with me?"

"Good God no!"

"Vasilou had it, in a card index in his study."

"Is everything . . . allright?"

"Better now. But it's been a terrible week, Vasilou is suddenly *affectionate,* back early from the office, wanting, you know. But poor Demetria has eaten a bad fish. He is enraged, shouting. He will buy the restaurant and fire the cook! Meanwhile, I hide in the bathroom." A memory of that moment drew from her a kind of amused snort. "Anyhow, at last I'm free to telephone. It is the servants' night out but they dawdled before they left and I realized you wouldn't be at work."

"Can you come here now? Even for a little while? Just to see you. . . ."

"Oh Costa I can't." But with her voice she let him know how much she wanted to, and, almost better, she had never said his name before and hearing it thrilled him.

"Tomorrow?"

"The day after. He is off to Athens, the maids are going to a christening, and I told everyone I was invited to a mah-jong party. So I can see you at five, and we will have two hours, unless . . ."

"Unless what?"

"I must warn you, Costa, he is a dangerous enemy, a very dangerous enemy. Some of the people who work for him, they will do . . . anything."

He wondered why she thought Vasilou would discover them so quickly, then he knew. "Demetria, do you want to tell him? Now? Leave him and stay with me?"

The line whispered. Finally she said, "Not now. Not yet."

She was, he thought, testing him. *I know you will lie in bed by me, but will you stand by me?* "I am not afraid of him, Demetria."

"You are not afraid of anybody, are you."

"No. And the day, the hour, you want to leave, it's done." When she didn't speak he said, "Do you still love him?"

"No, I never did, not really. I thought I might, at one time, yes, I suppose I did think that." After a moment, she continued. "I am, you know, his third wife — he simply wanted something different, a new possession, but even so, I hoped. He was forceful, masculine, rich — who was I to refuse him as a husband? And I had been married — and all that that means in this country — so I was grateful, and he was honorable; he went to my father and asked for my hand. Very old-fashioned, very traditional, and it *affected* me. I was alone, and getting older, and here was, at least, a luxurious life."

"That can happen, I think, to anyone."

"Yes, I guess it might. And I *am* 'anyone,' Costa, inside . . . all this."

"I'm afraid you're not just 'anyone,' not to me."

"I know. I saw that. From the car when you and Vasilou came out of the club." She hesitated, then sighed. "I want to tell you everything, but not on the telephone." A pause, then, "You haven't told me where you live."

"There are no numbers on Santaroza Lane, but it's the fourth house up from the corner toward the bay, the door is old wood, unpainted. I have the second floor."

She waited, said, "So," then, "I have to go now. But it's only two days. One day, and part of another."

"At five," he said.

"Yes, at five," she said, her voice lovely,

and hung up the phone.

Salonika's best gun shop was at the western
end of the Via Egnatia, in what had been,
before the Great Fire, the city's Jewish
district. The owner, called Moises, the
Sephardic version of the name, had been
there forever, more than thirty years. Still,
his sidelocks were not quite gray. He always
wore a black Homburg, a formal hat, with a
vest and a colorful tie, his shirtsleeves buttoned decorously at the wrists. The shop
smelled of gun oil, not far from bananas.
Policemen had always received a discount
from Moises, so Zannis showed his badge.

Moises said, "You are Costa Zannis, no?"

"That's right."

"What can I do for you?"

"I need a Walther, the PPK detective's
model, and a holster. Also a box of ammunition."

Grimly, Moises shook his head. "I thought
maybe you wanted something repaired."

"No, a new sidearm."

"Ach, forgive me, but I haven't got one."

"Well then, used. Maybe even better."

"All gone, I'm afraid. New, used, everything."

"What do you mean, all gone?"

"I'm down to practically nothing — everything's been bought up: hunting rifles, shotguns, all the handguns." He shrugged. "I wish I could help you. I write the Walther company, they say next month."

Zannis thought it over. "Moises, I have to ask you, as a special favor to me, to try and buy one back. I'll pay whatever it costs."

Moises scratched the back of his head and looked doubtful. "I don't know, I've never done such a thing. Once the customer buys, it's his, that's that."

"Of course. But, this time, I must have one. A PPK."

"Well, I had one customer who bought twenty model PPKs, I suppose he might make do with nineteen. I wonder, maybe it's better if you ask him yourself."

"Would he mind, that you gave me his name?"

Moises considered it. "Not you. Anybody in this city can tell you anything. And, come to think of it, I'd imagine you're acquainted with him."

"Who is it?"

"Elias, the man with one name. You know, the poet."

"Twenty handguns?"

"Not so strange. Who can see into the future?"

282

"Maybe Elias can. I'll get in touch with him."

"Tell him, tell him I was reluctant, to give you his name."

"He won't care."

"Poets buying Walthers," Moises said. "I don't remember anything like that, and I've been here forever."

Zannis walked back to the office. *Fucking war,* he thought. Salonika was preparing for resistance, people buying weapons and hiding them. But Elias, one step ahead of the game, meant to go — bearing gifts — up into the mountain villages where, once the Germans came, the bandits would once again become *andartes,* guerrilla fighters, as they had during the Turkish occupation.

Zannis telephoned, then met with Elias at a *kafeneion* an hour later. He'd come away from the gun shop with a belt holster and ammunition, now, ceremoniously, Elias handed over a box containing a Walther. When Zannis reached into his pocket, Elias held up a hand. "Not a drachma shall I take from you, Officer Costa. This is my pleasure. My gift, my gesture. For it's my job, as a Greek poet, to be oracular, to see into the future, so I know what this weapon will do, and to who. As I said, my pleasure."

283

■ ■ ■ ■

29 January. An excited Costa Zannis left his office at three to pick up the sheets he'd taken to be washed "and *ironed,* Elena." Then, once back at the apartment, he made the bed and started to sweep the floor, but stopped, realizing that this chore had to be preceded by another, and began to brush Melissa. Probably she liked food more than a brushing, but it was surely a close second. She rolled over on her side, paws out, tongue lolling out of the side of her mouth, so Zannis could brush her chest. "Yes, Melissa, we are going to have a guest. An important guest." Melissa's tail gave a single thump against the floor.

He was humming some song, the words forgotten, when there was a sharp knock at the door. Zannis looked at his watch. *She's early!* It was not much after four but, who cared; they would have more time together. He opened the door and there stood a detective — Tellos? Yes, he thought so, a few years earlier they'd served in the same squad. What the hell was he doing here?

"Come in," Zannis said.

"Vangelis sent me to find you," Tellos said, apologetically. "I went to the office, but you weren't there. I have a car downstairs."

"What's wrong?"

"You haven't heard?"

"No."

"General Metaxas has died. In a hospital in Athens."

"Assassinated?"

"No, though people are saying all sorts of things — poisoned by the Italians, you name it, conspiracies of every sort."

"But not true."

"No. Vangelis talked to people in Athens. The general had a tonsillectomy and died of toxemia. Anyhow, we may have to deal with demonstrations, riots, who knows what, so there's a meeting at the mayor's house, east of the port, and Commissioner Vangelis wants you there."

Zannis was enraged. He feared Tellos would see it and covered his face with his hands. *What evil fate contrived to take from him the thing he wanted most in the world?*

Tellos rested a sympathetic hand on his shoulder. "I know," he said. "This man saved Greece, and now he's gone."

30 January. There were no riots. The Metaxas government had never been popular; surely half the population would have preferred a republic, long championed by

the noble voice of Greek democracy, Venizelos. But Venizelos had died in exile in 1936, while Metaxas, dictator though he was, had led the country well in war. Now King George II had named one Alexandros Koryzis, a former governor of the Bank of Greece, as the new prime minister. Hardly anyone had ever heard of him. Therefore, no marching in the streets. Instead, melancholy and silence. Poor Greece, no luck at all, why did fate treat them so badly?

Zannis might have had similar feelings, but there was barely room in his wretched heart for emotion about the national politics, for he had to go to Paris the following day and, if the operation went wrong, he would never again see Demetria. It tore at him, this loss. If only they'd been able to meet, if only they'd made love. Two stolen hours, was that too much to ask? So it seemed — their hours together stolen in turn by a bizarre twist of destiny: a man got tonsillitis. Zannis couldn't stop brooding, angry and sad at the same moment.

But then he had to, because he had difficulties beyond this, and these he'd brought on himself. He knew he would be away for at least ten days, and during that time it was more than likely that a letter from Emilia Krebs would arrive at the office. And so he had no choice but to designate Gabi Saltiel — and Sibylla, she could no longer be excluded — as his deputies in running the Salonika end of the escape line. Saltiel never said a harsh word, but Zannis could tell his feelings were hurt — why hadn't he been trusted from the beginning? As for Sibylla, feelings didn't enter into it, she was simply intent on getting everything right.

Not all that easy. "You melt six Panadon in a glass of water and use a clean pen with a sharp point." And the rest of it: the iron, the lawyer's address in Berlin, the teletype numbers for the detectives in Zagreb and Budapest. "You can depend on us, chief," Sibylla said. And, Zannis realized, she meant it.

That done, Zannis's eye inevitably fell on the telephone. He didn't *dare.* Umm, maybe he did. Oh no he didn't! Oh but yes, he did. Vasilou would still be in Athens, and Zannis just could not bear to leave the woman he loved, perhaps forever, with no more than an unanswered knock on a door.

Very slowly, tempting fate but unable to stop, he worked the dial with his index finger, running each number around to the end. But then, at last, good fortune: it was Demetria who picked up the receiver. He spoke quickly, in case she had to hang up.

"I'm sorry, I was taken away to a meeting. Because of Metaxas."

"I see," she said, voice breathy and tentative; the call had frightened her. "Perhaps . . . I could try . . . next week?" Then, her mind now working quickly, she added, "For another fitting."

From the background: "Now who the hell is that?"

Skata, Vasilou!

"It's the seamstress, dear."

"Well, make it snappy. I'm expecting a call."

"Yes, dear, just a minute."

"Oh Lord," Zannis said, "I didn't realize . . ."

"The hem is just too long, so —"

"I'll be away, for ten days. I'll call you."

The sound of approaching footsteps. "Can't hang up?" Vasilou shouted. "Then let me show you how it's done!" The footsteps grew louder.

"I have to say good-bye." Her voice wobbled. "But, please —"

The receiver was slammed down.

At Gestapo headquarters, on the Prinz-Albrechtstrasse in Berlin, Hauptsturmführer Albert Hauser studied a long list of names typed on yellow paper. When a name caught his attention, he riffled through a metal tray of five-by-eight cards, where, in alphabetical order, information about each of the names was recorded. If that was insufficient, he had dossiers for most of the names, dossiers filled with pages of information obtained from surveillance, paid informants, denunciations, and interrogation. The yellow list was a sort of Who's Who of dissidents in Berlin, all suspected — some more than suspected — of activity against the interests of the Reich. Rather loosely defined, those interests; thus it wasn't difficult to say the wrong thing, to know the wrong person, to own the wrong book. *Welcome to the list!*

So then, A to Z, six and a half pages long. Some of the names had a mark next to them, Hauser's symbolic note to himself: question mark, exclamation point — you didn't want that! — asterisk, and others, even an x — the last, for instance, beside a couple whose names appeared early in the D section. This couple was believed, after coming under pressure from the Gestapo, to have committed suicide, but, Hauser thought, committed suicide in an irritating way, so that their bodies would not be identified when found. Spiteful, wasn't it. To go to some distant city and manage the business in some little hotel room, having first burned one's identity papers. Defiant even in death and, really, very annoying.

He turned the page. Beside the name GRUEN, two entries for man and wife, two question marks. On what had been meant to be their final day of freedom, missing. Fled? Fled where? One word used by these people — Jews, communists, even aristocrats — was *submerge.* It meant hiding in an apartment, sharing a friend's food obtained with ration coupons, rarely if ever going outside, and then only with borrowed or false identification.

Others, like the couple D, killed themselves. Still others contrived to flee the country — into Switzerland, if they were lucky. Or, sometimes, to the unoccupied zone of France, where the Vichy police agencies were dedicated to catching them, but not always. The trouble with the unoccupied zone, the southern part of the country, was that fugitives might make their way to Marseille. And, once in Marseille, with some money to spend, one could do just about anything. *That's how it is,* Hauser thought, *with port cities,* like Naples. Or Odessa — even under the rule of the ruthless NKVD, for so Hauser thought of them. Where else? Hauser's inner eye wandered over an imaginary map of Europe. Constanta, in Roumania? A long way to go, for a fugitive. Equally Varna, on Bulgaria's Black Sea coast.

Go to work, lazybones, Hauser told himself, stop woolgathering. Where were these Gruens? He rose and walked over to the wall, where large sheets of brown paper showed diagrams of relations between the dissidents. Solid lines, dotted lines, some in red pencil: who met with who, who worked with who, who telephoned who, and on and on. Hauser located the circle containing the name GRUEN and traced the radiating lines with his index finger. Popular, weren't they. Here was, for example, the circled name of KREBS. And who was that?

He returned to his list and flipped over to the Ks: KREBS, EMILIA, and KREBS, HUGO. The latter was marked with a triangle, which meant, in Hauser's system, something like *uh-oh.* Now to the three-by-five cards. Yes, there it was, definitely worth a triangle; this Krebs was a colonel on the Oberkommando Wehrmacht, the General Staff, and *not* to be pestered. *Scheiss!* You had to be careful in this work. You had to be on your toes! Or you'd wind up in Warsaw, God forbid. Still, he wondered, and had a look at KREBS, EMILIA. Close and longtime friend of the Gruens, neighbor in Dahlem, Jew.

291

Hunh, look at that. This Colonel Krebs must be powerful indeed to have a Jewish wife and get away with it.

He was distracted from this line of thinking by two taps on the door and the entry of the department's chief clerk: tall, fading blond, and middle-aged. Something of a dragon, Traudl, with her stiff hair and stiff manner, but smart, and relentless in her commitment to the job. No surprise there, at one time she'd worked for some of the better — mostly Jewish, alas — law firms in the city. Then, with Hitler's ascension, she'd seen the light and come to work for the Gestapo. "Hauptsturmführer Hauser?" she said. "Pardon the intrusion, but I have brought your morning coffee."

"Thank you, Traudl." He set the steaming cup on his desk.

"Will there be anything else, sir?"

"No, thank you," Hauser said. "I'll be going out for a bit."

He took a sip of the coffee. Real coffee, and strong — oh, the little pleasures of this job. He returned to his paperwork, drumming his fingers on the yellow list. *So, who wants to see the Gestapo today?* But he already knew that, some tiny clicker in his brain had decided to go out to Emilia Krebs's house. That wasn't pestering the

292

husband, was it? No, certainly not, he would never know about it, because she would never know about it. Just a little spur-of-the-moment surveillance. Just a look-see.

Hauser picked up his phone and dialed a two-digit number, which connected him with the office of Untersturmführer, Lieutenant, Matzig, his partner. "Matzi?"

"Yes, Albert?"

"Let's go for a little ride, I need some air."

"I'll bring the car around," Matzig said.

So, yet another ride out to Dahlem. Lord, this neighborhood was a dissident *nest!* But, in the end, there wasn't much to see. Hauser and Matzig sat in the front seat, talking idly from time to time, waiting, the principal activity of the investigative life. The winter darkness came early, a light snow began to fall, and eventually the colonel came home from work, dropped off at his door by a Wehrmacht car. The colonel disappeared into his house and, though the two officers waited another hour, that was it for the day.

They tried earlier the following day, waited longer, and were rewarded with a view of the Krebses going out for dinner. Thus Hauser and Matzig got to wait outside Horcher's while the couple dined. No fun at all, visiting the best restaurants in Berlin, but not a morsel of food. After dinner, the couple went home. Matzig drove the Mercedes to their chosen vantage point, Hauser lit a cigar and said, "Let's go home, Matzi. We'll give it one more day, tomorrow." All he could afford, really, because like any job you had to show your bosses some success, some production, and there was nothing yet to warrant even the most diffident interview.

But then there was. Patience paid off, at least sometimes, because just after five on the third day, the lovely Emilia Krebs, in sober gray coat and wide-brim gray hat, briefcase in hand, left her house, walked quickly down the path that led to the sidewalk, and turned left, toward downtown Berlin. As she passed the low hedge that bordered her property, here came a fellow in a dark overcoat: half-bald, heavy, wearing glasses — some sort of intellectual, from the look of him. For the length of a block, he matched her pace. Hauser and Matzig exchanged a look; then, no discussion required, Matzig turned on the ignition, put the car in gear, and drove past Emilia Krebs to a side street with a view of the nearest tram stop.

She arrived soon after, followed by the man in the dark overcoat. They stood at a distance from each other, mixed in with a few other people, all waiting for the trolley. Five minutes later it appeared, bell ringing, and rolled to a stop. Emilia Krebs and the others climbed on, but the man in the overcoat stayed where he was and, once the trolley moved away, he turned and walked back the way he'd come.

"Did you see what I saw?" Hauser said.

"A trailer, you think?" The function of a trailer, in clandestine practice, was to make sure the person ahead wasn't being followed.

"What else?"

6 February. Paris. Occupied Paris: triste and broken, cold and damp, the swastika everywhere. Following the operational plan, Zannis played the role of a Greek detective in Paris, come to escort a prisoner back to Salonika. In trench coat and well-worn blue suit, heavy shapeless black shoes, and holstered pistol on his belt, he took a taxi to the commercial hotel Escovil had named — on a little street near the Gare du Nord — and slept all afternoon, recovering from days of train travel. Then, around eight in the evening, he ventured forth, found a taxi, and went off in search of Parisian food and Parisian sex. So, if anybody was watching,

that's what they saw.

He left the taxi at the Place de la Bastille, found the proper café on the second try, and the woman right away. She was, according to plan, reading *Le Soir,* the evening tabloid, and marking the classified ads with a pencil.

"Excuse me," Zannis said, "are you waiting for Émile?" He hadn't been in France since the time he'd worked as a Parisian *antiquaire,* more than ten years earlier, but the language, though halting and awkward, was still there.

"I'm waiting for my grandfather," she said, completing the identification protocol. Then, looking at her watch, added, "We'd better be on our way. You shall call me Didi."

Didi! Good God. For whoever she was — and she'd given *Didi* her best effort: neckline much too low, "diamond" earrings, scarlet lipstick — this woman had never been picked up in a café, she'd never *met* a woman who'd been picked up in a café. What was she, a baroness? Possible, Zannis thought: narrow head, small ears, thin nostrils, aristocratic tilt to the chin. Didi? *Oh fuck, these people are going to get me killed.*

"Off we go, honey," Zannis said, with a

coarse grin, a nod toward the door, and a proffered arm.

The aristocrat almost flinched. Then she recovered, stood, took his arm, pressed it to her champagne cup of a noble breast, and off they went — circling the Place Bastille, heading for a brasserie down a side street. Zannis took a deep breath. These people were brave, were resisting the Occupation, were putting their lives in jeopardy. They were, he told himself, doing the best they could.

So the Greek detective, in case anybody was watching — and there was no way to know whether they were or not — had found a girl for the evening and would now take her out for dinner. The restaurant was called the Brasserie Heininger, a man in an apron and a fisherman's waterproof hat was shucking oysters on a bed of shaved ice by the entryway.

When Zannis opened the door, the interior hit him hard — much fancier than any place he'd been to when he'd lived in Paris. The brasserie was fiercely Belle Epoque: red plush banquettes, polished brass, and vast gold-framed mirrors lining the walls, the waiters in muttonchop whiskers, the conversation loud and manic, the smoky air scented by perfume and grilled sausage.

And, as the maître d' led them to a table —
that sexy slut Didi had reserved ahead —
Zannis saw what looked to him like half the
officer class of occupied Paris, much of it in
Wehrmacht gray, with, just to set off the
visual composition, a sprinkling of SS black.
As they wove their way among the tables,
the aristocrat crushed Zannis's arm against
her breast so hard he wondered why it
didn't hurt her, or maybe she was so scared
she didn't notice. At last they were seated,
side by side on a banquette at a table where
the number 14 was written on a card supported by a little brass stand. The aristocrat
settled close to him, then took a deep
breath.

"You're allright?" Zannis said.

She nodded, gratitude in her eyes.

"Good girl," he said. "Didi."

She gave him a conspiratorial smile; the
waiter brought menus in golden script.
"Here one takes the *choucroute garnie*," she
said. "And order champagne."

Sauerkraut? Oh no, not with the way his
stomach felt. On the surface, Zannis showed
a certain insouciant confidence, but every
muscle in his body was strung tight; he was
ready to shoot his way out of this restaurant
but not at all prepared for sauerkraut.
"Maybe they have a fish," he said.

"Nobody orders *that*."

He searched the menu. "Shellfish," he said.

"If you like."

He looked up for a moment, then said, "What the hell is that? Behind your shoulder, in the mirror."

"It's very famous," she said. "A memorial to a Bulgarian waiter, slain here a few years ago."

"It's a *bullet* hole."

"Yes, it is."

"They don't fix it? Back where I come from, they have them fixed the next day."

"Not here."

The waiter returned. *" 'Sieur et 'dame?"*

Zannis ordered the seafood platter, which he would try to eat, followed by the *choucroute,* which he would not, and a bottle of champagne. As the waiter hurried off, Zannis discovered his neighbors in the adjacent booth: two SS officers with French girlfriends; puffy and blond, green eyeshadow, pouty lips. One of the SS men looked like a precocious child, with baby skin, a low forehead, and eyeglasses in tortoiseshell frames. The other — Zannis understood immediately who he was, what he was — turned to face him, rested an elbow on the plush divider, and said, *"Bonsoir, mon ami."*

The set of his face and the sparkle in his eyes suggested a view of the world best described by the word *droll,* but, Zannis saw, he was a certain kind of smart and sophisticated German who'd found, in the black uniform and death's-head insignia, a way to indulge a taste for evil.

"Bonsoir," Zannis said.

"Your girl's a real looker." He moved his head to get a better view of Didi, said, "Hello, gorgeous," with a sly smile and waggled his fingers by way of a waved greeting. The aristocrat glanced at him, then looked down. The SS officer, at that stage of inebriation where he loved the world, said, "Aww, don't be shy, gorgeous."

Zannis turned back and began to make conversation. "Had much snow this winter?"

From behind him: "Hey! I was talking to you!"

Zannis faced him and said, "Yes?"

"You Frenchmen can be very rude, you know."

"I'm not French," Zannis said. Maybe the SS officer wouldn't figure it out but the girlfriends certainly would.

"No? What are you?"

"I'm from Greece."

The officer spoke to his friends. "Say, here's a Greek!" Then, to Zannis, "What brings you to Paris, Nick?"

Zannis couldn't stop it: a hard stare that said *Shut your fucking mouth before I shut it for you.* Then, making sure his voice was soft, he said, "I'm a detective, I'm here to bring back a murderer."

"Oh," the officer said. "I see. Well, we're friendly types, you know, and we were wondering what you were doing after dinner."

"Going home," Zannis said.

"Because I have this very grand apartment up on the avenue Foch, and you and Gorgeous are invited, for, well, some . . . champagne."

The aristocrat sank her clawed fingernails into Zannis's thigh; he almost yelped. "Thanks, but the lady is tired, I'll take her home after dinner."

The officer glared at him, his head weaving back and forth.

The woman beside him said, "Klaus? Are you ignoring us?"

Thank God for Frenchwomen, puffy blond or not! "Enjoy your evening, my friend," Zannis said, employing a particular tone of voice — sympathetic, soothing — he'd used, all his years with the police, for difficult drunks.

And it almost worked; the officer couldn't

decide whether he wanted to end this battle or not. Then he lurched, and his face lit up. What went on? Maybe his girlfriend's hand had done something under the table, something more enticing than the aristocrat's. Whatever it was it worked, and the officer turned away and whispered in girlfriend's ear.

"Plat de la mer!" the waiter cried out, wheeling to a stop at the table, a gigantic platter of crustaceans held high, balanced on his fingertips.

A taxi was waiting in front of the brasserie, and Zannis directed the driver back to his hotel. A much-relieved aristocrat sank back against the seat and said, voice confidential, "Thank God that's over. I was afraid you were going to shoot him."

"Not likely," he said. *This thing in the holster is just for show.* And so he'd believed, until his third and final meeting with Escovil. Who'd said, just before they parted, "Finally, I must say something a bit . . . *sticky.* Which is, you mustn't allow Byer to be taken by the Germans, we *cannot* have him interrogated. So, if it looks like the game is up, you'll have to, to, to do whatever you must." Zannis hadn't answered: at first he couldn't believe what he'd heard, then he had to, but such madness, murder, was far beyond what he was willing to do.

At war, the city was blacked out; every window opaque, the occasional lighted streetlamp painted blue, car headlights taped down to slits, so the taxi moved cautiously through the silent, ghostly streets. When they reached the hotel and were alone as they approached the doorway, his companion said, "Not long now. Your friend has been brought to the hotel, and you're meant to catch the early train."

"The five-thirty-five."

"Yes, the first train to Berlin. You have all the papers?"

"Stamped and signed: release from the Santé prison, exit visas, everything."

The night clerk was asleep in a chair behind the reception desk, a newspaper open across his lap. They made sure they didn't wake him, climbing the stairs quietly as he snored gently down below. When they reached the third floor, Zannis stood by his door and said, "Where is he?"

The aristocrat made an upward motion with her head. "Forty-three."

In his room, Zannis shed his trench coat and had a look at his valise, which appeared to be undisturbed, but, he well knew, an experienced professional search would leave no evidence. The aristocrat, waiting at the door, said, "Ready to go?" In her voice, as much impatience as, true to her breeding, she ever permitted herself to reveal. These people were amateurs, Zannis thought, and they'd had all they wanted of secrecy and danger.

They climbed another flight, the aristocrat tapped twice on the door, then twice again, which was opened to reveal a darkened room. The man who'd opened the door had a sharp handsome face, dark hair combed straight back, and stood as though at attention. A military posture; he was perhaps, Zannis thought, a senior officer. The aristocrat and the officer touched each other's cheeks with their lips, Paris style, murmuring something that Zannis couldn't hear but certainly an endearment. So these two were husband and wife. The officer then said, to Zannis, "I can't tell you my name," as though it were an apology. "You are Zannis?"

"I am."

They shook hands, the officer's grip powerful and steady. "Your problem now," he said, nodding toward the interior of the room.

In the shadows, the silhouette of a small man sat slumped on the edge of the bed.

Zannis said, "Harry Byer?"

A white face turned toward him. "Yes," the man said in English. "More or less."

Zannis went downstairs to his room and collected his trench coat and valise. When he returned to Room 43, the officer said, "We've arranged a car. At oh-four-forty hours. A police car, actually. So your arrival at the Gare du Nord, which is closely guarded, will look authentic."

"Stolen?"

"Borrowed."

"Better."

"And driven by a policeman. Well, at least somebody wearing the uniform."

The aristocrat laughed, silver chimes, at the idea of whatever old friend this was, playing the role of a policeman. As she started to remove her earrings, Zannis noticed a bare ring finger. Now he realized that these two were probably not married but were, instead, lovers. This sent his mind back to Salonika and a fleeting image of Demetria, by his side, in an occupied city.

Zannis crossed the room, the bare boards creaking beneath his weight, and shifted the room's single chair so that he sat facing Byer. Then, very laboriously, in his primitive English, he explained how the operation would work. When he showed Byer his photograph in the Greek passport, he was rewarded with at least a flicker of hope in the man's eyes. "It might even work," Byer said. He took the passport and studied it. "I do speak a little French, you know. I took it at school."

"He does," the officer said. "If you speak slowly."

Zannis was relieved and switched to a mix of the two languages, making sure at the end of every phrase that Byer understood what he'd been told. "At the borders, Harry, and on the trains — at least as far as Yugoslavia — you can't say anything at all, because you're supposed to be Greek. And nobody will speak to *you,* once you're wearing these." He took a pair of handcuffs from his pocket. Byer stared at them. Zannis said, "Better than a POW camp, right?"

Byer nodded. "What did I do, to be in the Santé?"

"You murdered your wife and her lover, in Salonika."

After a moment, Byer said, "Not the worst idea."

Zannis ignored the irony. "It had to be a murder of some kind, for the Germans to believe that we'd gotten the French police to arrest you, after you'd fled to Paris." He paused, then said, "The only plausible crime would be a crime of passion. You don't much look like a gangster."

Zannis stood, took a cigarette from his packet, then offered the packet around. Only the officer accepted, inhaling with pleasure as Zannis extinguished the match. He started to speak, but something caught his attention and he looked at his watch and said, almost to himself, "It's too early for the police car." Then, to Zannis, "Can't you hear it?"

In the silence of the room, Zannis listened intently and discovered the low beat of an idling engine. The officer went to the window and, using one finger, carefully moved the blackout curtain aside, no more than an inch. "Come have a look," he said.

Zannis joined him at the window. Across the street from the hotel, a glossy black Citroën, the luxury model with a long hood and square passenger compartment, was parked at the curb. The air was sufficiently cold to make the exhaust a white plume at the tailpipe.

The officer kept his voice low, his words meant for Zannis and nobody else. "The only people who drive these things in Paris are the Gestapo and the SS. It's the official German car."

Zannis understood immediately, though he found it hard to believe. "We had a problem at the restaurant," he said, "with an SS officer. It seems he followed us back here."

"Why would he do that?"

"He wanted your woman friend. He was very drunk."

"Then let's hope it's him."

"Why?"

"Because if it isn't, we've been betrayed."

"Is that possible?"

"I'm afraid it is."

The aristocrat joined them at the window. "What's going on?"

"There's a car out there. See it? Zannis thinks some SS man followed you home from the restaurant."

The aristocrat peered past the curtain. She swore, then said, "Now what?"

"We'll have to think of something."

"Will they search the hotel?" she said.

Byer said, "What's going on?" His voice rose to a whine. "What is it?"

The officer said, "Keep quiet, Harry." Then, "They might search the hotel. Maybe he's waiting down there for a squad to show up."

"Is there a back door?" Zannis said.

"There is, but it's padlocked. And, even if

we got out that way, what happens when our friend shows up with the police car?"

They were silent for a moment. The officer again moved the curtain and said, "He's just sitting there."

"There were two of them, and their girl-friends," the aristocrat said. "Maybe they'll just go away. They have to assume I'm in this hotel for the night."

"Maybe they will. Or maybe they'll wait until morning," the officer said.

"Could anybody be . . . that crazy?"

Nobody answered. Finally Zannis said, "Can you somehow contact your friend and warn him off?"

The officer looked at his watch. "No, he's left his hotel by now. The police car is up at Levallois, in a garage. The owner helps us."

Again, silence.

Zannis's mind was racing. He had seen, when he'd first entered the hotel, a metal shutter pulled down over a broad entryway. Not a shop, he guessed, because the sidewalk ended at either side of the shutter and a cobblestone strip led to the street. "If Byer and I aren't here," he said, "would it matter if a Gestapo squad searched the hotel?"

The officer thought it over. "No, it would just be the two of us in a room. And, when our friend arrives, he'll see the Gestapo vehicles and drive away."

"I think we'd better do something now," Zannis said. He put on his trench coat and grabbed the handle of his small valise.

"Good luck," the officer said. He shook Zannis's hand, and the aristocrat kissed him on both cheeks and said, "Be careful."

"Let's go, Harry," Zannis said.

In the dark lobby at the foot of the staircase, the night clerk snored on, dead to the world. Zannis shook him by the shoulder and he woke with a start and said, "What . . . what do you want?" His breath smelled of sour wine.

"Is there a garage in this hotel?"

"Yes."

"What's in there?"

"A car, belongs to the guy who owns the hotel. He can't drive it — the Bosch tried to confiscate private cars, so some people hid them."

"Is the car locked?"

The clerk sat up straight. "Say, what do you think —" Zannis drew the Walther and showed it to the clerk, who said, "Oh," then, "The key's in the office, in the desk."

Zannis gestured with the Walther and the clerk stood up, went into the office behind the reception desk, and searched in the bot-

310

tom drawer until he found car keys on a ring.

"And next," Zannis said, "I'll want the key for the back door."

"On a nail, just next to you."

"Harry?"

Byer came around the desk; Zannis gave him the key. "Run this upstairs. Tell them to open the back door and get out right away."

Byer hurried off and Zannis turned back to the clerk. "The shutter over the garage doorway, it's locked?"

"Of course."

"From inside? Is there an entry from the hotel?"

"No, it has a lock at the bottom, you have to go out to the sidewalk."

"Get the key."

Muttering under his breath, the clerk searched the middle drawer, threw pens, a rubber stamp, an ink pad, and miscellaneous papers on the desk. At last he found the key, and started to hand it to Zannis, who waved him off. "Is there gas in the car?" Zannis said.

"Yes."

"Battery connected? Tires still on?"

"I charge the battery twice a week, late at night. The boss wants it ready to drive."

"He does? Why?"

"The hell would I know? Maybe he wants to go somewhere."

Zannis heard Byer, running down the stairs, likely waking every guest in the hotel. *This will not work,* Zannis thought. There was no way he could get this man back to Salonika. A moment later, Byer, breathing hard, arrived at the reception. "They said thank you."

"Now it's time," Zannis said to the clerk, "for you to go outside, unlock the shutter, and roll it up."

"Me?"

"You see anybody else?"

"Why can't your pal do it?"

Zannis rapped him on the shoulder blade with the barrel of the Walther, just hard enough.

The clerk mumbled something Zannis was not meant to hear and said, "Allright, whatever you want."

Keeping Byer behind him in the darkened lobby, Zannis unlocked the hotel door and watched as the clerk went out the door and turned left, toward the shuttered garage. Across the street, the Citroën idled, but Zannis could see only dim shapes behind the steamed-up windows.

The clerk came quickly through the door. "Done," he said. "That Citroën out there, are they . . . ?"

"Go back to sleep," Zannis said.

"What about the boss's car?"

"Send me a bill," Zannis said. "After the war." He turned to Byer. "Ready, Harry? We're not going to run, we're going to walk quickly. You get in the back and lie on the floor."

"Why?" Byer's eyes were wide.

"Just in case," Zannis said.

Keeping Byer on his left — the side away from the Citroën — and the gun in his hand in his coat pocket, Zannis walked through the hotel door. The shutter was rolled up to reveal an old Peugeot sedan, the metal rims around the headlights spotted with rust. He thought he might get away with it: the SS officer hadn't seen him in his trench coat, the seductive Didi wasn't with him, and the people in the Citroën wouldn't be able to see much of anything through the cloudy windows.

On the first try, wrong key — trunk key, of course — then the driver's door opened, Zannis unlocked the back door, and Byer, as ordered, lay flat on the floor. As Zannis settled behind the wheel, the driver's door of the Citroën swung open and the baby-faced SS he'd seen at the brasserie started to get out, then turned his head as though somebody in the backseat had spoken to him. Zannis searched for the starter button, found it, and pressed it with his thumb. Nothing. *Betrayed.* By night-clerk malice, or by an old car on a damp night, it came to the same thing.

"What's going on?" Byer said.

Zannis pressed again.

Now the other SS officer climbed out of the Citroën. From the Peugeot's engine, a single, rather discreet, cough. The SS man heading for the garage wasn't in a hurry. A little unsteady on his feet, he kept one hand out of sight behind his leg. Zannis held the button down, which produced a second cough, another, and one more. Then the engine grumbled and came to life. Zannis shoved the clutch pedal to the floor and put the car in what he thought was first gear. It wasn't. As the clutch pedal came up, the Peugeot stalled. The SS man, now ten feet away, was amused and shook his head — a world populated by fools, what was one to do?

The starter worked once again and this time Zannis found first gear and gave the engine as much gas as he dared. The SS man's hand came out from behind his leg, Luger pistol held casually, barrel facing down. He changed direction in order to block the Peugeot and held up his other hand — the amiable traffic cop. Zannis slammed on the brake, the Peugeot lurched to a stop and then, looking sheepish and embarrassed, he cranked the window down. He had almost hit a German officer, what was *wrong* with him?

The SS man smiled, *that's better,* and, obviously very drunk from the way he walked, approached the driver's side of the car. He was just starting to bend over so he could have a word with the driver when Zannis shot him in the face. He staggered backward, his hat fell off, blood ran from his nostrils, and Zannis fired twice more; the first clipping off the top of his ear, the second in the right eyebrow. That did it, and he collapsed.

Zannis hit the gas pedal, first gear howling. As he swung into the street, the baby-faced SS scrambled out of the Citroën. *Idiot.* Zannis snapped off two shots but the car was moving and he didn't think he'd hit him. Or maybe he had, because the last Zannis saw of him he was limping back to his car. Just as, in the rearview mirror, Zannis saw the two puffy blondes take off like rabbits, high-heeled shoes in hand, running for their lives down the dark street. *Go fuck*

Germans and see where it gets you, Zannis said to himself.

From the back, Byer said, "What happened? What happened?"

Zannis didn't answer. Finally put the Peugeot into second gear — he could smell burning clutch — then third, and turned hard right into a side street, then right again, so that he was now headed north, toward the Porte de Clignancourt.

Slowly, Zannis worked his way through the back streets, which angled off the main boulevards, so, a series of diagonals. But Zannis couldn't have gone much faster if he'd had to — the untaped headlights were turned off, and it was hard to see in the blacked-out city. After ten minutes of driving, he stopped the Peugeot so Byer could move to the passenger seat and Zannis told him the details. Byer took it well enough; after everything he'd been through since the Wellington went down, this was but one more nightmare. As Zannis again drove north, he heard the high-low sirens in the distance, converging on the hotel, but he was well away from it. A few blocks on he passed a pair of French policemen, in their long winter capes, pedaling easily on their bicycles. One of them gave him a sour look,

316

and Zannis wondered if Paris was under curfew, often the case in occupied cities. He didn't know but, if it was, it was a German curfew, and the policemen couldn't be bothered to stop him.

Of course that would change, violently, in the morning. The Gestapo and the French Sûreté would turn Paris upside down, looking for him — they'd have a good description — and for the Peugeot. Maybe, he thought, he should have tied the clerk to a chair, evidence that the man wasn't complicit in the crime, but he hadn't thought of it and he'd been intent on escaping from the hotel. In any event, the escape south by railway was no longer possible, he'd have to find another way to get out of the country.

He reached Saint-Ouen soon enough, wondering if Laurette, his lover when he'd lived here, was still in the apartment they'd shared. It didn't matter if she was; he couldn't go anywhere near her. Moments later, at the edge of Saint-Ouen, he entered the vast flea market, a labyrinth, endless twisting lanes lined by shuttered stalls. Clignancourt didn't precisely have borders, it faded away to the north in a maze of alleys and storage sheds, and here Zannis found an open courtyard behind a workshop with boarded-up windows. He parked the car and lit a cigarette. Dawn was still hours away, and ten in the morning farther yet. He was very tired, nothing more than that, and, in time, both he and Byer dozed, woke up, and dozed again.

10:15 A.M. Zannis left Byer in the Peugeot and made his way to stall number fifty-five of the section known as Serpette. The market was nearly deserted, many of the stalls unopened, only a few shoppers wandering listlessly among the aisles, past old chinaware, old clothes, old maps and books, antlers for the wall above the fireplace, a collapsible opera hat. You had to be clever here, to find that priceless object, its value unknown to the owner of the booth, then you had to bargain hard to get the meagre price lower, so the *antiquaire* never suspected you were cheating him out of a fortune. Day in, day out, year in, year out, the devious customers carried off their treasures, displayed them in their parlors, and boasted to their friends.

Zannis was relieved to find his uncle, seeing him from behind as he sat with two friends, playing cards on a mahogany tabletop held up by three upended fruit crates. Zannis's heart lifted — that bald pate, freckled and scarred, with its fringe of wiry

318

gray hair, could belong to no one else. "Anastas?"

His uncle turned, his eyes widened with disbelief, then he shouted, "Constantine!," rose to his feet, and embraced his nephew. Strong as an ox, Uncle Anastas, who held him tight while Zannis felt, on his cheek, tears from his uncle's eyes. "Oh my God, I thought I'd never see you again," Anastas said. Then took him by the arms, stepped back, stared at him lovingly, and said, "Constantine, my own nephew, what the fuck are you doing *here?*"

"A long story, uncle."

"My brother's son," Anastas said to his friends. "*Look* at him."

"A handsome boy," one of them said, in Greek.

"Are you still playing, Anastas?" said the other.

"I fold my cards," Anastas said, wiping his eyes.

Uncle Anastas wanted to show him off at the *antiquaires'* café but Zannis told him, as gently as he could, that they should close the booth and speak inside, so Anastas shooed his friends off, lowered the shutter over the front of the stall, then went to the café and returned carrying coffees spiked with Calvados. Zannis had meanwhile discovered — lying on a demi-lune table artfully coated with dust — a copy of that morning's *Le Matin.* On the front page a headline: SS MAJOR SHOT BY JEWISH GANGSTERS!

His uncle, having had time to think things over on his walk to the café, was good and worried by the time he returned. He waited one sip of coffee, then said, "You better tell me the story, Constantine."

Zannis held up the newspaper.

"*Skata!* You're not a Jew."

"Not a gangster either."

Anastas switched on a lamp with a colored-glass shade, read the first few sentences of the article, then said, "Well, it's in the Zannis blood. I got my first Turk when I was sixteen. A gendarme, but only a corporal, not a *major.*"

"I remember the story," Zannis said.

Anastas put the paper down and looked puzzled. "But tell me something, why did you have to come all the way to Paris to do this thing? You could've waited, you know, they'll be in Greece soon enough."

"I came up here to rescue an Englishman, Uncle Anastas."

"Oh, I see. You're involved in . . . secret work?"

"Yes."

"Bad business, dear nephew, they kill people who do that."

"I know. But what happened last night was accidental — we were supposed to leave here quietly. Now we're stuck."

"Oh, 'stuck' I don't know. All sorts of people in hiding here, waiting for the war to end, waiting for the Americans to stop sitting on their asses and do something."

"I can't wait, uncle. I have to get out, and I have to get my Englishman out."

Anastas thought it over, finally said, "Not easy."

"No, it isn't."

"But not impossible. Do you have any money?"

"Plenty. Grandma sewed it in the lining of my jacket."

"Because that's what it takes. And if you don't have enough —"

"No, uncle, I have a lot. In dollars."

"Dollars! *Skata,* I haven't seen dollars in a long time. How much, hundreds?"

"Thousands."

"Constantine!"

"It's the war, uncle. Everything's expensive."

"Still, you must be very important. I mean, *thousands.*"

"The English do *not* want this man captured."

From outside the stall, a low two-note whistle. Zannis could see, in the space between the bottom of the shutter and the ground, a pair of shoes, which then moved away. "What goes on?" he said.

"Police." He tugged the little chain on the lamp, darkening the stall, then rested an elbow on his knee and rubbed the corners of his mouth with thumb and index finger. "What to do with you," he said. "Where have you hidden your Englishman?"

Zannis described the building and the courtyard.

"He'll be safe there, but not for long. When these clowns go away, you'll bring him to my apartment."

"Thank you, Anastas," Zannis said.

"What the hell, you're family. And maybe I have one idea."

"Which is?"

"I know somebody."

"Always good, to know somebody."

"You'd better," Anastas said. "Otherwise . . ."

In the apartment, Zannis and Byer settled down to wait. Byer would sleep on a chaise longue, Zannis on a tasseled couch. And, later that morning, one of Anastas's card-playing friends took a can of blue paint and a license plate over to the courtyard where they'd hidden the Peugeot. He then drove the newly painted car to a nearby village, parked it on a mud flat by the river, and took a train back to Paris. "I suspect it was gone before I got on the train," he told Anastas. "Into a barn until the war ends."

"Harder than I thought," Anastas said at dinner. His French wife had prepared steaks, with spinach and onions sautéed in oil, and they drank a *very* good red wine in unlabeled bottles. "The man I know . . . ?" Anastas paused to chew his steak, then took a sip of the wine. "Well, he had to go to a man *he* knows." Anastas met his nephew's eyes, making sure he understood the magnitude of such an event. "So prepare to pay, nephew."

"When do I meet him?" Zannis said.

"After midnight, two-thirty. A car will come for you."

Byer looked up from his plate and said, "Thank you, madame, for this wonderful dinner."

"You are welcome," she said. "It is in your honor, monsieur, and Constantine's. To wish you safe journey." She smiled, warm and affectionate. If the occupation had affected her, there was no evidence that Zannis could see.

"We drink to that," Anastas said. And they did.

2:30 A.M. The glossy black automobile was surely worth a fortune, Zannis had never seen one like it and had no idea what it was. It rolled to a stop in front of Anastas's apartment building in Saint-Ouen, the back door swung open, and Zannis climbed in. The interior smelled like expensive leather. The driver turned to face him, holding him with his eyes for a long moment, likely making sure Zannis knew who he was dealing with. He knew. He recognized the breed: confident young men to whom killing came easily and smart enough to profit from it. Then the driver rested his hands on the wheel but the car never moved, simply sat there, the huge engine purring softly.

Zannis had known corrupt men of every sort, high and low, over the years he'd been with the police, but the friend of the friend, sitting next to him, was something new. He looked, Zannis thought, like a French king; prosperously stout, with fair, wavy hair parted to one side, creamy skin, a prominent nose, and a pouch that sagged beneath his chin. "I'm told you wish to leave France," he said, his voice deep and used to command.

"That's right."

"The price, for two individuals, is two thousand dollars. Have you the money with you?"

"Yes."

"I believe you are the man who shot a German officer. Did you do this because you have a hatred of Germans?"

"No. My friend was lying on the floor of the car, the officer would have seen him, so I had to do it. Why do you want to know?"

"To inform certain people — the people who need to know things. They don't care what is done, they simply require information."

"Germans?"

The man was amused. "Please," he said, not unkindly. Then, "It doesn't matter, does it?" It was as though he enjoyed innocence, found Zannis so, and instinctively liked him. "Now," he said, "there are two ways for you to leave France. The first choice is a freight train controlled by communist railway workers. Traveling in this way you may go to Germany, Italy, or Spain. However, once you've crossed the border — there will be no inspection of papers — you are on your own. Hopefully, you've made arrangements that will allow you to proceed from one of those countries."

"I haven't."

"I see. In that case, you may wish to travel by airplane."

"By airplane?" Zannis was incredulous.

"Yes, why not? Are you reluctant to fly?"

"Just . . . surprised."

The man's shrug was barely detectable. "If you wish to leave tomorrow, and for you that might not be a bad idea, the plane is going to . . ." He leaned forward, toward the driver, and said, "Leon?"

"Sofia."

"Yes, Sofia."

"That would be best," Zannis said.

"Very well." He held out a hand, creamy and fat, palm up, and said, "So then . . ."

Zannis had removed the money from his jacket lining and put the thick wad of bills in the pocket of his coat; now he counted out two thousand dollars in fifty-dollar bills. The man next to him, the French king, stowed the money in a leather briefcase, probing first to make room for it. Then he gave Zannis directions: the name of a village, how to identify the road that led to an airstrip, and a time. "All memorized?" he asked Zannis.

"Yes, I won't forget."

"When you describe your adventures in France, as no doubt you will have to, I would take it as a personal favor that you remain silent about this particular chapter, about me. Do I have your word?"

"You have it."

"Do you keep your word?"

"I do."

"Then good evening."

Uncle Anastas had a friend — also an émigré Greek, it turned out — who owned an ancient truck, and he picked them up at dawn. A few minutes later they joined a long line of produce trucks, coming back empty after delivery to the Paris produce markets, and the soldiers waved them through the control at the Porte Maillot. Then he headed northwest from Paris on the road that followed the Seine, with signs for DIRECTION ROUEN. A wet, steady snow that morning, from a low sky packed with gray cloud. "We won't fly today," Byer said, staring anxiously out the window.

"We may have to wait," Zannis said. "But I expect we'll take off."

"Not in this." After he spoke, Byer swallowed.

Zannis studied him. What went on? "Everything all right?" he said.

Byer nodded emphatically. Nothing wrong with *me.*

It was hard to see, the windshield wiper smeared snow and road grime across the window, not much more than that, and the driver leaned forward and squinted, cursing eloquently in Greek. Finally he found the *route départementale* for La Roche–Guyon, the truck skidding as he made the last-minute turn. The narrow road wound past winter farmland for a long time, then it was Zannis who spotted the stone marker with a number chiseled into it, and the truck drove, in low gear, up a muddy, deeply rutted path. Finally, when they knew they'd taken the wrong turn, they saw an airplane in a plowed field. A compact twin-engine aircraft, a workhorse used for a few passengers or a small load of freight, with a white cross in a red circle insignia behind the cockpit. *Swiss markings,* Zannis thought. *What a clever king.* Two men were loading crates into the plane, through a cargo hatch on the underside of the fuselage. "You can walk from here," the driver said. As he worked at getting the truck turned around, Zannis and Byer trudged across a field, wind-driven snow in their faces. When they neared the plane, one of the men saw them, stopped loading, and waited until they reached him. "You are the passengers?"

"Yes."

"Bad morning."

"Will we be able to fly?" Byer said.

"Me?" The man grinned. He had high, sharp cheekbones, hair sheared off close to the scalp, and, Zannis could hear it, a hard Slavic edge to his French. A Russian? A Serb? He wore a leather jacket and a dirty white scarf spotted with oil — a cinema aviator — with a holstered revolver on his hip. "You give us a hand," he said. "We'll take off sooner."

The crates were heavy, MAS 38 stenciled on the rough wooden boards. Zannis wasn't certain, but he had a pretty good hunch he was loading French machine guns. When they were done, the pilot's helper headed toward a farmhouse on the horizon. The pilot rubbed his hands and looked up at the sky. "One of you can sit on the crates, the other can use the co-pilot seat." He led them around the plane, to a door behind the cockpit with a short steel-frame ladder propped against the bottom of the doorway.

Standing at the foot of the ladder, Zannis waited for Byer to climb up. When he didn't, Zannis said, "Time to go." He sounded cheerful, but he knew he had trouble.

Byer stood there. He was in a trance, face dead white, eyes closed.

"Harry?"

No answer.

"Let's go," Zannis said sharply. *No nonsense, please.* The pilot was staring at them through the cockpit window.

But Byer was rooted to the earth. Zannis guessed that something had happened to him when the Wellington went down, and now he couldn't get on the plane.

The pilot's patience was gone, the engines roared to life and the propellers spun. Zannis tried once more, raising his voice over the noise. "One foot in front of the other, Harry, your way back to England. Think about England, going home."

Byer never moved. So Zannis took him by the back of the collar and the belt, hauled him up the ladder, and shoved him into the plane. Then he sat him down on a pile of crates. From the cockpit, the pilot called out, "I have a bottle of vodka up here, will that help?"

"No, it's all right now," Zannis yelled back, closing the door, pulling a bar down to secure it.

The plane began to bump across the field,

gathering speed, then, heavily loaded, it wobbled aloft and climbed into the gray cloud.

Melissa stood on her hind legs, tail wagging furiously, set her great paws on his chest and licked his face. "Yes, yes girl, I'm back, hello, yes." The welcome from his family was no less enthusiastic — they knew he'd been up to something dangerous and were relieved that he'd returned. A demand that he stay for dinner was gently turned aside; he wanted to go back to his apartment, to his bed, because he wanted to sleep more than he wanted to eat. So he promised he would return the following night and, by the time he let Melissa out the door, his grandmother was already at her sewing machine, working the pedals, restitching the lining of his jacket. As he walked down the hill toward the waterfront, Melissa ran ahead of him, turning from time to time to make sure he hadn't again vanished, a sickle slice of moon stood low in the night sky, the streets were quiet, it was good to be home.

The flight to Bulgaria had been uneventful. At one point — was it Germany down there? Austria? — a pair of patrolling Messerschmitts came up to have a look at them, then banked and slid away. Perhaps the French king had permission to fly his crates over Germany — from some office, in some building. Perhaps more than one office, perhaps more than one building, perhaps more than one country. Perhaps the French king could do whatever he wanted; it had not been easy for him to find room in his briefcase for the two thousand dollars. Zannis had, in time, accepted the pilot's invitation to sit in the co-pilot's seat. From there he watched the passage of the nameless winter land below, the hills and the rivers, and wondered what to do about the crates. Machine guns to Bulgaria? For who? To shoot who? So, say something to Lazareff? Who worked for the Sofia police. Tell them? Tell Bulgaria — the historic enemy of Greece? He'd given his word to the French king, he would keep it. Did that include the crates?

In the end, it didn't matter.

Because the pilot landed at a military airfield north of Sofia, and a squad of Bulgarian soldiers was waiting to unload the shipment. The officer in charge at the airfield had no idea what to do with unexpected, and unexplained, passengers, and had pretty much decided to hold them at the base and await orders from above. But then, at Zannis's insistence, he'd made a telephone call to Captain Lazareff, which produced a police car and a driver, who dropped them off at a restaurant in Sofia.

There, over plates of lamb and pilaf, accompanied by a bottle of Mastika, Lazareff and Zannis conversed in German, which excluded Byer, who, now back on solid ground, hardly cared. Lazareff inquired politely about the flight, Zannis responded politely that it had been smooth and easy. Lazareff suggested — still polite, though with a certain tightness at the corners of the mouth — that it would be better if Zannis were to forget he'd seen the plane's cargo.

"What cargo?"

"You'll tell your friend there? Whoever he is?"

"What friend?"

"Ha-ha-ha!"

More Mastika, tasting like anise, and lethal.

"By the way," Lazareff said, "the situation in Roumania is a little worse than the newspapers are letting on. We calculate six hundred and eighty thousand troops, maybe sixty Wehrmacht divisions, artillery, tanks, all of it. They have to be fed, it isn't cheap, so they're obviously there for a reason.

Probably they're meant to intimidate us or, if it comes to that, invade. Or maybe they're there to threaten the Serbs, or maybe Greece. Our response, so far, has been to tell Hitler that we're not quite ready to sign his pact."

"Not quite ready?"

"Not quite. We've destroyed the bridges over the Danube."

"That would be a message, I'd think."

"A tantrum. We've seen the matériel, struts and floats, that can be assembled into pontoon bridges."

"I appreciate your telling me," Zannis said.

"I expect your generals know all about it," Lazareff said. "But I think you should know also, Costa, so you can make your own, personal . . . arrangements. If you see what I mean."

From there, they'd moved to lunchtime conversation. And by midafternoon, after Zannis had telephoned Escovil, and with exit visas provided by Lazareff, Zannis and Byer were on the train to Salonika. At six-thirty in the evening, Byer was delivered to Escovil at the Pension Bastasini. "How did you get here so quickly?" Escovil said, accusation in his voice.

"It's a long story," Zannis said. "For another time."

"You didn't travel on the trains," Escovil said. It wasn't a question.

"You were watching, weren't you."

"Of course. So we'll want you to explain."

"Later," Zannis said. "I'm going to see my family." He was exhausted, at the last available edge of patience. Escovil knew what came next, so left it there and, a brief taxi ride later, Melissa came to the door to greet the returning hero.

Back at his apartment, the hero was exhausted — threw the mail on the kitchen table, washed his hands, and flopped down on the bed. But then, his mind charged with the images of the past few days, he realized he was not going to be able to sleep any time soon, so took off his shoes and socks and covered himself with a blanket. He tried to return to Inspector Maigret, waiting on his night table, but memories of the real Paris intruded and the book lay open on his chest while he brooded about them. Uncle Anastas was a shining example of survival, even prosperity, in an occupied city, but that was Anastas, who could deal with anything. So could he, come to that, but his family couldn't. According to Lazareff, time was growing short, the Balkans would be overrun, and Zannis had to make plans to save

335

his family. Where could they go? How, once he became involved in resistance and likely in hiding, would he support them? The Germans would eventually figure out who had shot their SS officer, would they dare to come after him in Greece? Maybe not, but they would be looking for him the day they entered the city.

For these problems he had no solutions, so tried Maigret again but couldn't concentrate — *Madame Cavard was who?* Time *was* running short — so why was he alone on this bed? What was Demetria doing? In bed herself? In bed with Vasilou? What a bastard, the bully he'd heard on the telephone. So, there was also Demetria to save. *What if he telephoned . . . ?*

He woke with a start, then turned off the lamp. While he'd slept, Maigret had disappeared. No, there he was, under the blanket.

ESCAPE FROM SALONIKA

10 February, 1941.

Well before dawn, Costa Zannis woke from a night of bizarre and frightening dreams. He lay there with his eyes open, supremely grateful that none of it was real and so, fearing that further horrors awaited him if he went back to sleep, forced himself to get out of bed. He washed, dressed for work, let Melissa out the door, and walked down to the waterfront corniche, to a *kafeneion* that stayed open all night for the stevedores and sailors of the port. There he drank coffee, smoked cigarettes and stared out the window, where the sky was streaked with red cloud as the sun, coming up over the Aegean, lit the whitecaps in the bay and the snow on Mount Olympus in the distance. The fishing caïques were headed out to sea, attended by flocks of seagulls, their cries sharp in the morning silence.

The *kafeneion* was quiet, only the sleepy

waiter, a fiftyish prostitute with dyed-red hair, and a man dressed in merchant seaman's sweater and wool watch cap. Zannis took a morning paper from the counter and looked at the headlines: somebody had taken a potshot at the mayor, the bullet punching a hole in his briefcase and coming to rest in the sheaves of official paper packed inside.

The prostitute was watching Zannis as he read and said, "Terrible thing."

Zannis mumbled an assent — it was too early in the morning to talk, and, once he went to work, a full day's talking lay ahead of him.

Turning to the seaman, she said, "Don't you think? Shooting at a mayor?"

The man raised his hands and shrugged; he did not understand Greek.

"Always something here," the waiter said. "They never catch them, people like that."

But, Zannis found when he reached the office, they already had. Sort of. "What they say in the papers" — Saltiel had his feet up on the desk, his jacket over the back of the chair — "is that he was shot at, yesterday morning, while getting into his car. True, as far as it goes. But the detective who questioned the mayor told me that he was get-

340

ting into the backseat, because he has a driver, and his left foot was up on the floorboard as he bent over to go through the door, with his briefcase in his left hand, swung slightly behind him. Try it, Costa, and you'll see what went on."

"What?"

"The way the detective sees it, somebody tried to shoot him in the backside."

"A warning?"

"More like a lesson. I talked to some people, especially the mayor's secretary, who knows all, and what happened is that the mayor's wife caught him in bed with his girlfriend and made him cut her loose. Girlfriend doesn't like it — she thought she was the one and only — so she goes out and hires somebody to pop him one in the ass. Or maybe she did it herself. She's nobody to fool with, according to the secretary."

"The mayor never turned around? Never saw anybody?"

"At the time they thought, the mayor and the driver, they'd heard a car backfire. Or at least that's what they told the detectives." Saltiel raised his eyebrows. "According to the mayor, he didn't realize he'd been shot at until he got to his desk and opened the briefcase. The bullet stopped right in the middle of *Papadopoulos v. City of Salonika.*"

"So, case closed," Zannis said.

"Not around here, it isn't. The mayor can't have *that* in the newspapers, so the investigation is transferred to this office and we're supposed to question a few communists, or Macedonian terrorists, or whatever we can think up. At least tell the press we're doing it."

"Maybe a disappointed office seeker," Zannis said.

"Yes, that's good. Or a lunatic."

"Well, we're not going hunting for lunatics, but somebody better talk to the girlfriend and tell her not to try *that* again."

"Somebody?" Saltiel said.

"All right, Gabi, get me a telephone number."

There was more that had gone on in his absence. Saltiel opened his desk drawer and handed Zannis a message from Emilia Krebs. In ochre letters above the lines of the typed commercial paragraphs she said that three men and two women would be leaving Berlin on the eleventh of February, adding that she had no knowledge of the man seen on the platform of the Zagreb railway station. The secret writing was far more legible than what Zannis had been able to produce. "Who heated the letter?"

he asked Saltiel.

"Sibylla. I never used an iron in my life."

"Well done, Sibylla," Zannis said. "Did you send the teletypes?"

"I did," Sibylla said. "They were confirmed, and I made copies for you."

"Thank you," Zannis said. "And I mean it."

"Oh, you're welcome," she said, both surprised and pleased that Zannis was so grateful. "I'll do the next one too, if you like."

As Saltiel returned to his desk, Zannis prepared to telephone Demetria's house. He'd almost done it the night before, because the time he'd spent in Paris — the Germans, the shooting, the escape — had had its effect on him. On the flight to Sofia he'd thought, in fact told himself, *your time is running out,* and more than once. Now he was going to reach for her, any way he could, and to hell with the consequences. But, as his hand moved toward the telephone, it rang.

"Yes? Hello?"

"Hello. I'm calling from the Bastasini."

Escovil. "And?"

"I understand you were tired last night, but I would like to talk to you, as soon as possible." Escovil was trying to sound

343

casual, but his voice was strained and tense.

"I can't, right now," Zannis said, cold as ice. "I'm busy."

The line hissed. "Some people I know are very, *concerned*."

"Why? They got what they wanted."

"They'd like to know — the details."

"Ask *him*."

"Um, he isn't sure how it worked. So they're, well, anxious to hear your story. And this would be better in person, not on the telephone."

Instead of attacking Escovil, because the urge to do that was very powerful, Zannis took a deep breath. "You know where I am."

"Yes."

"I'll see you downstairs, in the vestibule, in ten minutes. There's something I have to do first, so you may have to wait for me."

When Escovil answered, it sounded as though he were reading a sentence he'd written out beforehand. "Actually, my friends would like to meet you. To thank you. In person."

"Come over here in ten minutes, and come alone. Understood?"

Escovil hesitated, then said, "I'm on my way."

Zannis hung up, but didn't leave the receiver on the cradle long enough for a dial tone, so had to do it again.

A maid answered.

"Is Madam Vasilou there?"

"Gone away." This was a different maid; she barely spoke Greek.

"What do you mean, 'gone away'?"

She tried harder, raising her voice. *"They gone."*

"Where did they go?"

"Gone away," the maid said, and hung up.

Zannis made himself wait ten minutes, then walked down the stairs. He couldn't believe what had happened; where were they? Had they left the country? He wanted to break something. And here, on top of it all, was Escovil. Who hadn't put on a coat, had instead looped a woolen scarf around his neck, stuffed the ends inside his buttoned jacket, and turned the collar up. With the addition of brown leather gloves, he looked like a country squire going up to London on an autumn day.

If Escovil was already anxious about the meeting, the expression on Zannis's face did nothing to reassure him. "I hurried straight over," he said.

"What do you want from me?" Zannis said.

"Byer told us you flew from Paris to Sofia.

How did you manage that?" After a moment he added, "The people I work for would like to know how you did it." *It isn't me.*

"I was helped by some friends in Paris, people I met when I lived there."

"And they are . . . ?"

"Friends in Paris. And now, let me ask *you* something. Who had the idea that I should go to a *restaurant?* Because I'm sure Byer told you what happened."

Escovil hesitated. "A senior person, in London, felt you should act like a visitor. The original idea was the Eiffel Tower, but the time didn't work. So, a brasserie."

"Very clever," Zannis said. "Except that it wasn't."

"We need to know about the airplane," Escovil said, desperation in his voice. "It could be very important, *very* important."

"Well, you know as much as I'm going to tell you. I understand what your people want, they want to be able to use what I used, any spy service would, but they'll have to find their own way."

"Would you at least meet with them?"

Zannis stared at Escovil. "No," he said.

A muscle ticked in Escovil's cheek. He half-turned toward the door, then turned back to face Zannis. "I'm serving in a war, Zannis. And so are you, no matter whether you like it or not." He reached the door in two strides and, over his shoulder, said, "I'd think about that if I were you."

It was just after six when Zannis got back to Santaroza Lane. As he took Melissa's butcher scraps from his tiny refrigerator, he saw the mail he'd tossed on the table when he'd come home the night before. He fed Melissa, then, looking for anything commonplace to make him feel, if not better, at least occupied, he began to look through the pile of envelopes. A few bills, an invitation to a formal party, a letter. No return address. Inside, a single sheet of paper:

5 February

C.
We have left Salonika and gone to Athens. I have said my mother is ill and I had to come here, to Kalamaria, to take care of her. She has a telephone, 65-245. I don't know how long I can stay here, and I don't know where you are. I hope you read this in time.

D.

He called immediately and was out the door minutes later. Kalamaria wasn't far away, maybe ten miles south, down the peninsula. Out on the corniche he found a taxi and paid the driver extravagantly to take him to the village, where, Demetria had told him, there was only one hotel, the Hotel Angelina. He arrived at seven-ten and took a room. The hotel was barely open, in February, but a boy led him up to Room 3 — likely their finest, since Zannis was their only guest — and lit a small oil heater in the corner. It produced a loud pop and a flash, and the boy swore as he jumped aside, but the thing worked and, ten minutes later, the room began to warm up.

The Hotel Angelina was on the bay and the room had one large window that faced west, over the sea. Not so bad, the room. Whitewashed stucco walls, a narrow bed with a winter blanket, a lamp on a night table, a wooden chair, and an armoire with two hangers. Zannis hung his trench coat and jacket on one, and left the other for his guest. He tried sitting in the chair, then lay on the bed, set his glasses on the night table, and waited. There were rain squalls on the bay that night, accompanied by a gusting wind that sighed and moaned and rattled the window. Eight o'clock came and went. Eight-fifteen. Where was she? Eight-twenty. Two light knocks on the door.

When he opened it, there she was. Beautiful, yes, but unsmiling and, he sensed, maybe a little scared. He'd planned to embrace her — *finally, at last!* — but something told him not to, so he rested a light hand on her shoulder and guided her into the room. "Hello, Demetria," said the passionate lover. "May I take your coat?" She nodded. He could smell her perfume on the collar as as he hung it up in the armoire.

Sitting on the edge of the bed, she wore a heavy slate-colored wool sweater and skirt, with thick black cotton stockings and lace-up shoes. "Oh lord," she said.

"Yes, I know."

"You can sit down," she said.

He was standing there, hesitant, and as tense as she was. "I can go downstairs. Maybe there's some retsina, or wine."

She brightened. "Whatever they have. It's *cold* in here."

He went downstairs. The hotel didn't exactly have a bar; a shelf with bottles stood above a square plank table. The door by the table was ajar, Zannis could hear a radio. "Hello?" he said. When the woman who had rented him the room came out, he bought a bottle of retsina and she gave him two cloudy glasses, then said, "Good night, sir."

Demetria was sitting exactly where he'd

left her, rubbing her hands.

"What a night," Zannis said. He poured retsina into the glasses and gave her one. When he sat by her side, the bed sagged beneath them.

Demetria laughed. "Ah, Kalamaria."

"Did you live here? As a child?"

"No, my mother came here after my father died. Returned. It was her home village."

"Is she actually ill?"

"Oh no, not her. Never. Not that I can remember."

"You told her, ah, what you're doing?"

From Demetria, a tight smile. "She knows, Mama does. Knows her daughter."

They clinked their glasses together and drank. The retsina was strong.

"Not so bad," Zannis said.

"No, not bad at all. A good idea." She put her glass on the floor and rubbed her hands, trying to get warm.

"Shall we get drunk and forget our woes?"

"Not *that* drunk."

When she again picked up her glass, Zannis saw that she wasn't wearing her wedding ring. And she'd pulled her hair back with an elaborate silver clip.

"I called your house, this morning," he said. "I came home last night but I didn't see your letter until just before I called you."

"I knew . . . I knew you would call. I mean, I knew you would call to the house in Salonika, so I telephoned, from Athens. Nobody answered. . . ." She put her glass on the floor, rubbed her hands and said, "My hands are so cold." *You dumb ox.*

"Give them to me." He held her hands, which weren't all that cold, and said, "You're right. They need to be warmed up." He took her left hand in both of his and rubbed the back, then the palm.

After a time she said, just the faintest trace of a hitch in her voice, "That's better." With her free hand, she drank some retsina, then put her glass on the floor.

"Now the other. You were saying?"

"That I called, from Athens. . . ."

He worked on her hand, his skin stroking hers. "And?"

She leaned toward him a little. "And you . . . weren't home."

"No." He noticed that the dark shade of lipstick she wore flattered her olive skin. "No . . . I wasn't."

"So I wrote it." She was closer now.

He took both her hands, meaning to move her toward him but she was, somehow, already there. "I did get it."

"I know." Her face was very close to his, so she spoke very softly. "You said."

351

He pressed his lips against hers, which moved. After a time he said, "So . . ." They kissed again, he put a hand on her back, she put a hand on his. With his lips an inch away from her mouth he whispered, ". . . I telephoned." The wool of her sweater was rough against his hand as it went up and down.

It was awkward, sitting side by side, but they managed, until he could feel her breasts against him. When she tilted her head, her lips lay across his, and she spread them apart, so that his tongue could touch hers. Involuntarily, he shivered.

He knelt on the floor and began to untie the laces of her shoes. As he worked at one of the knots, she ran her fingers through his hair, then down the side of his face. "Can you do it?"

The knot came undone.

They had set the hard pillows against the iron railing at the foot of the bed in order to see out the window, where, across the bay, a lightning storm raged over Mount Olympus. The mountain was famous for that. Almost always, in bad weather, forked white bolts lit the clouds above the summit — which meant that Zeus was angry, according to the ancient Greeks. Zannis was anything but. Demetria lay sideways against him, the silver clip cold where it rested on his shoulder.

When he'd finished with her shoes, he had returned to her side and taken the hem of her sweater in his hands but she held them still and said, her voice low and warm, "Let me do this for you." Then she stood, turned off the lamp, and undressed. It wasn't overly theatrical; she might have been alone, before a mirror, and took her time because she always did. Nonetheless, it was a *kind* of performance, for she clearly liked being watched. Carefully, she folded her clothing and laid each piece on the chair, using it as — a prop? She wore very fancy silk panties over a garter belt and, after she'd slid them down, she turned partly away from him and braced her foot on the chair in order to remove her stocking. From this perspective, her bottom was fuller, as it curved, than promised when she'd leaned against the back of a sofa. And the angled form of a woman in that position suggested a seductive painting, though it was a natural, a logical, way to go about removing a stocking.

Was it not?

When she'd laid the garter belt on top of her clothes, she stood there a moment, head canted to one side. *So, here is what you shall have.* Was it what he'd hoped for? She was heavier, sturdier, than the naked Demetria of his imagination, with small breasts, small areolae, erect nipples.

Demetria may have taken time to undress, Zannis most certainly did not. He shed his clothes, took her in his arms and drew her close, savoring the feel of skin on skin. And here, pressed between them, was an emphatic answer to her silent question. Until that evening, Zannis had been in a way ambivalent; for in his heart a tender passion, which he thought of as *love,* had warred with the most base desire. But tender passion, as it turned out, would have to wait. And he was only half to blame. Maybe less.

And so?

Lightning flickered in the distance and, when a squall passed over the Hotel Angelina, wind-blown rain surged against the window. "You could, you know" — Zannis spoke the words slowly — "never go back to Athens."

She didn't answer, and he couldn't see her face, but she nestled against him, which meant *no* and he knew it.

"No?" he said, making sure.

"It is . . . ," she said, suppressing the *too*

354

soon, then started over. "It would be very sudden."

"You have to go back?"

"Don't," she said.

He didn't. But, even so, she rolled away from him and lay on her stomach with her chin on her hands. He stroked her back, a deep cleft in the center. "Can you stay until the morning?"

"Well, I'm surely not going anywhere now."

"Is it a long walk? To your mother's house?"

"Not far. It's on the water, just around the bay. One of those stucco villas."

"Oh?"

" 'Oh?' " she said, imitating him. "Yes, my love, now you know."

"Know what?"

"That she could never afford such a thing. Nor could I. And you should see where my sister lives, in Monastir."

"Oh."

"You think I'm paid for, like . . . I won't say the word."

"That isn't true."

She shrugged.

"So he's rich, so what?"

"That barely describes it. He buys French paintings, and Byzantine manuscripts, and carved emeralds. He spends money like water, on anything that takes his fancy. Have you noticed a small white ship, practically new, that stays docked in Salonika? I think it was an English ship, one of those that carried mail and passengers to the Orient. Anyhow it sits there, with a full crew on board, ready to go at an hour's notice. 'In case,' as he puts it, 'things go badly here.' Then we will all sail away to safety."

"Not a yacht?"

"The yacht is in Athens, in Piraeus. Not meant for an ocean in winter."

"You will leave with him, if 'things go badly'?"

"I don't know. Maybe. Maybe not." She thought for a time. "Perhaps I won't be invited, when the day comes. He has a girlfriend lately, seventeen years old, and he hasn't been . . . *interested* in me for a while. So, when I return, I don't want you to think that I . . ." She left it there.

Zannis sighed and settled down next to her, in time laying his leg across the backs of her knees and stroking her in a different way. She turned her head so that their faces were close together. "I get the feeling you're not ready to go to sleep."

"Not yet."

■ ■ ■ ■

11 February. The rains continued. Hanging from a clothes tree in the corner of the office, three coats dripped water onto the floor. When Zannis reached his desk, a note from Saltiel — a name, a telephone number — awaited him. "This would be the mayor's girlfriend?"

"It would." Saltiel was not only amused, he was anticipating the performance.

"Hello? Madam Karras?"

"Yes?"

"My name is Zannis, I'm with the Salonika police department."

"Yes?" The way she said it meant *What could you want with me?*

"I have a favor to ask of you, Madam Karras."

"What favor?"

"That you refrain, in the future, from shooting at the mayor. Please."

"What?"

"You heard me. We know you did it, or hired somebody to do it, and if I can't be sure you'll never try it again, I'm going to have you arrested."

"How *dare* you! What did you say your name was?"

357

"Zannis. Z-a-n-n-i-s."

"You can't just —"

"I can," he said, interrupting her. "The detectives investigated the incident and they know how it came about and so, instead of taking you to jail, I'm telephoning you. It is a *courtesy,* Madam Karras. Please believe me."

"Really? And where was *courtesy* when I needed it? Some people, I won't mention any names, need to be taught a *lesson,* in courtesy."

"Madam Karras, I'm looking at your photograph." He wasn't. "And I can see that you're an extremely attractive woman. Surely men, many men, are drawn to you. But, Madam Karras, allow me to suggest that the path to romance will be smoother if you don't shoot your lover in the behind."

Madam Karras cackled. "Just tell me that bastard didn't have it coming."

"I can't tell you that. All I can tell you is to leave him alone."

"Well . . ."

"Please?"

"You're not a bad sort, Zannis. Are you married?"

"With five children. Will you take this call to heart?"

"I'll think about it."

"No, dear, make a decision. The handcuffs are waiting."

"Oh all *right.*"

"Thank you. It's the smart thing to do."

Zannis hung up. Saltiel was laughing to himself, and shaking his head.

12 February. Berlin was glazed with ice that morning, perhaps the worst of the tricks winter played on the Prussian city. At Gestapo headquarters on the Prinz-Albrechtstrasse, Hauptsturmführer Albert Hauser was trying to figure out what to do about Emilia Krebs. His list of names was shrinking: some of the suspects had been arrested, success for Hauser, yet some had disappeared, failure for Hauser. That couldn't continue, or he really would wind up in Poland, the Hell of German security cosmology. But he couldn't touch her. He worked, alas, for a moron, there was no other way to put it. The joke about Nazi racial theory said that the ideal superman of the master race would be as blond as Hitler, as lean as Göring, and as tall as Goebbels. But the joke was only a joke, and his superior, an SS major, was there because he was truly blond, tall, and lean. And a moron. He didn't think like a policeman, he thought like a Nazi: politics, ideology, was,

to him, everything. And in that ideology rank meant power, and power ruled supreme.

Hauser had gone to see him, to discuss the Krebs case, but the meeting hadn't lasted long. "This man Krebs is a Wehrmacht colonel!" he'd thundered. "Do you wish to see me crushed?"

Hauser wished precisely that, but there was no hope any time soon. Still, brave fellow, he wondered if he might not have the most private, the most genial, the most *diffident* conversation with Emilia Krebs. Where? Certainly not in his office. Neutral ground? Not bad, but impossible. To the dinners and parties of her social circle, Hauser was not invited. And they did not yet have an agent inside her circle who could find a way to get him there. Down the hall, another Gestapo officer was working on the recruitment of a weak and venal member of the group — they were everywhere, but one had to fish them out — as an informant, but he wasn't yet theirs. So, no parties. That left the Krebs home, in Dahlem.

Alarm bells went off in Hauser's mind. "Darling, the Gestapo came to see me today." What? To my house? To my *home?* The home of the important Colonel Krebs?

Of the Wehrmacht? An organization that didn't care for the Nazis and loathed the SS. No, a simple telephone call from Krebs, going upward into the lofty heaven of the General Staff, and Hauser would be shooting Poles until they shot him. Those people were crazy, there was absolutely no dealing with them. So, better not to offend Colonel Krebs.

However . . .

. . . if the Krebs woman was involved with an escape operation, and Hauser pretty much knew she was, would the husband not be aware of it? And, Hauser reasoned, if he was, would his first instinct not be to protect her? How would he do that? By calling attention to the fact that the Gestapo considered her a 'person of interest'? Or, maybe, by hushing the whole thing up? And how would he do *that?* By telling her to end it. Stop what you're doing, or our whole lives will come crashing down around us.

Hauser, in the midst of speculation, usually looked out the window, but that morning the glass was coated with frost and he found himself staring instead at the photograph of his father, the mustached Düsseldorf policeman, that stood on his desk. *So, Papa, what is the safest way for Albert?* Papa knew. *The list!* True. What mattered was the list. It couldn't keep shrinking because, if it did, so much for Hauser. Safer, in the long run, to have a chat with the Krebs woman.

Who should he be? He would dress a little for the country, a hand-knit sweater under a jacket with leather buttons. A pipe? He'd never smoked a pipe in his life but how hard could it be to learn? *No, Albert!* A policeman with a Prussian haircut, sheared close on the sides — smoking a *pipe?* And then, clumsy with the thing, he'd likely burn a hole in the colonel's carpet.

And the colonel wouldn't like that. But, on the other hand, he couldn't dislike what he didn't know about. In fact, Hauser thought, if the meeting was properly managed there was at least a chance that she wouldn't tell him! Simply stop what she was doing in order to protect her husband. And oh how perfect that would be.

Therefore, no pipe.

But maybe eyeglasses.

Hauser walked down two flights of stairs to a department where objects of disguise were available. Not much used, this department. True men of the Gestapo did not deign to disguise themselves, they showed up in pairs or threes and hammered on the door. Here is the state!

But not always. The clerk who maintained

the department found him a pair of steel-framed eyeglasses with clear lenses. Hauser looked in the mirror: yes, here was a softer, more reflective version of himself. *Frau Krebs, I am Hauptsturmführer* — no, *I am Herr Hauser. Please pardon the intrusion. I won't keep you long.*

In Salonika, in the morning papers and on the radio, the news was like a drum, a marching drum, a war drum. On the tenth of February, Britain severed diplomatic ties with Roumania, because the government had allowed Germany to concentrate numerous divisions of the Wehrmacht, munitions, and fuel, within its borders. And this, according to the British, constituted an expeditionary force.

Then, on the fifteenth of February, it was reported that Hitler met with certain Yugoslav heads of ministries at his alpine retreat in Berchtesgaden, known as the Eagle's Nest. Accompanied by a photograph, of course. Here was the eagle himself, surrounded by snowy peaks, shaking hands with a Yugoslav minister. Note the position of the minister's head — is he bowing? Or has he simply inclined his head? And what, please, was the difference? The ministers had been informed that their country would have to comply with certain provisions of the Axis pact, whether they signed it or not. To wit: increased economic cooperation with Germany — *sell us what we want, we'll name the price* — permission for the transit of German men and arms through Yugoslavia, and passivity in the event of a German occupation of Bulgaria.

What wasn't in the newspapers: BULGARIA CALLS FOR GENERAL MOBILIZATION! And what, on the sixteenth of February, was: BULGARIA SIGNS NON-AGGRESSION PACT WITH TURKEY! Over his morning coffee, Zannis read a quote from the agreement about the two countries' intention "to continue their policy of confidence toward each other, which policy assures the security of peace and quiet in the Balkans in a most difficult moment, through mutual consideration of their security." Which meant: When Bulgaria invades Greece, Turkey will not join the fighting. *If* Bulgaria invades Greece? The Salonika journalist didn't think so. Neither did Zannis. And the phrase "peace and quiet in the Balkans" did not originate with either Bulgarian or Turkish diplomats, it was Hitler's phrase.

So, now everybody knew.

■ ■ ■ ■

Three days later, on the nineteenth of February, some time after ten in the evening, Costa Zannis lay stretched out on his bed, trying not to think about Demetria. A restless reader, he'd put Inspector Maigret aside in favor of a novel by the Greek writer Kostykas, a lurid tale of love and murder on one of the islands south of the coast. A yacht anchors off a fishing village, an English aristocrat falls in love with a local fisherman. So, who killed Lady Edwina? He didn't care. Staring blankly at the page, he returned to the night at the hotel, watching Demetria as she slept, the goddess at rest, sleep having returned her face to the composure he'd seen in the backseat of the Rolls-Royce. But she wasn't at all as he'd thought — now he knew her for an avid and eager lover, without any inhibitions whatsoever. In the past, he'd viewed fellatio as a kind of favor, performed when a woman liked a man to the extent that she would do it to please him. Hah! Not true. He had been simultaneously excited and astonished as he'd watched her, as she'd raised her eyes, pausing for an instant, to meet his. Such recollections were not conducive to reading, and he was about to put the book aside when the telephone rang. It was her!

"Hello," he said, his voice reaching for tenderness in a single word.

"Costa . . . ?"

Not her. Some other woman.

"It's me, Roxanne."

Roxanne? Why now? The ballet school, the love affair, the sudden departure on a small plane — it seemed a long time ago, and over forever, but apparently not. "Why are you calling?"

"I must speak with you, Costa. Please don't hang up."

"Where are you?"

"Nearby. I can be at your apartment in a few minutes."

"Well. . . ." How to say no?

"We can't talk on the telephone. What I have to say is, private." She meant *secret*. "See you right away," she said, and hung up.

Now what? But, in a general way, he knew. The newspaper stories told the tale: when the political tides shifted, certain deepwater creatures swam to the surface.

A few minutes later he heard a car. A black sedan, he saw out the window, which rolled to a stop in front of his building, there was barely room for it in Santaroza Lane.

As the car's headlights went dark, a figure emerged from the passenger seat. Zannis headed for the stairs, Melissa watching him, to answer the knock at the street door.

Only a few months since he'd seen her, but she was not the same. Well dressed, as usual, with a horsewoman's lean body and weathered skin, but had there always been so many gray strands in her hair? And now her eyes were shadowed with fatigue. As they faced each other in the doorway, she offered him a forced smile and touched his arm with a gloved hand. Over her shoulder, he could see that the driver of the sedan had his face turned away.

In the apartment, she kept her raincoat on as they sat at the kitchen table. Zannis lit a cigarette and said, "Would you like something to drink?"

"No, thanks. You're looking well."

"So are you."

"Forgive the sudden visit, will you?"

"Doesn't matter. I think I ought to let you know right away that I won't tell you any more about what went on in Paris than I told Escovil. I don't betray friends; it's that simple."

"We don't care, not now we don't; you can keep your secrets. Have you been reading the newspapers?"

He nodded.

"The situation is worse than what's written. Bulgaria will sign the pact, some time in the next two weeks. They've asked Moscow for help but, to turn the Bulgarian expression around, Uncle Ivan will *not* be coming up the river. Not this time, he won't. And, when that's done, Yugoslavia is next. The regent, Prince Paul, doesn't care; he stays in Florence and collects art. The real power is in the hands of the premier, Cvetkovic, who is sympathetic to the Nazis, and he will also sign. Then it's your turn."

"Not much we can do about it," Zannis said.

"Unless . . ."

"Unless?"

She hesitated, choosing her words carefully. "There is some reason to hope there will be a coup d'état in Belgrade."

Zannis was startled and he showed it — such a possibility had never occurred to him.

"A last chance to stop Hitler in the Balkans," she said.

"Will it stop him?"

"He may not want to fight the Serbs — most of Croatia will side with Hitler, their way out of the Yugoslav state."

Zannis wanted to believe it. "The Serbs

368

fight hard."

"Yes. And Hitler knows it. In the Great War, German armies tore Serbia to pieces; people on the street in Belgrade were wearing window curtains, because the German soldiers stole *everything.* The Serbs remember — they remember who hurts them. So, for the Wehrmacht, it's a trap."

"And Greece?"

"I don't know. But if Hitler doesn't want war in the Balkans, and the Greek army withdraws from Albania . . ."

From Zannis, a grim smile. "You don't understand us."

"We do try," she said, very British in the way she put it. "We understand this much, anyhow, Greeks don't quit. Which is why I'm here, because the same spirit might lead you to help us, in Belgrade."

"Us," Zannis said. "So then, *your* operation."

She shook her head. "It doesn't work like that, but we can help. And, if the Serbs mean to do it, we *must* help."

"And I'm to be part of this?"

"Yes."

Zannis crushed his cigarette out in the ashtray. "Why me? How the hell did I ever become so . . . desirable?"

"You were always desirable, dear." She

smiled briefly, a real one this time. Then it vanished. "But you are desirable in other ways. You can be depended on, for one, and you have real courage, for another."

"Why are *you* here, Roxanne? I mean you, and not Francis Escovil?"

"He does the best he can but he's an amateur. I'm a professional."

"For a long time?"

"Yes. Forever, really."

Zannis sighed. There was no way to refuse. "Well then, since you're a professional, perhaps you could be more specific."

"We know you have friends in the Yugoslav police, and we will need to control certain elements in the army General Staff, not for long, forty-eight hours, but they can't be allowed to get in our way."

Zannis was puzzled. "Isn't it always the army that stages the coup?"

"Air force." She paused, then said, "There are more particulars, names and so forth, but first make certain of your friends, then contact Escovil and you'll be told the rest. You won't know the exact day, so you'll have to move quickly when we're ready." She looked at her watch, then, as she stood, she raised a small leather shoulder bag from her lap and Zannis saw that it sagged, as though it carried something heavy. What was in there? A gun? "I have to say good night now," she said. "My evening continues."

He walked her as far as the top of the stairway. "Tell me one more thing," he said. "When you came to Salonika, was it me you were after? A target? A recruit? It doesn't matter now, you can tell me, I won't be angry."

She stopped, two steps below him, and said, "No, what I told you at the airfield was the truth — I was in Salonika for something else. Then I met you and what happened, happened." She stayed where she was, and when at last she spoke her voice was barely audible and her eyes were cast down. "I was in love with you."

As she hurried down the stairs, Zannis returned to his kitchen and lit another cigarette. In the street below, an engine started, lights went on, and the sedan drove away.

1 March. Zannis and Saltiel went to lunch at Smyrna Betrayed and ate the grilled octopus, which was particularly sweet and succulent that afternoon. Always, a radio played by the cash register at the bar, local music, bouzouki songs, an undercurrent to the noisy lunch crowd. Zannis hardly noticed the radio but then, as the waiter came

to take away their plates, he did. Because —
first at the bar, next at the nearby tables,
finally everywhere in the room — people
stopped talking. The restaurant was now
dead silent, and the barman reached over
and turned up the volume. It was a news
broadcast. King Boris of Bulgaria had
signed the Axis pact; German troops were
moving across the Danube on pontoon
bridges constructed during the last week in
February. The Wehrmacht was not there as
an occupying force, King Boris had stated,
because Bulgaria was now an ally of Germany. They were there to assure stability
"elsewhere in the Balkans." Then the radio
station returned to playing music.

But the taverna was not as it had been.
Conversation was subdued, and many of
the customers signaled for a check, paid,
and went out the door. Some of them
hadn't finished their lunch. "Well, that's
that," Saltiel said.

"When are you leaving, Gabi? Are you,
leaving?"

"My wife and I, yes," Saltiel said. "Is your
offer, of Turkish visas, still possible?"

"It is. What about your kids?"

"My sons talked it over, got their money
out of the bank, and now they have Spanish
citizenship. It was expensive, in the end I

372

had to help, but they did it. So they can go and live in Spain, though they have no idea how they will support their families, or they can remain here, because they believe they'll be safe, as Spanish citizens, if the Germans show up."

Zannis nodded — that he understood, not that he agreed — and started to speak, but Saltiel raised his hands and said, "Don't bother, Costa. They've made their decision."

"I'll go to the legation this afternoon," Zannis said.

"What about your family?"

"That's next."

"Let's get out of here," Saltiel said.

They paid the check and returned to the Via Egnatia. At the office, Zannis draped his jacket over his chair and prepared to work but then, recalling something he'd meant to do for a while, went back down the five flights of stairs. On the ground floor he passed beneath the staircase to a door that opened onto a small courtyard. Yes, it was as he remembered: six metal drums for the garbage. Two of them had been in use for a long time and their sides had rusted through in places, so there would be a flow of air, just in case you wanted to burn something.

■ ■ ■ ■

Late that afternoon, the bell on the teletype rang and, as Zannis, Saltiel, and Sibylla turned to watch it, the keys clattered, the yellow paper unrolled, and a message appeared. It was from Pavlic, in Zagreb. Zannis had been worrying about him over the last few days because he'd sent Pavlic a teletype — in their coded way requesting a meeting — the morning after Roxanne said, "Make sure of your friends," but there had been no answer. Now Pavlic explained, saying he'd received the previous communication but had been unable to respond until their machine was repaired. However, as he put it:

PER YOUR REQUEST OF 23 FEBRUARY WILL ALERT LOCAL AUTHORITIES TO APPREHEND SUBJECT PANOS AT ARRIVAL NIS RAILWAY STATION 22:05 HOURS ON 4 MARCH

Zannis had only inquired if they could meet, but Pavlic had sensed the import of Zannis's query and set a time for the meeting. Nis was seven hours by rail from Zagreb and four hours from Salonika, but this business had to be done in person.

374

■ ■ ■ ■

At six o'clock, on the evening of the first of March, Zannis joined the jostling crowd at a newspaper kiosk and eventually managed to buy an evening edition. In the five hours since he'd heard the report on the taverna radio, the situation had changed: armoured Wehrmacht divisions were said to be moving south, to take up positions on the Greek border. Well, as Saltiel had put it, that was that, and Zannis could no longer postpone telling his family they would have to leave Salonika. Newspaper in hand, he went looking for a taxi.

As the driver wound his way through the old Turkish quarter, past walled courtyards and ancient fountains, Zannis rehearsed what he would say, but there was no way to soften the blow. Still, in the event, it was not as bad as he'd feared. His mother insisted on feeding him, and then he explained what had to be done. The family must go to Alexandria, and go soon. There was a large Greek community in the city and he would give his mother enough money to secure an apartment in that quarter where, as he put it, "there are Greek shops and Orthodox churches and our language is spoken everywhere."

However, he would soon enough be fighting in the mountains of Macedonia, and he would not be able to send them any more money. He didn't say the word *charity* because, at that moment, he couldn't bear to. His mother, silent in the face of new and frightening difficulties, responded with a stoic nod, and Ari, who could not hide what he felt, was close to tears. But his grandmother, whose relatives had fought the Turks for decades, simply walked over to the table where she kept the sewing machine, removed its cloth cover, and said, "As long as we have this, my beloved Constantine, we shall not go hungry." And then, moved by his grandmother's example, Ari said, "I will find something, Costa. There's always something. Perhaps they have tram cars in Alexandria." Zannis, swept by emotion, looked away and did not answer. When he'd steadied himself, he said, "I will take you to the Egyptian legation tomorrow, so you will have the proper papers, and then I will buy the steamship tickets. After that, you should probably begin to pack."

Back at Santaroza Lane, as he stroked Melissa's great, noble head, his voice was gentle. "Well, my good girl, you will be going on a sea voyage."

Melissa wagged her tail. *And I love you too.*

There was yet one more soul he cared for, but, once again that day, no letter in his mailbox, and the telephone, no matter how hard he stared at it, was silent.

4 March. Nis was an ancient city, a crossroads on the trade routes that went back to Roman times. A certain darkness in this place — as the Turks had built a White Tower to frighten their subjects in Salonika, here, in the nineteenth century, they had built a tower of skulls, employing as construction material the severed heads of Serbian rebels.

The station buffet was closed, an old woman on her knees was attempting, with brush and bucket, to remove the day's — the month's, the century's — grime from what had once been a floor of tiny white octagonal tiles. Zannis, his train an hour late getting in, found Pavlic sitting on a wooden bench, next to a couple guarding a burlap sack. Pavlic was wearing a suit and tie but was otherwise as Zannis remembered him: brush-cut, sand-colored hair; sharp crow's-feet at the corners of narrow, watchful eyes. He looked up from his newspaper, then stood and said, "Let's go somewhere else, I'm getting a little weary of this." He nodded toward the burlap sack from which, as he gestured, there came a single emphatic cluck.

Seeking privacy, they walked out to the empty platform; no more trains were running that night, some of the people in the crowded station were waiting for the morning departures, others were there because they had nowhere else to go. On the platform, Zannis and Pavlic found a wooden handcart that would serve as a bench. They were, without saying much, pleased to see each other; the closer war came, the more conspiracy was a powerful form of friendship. They chatted for a time — the fugitive Jews coming from Berlin, the Germans in Bulgaria — then Zannis said, "I've heard that if the Cvetkovic government signs the pact, it may be overthrown."

"So they say. In every coffeehouse and bar. 'Pretty soon we'll kick those bastards out!' They've been saying it for ten years, maybe more."

"It's the British, saying it this time."

Pavlic took a moment to think that over. There had to be a good reason Zannis put him on a train for seven hours, now here it was. "You mean it might actually happen."

"I do, and, when it does, if it does, they

want me to work with them. And I'm asked to organize a group of police to help. Detectives, I would think," Zannis said.

"Like me," Pavlic said.

"Yes."

"And like my friends in Belgrade."

"Them too."

"Which British are we talking about? Diplomats?"

"Spies."

"I see," Pavlic said.

Zannis shrugged. "That's who showed up."

Pavlic was quiet for a time, then he said, "I might as well help out, if I can. No matter what I do, things won't stay the same here. If Cvetkovic signs, there's a good chance we'll have a guerrilla war in Serbia. Not in Croatia — the Ustashi have been taking money from Mussolini for years, because they want Croatia to be an independent state, an ally of Rome. But the Serbs won't be governed from Berlin. As soon as Hitler starts to push them around — tries to send the army into Greece, for example — they'll fight. It will start in the cities and spread to the villages. Assassination, bombing, the traditional Black Hand style."

"And your friends in Belgrade?"

"They're Serbs. They're going to be caught up in whatever happens, but if we get rid of Cvetkovic and his cronies, we might get a few months of peace. What passes for it these days, anyhow — threats, ultimatums, the occasional murder. And, you know, Costa, with *time* anything can happen. America joins the war, Germany invades Russia, Hitler is assassinated, or who knows what. They'll take the gamble, my friends will, I think, but I've got to tell them what they're supposed to do."

"Our job is to make sure that certain elements of the General Staff are kept quiet. Not for long, forty-eight hours."

"Why would they resist?"

"Cvetkovic allies? Maybe reached by German money? You can't be sure, down here, about motives. And all it takes, like Sarajevo in nineteen-fourteen, is one determined man with a pistol."

"How much time do I have?"

"It could happen any day now. In a way, it's up to Cvetkovic . . . he might decide not to sign."

"He will, Costa. Under pressure, he'll give in." Pavlic looked at his watch, got down from the cart, and brushed off the seat of his pants. "I think we'd better find somewhere we can get rooms for the night, before they lock the hotels. We'll talk on the way."

When he reached Salonika, the following afternoon, Zannis stopped by the Pension Bastasini and told Escovil that his friends in Belgrade would agree to join the operation. Escovil was clearly relieved; one of many things he had to do was now accomplished. Maybe too many things, Zannis thought — he could smell alcohol on Escovil's breath. "We'll be in contact," he told Zannis. What they had to do now was wait.

Back in his office, Zannis made a telephone call to Vangelis, then walked over to see him.

"You may as well close the door," Vangelis said, a St. Vangelis glint in his eye. He was very much a ruler of the civic kingdom that afternoon, in his splendid office with a view of the harbor: his shirt crisp and white, his tie made of gold silk, his suit perfectly tailored. "Thank you for taking care of our esteemed mayor," he said. "And, by the way, the lovebirds are back together, all is forgiven." This was accompanied by a mischievous flick of the eyebrows. "So then, what's going on with you?"

"I will have to go away for a few days, commissioner, some time soon, but I don't

381

know exactly when."

"Again," Vangelis said.

Zannis nodded. "Yes, sir," he said, apology in his voice. "Again."

Vangelis frowned. "Saltiel will take care of the office?"

"He will."

"What are you doing, Costa? Does your escape line need tending?"

"No, sir, this time it's . . . a British operation."

Vangelis shook his head: *what's the world coming to?* "So now I've got a secret service running on the Via Egnatia, is that it?" But he was only acting his part, stern commissioner, and suddenly he tired of it — perhaps he slumped a little, behind his grand desk — because he knew precisely what the world was coming to. "Oh fuck it all, Costa, you better do whatever you want, and you better do it quickly."

"Thank you, sir."

"It's probably what you should be doing, that sort of thing, though I don't like admitting it. What's the matter with me?"

"Nothing, sir."

"I wish you were right, but you're not. Anyhow, you should likely go back to work, as long as you can, and I'll just say farewell."

The word puzzled Zannis who, having been dismissed, rose slowly from his chair.

"What I mean to say, is, well, may God watch over you, Costa."

"Over us all, sir."

"Yes, of course," Vangelis said.

Somebody was certainly watching over something. Zannis eagerly checked his mailbox when he got home, but what he was looking for wasn't there. Instead, an official letter from the Royal Hellenic Army, informing Lieutenant Zannis, Constantine, that he was as of this date relieved of active duty in the event of a call-up of reserve units, by reason of "medical condition." Signed by a colonel. What was this? Zannis read it again. Not, he thought, an error. Rather, it was as though he'd been moved a square on an invisible board by an unseen hand, because he had no medical condition. On the seventh of March, sixty thousand British Commonwealth troops, mostly Australian and New Zealand divisions, disembarked from troop ships at various Greek ports. In Salonika, they were welcomed with flowers and cheers. Help had arrived. And, Zannis thought as the troops marched along the corniche, any nation that would do that might do all sorts of extraordinary things.

Finally, she telephoned.

The call came to the office, late in the afternoon. "I'm at a friend's house, in Athens," she said. To Zannis she sounded defeated, weary and sad.

"I was wondering," Zannis said. "What happened to you."

"I was afraid of that. Maybe you thought I . . . didn't care."

"No. Well, not really."

"I'm miserable," she said.

"Demetria?"

"Yes?"

"Get on a train. Tonight. Call, and I'll be waiting at the station."

"I *want* to. . . ."

"Well then?"

"I don't know what to do." Now she was crying.

"I love you, Demetria. I think about you, I want you with me. Is there something you want me to say? Promise? *Anything.*"

"*No!* It's beautiful . . . what you say."

"And so?"

Now she didn't speak.

"Please, don't cry."

"I can't help it." She snuffled. "Forgive me."

384

He paused — was there a worse time to say what now had to be said? "There is something I have to tell you."

"What?" He'd frightened her.

"I'll be going away, soon, I don't know when, and not for long. But I'll leave a key with the neighbor downstairs, I'll tell her to expect you."

"Where are you going?"

"It's for work. A few days, only."

For a time she was quiet, then she said, in a different voice, "I understand, you can't say. But, what if you don't come back?"

"I will, don't worry about that."

"Do you have a pencil?"

"Yes."

"My friend's number is Athens, 34-412. Her name is Theodora. Telephone her when you return."

"Three, four? Four, one, two?"

"Yes. You don't know when you're leaving?"

"Days, maybe a week, maybe more. It doesn't matter."

"It doesn't? What if the war comes?"

Then you will be safe only with Vasilou. On his white ship. Finally, resignation in his voice, he said, "I don't know."

She sighed. "Nobody knows. All they do is talk." She regretted having asked him a question he couldn't answer, so now they would be strong together, not like the people who just talked.

"You won't come here now?"

"Telephone when you return," she said firmly. "Then I'll be ready. I'll be waiting."

He said he would. He told her again that he loved her, and they hung up.

Zannis looked around the office, Saltiel and Sibylla had their heads down, engrossed in their work.

On 13 March, Hitler again demanded that Yugoslavia sign the Axis pact. They didn't say no, they said, *We're thinking about it,* the "no" of diplomacy. Which might have worked, but for the weather. Spring, the war-fighting season in Europe, was just beginning: once the fields were planted, the men of the countryside would take up their weapons, as they had since the Middle Ages. The March chill receded, the rain in Central Europe and the Balkans was a light rain, a spring rain, a welcome rain. Winter was over, now it was time for action, no more speeches, no more negotiation — certain difficult matters had to be settled, once and for all. Hitler loved that phrase, "once and for all," and so, on the nineteenth of March, he issued an ultimatum. Do what I say, or you will be bombed and invaded. Costa Zannis paced his bedroom, smoked too much, found it hard to sleep. Yes, he had papers and steamship tickets for his family, but the earliest sailing he'd been able to reserve was on 30 March. Eleven days in the future. Would Hitler wait?

On the afternoon of the twentieth, he stood on the railway platform where passengers were boarding the express to Istanbul and said good-bye to Gabi Saltiel and his wife. As the train rolled out of the station, Zannis watched it go by until the last car disappeared in the distance. He wasn't alone, there was a line of people, all up and down the platform, who waited until the train was gone.

24 March. Belgrade was quiet that night, people stayed home, or spent long hours in the coffeehouses. In the larger towns, special Serbian police had been assigned to ensure peace and quiet in the streets. The newspaper *Politika,* the most esteemed journal in the Balkans, and read by diplomats all across Europe, had that morning been forced to print an editorial supporting Yugoslavia's signature on the Axis pact. Just before midnight, two armoured cars brought Premier Cvetkovic and his foreign minister

to Topchidersko railway station so they could board a train to Vienna. There they would sign.

Costa Zannis had arrived in Belgrade that same evening, met by Pavlic and taken to the Hotel Majestic on the Knez Mihailova, the main shopping street in the city. As they drove down the avenue, Zannis saw a huge swastika flag hung from the balcony of a five-story office building. "What's *that?*" he said.

"The office of the German Travel Bureau," Pavlic said. "Getting an early start on the celebration."

In the Majestic, Zannis stowed a small valise in his room and went downstairs to the hotel bar. There, Pavlic introduced him to a bulky pale-haired Serb called Vlatko — from the spread of his shoulders and neck, every inch a cop. "He's from the homicide office," Pavlic said, as the two men shook hands. "And he speaks German."

They ordered slivovitz, then Vlatko said, "It's quiet here, but that's just on the surface. The people are in shock."

"It won't last," Pavlic said.

"No, big trouble tomorrow." With this he grinned. He took, Zannis realized, great pleasure, a patriot's pleasure, from the anticipation of big trouble.

Both Pavlic and Vlatko, taking turns, told Zannis the news of the day: a terrific fist-fight in the bar of Belgrade's best hotel, the Srbski Kralj, King of Serbia. Two American foreign correspondents and an Italian woman, their translator, on one side, five Wehrmacht officers — from the German legation — on the other. The Americans ordered whiskies, the Germans ordered schnapps; the Germans demanded to be served first, the barman hesitated. Next, savage insults, tables turned over, broken dishes. The Italian woman had thrown a drink in a German's face, he hit her on the head, then the *New York Times* reporter, a good-sized Texan, had fought two of the Germans. "Knocked them down," Vlatko said, ramming a huge fist into a meaty palm for emphasis. "Out *cold.* On the floor." Once again, he grinned.

"And broke his hand," Pavlic said.

"Both hands, I heard."

"One hand," Pavlic said. "I hope we can do without that, tomorrow."

Vlatko shrugged. "We shall see."

From his inside pocket, Zannis brought out the sheet of paper Escovil had given him: a typed list of twenty-seven names. He laid it on the table and smoothed out the folds with his hands. "Here it is," he said.

"We have a day to find out the addresses."

Pavlic and Vlatko put their heads together over the list. Vlatko said, "Who are these people? Military, some of them, I can see that."

"Not people who get their names in the newspapers," Zannis said.

"Traitors," Vlatko said.

"Possible troublemakers, anyhow," Zannis answered.

"Well, we'll find them."

"Tomorrow night," Zannis said. "When they're at home. We don't want to arrest them at staff headquarters, we don't want gun battles."

"No, I guess not," Vlatko said, bringing forward, with some effort, the sensible side of his nature. "Pavlic and I have enlisted fifteen detectives, so we'll work in groups of three — that should be sufficient. Do these people," he paused, then said, "form a conspiracy?"

Zannis didn't think so. "I doubt it," he said. "The wives won't warn their husbands' friends, if that's what you're thinking."

"Would be best to start at seven — before people go out to restaurants or whatever it is they do."

"They won't go out tomorrow night," Pavlic said. "They'll stay home with the radio on."

"We can't all come here," Zannis said. "Vlatko, can you have them meet at six? You'll have to distribute the names this afternoon, so we'll divide up the names now and make new lists."

"Where do we take them?"

"There's a holding cell," Pavlic said, "at the prefecture near the foreign legations, on Milosha Velikog. They're going to move their prisoners — to make room for ours."

"Stack them one on the other," Vlatko said. "Who cares?"

"These people might be needed later," Zannis said. "We want them out of circulation for a day and a half — for them an anecdote, not a nightmare. We'd put them in a spa, if we could."

Vlatko looked at him. "You're very kind, in Salonika."

"As long as it works, we are. If it doesn't, then we do it the other way."

"Really? I guess we think differently, up here."

A group of men came laughing into the bar, calling for slivovitz. They wore — Pavlic explained in an undertone — the black fur hats of the Chetniks, the ancient Serbian resistance movement, with skull and crossbones insignia on the front.

"They've come in from the villages," Pavlic said. "They're gathering."

Back upstairs, Zannis was restless. The street below his window was deserted, the city quiet. No, not quiet, silent, and somehow sinister. Thousands of conversations in darkened rooms, he thought; they could not be heard but they could be felt, as though anger had its own special energy. And this, despite his better, too-well-learned instincts, he found exciting.

At seven the following morning, the telephone rang in his room, no name, no greeting, just an upper-class British voice, clipped and determined.

"Have you everything you need?"

"I do."

"Tomorrow's the day. I know you'll do your best."

"Count on it," Zannis said, hoping his English was proper.

"That's the spirit."

No way to go back to sleep. He dressed, holstered his Walther, and went downstairs for coffee. When he returned, an envelope had been slid beneath his door: a local phone number, and a few words directing him to maintain contact, using street call boxes or telephones in bars, throughout the following day. Pavlic was going to pick him up at ten and drive him around the city. Until then, he didn't know what to do with himself so he sat in a chair.

Outside, the people of the city began their day by breaking glass. Big plate-glass windows, from the sound of it, broken, then shattering on the pavement. Accompanied by a chant: *Bolje rat, nego pakt!* This much Serbo-Croatian he could understand: *Better war than the pact!* Outside, more glass came crashing down. He could see nothing from his room but, going out into the hall, he found a window at the end of the corridor. Down in the street, students were chanting and breaking store windows. As cars drove by, the drivers honked furiously, waved, and chanted along with the students: *"Bolje rat, nego pact!"* One of them stopped long enough to tear up a copy of *Politika* and hurl it into the gutter.

At nine-fifty, Pavlic's car rolled to the curb in front of the Majestic. Vlatko was sitting in the passenger seat so Zannis climbed in the back where, on the seat beside him, he discovered a pump shotgun with its barrel and stock sawed off to a few inches. As Pavlic drove away, a group of students ran past, waving a Serbian flag. "Brewing up nicely, isn't it," Pavlic said.

Vlatko was wearing a hat this morning, with the brim bent down over his eyes, and looked, to Zannis, like a movie gangster. He turned halfway round, rested his elbow on top of the seat and said, "They're out on the streets, in towns all over Serbia and Montenegro, even Bosnia. We've had calls from the local police."

"They're trying to stop it?"

From Vlatko, a wolf's smile. "Are you kidding?"

"Rumors everywhere," Pavlic said. "Hermann Göring assassinated, mutinies in Bulgarian army units, even a ghost — a Serbian hero of the past appeared at Kalemegdan fortress."

"True!" Vlatko shouted.

"Well I'll tell you what *is* true," Pavlic said. "At least I think it is. Prince Peter, Prince Paul's seventeen-year-old cousin, has supposedly returned from exile. Which means he'll be crowned as king, and the regency is over, which is what the royalists have wanted for years, and not just them."

Zannis liked especially the ghost; whoever was spreading the rumors knew what he was doing. Ten minutes later, Vlatko said, disgust in his voice, "Look at that, will you? Never seen *that* in Belgrade." He meant two SS officers in their black uniforms, strolling up the street in the center of the sidewalk. As Zannis watched, two men coming from the opposite direction had to swing wide to avoid them, because they weren't moving for anybody. Pavlic took his foot off the gas and the car slowed down as they all stared at the SS men, who decided not to notice them.

They drove around for an hour, locating the addresses that made up their share of the list. Two of the men lived in the same apartment building, two others had villas in the wealthy district north of the city, by the Danube — in Serbia called the Duna. Heading for the prefecture with the holding cell, they drove up the avenue past the foreign legations. The Italian, Bulgarian, and Hungarian legations, in honor of the newly signed pact, were all flying the red-and-black swastika flag. "Does that do to you what it does to me?" Pavlic said.

"It does," Zannis said.

Vlatko stared out the side window. "Wait until tomorrow, you bastards."

As they neared the prefecture, Zannis said, "If Prince Peter becomes king, who will run the government?"

"Whoever he is," Vlatko said, "he'd better be a war leader."

Zannis, hoping against hope, said, "You don't think Hitler will accept a new government? A neutral government?"

Vlatko shook his head and said to Pavlic, "A real dreamer, your friend from Salonika."

At the prefecture, the detectives had been listening to the radio and told Vlatko and Pavlic the news.

"What's happened?" Zannis said.

"It's what hasn't happened that's got them excited," Pavlic said. "Cvetkovic was supposed to give a speech at ten, but it was delayed until noon. Now it's been delayed again. Until six this evening."

"When it will be canceled," Vlatko said.

"Why do you think so?" Zannis said.

"I know. In my Serbian bones, I know it will be canceled."

And, at six that evening, it was.

7:22 P.M. A warm and breezy night, spring in the air. Pavlic pulled up in front of a villa; the lights were on, a well-polished Vauxhall sedan parked in the street. "They're home," Pavlic said.

"You don't want this, do you?" Zannis said, nodding toward the shotgun.

"No, leave it. It won't be necessary."

There was no doorbell to be seen, so

Vlatko knocked on the door. They waited, but nobody appeared, so he knocked again. Nothing. Now he hammered on the door and, twenty seconds later, it flew open.

To reveal one of the largest men Zannis had ever seen. He towered above them, broad and thick, a handsome man with blond hair gone gray and murder in his eye. He wore a silk dressing gown over pajamas — perhaps hurriedly donned because half the collar was turned under — and his face was flushed pink. As he gazed down at them, a woman's voice, a very angry voice, yelled from upstairs. The giant ignored her and said, "Who the hell are you?"

"General Kabyla?" Pavlic said.

"Yes. So?"

Again the voice from upstairs. Kabyla shouted something and the voice stopped.

"We have orders to take you to the prefecture," Pavlic said. Zannis didn't get all of it but followed as best he could.

"From who?"

"Orders."

"Fuck you," said the general. "I'm busy."

Vlatko drew an automatic pistol and held it at his side. "Turn around," he said, producing a pair of handcuffs from his jacket pocket.

"I'm under arrest? Me?"

"Call it what you like," Pavlic said, no longer patient.

As the general turned around and extended his hands, he said, "I hope you know what you're doing."

In answer Vlatko snapped the handcuffs closed, took the general by the elbow, and guided him toward the door. Where he stopped, then shouted over his shoulder so his voice would carry upstairs, "Stay right there, my duckling, I'll be back in twenty minutes."

At the prefecture, there were already three men behind bars. Two of them, disconsolate, sat slumped on a bench suspended from the wall by chains. A third was wearing most of a formal outfit — the white shirt, black bow tie, cummerbund, and trousers with suspenders, but no jacket. He was a stiff, compact man with a pencil mustache and stopped pacing the cell when a policeman slid the grilled door open. As Vlatko unshackled the general, the man in evening wear took a few steps toward them and said, "We'll find out who you are, you know, and we will settle with you."

Vlatko shoved the general into the cell, then took a step toward the man who'd threatened him but Pavlic grabbed his arm. "Forget it," he said.

The man in evening wear glowered at them. "You can bet we won't."

"Say another word and we'll throw you in the fucking river," Vlatko said.

The man turned and walked away, joining the other two on the bench.

By ten-thirty they were sitting in the bar at the Majestic, having rounded up the other three men on their list, stowing all three in the back of the car, where one of them had to sit on another's lap to make room for Zannis. When the man complained, his dignity offended, Vlatko offered to put him in the trunk and he shut up. On the way to the prefecture the overloaded car crawled along the Milosha Velikog, where Pavlic had to stop twice, tires squealing, when armoured cars came roaring out of side streets and cut them off.

Throughout the next few hours, until well after midnight, detectives showed up at the bar to report on the evening's work, while Zannis and Pavlic kept score on the master list. Around one in the morning it was over, they had twenty-two of the twenty-seven men in the holding cell at the prefecture. Two of the named subjects didn't exist, according to the detectives — no trace in police or city records of their names. A third had escaped, having run out a back door and, as the story was told, "simply vanished, he's hiding out there somewhere but we hunted for an hour and couldn't find him." A fourth was said, by a woman living at the house, to have been in Vienna for two years, and a search had revealed nothing — no men's clothing. The last wasn't home. The detectives had broken into his apartment and looked for him, but he wasn't there. The neighbors shrugged, they didn't know anything. One of the detectives had remained, in case he came home, and would stay until the morning.

There had, of course, been a few problems. One of the subjects, having gone for a pistol in a desk drawer, had been knocked senseless. Several bribes had been offered, and there'd been a number of arguments and threats. One of the detectives had been bitten by a dog, another had been scratched on the face. "By his woman," the detective said, "so we arrested her, and now she's in with the rest of them." On two occasions, Pavlic was asked, "What will become of these people?"

"According to the plan, they are to be released in a day or so," Pavlic said, and left it at that.

Many of the detectives stayed at the bar;

this was an important night in the national history and they wanted to savor their part in it. Zannis encouraged them to eat and drink whatever they liked — the hotel kitchen produced roast chickens, the slivovitz flowed freely — as the money provided for the operation would easily cover the bill. At two in the morning, while the celebration raged around him, Zannis used the telephone at the bar and called the number he'd been given. A woman's voice answered on the first ring. "Yes? Who's speaking?" Her voice had a foreign accent but Zannis couldn't place it.

"This is Zannis. We have twenty-two of twenty-seven. Locked up in prefecture."

"Names, please."

Zannis worked his way down the list.

"Wait," she broke in. "You say Szemmer doesn't exist?"

"No record. He is Serbian?" Zannis had wondered about the name.

"A Slovene. And he does exist. He is very dangerous."

"They couldn't find him. You know where to look, I'll go myself."

"No. Captain Franko Szemmer, that's all we know."

"Maybe, an office?"

"Where are you?"

"The bar, at the Hotel Majestic."

"If I can find something, you'll be contacted."

After the telephone call, Zannis decided to go outside for a time, have a smoke, look at the stars, try to calm down. The front door was locked but the bolt turned easily and Zannis stepped out onto the sidewalk.

Half a block away, up at the cross street, somebody else had the same idea, on a tense night in Belgrade, and Zannis saw the red dot of a cigarette. There *was* one difference, between Zannis and his fellow star-gazer, the latter was sitting on the turret of a tank, its long gun pointing down the Knez Mihailova.

Zannis finished his cigarette and returned to the bar. "Maybe bad news," he said. "There's a tank out there."

Pavlic swore, a nearby detective noticed the exchange and asked if something had gone wrong. Pavlic told him. "It could be," he said, "that Cvetkovic has called out the army."

Very quickly, the word spread. "If that's true," one of the detectives said, "we're in for it." He rose, went outside to see for himself, then came back looking more than worried. He spoke rapidly, Pavlic telling

Zannis what he'd said. "I think we'd better find the back door." As most of the detectives left, a heavy engine went rumbling past the hotel and the floor trembled. Zannis went to the door, then said, "Another one. Now they've got the street blocked off."

Vlatko stood up, finished his drink, and said, "I'm going to find out what's going on." A few minutes later he returned. "They won't talk to me," he said. "Just told me not to ask questions."

Zannis called the telephone number. When the woman answered, he said, "There are tanks here, blocking Knez Mihailova."

"I will see," said the woman, who took the telephone number, and hung up.

Out in the lobby of the hotel, by the over-stuffed chairs and potted rubber trees, a large Philco radio stood on a table. Pavlic turned it on and searched for a station, but all he got was a low, buzzing drone.

Zannis stayed up until four-fifteen, waiting by the telephone, but it didn't ring. *The hell with it,* he thought, and decided to go to bed. The faithful Vlatko, the last of the Serbian detectives in the bar, wished him a good night, and headed for a kitchen door that led to a back alley.

26 March. 7:30 A.M. Zannis had taken off

403

his shoes, set his eyeglasses and Walther on the night table, and dozed. The roar of engines and rattle of tank treads woke him again and again, and finally he just gave up. He wouldn't desert his post, but if the army had been called out that was the end of the coup d'état, and he'd have to slip away somehow and make his way back to Salonika. Soon enough, somebody would discover the Cvetkovic loyalists at the prefecture and then, he hadn't a doubt in the world, they would enlist their own thugs and come looking for him. So, no trains. Perhaps, he thought, he could steal a car. He would, at least, propose the idea to Pavlic, whose problem was severely worse than his own; he might well have to leave the country. *Skata!* Well, they had tried, and now he would have company on the run. Where to go? East to Bulgaria was closer than south to Greece, but he well remembered the swastika flag flown by the Bulgarian legation. Would Lazareff help them? Maybe. Maybe not. Maybe, more than wouldn't, couldn't.

He walked down the corridor and knocked on Pavlic's door. Pavlic answered immediately, wearing only his underwear, and holding his own Walther PPK by his side. "Oh, it's you," he said. "Well, good morning.

Any news?"

"No. We'll have to run for it, I'm afraid. Marko, I —" He'd started to apologize, but Pavlic waved him off.

"Don't bother. I knew what I was getting into. Let's try to find out what's going on, at least, before we take off."

He waited while Pavlic shaved — very much his own inclination at difficult moments. If you were going to face danger, even death, better to shave. After Pavlic got dressed, they went downstairs together and found the lobby deserted; no guests, no clerk, eerie silence. Pavlic unlocked the hotel door and they took a walk up the street. The tank crews were sitting on their machines, waiting for orders, content to relax while they had the opportunity.

Pavlic talked to the soldiers, his Serbo-Croatian much too fast for Zannis to follow. Brave sonofabitch, he really laid into them. Finally the sergeant commander got tired of him, sauntered off, and returned with an officer. Pavlic's tone now altered — serious and straightforward, as though saying, come now, we're fellow countrymen, you shouldn't keep me in the dark. But, no luck. The officer spoke briefly, then walked away, back toward a wall of sandbags stacked across a doorway — the barrel of a

405

machine gun poking out of a space that left it room to traverse.

"Well, what did he say?"

Pavlic's face was alight. More than a smile — the cat had not only eaten the canary, he'd drunk up a pitcher of cream and got laid in the bargain. So, there was a joke all right, but Pavlic wasn't ready to share it. "He didn't say much, only that it would all be cleared up as the day went on."

Zannis was puzzled; one certain detail had provoked his curiosity. "Tell me," he said. "Why was the officer wearing a blue uniform?"

Pavlic jerked his head back toward the hotel and, as they began to walk, he put an arm around Zannis's shoulders. "He wore a blue uniform, my friend, because he is in the air force."

As instructed, Zannis left as soon as he could — the first train out at midday. But they made slow progress; stopped for a herd of sheep crossing the track, stopped because of overheating after a climb up a long grade, slowed to a crawl in a sudden snowstorm, stopped for no apparent reason at a town on the river Morava, somewhere north of Nis, the name on the station not to be found on the timetable. It was the fault of the engineer, someone said; who had halted the train for a visit with his girlfriend. Late at night, Zannis arrived in Nis, where the train that was to take him south was long gone.

At two-thirty on the afternoon of 27 March, he was again under way, headed for Skoplje. On this train he discovered — wedged into a space beside the seat where it blocked a savage draft — a Greek newspaper, printed early that morning. A new government in Yugoslavia! A coup led by General Simovich and the officer corps of the air force, joined by an army tank brigade. Being a Greek newspaper, it spoke from the heart: the people of this proud Balkan nation were "defiant," they had "defied the Nazis," and would continue to "defy" them — the journalist couldn't get enough of it! "Hitler denied a victory," "fury in Berlin," "a defeat for Fascism," Yugoslav "bravery," "determination," and, here it came again, "defiance."

On the front page, a grainy photograph: a street packed with marching Serbs, their mouths open in song, some carrying flags and banners, others with pictures, taken down from walls and mantelpieces, of Prince Peter. Whose radio speech from the afternoon of the twenty-sixth was excerpted in a separate story on page two:

407

Serbs, Croats, Slovenes! In this moment so grave for our people, I have decided to take the royal power into my own hands. . . . The Regents have resigned. . . . I have charged General Simovich with the formation of a new government. . . . The army and the navy are at my orders. . . .

The newspaper story carried supportive statements from American and British politicians. The Americans were passionate and blunt, while the British, as was their custom, were rather more reserved.

That same day, in Berlin, the newspapers wrote about Yugoslav "criminals and opportunists," claiming that ethnic German minorities in northern Serbia and the Banat region were being attacked by Serbian bandits: their houses burned down, their shops looted, their women raped. This was handwriting on the wall. Because such falsehoods had by now become a kind of code: used first in Poland, then in Czechoslovakia, as pretexts for invasion. So the fate of Yugoslavia was that morning already in preparation, and stated openly, for all to see.

One of the people who saw it was Emilia

Krebs. She had done no more than skim the newspaper, being occupied with the departure of yet one more friend who had come to the attention of the Gestapo. This was a tall gray-haired woman of Polish descent, the eminent ethnologist and university professor known simply as Ostrova. *You know he studied with Ostrova. We went to a lecture by Ostrova.* But now, eminence had failed her, and her situation had become perilous. Thus, by eight-thirty, Emilia Krebs had served rolls and coffee, handed Ostrova a set of false documents, and wished her safe journey. Surely the news that morning was disquieting, and they'd talked it over. Yes, there would be war in the Balkans, but not yet. Maybe in a week, they thought. "So I'd better leave today," Ostrova said and, if the Hungarians had been forced to close the border, she would find a way through the countryside. The two women embraced, and a determined Ostrova set out for the train to Vienna.

Twenty minutes later, Emilia Krebs was having a second cup of coffee when she heard the chime of the doorbell. Now who could be calling at this hour? Likely one of her fellow conspirators, she guessed, properly afraid to trust the telephone.

However, when she opened the door she

409

faced a man she knew she'd never seen before. Heavily built, with a Prussian haircut, he wore steel-rimmed eyeglasses and looked, she thought, something like a mathematics teacher at a military academy. But he wasn't that. He announced himself as "Herr Albert Hauser," but, as it turned out, he wasn't that either, not quite. What he was, he revealed as he sat on her couch, was *Hauptsturmführer* Albert Hauser, of, as he put it, "the Geheime Staatspolizei." An official title, the secret state police, simply one more government organization. But in Germany it was common usage to abbreviate this title, which came out "Gestapo."

"Oh, that name, it's become so . . . ," he said, hunting for a polite word but not finding one, and instead finishing, ". . . you know what I mean, Frau Krebs."

She did.

"I called because I was wondering if you could shed some light on the whereabouts of a certain couple. Herr and Frau Gruen?"

Ah yes, she'd known them.

"Good friends of yours?"

Acquaintances.

"Well, it was reported to the local police that they'd disappeared, back in December this was, and when the detectives made no progress, it became my . . . concern."

410

Not *case,* she thought. *Concern.* This Gestapo man seemed quite the gentle soul. Perhaps one could be, umm, *forthcoming* with him.

In a pig's eye.

Emilia's hands lay modestly folded in her lap, because she didn't want Hauser to see that they were trembling.

"Unfortunately," Hauser said, "I must consider the possibility that they met with foul play. They haven't been seen since then, and there's no record of their having — emigrated."

They ran for their lives, you Nazi filth. No, she hadn't heard that they'd emigrated, but still, they might've done so. Could the records be at fault?

"Our records, Frau Krebs?"

"Yes, Hauptsturmführer. Yours."

"I would doubt that."

Very well. In that case, there was little she could add.

"Please, Frau Krebs, do not misunderstand the nature of this inquiry. We both know that the Gruens were . . . of the Jewish faith. But, even so, our security institutions are responsible for the protection of *all* our German citizens, no matter what people say."

What people say. Do you mean that you are

411

Jew murderers and should roast in hell for all eternity — that sort of thing? "Yes, I'm aware of what people say, Herr Hauptsturmführer. Some people."

"What can we do, *meine Frau?*"

You poor thing.

It went on, but not for long, and Hauser's exterior never showed the slightest fissure — he was, certainly, beyond courteous. Still, there he was, in her living room, the coffee cup of the fugitive Ostrova sitting on the kitchen counter. He hadn't come in uniform, with three fellow officers, he hadn't kicked down the door, he hadn't smacked her face. Yet, nonetheless, there he was. And, as he prepared to leave, her hands shook so hard she had to clasp them behind her back.

"I wish you a good day, Frau Krebs. I hope I have not intruded."

He closed the door behind him, it clicked shut, she called an office at the General Staff headquarters, and Hugo was home twenty minutes later. It was the worst conversation they ever had. Because they had to part. She was obviously a suspect, so obviously under surveillance but, as long as he stayed where he was, she was safe, she could leave Germany. If they were to attempt to leave together, they would both be arrested.

■ ■ ■ ■

She took the train to Frankfurt that afternoon. Was she watched? Impossible to know, but she assumed she was. At the grand house in which she'd been raised, she spoke with her grandfather, and together they made their plans. If, he said, it was time for her to leave, then it was also time for him. Since the rise of Hitler in 1933 he'd hoped for the sort of catastrophe that always, sooner or later, brought such people down, but it hadn't happened. Instead, triumph followed triumph. So now came the moment to abandon such folly, as Emilia's grandfather put it, "and leave these people to their madness." The next morning, with a single telephone call, he procured exit visas for a week-long vacation in Basel. He did not have to visit an office, he simply sent a clerk over for the papers. "The general's aide asked that I convey the general's warmest wishes for a pleasant stay in Switzerland," said the clerk, as he handed Adler a manila envelope. No more than expected, from this general, for Adler had made him a very wealthy general indeed.

It was a long drive, ten hours, from Frankfurt to the Swiss border, but Emilia Krebs and her grandfather were comfortable in the luxurious Mercedes automobile. The cook, saddened because she suspected she would never see them again, had made up a large packet of sandwiches, smoked liver-wurst and breast of chicken, and filled a large thermos with coffee. The cook knew what they knew: that even traveling in a chauffeur-driven Mercedes, and looking like powerful and protected people, it was better not to stop. There were Nazi luminaries everywhere along the way and when they drank, which was often, they were liable to forget their manners. The chauffeur drove steadily through the gusty March weather, Emilia Krebs and her grandfather watched the towns go by and, even though the glass partition assured them privacy, only conversed now and then.

"How many did you save, Emmi?" the elder Adler asked.

"I believe it was forty, at least that. We lost one man who was arrested at the Hungarian border, we never learned why, and a pair of sisters, the Rosenblum sisters, who simply vanished. They were librarians, older women; God only knows what happened to them. But that was in the early days, we managed better later on."

"I am proud of you, Emmi, do you know

that? Forty people."

"We did our best," she said.

And then, for a time, they did not speak, lost in their own thoughts. Emilia didn't cry, mostly she didn't, she held it in, and kept a handkerchief in her hand for the occasional lapse. Her grandfather was, in his way, also brokenhearted. Seven hundred years of family history in Germany, gone. Finally he said, some minutes later, "It was the honorable thing to do."

She nodded, in effect thanking him for kind words. *But we pay a price for honor,* she thought.

So now she paid, so did her husband, so did her grandfather, and, for that matter, so would the Yugoslavs, and the Greeks. *Such a cruel price.* Was it always thus? Perhaps, it was something she couldn't calculate, life had somehow grown darker, at times it did. Perhaps that was what people meant by the phrase *the world is coming apart.* But mostly you couldn't question what they meant, because mostly they said it to themselves.

Hours later, they reached the Swiss border. The German customs officer glanced at their papers, put two fingers to the brim of his cap, and waved them through. The Swiss officer, as the striped barrier bar was lowered behind them, did much the same. And then they drove on, a few minutes more, into the city of Basel.

29 March. There was little to do in the office — only Sibylla and Zannis there now, and Saltiel's bare desk, his photographs gone. The telephone rang now and then, the Salonika detective units continuing to work because they might as well, while they were waiting. Zannis read the newspaper as long as he could stand it, then threw it in the wastebasket. German troop formations moving south, diplomats said this and that; now it was only a matter of time.

"What will you do, Sibylla, when we close the office? Do you need help? With anything?"

"I've made my arrangements, chief."

"Yes?"

"I have a job, as a bookkeeper, at the hotel where my husband works. Nice people, the couple that own the place."

"And if the Germans question you?"

"Maybe they will, maybe they won't, but, if they should, I don't know anything, I was just a secretary. And there's a chance they'll never know I was here. The owners said they would backdate the employment records, if I wanted them to."

"Will you do that?"

416

"Maybe. I haven't decided." After a moment she said, "I don't know what you have in mind, but, whatever that might be, if you need somebody to help out you only have to ask."

"Thank you, Sibylla."

Zannis sat out the day, then went up to see his family at six. This he dreaded, and found what he'd known he would: the chaos of departure. The open suitcases, piles of clothing that were never going to fit, a blackened pot that sat on the table, waiting for a miracle. In the middle of all this, his mother was cooking a lamb roast. "We have a lot to give away," she said.

"Why not just leave it here?"

"It will be stolen."

"Oh, you can't be sure of that."

His mother didn't answer.

"The *Naxos* sails at one-thirty," he said. "We'll go an hour early."

"Well, we have packing to do in the morning. The bedding. . . ."

Zannis found the retsina and poured himself a generous portion. "One for me too, Constantine," his grandmother said, staring at a ladle, then putting it aside.

The following morning, he telephoned Sibylla and told her he wouldn't be in the office until later, maybe two o'clock. Then he set out for the central market, Melissa rambling along with him, for the errand he couldn't face but now had to. After hunting through the goods in several stalls, he bought a khaki pouch with a shoulder strap, possibly meant for ammunition, from some army in the city's history. Returning home, he went to the kitchen, washed Melissa's dinner and water bowls, wrapped them in newspaper, settled them in the pouch, and added her leash; she might just *have* to wear it. Then he went into the other room, but Melissa wasn't there.

The door to the apartment stood open. He only locked it at night, its latch hadn't worked for years, Melissa could push it open with her head. *Oh no.* Hoping against hope, he looked under the bed. No dog. "Melissa? *Melissa!*"

She knew. Strange mountain beast, she knew what it meant — her only possessions packed up in a khaki pouch.

Zannis trotted down the stairs. He'd thought this through — there was no possibility she could stay with him. Fighting in the mountain villages meant near starvation — crops burned, houses destroyed — and the animals, even beloved animals, didn't survive it. Out on Santaroza Lane, he called

418

her name, again and again, but there was only morning silence.

He set out on her daily route, finding no help along the way because the street was deserted. He went as far as the corniche, then worked back toward the top of the lane, past the fountain, searching every alley and looking at his watch. By now, he was supposed to be with the family. Where had she gone? Finally he turned into the alley where a neighbor kept her chicken coop and, at the very end, there she was. Lying on her stomach, head resting on crossed paws, looking as miserably sad as any dog he'd ever seen. He squatted by her side and stroked her head. "I'm sorry," he said. "You know you're going away, don't you. Well, good girl, it has to be. Now you have to take care of the family." When he stood up, so did she, and walked back to the apartment, head carried low, close to his side. Facing the inevitable.

He arrived at the house in the Turkish quarter after eleven and shooed the family along in the last hectic stages of packing — God only knew what would be forgotten. He made sure that his mother put a packet of money in a safe place — the envelope pinned to the inside of her coat. Made Ari responsible for Melissa's traveling bag, looping the strap over his shoulder. Secured his grandmother's valise with a length of cord. And found a taxi.

By twelve-thirty they reached the dock; the *Naxos* already had steam up. Spreading out from the foot of the gangway, a great mob of people, some two hundred of them. And loud — babies wailing, people arguing and swearing, or shouting to friends. He maneuvered the family toward the gangway, then settled in to wait until they would be permitted to board. The tickets! Frantically he patted his clothing, eventually discovering he'd moved them to a safer pocket. Now a few harassed customs officials appeared and tried to form the mob, hauling trunks and suitcases and bags, into a line. But, clearly, that wasn't going to work.

Suddenly, gunfire.

The rhythmic thump of Bofors cannon. Amid screams, as people dove to the ground, Zannis searched the horizon. Far above the puffs of exploding shells in a blue sky, a small aircraft, perhaps a German reconnaissance plane. Some officer at the antiaircraft battery down the bay had evidently spotted the insignia with his binoculars and given the order to fire. No chance of hitting it, not at that altitude. And the plane didn't evade, simply circled the city, then turned out to sea and disappeared into the haze. From the crowd, more than a few cheers. An old man, standing near Zannis, said, "Where is our air force?"

The gunfire had certainly affected the passengers on the wharf. What had been an unruly mob now formed itself into a long line, leading to a wooden table and two customs officers sitting on folding chairs. When it came the turn of the Zannis family, he hugged and kissed them all, knelt and embraced Melissa, now miraculously wearing her leash, and, taking his glasses off to wipe his eyes, watched their blurred forms wave good-bye as they climbed the gangway.

In the office, a telegram awaited him, sent from Basel.

HAD TO GO AWAY STOP BUSINESS CLOSED
STOP MAY GOD WATCH OVER YOU STOP
SIGNED FRIEND FROM BERLIN

"At least she's safe," Sibylla said. "And I suppose the operation couldn't go on forever."

"No, I guess it couldn't. Maybe someone else might have taken over, but with war coming in Yugoslavia that won't be possible."

"She did what she could," Sibylla said.

"Yes," Zannis said. "She did."

Next he went off to the Bank of Commerce and Deposit on Victoros Hougo Street. He'd paid for the family steamship tickets with his own money, but he wasn't going to abandon the secret fund — money was crucial to resistance. He was, however, not the only person in town that afternoon clearing his account. There were fourteen people ahead of him on line — all waiting for the bank officer who handled "special accounts."

The man was not holding up well; he seemed to Zannis pale and anxious. "I regret, sir, there are no dollars, not anymore. Maybe tomorrow, we might have some, but I wouldn't wait, if I were you."

"No British money? Gold sovereigns?"

The man closed his eyes and shook his head. "No, sir. Not for weeks. Gold is very desirable now."

"What do you have left?"

"Drachmas, of course. Spanish pesetas, and Swiss francs."

"Swiss francs," Zannis said.

The officer, having set the account's file card down before him, went into the vault and returned with a metal drawer that held packets of Swiss francs, a pin forced through the corner of each stack of one hundred. "Do you have a briefcase, sir?"

Zannis produced it and, recalling the French king in the back of his royal automobile, slid the packets into the case.

When he returned to the office, he found a message to telephone a detective in the second district. "Costa Zannis," he said. "You telephoned?"

"Somebody threw a brick through the window of the German legation," the detective said. "Would that be something for your office?"

"Did you talk to them?"

"Yes. I went over there and wrote up a report. The consul was in a real fury."

"He was, was he."

"Oh yes. Red in the face, sputtering."

Zannis laughed. "First good news today."

"I guess that means you don't care."

"Well, I can't help him."

"You should've seen it," the detective said. "It was really wonderful."

Eventually, Zannis had to return to Santaroza Lane; he had nowhere else to go. Spring was heavy in the air that afternoon, and the two old women had their kitchen

chairs out, gossiping in the last of the
sunshine. As always they were pleased to
see him. One of them said, "By the way,
your telephone's been ringing most of the
afternoon."

"It has?"

"Somebody's been trying to reach you."

Zannis hurried upstairs. The apartment
was very still without Melissa. He sat on the
edge of the bed and waited, but the phone
didn't ring for another forty minutes. "Yes?
Hello?"

"Finally! It's me, Costa." Demetria, her
voice strong and sweet.

"Where are you?" The connection was
suspiciously clear.

"Not far. I'm in Salonika."

"You've come home?" he said.

"No, that's finished." She paused, then
said, "I'm at the Lux Palace, in 601, the
suite on the top floor."

"I'll be right there," he said.

It turned out to be the same suite where
he'd first met Emilia Krebs. When Demetria opened the door, they stared at each
other for a long moment. *Well, now it's happened, I hope you meant it.* He rested his
hands on her shoulders, wanting a good
long look at her, his prize. She was wearing
the bronze silk blouse and pearl necklace

424

she'd had on the first time he'd seen her, in the back of the Rolls-Royce. Finally she raised her face, and he touched his lips to her smile.

"Well then," she said. "Maybe you should come inside."

She gestured to the sofa, sat down at the other end, then moved closer. For a time they didn't speak, their alliance settling on them amid the ambient sounds from the open window — seagulls, car horns, voices in the street. At last he said, "Was it very bad?"

"Bad enough," she said. "I'm going to call down for something to drink, what would you like?"

"French wine? Champagne?"

As she went to the telephone, he watched her walk. Not that she overdid it, but she knew his eyes were following her. After she'd ordered champagne, she returned to the sofa. "I guess I could have done that while you were on the way but then I didn't know if you'd want a room service waiter . . . knocking on the door . . ."

"We have time," he said. "What a luxury that is."

She looked into his eyes, excited to be with him, in love with him, and put a warm hand atop his. But she did this instead of responding to what he'd said. Because there wasn't very much time, she just didn't have the heart to say it. "Yes," she said. "A luxury."

His eye fell on an open suitcase that stood on a luggage rack. "Is that all you brought?"

"Oh no, there's more in the baggage room. You should see what I brought. That's why I waited until we came back to Salonika. Then I told him."

"How did he take it?"

"He was ice cold. He knew, I think. Either in his mean little heart, sensed I wasn't with him any more, or his spies told him what was going on."

"It doesn't matter."

"No, he's too busy settling his affairs before he leaves, to think about revenge."

"He's going to America?"

She nodded. "I would've liked to see it, but —"

A knock on the door. "Room service."

They drank the champagne, touching glasses in a silent toast. Zannis poured a second, then a third, and the effect was powerful. Darkness gathered outside the window, the last drifts of sunlit cloud low on the horizon. Demetria said it was beautiful, then she yawned. "Oh God, forgive me

426

— I couldn't help it."

"You're tired, I'm not surprised, and the champagne . . ."

"I'm exhausted."

"Me too. A very difficult day, until you called."

"Maybe we should sleep."

"Why not? We'll stay here tonight, then —"

"Oh we can stay as long as we like."

"It's expensive, no?"

She shrugged. "I don't think I'm rich, but I have a lot of money. He gave me money, I saved it. And there's more."

"More?"

"I'll show you." She went to her suitcase and returned with a slim elongated package — heavy oilcloth wound tight and secured with a waxed cord. "A gift from Vasilou," she said. "He used to go up to the monasteries and buy things from the monks." Carefully, she unwound the oilcloth, then burlap sacking, and held up a parchment scroll wrapped around a spindle. Very delicately, she extended the parchment. "See? It's a royal decree, from Byzantium."

The writing was strange; Zannis couldn't read it. At the bottom, a series of flourishes that glittered in the lamplight.

"The emperor's signature," she said.

"Basil II. When the emperor signed a decree, it was sprinkled with gold dust and ground cinnabar, that's why it sparkles."

Zannis peered at it. "Well, if you're going to sign a decree . . . Seems like we've lost something in the modern government service."

She smiled, carefully rewrapping the scroll. "Vasilou had a professor at the university read it. It orders a water system — for some city that no longer exists."

As she returned the package to her suitcase, Zannis laid his head back against the sofa and, for a moment, closed his eyes. Then she said, "Very well, that does it."

She turned out the lamp and they undressed, she down to bra and panties while he, following her example, stayed in his underwear. She took his hand and led him to the bed, they crawled under the covers — exquisitely soft and fluffy in there — held each other, and fell asleep. For an hour. Then he woke, because she had unbuttoned the front of his underpants and was holding him in her hand.

Later, they really slept. And the next thing he knew she'd woken him by kissing him on the forehead. "What time is it?" she said, urgency in her voice.

He reached a hand toward the night table,

found his watch, put on his glasses, and said, "Eight minutes after six."

"Something I want to see, so don't go back to sleep."

They waited until six-thirty; then she led him to the window. From here — standing naked, side by side and holding hands — they could look out over the span of the harbor. Down at the dock, the white ship sounded its horn, two blasts, and moved slowly out into the Aegean. "There it goes," she said.

They put it off — a certain conversation, the inevitable conversation. Were very determined to leave it in the future, because they meant to have as much of this love affair as they could. So they made love in the late afternoon — first one kind of seduction, then another — decided to see every movie in Salonika, and ate everything in sight. A taverna he knew, one she knew, why hold back? Not now, they wouldn't, and money no longer mattered. They ate spiced whipped feta, they ate calamari stuffed with cheese, they ate grilled octopus and grilled eggplant and mussels with rice pilaf and creamy thick yogurt with honey. Zannis didn't go to the office on the first day, he just didn't, and then he did it again. They walked along the sea, over to the amusement park in the Beschinar Gardens and rode the Ferris wheel. Of course, being out in the streets, there were traps laid for them: newspaper headlines in thick black print, posted on the kiosks. Reflexively, he started to comment on one of them but she put a finger to his lips and her eyes were fierce. So much warrior in Demetria, it surprised him. They weren't so different.

Finally, after two lost days, he went to the Via Egnatia on the third of April. No more than a raised eyebrow from Sibylla. "A certain Englishman has been frantic to reach you," she told him. "He called and called and then, yesterday morning, he showed up here. Escovil, is that the name? Anyhow, he had a valise with him, and he left you an envelope. On your desk."

Zannis sat in his chair and stared at it, an oversize yellow envelope, thick paper, you couldn't buy a more expensive envelope than that, he thought. Still, fancy as it was, only a paper envelope, and, with thumbs and forefingers, you could rip it in half. Sibylla was busy typing something, clackety-clack, what the hell had she found to do as the world came to an end? In his mind, he saw himself as he tore the envelope in two; then he opened it. A single sheet of notepaper, the message handwritten in Greek. "This is for 5 April; you won't be able to travel after that." No signature. And what was "this"? *The hand of the gods,* Zannis said to himself. Because it was a steamship ticket for, of all ships, the *Bakir* out of Galata, Istanbul, the same tramp steamer that had brought a German spy to Salonika last October. A Turkish ship, the ship of a neutral nation, thus safe from German submarines and bound, at 2100 hours on 5 April, for Alexandria, Egypt.

So now they would have to have the conversation. Zannis, the ticket folded up in the inside pocket of his jacket, walked slowly, as slowly as he could, back to the Lux Palace. It just wasn't far enough away, not at that moment it wasn't, and, too soon, he rode the ancient grilled elevator to the sixth floor. At his knock, Demetria swept the door wide and gestured with the hand of a stage magician. Presto! Believe your eyes if you can! She had bought at least two dozen vases, no, more, and filled each of them with flowers, red and yellow, white and blue, anemones, roses, carnations, an entire flower stall it seemed. The air was dense with aroma. "I took two hotel porters to the market," she said. "And I could have used another. We *staggered.*"

431

Enchanting. Well, it was. He touched a finger to the steamship ticket in his pocket, but he couldn't show it to her now — not when she'd done all this. Demetria circled around him and slid his jacket down his arms. "Come sit with me on the sofa," she said. "And behold! Demetria's garden."

4 April. 7:20 A.M. Half awake, he reached out for her — he would stroke her awake, and he would do more than that. But he found only a warm place on her side of the bed, so opened one eye halfway. She was all business, getting dressed. "Where are you going?"

"To St. Cyril's, to the eight o'clock mass."

"Oh."

Soon he watched her go out the door, then fell back to a morning doze. But fifteen minutes later, she reappeared, looking grim and disappointed. "What happened?" he said.

"Jammed. Packed solid. I couldn't even get in the door."

Finally, at mid-morning, as they lazed around the suite, it was time. He'd let it go for a day, but now the moment had come; she would have only that day and the next — the *Bakir* was due to sail at nine in the evening — to prepare to leave. She was reading in an easy chair by the window — they'd found other uses for that chair — and he retrieved the ticket from his jacket and laid it on the table by her side.

"What's that, Costa?"

"Your steamship ticket."

She was silent for a time, then said, "When?"

"Tomorrow night."

"What makes you think I'll use it?"

"You must, Demetria."

"Oh? And you?"

"I have to stay."

She stared at the ticket. "I guess I knew it would be this way."

"What did you intend to do, if the war came here?"

"Stay in Salonika. Even if we lose, and the Germans take the city, it won't be so bad. They say Paris isn't bad."

"This isn't Paris. To the Germans, it's closer to Warsaw, and Warsaw is very bad. No food. No coal. But that isn't the worst of it. You are a very beautiful and desirable woman. When you walk down the street, every man turns his head, and such women are like . . . like treasure, to an occupying army, and they *take* treasure."

"I can dye my hair."

From Zannis, a very rueful half-smile: *as though that would matter.*

She thought for a time, started to say something, thought better of it, then changed her mind again. "I thought you would protect me." *From Vasilou, from the world.*

"I would try, but . . ." He left it there, then said, "And they will come after me, they have a score to settle with me, and these people settle their scores. So I will work against them, but I believe I'll have to go up to one of the mountain villages and fight from there. Not right away, the war could go on for six months, maybe more. Look what we did with the Italians."

"These are not Italians, Costa."

"No, they're not. So . . ." He nodded toward the ticket. "It isn't forever. I'll find you, we'll be together again, no matter what it takes."

"I love you, Costa, with all my heart I love you, but I am Greek, and I know what goes on when we fight in the mountains." She reached out and gripped his hand. "As God wills," she said, "but I can only *hope,* to see you again." She looked away from him, out the window, then down at the floor. Finally, her eyes turned back to his. "I won't resist," she said quietly. "I'll go, go to" — she squinted at the ticket — "to Alexandria. Not Istanbul?"

"The ship is going to Alexandria."

"Won't I need a visa?"

"Too late. The Egyptians will give you one when you land; you'll have to pay for that but they'll do it."

She nodded, then let go of him and covered her eyes with her hands, as though she were very tired. "Just fuck this horrible world," she said.

And then, it all came apart.

They decided that Demetria would repack for the voyage: take what was valuable, then bring the rest out to the house in Kalamaria and say good-bye to her mother. Meanwhile, Zannis had several things to do, and they agreed to meet back at the hotel at three.

Zannis went first to his apartment, to retrieve the Walther — better to carry it, now. The weather had turned to gray skies and drizzling rain, so the ladies were not out on their kitchen chairs, but one of them must have been watching at her window. Upstairs, he wandered around the apartment, coming slowly to understand that all was not as it should be. Had he been robbed? He didn't think so; he could find nothing missing. Still, the door to the armoire was ajar, had he left it like that? Usually he didn't. He tried to remember, but that night was a blur; he'd hurried away when Demetria called, so . . . But then, a chair was pushed up close to the table — a neat and proper position for a chair, but not its usual place.

As he poked around, he heard a hesitant knock at the door. It was one of his neighbors. He asked her in, but she remained on the landing and said, "I just wanted to tell you that some friends of yours came to see you yesterday."

"They did?"

"Yes. Two men, well dressed; they didn't look like thieves. We saw them go into the house, and my friend on the first floor wasn't home, so they must have been . . . waiting for you. That's what we decided."

"How long were they there?"

"An hour? Maybe a little less."

"Any idea who they were?"

"No, not really. I don't think they were Greek, though."

"You . . . overheard them speak?"

"It's not that, they didn't say anything, just . . . something about them. I'm probably wrong, perhaps they came from Athens."

436

Zannis thanked her, then retrieved his Walther and ammunition and headed for the Via Egnatia. *They're already here,* he thought. *And I must be high on their list.*

At the office, he hung up his coat and left his umbrella open so it would dry. Then he said, "I think today's the day, Sibylla. For getting rid of the files."

She agreed. "It's any time now, the Yugoslavs have mobilized."

"I haven't seen the papers."

"Well, all the news is bad. The German army is now at the border between Hungary and Yugoslavia. Though the Hungarians, according to the newspaper, have issued a protest."

"To who?"

"I don't know, maybe just to the world, in general." She started to go back to work, then stopped. "Oh, before I forget, two men showed up here yesterday, asking for you."

"Who were they?"

"Greek-speaking foreigners. Polite enough. Were you expecting them?"

"No."

"What if they return?"

"You know nothing about me, get rid of them."

It took, for Sibylla to understand, only a

beat or two. Then she said, "Germans? Already?"

Zannis nodded. "It doesn't matter," he said. "And we have work to do." He began to take his five-by-eight card files out of the desk drawer. "We'll have to burn the dossiers as well," he said.

"You read the name," Sibylla said, "and I'll pull them."

He looked at the first card — *ABRAVIAN, Alexandre, General Manager, Shell Petroleum Refinery* — and said, "Abravian."

In time, they carried the first load down the stairs. Out in the tiny courtyard, enclosed by high walls, the sound of the rain pattering on the stone block had a strange depth to it, perhaps an echo. One of the rusty old barrels Zannis had chosen was half full, so he decided to use the other one. He crumpled up pages from Sibylla's newspaper and stuffed them in the bottom, knelt, and used a rusted-through slit to start the fire. Burning papers, that ancient tradition of invaded cities, turned out to be something of an art — best to drop them in a few at a time so you didn't starve the fire of oxygen. A grayish-white smoke rose into the sky, along with blackened flakes of ash that floated back down into the puddles on the floor of the courtyard.

It took more than an hour, Sibylla working with mouth set in a grim line. She was very angry — this had been her work and she had done it with care and precision — and they didn't converse, beyond the few words necessary to people who are working together, because there was nothing to say.

When they were done, they returned to the office. Zannis stayed for a time, making sure there was nothing there for the Germans to exploit, then put on his coat. As he was doing up the buttons, the telephone rang and Sibylla answered. "It's for you," she said.

"Who is it?" He didn't want to be late getting back to the hotel.

"The commissioner's secretary. I think you'd better talk to her."

Zannis took the phone and said, "Yes?"

The voice on the other end was strained, and barely under control — somewhere between duty and sorrow. "I'm afraid I have bad news for you. Commissioner Vangelis has died, by his own hand. At one-thirty this afternoon, he used his service revolver."

She waited, but Zannis couldn't speak.

"He left," she took a deep breath, "several notes, there's one for you. You're welcome to come over here and pick it up, or I can read it to you now."

"You can read it," Zannis said.

" 'Dear Costa: you have been a godson to me, and a good one. I have known, over the years, every sort of evil, but I do not choose to tolerate the evil that is coming to us now, so I am leaving before it arrives. As for you, you must go away, for this is not the time and not the place to give up your life.' And he signs it, 'Vangelis.' Shall I keep the note for you?"

After a moment, Zannis said, "Yes, I'll come by and pick it up. Tomorrow. What about the family?"

"They've been told."

"I'm sorry," he said. "He was —"

She cut him off and said, "There will be a service, we don't know where, but I'll let you know. And now, I have other calls to make."

"Yes, of course, I understand," Zannis said and hung up the phone.

5 April. 8:20 P.M. The captain of the tramp steamer *Bakir* had six passengers for Alexandria and no empty cabins, so he showed them to the wardroom. At least they could share the battered couches for the two-day trip across the Mediterranean — it was the best he could do and he knew it really didn't matter. The other five passengers — an

440

army officer, a naval officer, and three civilians — had obtained passage, Zannis suspected, the same way he had: by means of the discreet yellow envelope. One of the civilians was prosperously fat, with a pencil-thin mustache, very much the Levantine, all he needed was a tarboosh. The second, thin and stooped, might have been a university professor — of some arcane discipline — while the third was not unlike Zannis; well-built, watchful, and reserved. They spoke a little, the man knew who Zannis was and had worked, he said, for Spiraki. And where was Spiraki? Nobody knew. He said. And if they were surprised to find that a woman, a woman like Demetria, was joining them, they did not show it. What the British did, they did, they had their reasons, and here we all are.

At twenty minutes to nine, the captain appeared in the wardroom. Zannis stood up — if the ship was about to sail, he had to get off. "You can sit back down," the captain said. "We're not going anywhere. Not tonight we're not, problems in the engine room. We'll get it fixed by about eight, tomorrow morning, so, if you and your wife, or any of you, want to spend the night ashore, you may do that."

Zannis and Demetria looked at each

other, then Zannis gestured toward the passageway. He picked up Demetria's two suitcases, one of which was very heavy. "Silver," she'd told him when he asked. "Something you can always sell."

Back at the Lux Palace, Suite 601 had not been taken, so Zannis and Demetria rode back up on the elevator. The flowers were gone. "Likely the maids took them home," Demetria said. "I hope so, anyhow."

"Are you hungry?"

"No. The opposite."

"Me too."

"I was ready to leave," she said. "Now this."

Zannis sat on the sofa. "Well, a few more hours together," he said. He certainly didn't regret it.

She managed a smile, weak, but a smile. Without saying anything, they agreed that the idea of making love one last time did not appeal to either of them, not at that moment it didn't. They talked for a while, and eventually undressed and tried to sleep, without much success, lying silent in the darkened room. And they were still awake at dawn, as early light turned the clouds to pearl gray, when the first bombs fell on Salonika.

The first one hit somewhere near the hotel — they could feel the explosion and the sound was deafening — and sent Zannis rolling onto the floor, pulling the blankets on top of him. He struggled to his knees and looking across the bed saw Demetria — the same thing had happened to her — staring back at him. He got to his feet and headed for the window, which had cracked from corner to corner. She was immediately behind him, her arms wrapped around his chest, her body pressed against his back. Down on the waterfront he was able, after searching the line of docked ships, to find the *Bakir*. She was tilted awry, with a column of heavy black smoke rising from the foredeck. "Can you see the *Bakir?*" he said.

She looked over his shoulder. "Which one is it?"

"The one on fire. I mean, the second one on fire, in the middle."

"What should we do?"

Toward the eastern end of the city, the smoke and thunder of an explosion; then, two seconds later, another one, closer, then, two seconds, another, each one marching toward them as bombs tumbled down from the clouds. Her arms tightened around him — all they could do was watch and, silently, count. Three blocks away, the roof of a building flashed and a wall fell into the street. One second, two. But there it stopped. From the far end of the corniche, long strings of orange tracer rounds floated upward, aimed at a dive-bomber headed directly at the battery. The gunners didn't stop, the pilot didn't pull up, and the plane caught fire just before it crashed into the guns.

After that, silence. Well to the east, where the oil storage tanks were located, the rolling black smoke of burning oil had climbed high into the air. "The railway station," Zannis said. "Our only chance." They dressed quickly and took the stairs down to the first floor, Zannis carrying Demetria's suitcases.

In the lobby, the hotel staff and a few guests were gathered around a radio. "The Germans have set Belgrade on fire," the bell captain said, "and they're attacking Fort Rupel with paratroops, but the fort still holds."

The Rupel Pass, Zannis thought, fifty miles north of Salonika. He'd found photographs of the fort carried by a German spy in the Albala spice warehouse, back in October. Now, if the Wehrmacht broke through, they'd be in the city in a few days. "Is there a train this morning?" Zannis said. "Headed east?"

The bell captain looked at his watch. "It's gone. Should have left twenty minutes ago but who knows, this morning. Still, if they can run they will, that's how it is with us."

Zannis picked up Demetria's suitcases. As he did he saw Sami Pal, sitting in a chair in the corner, reading a newspaper, a cup of coffee by his side. Sami Pal? The Hungarian gangster? At the Lux Palace? But Sami seemed to be doing well, wore an expensive sky-blue overcoat, and, absorbed in his reading, apparently did not see Zannis.

Out in the street, a carpet of shattered glass sparkled in the early light. "Off we go," Zannis said. There were no taxis, no cars of any kind, though he could hear sirens in the distance. Demetria and Zannis moved at a fast trot, taking the corniche, coughing from the acrid smoke that hung in the air. "Are you allright?" Zannis said.

Demetria nodded, breathing hard, a line of soot around her mouth and below her nostrils. "We'll get there," she said.

It took fifteen minutes. The station had been hit — a hole in the roof and a black crater in the floor of the platform — but there was a train. Perhaps it had been scheduled to leave but people were still trying to jam themselves into the cars. A conductor stood by the door of one of the

445

coaches. "Where's it going?" Zannis said.

"It's the Athens-Alexandroupolis Express, one stop at Kavala, but it may go all the way to Turkey."

"Why would it go to Turkey?" Demetria said.

"Because it's a Turkish train. Eventually it goes to Edirne, but, today . . ."

"Do we need tickets?" Zannis said.

The conductor laughed. "We don't care this morning, try to get on if you can."

The train was packed. At the far end, only four people were standing on the steps of the coach and there was room for one more. Demetria forced her way onto the first step, then put a foot on the second. Above her, a large angry man shoved her back. "No room up here," he said. His face — pitted skin, a well-trimmed beard — was knotted with rage.

"Make a space for the lady, sir," Zannis said. He started to help Demetria up to the step, but this time the man pushed with both hands on her shoulders. Zannis led her back down onto the platform, then turned, climbed on the first step and hit the man in the throat. The man made a choking noise, a woman screamed, and Zannis hit him again, knuckles extended, between the ribs, in the heart, and he folded in two.

446

The woman next to him had to grab him or he would have fallen. "Now make room," Zannis said. "Or I will finish this."

The man moved aside, Demetria stood with one of the suitcases upended between her legs. Zannis was wondering what to do with the other suitcase when Demetria reached down and grabbed him by the lapel. "Please don't leave me here," she said. Beside her, the bearded man was staring at her with pure hatred. Zannis climbed up on the first step and held on to the railing, straddling the second suitcase. He would, he thought, get off at Kavala. When the train jerked forward, Zannis stumbled, put one foot on the platform, and, using the hand-rail, hauled himself back on. The train jerked again, the crowd on the platform was still trying to find a way to board. Somebody yelled, "The roof! Get on the roof!" Slowly, the train picked up speed. One more man climbed on the bottom step, forcing Zannis against the railing. "Beg pardon," the man said.

"Can't be helped," Zannis said.

An hour passed, then another. They crossed from Macedonia into the province of Thrace, the train chugged past flat farm fields, always twelve miles from the coast. The Turks had built this railroad in the days of the Ottoman Empire and set the tracks inland so that military transport trains could not be bombarded by enemy naval vessels. Zannis hung on every time the train rounded a curve, the gravel by the track only inches from his feet, his hand freezing where it gripped the iron railing. They would soon be in Kavala, where he'd intended to leave the train, but he had two problems. The bearded ape above him, swaying next to Demetria, and the Turkish border post — if the train went that far. Demetria had no entry visa and Zannis well remembered what had happened to Emilia Krebs when she'd tried to bribe her way past the customs officials.

In the event, it was the train's engineer who made the decision. He did not slow down for Kavala, he sped up. Zannis soon saw why. On the station platform, a huge mob of people yelled and waved as the train rumbled past them.

And then, another two hours on, at Alexandroupolis station, the same.

"Where's he taking us?" the man next to Zannis said.

"Edirne. Turkey."

"Well, my wife is waiting for me in Alexandroupolis. She will be extremely annoyed."

Zannis shrugged. "We're at war," he said.

Edirne. 3:50 P.M. Slowly, the passengers climbed down off the train and joined a long snake of a line, maintained by Greek and Turkish gendarmes who tapped their palms with wooden batons by way of enforcing discipline. Rumors ran up and down the line — some people had visas, and they were allowed to enter Turkey. Those who didn't were being sent back to Greece. This was apparently the case, since a crowd of passengers, looking weary and defeated, began to gather on the Greek side of the customs post.

"Will we get in?" Demetria said.

"We'll try."

"Do you need money?"

"I have Swiss francs, more than enough." *If they'll take them.*

But they wouldn't.

When Zannis and Demetria approached the desk, the Turkish officer said, "Passports and visas, please."

"Here are the passports," Zannis said. "We have no visas."

"You will return to Greece. *Next!*"

Zannis brought his hand from his pocket, holding a wad of Swiss francs. The officer met his eyes and began to tap a pencil on his table. "If you dare —" he said.

"Excuse me." This was reeled off in several languages: German, Spanish, French, and English, by a man who had somehow appeared at the table. The officer stared at him — what did he want? Who was he? Bald, with a fringe of dark hair, eyeglasses, and a sparse mustache, he wasn't much: a short, inconsequential little fellow in a tired suit, Mr. Nobody from Nowhere. Now that he had their attention, he consulted a slip of paper in his hand and, speaking to Zannis in French, said, "You are Strathos?"

"No, Zannis. Constantine Zannis."

The man studied the paper. "Oh, of course, my mistake, you're Zannis. Strathos is somebody else." He turned to the officer, drew an envelope from the inside pocket of his jacket, slid out a letter typed in Turkish, and showed it to the officer. Who stood, saluted Zannis, and said, "Forgive me, Captain Zannis, but I didn't realize. . . . You are not in uniform. The lady is with you?"

"She is."

"Please," he said, his hand extended, welcoming them to Turkey.

As the little man led them toward a dusty Renault, Zannis said, "Captain Zannis?"

"That's right. You're an officer in the British army. Didn't you know?"

"I didn't," Zannis said.

"Oh well," said the little man. "Always surprises, in this life."

Once the suitcases had been put in the trunk and they were under way, the little man got around to introducing himself. "S. Kolb," he said. "That's what some people call me, though most don't call me anything at all. And, unfortunately, there are those who call me terrible names, but I try, when that happens, to be elsewhere."

Zannis translated for Demetria, sitting in the backseat. Then said to Kolb, "We're going south, not to Istanbul."

"We're going to Smyrna, I mean, Izmir. I can never get used to that."

He was a woeful driver, gripping the wheel as though he meant to choke it, squinting through the cloudy window, slow as a snail and impervious to the horns honking behind him. After battling his way around a gentle curve, he said, "You'll work there, in Smyrna — ah, Izmir. Though I think they meant for you to be in Alexandria, to begin with. Meetings, you know, with the big brass."

"We couldn't get to Alexandria, a bomb hit the ship at the dock." Zannis wondered, briefly, how Kolb knew he'd come to Edirne by rail, then recalled Sami Pal, sitting in the

451

lobby of the Lux Palace.

"The *Bakir?*"

"Yes."

"Hmm, too bad, I liked the old *Bakir*. Anyhow, a lot of Greeks are coming out of the country, and a few of them we'll send back. Resistance operations, spy missions, the usual, into occupied Greece. And we want you to run the Smyrna part of that — it's an important job. Ever been there?"

"I haven't."

"Well, there's a big British expatriate community, and you'll find a way to get along with the Turks, no?"

"Of course," Zannis said.

"You'll have to sign a few papers, but there's time for that."

Zannis turned halfway around in the seat, hung his arm over the back, and told Demetria what Kolb had said. "Smyrna, of all places," was her only response, though she took his hand for a moment. A small gesture, for a couple who had indulged themselves in every possible intimacy, but it meant something, that late afternoon in Turkey, *we're safe for the moment, safe from a brutal world, and together,* something like that.

On 27 April, 1941, Wehrmacht forces occupied Athens and, at 8:35 that morning, German motorcycle troops appeared at the Acropolis and raised the swastika flag. Some weeks later, at the end of May, two Athenian teenagers slipped past German sentries and took it down.

From the *Tulsa Star-Tribune*, 5 June, 1942:

A new bookstore is coming to town. Two of our newer residents, the sisters Hedy and Frieda Rosenblum, will be opening The Bookmark tomorrow at 46 S. Cheyenne Ave. next to Corky's Downtown Cafe. The Rosenblum sisters, who've been working at the library, were brought to town under the sponsorship of Dr. Harry Gutmann, a local dentist, from New York City. Before that, they managed to escape from Hitler's Nazis and are writing a book about their experiences. The Bookmark will carry all the latest bestsellers and will have a special section for children's books.

ABOUT THE AUTHOR

Alan Furst is widely recognized as the master of the historical spy novel. Now translated into seventeen languages, he is the author of *Night Soldiers, Dark Star, The Polish Officer, The World at Night, Red Gold, Kingdom of Shadows, Blood of Victory, Dark Voyage, The Foreign Correspondent,* and *The Spies of Warsaw.* Born in New York, he now lives in Paris and on Long Island. Visit the author's website at www.alanfurst.net.

We hope you have enjoyed this Large Print book. Other Thorndike, Wheeler, Kennebec, and Chivers Press Large Print books are available at your library or directly from the publishers.

For information about current and upcoming titles, please call or write, without obligation, to:

Publisher
Thorndike Press
295 Kennedy Memorial Drive
Waterville, ME 04901
Tel. (800) 223-1244

or visit our Web site at:

http://gale.cengage.com/thorndike

OR

Chivers Large Print
published by AudioGO Ltd
St James House, The Square
Lower Bristol Road
Bath BA2 3BH
England
Tel. +44(0) 800 136919
email: info@audiogo.co.uk
www.audiogo.co.uk

All our Large Print titles are designed for easy reading, and all our books are made to last.